# THE
# WITCH
## OF THE HILLS

## J. M. FRASER

THE WITCH OF THE HILLS

Copyright © 2017 by Joseph Fraser

Cover art by Elle J Rossi
Interior formatting by Author E.M.S.

Published in the United States of America by J.M Fraser
ISBN-13: 978-1-946464-03-3

# Acknowledgments

**HOW DO I BEGIN** thanking people after this ten-year journey of a novel-writing experience? So many critique partners and beta readers have come and gone. But Mia Jo Celeste and Helen Johannes have always been there for me, and they stick around. Thanks you so much!

I also want to thank Elle J. Rossi for a fantastic cover that will certainly draw more readers than my meagre storytelling skills ever could.

Finally I do remember my two earliest beta readers who shared thoughts and suggestions with me at a time when this novel still needed a lot of work. Carolyn Fraser and Yvette Graff, thank you!

# CHAPTER ONE

A TINY SHAPE EMERGED at the shimmery point in the distance where highway squiggled into heat mirage. Brian squinted but couldn't make it out. Fence post?

Eastern Wyoming had so much to offer.

The distance closed fast, and the figure turned into a girl with her thumb out. A stiff breeze scattered dark hair across her face and ruffled her long country dress. She held her ground where the shoulder met the pavement, as if daring the next semi to take her down. Spunky, unconventional, interesting, this hitchhiker had arrived at the perfect time. Brian's earlier excitement at the prospect of his first-ever road trip alone had more recently faded into a slow slog of highway boredom.

As foot on the gas became foot off the gas became foot on the brake, the possibilities raced through his mind.

Together in the car, the two of them could crack jokes about the bland scenery. Bluffs, scrub brush, coal trains. *Let's stop and take a picture of those wicked telephone poles.*

They could swap life stories. Matching sets, most likely— parents, school, part-time jobs, rules, rules, rules, but also a vision of a promising future, a light at the end of the tunnel, the day when they might be old enough to start making the rules themselves or at least wouldn't have to follow every stinking one of them.

1

The universal need for a better half in life's many us-against-the-world scenarios had been weighing on Brian lately.

And yet, this girl wasn't the one who'd been tugging his heart in an otherwise disturbing series of midnight dreams. The hitchhiker's hair was black, not red. Scraggly, not straight. More importantly, she had rebellion in her eyes, not a calm resolve.

But this girl on the shoulder was *real,* not a dream. Whether she'd prove to be a soulmate or merely a passing stranger, if she needed a ride, he was here to help. A desolate road offered plenty of risk. Nobody should be standing alone with their thumb out.

He braked harder and cut over from the fast lane.

The girl allowed him some room to get off the road.

He stopped, and lowered the passenger window. "Want a lift?"

A car roared by, buffeting them with draft. She waited for it to muscle past them, waited until silence hung heavy in the air. "Not with the likes of you," she said.

The line was delivered with an undertone of anger cold enough to send a chill down his spine. Dizzying, almost stupefying in its intensity. Groping for some meaning in her harsh expression, he stumbled into a reboot of a conversation going bad.

"Aren't you hitching? I was just asking if—"

"I said no." She glared even more fiercely.

And to think, the day had started so well. His sister handed over the car keys without making him beg. But then came this long, highway trip through nowhere, followed by his big screw-up here—he'd crashed in on the girl uninvited, no doubt imagining she'd had her thumb out in his hope of finding a road-trip companion. The initial promise of a fun-filled day now caught in his throat like a dry-mouth swallow. He'd supremely annoyed somebody who needed space, not a ride.

"Can I give you some advice?" the girl asked.

A cold breeze frosted over him, as if her icy expression chilled the summer air. No good could come of this. He steeled himself for the gathering storm.

She swept a dark bang out of her eyes, freeing them to level an even harder stare at him. "This isn't a promising day for you. Stay clear of girls on the shoulder and *especially* ignore any macabre roadside signs trying to lure you in."

*Macabre*? The old-fashioned word summoned a cloud overhead, casting their confrontation into shadows. He tried to rally against the dispiriting gloom with a stab at humor. "What would we see on a billboard? There's nothing to sell out here but dry riverbeds and scrubby bushes."

She stepped back and then shimmered in the heat ever so slightly—just enough for him to realize the obvious and awaken from a dream.

But he didn't.

The girl turned her back on him and trudged away.

Brian threw the car into drive and tried to make sense of what just happened. Not that he held out much hope. Free phone apps didn't have a monopoly on pop-ups. Sometimes the real world hiccupped, too, and it didn't offer an interruption-free version for a buck ninety-nine.

An hour and a half later, two sodas and a candy bar later, an almost recovered sense of restored spirits later, he rounded a curve.

*Sidney: Lynching Capital of Nebraska*

The wacky message broadsided him with enough force to swerve the car. The billboard displayed a stagecoach, a few cowboys, and a huge noose dangling at the end of a rope. *Macabre*. The girl nailed it from a hundred miles away.

But she couldn't have imagined the stomach-churning effect this advertised hanging scene might specifically hold on him.

Brian had suffered through that weird nightmare again the night before. Not the dumb one where he forgot his locker combination. This one had teeth. A redhaired girl clung to a jagged cliff, just above a foaming sea. A girl he knew somehow, but couldn't remember from when. She meant everything to him, but he didn't know why. In this dream, a tree poked out of the rocks above her, and a *noose* hung down from its gnarly limb.

3

Brian thrashed awake every time, before he could save her from hanging, drowning, or whatever the glowing-eyed man had in store. Yeah, like most nightmares, this one had a villain, too.

First the dream, and now an echo. Time for a break. Again he cut over from the fast lane, this time to get off at the exit and check out a town so desperate for tourists it offered to hang them.

As he glanced back at the billboard for one more peek, the guitar-tone blast of his cell phone startled him onto a rough section of shoulder, rattling him from feet to hands. Luckily traffic was almost nonexistent. He righted the car and glanced at caller ID. *Mom.*

The sudden transition from dark reflection to mundane reality almost ushered a sense of relief, except the prospect of a grounding now threatened to swallow him whole. He took a deep breath. "Hey."

"Don't *hey* me! Where's your sister?"

"Kara?"

"Do you have another one I haven't heard about?" His mom was the world champion at employing sarcasm to tighten the screws.

He swallowed. "She hooked up with this girl, Cheryl, from Joliet. They're heading back in that girl's car."

"And you're driving a thousand miles alone? Why didn't you two run that by *me* first?"

*Because you would have said no?* His hands were getting clammy. "It's not like I don't have a license, Mom."

"You're only sixteen, Brian. How many times have I—"

The line went dead. Yay. Whoever forgot to plant a cell phone tower near the booming metropolis of Lynching Sidney just earned a high five. He'd call her back later. Maybe she'd cool off by the time he got to Iowa.

Brian slipped the phone into his pocket. By then he was off the interstate, cruising into a dusty town. The main street held nothing but the same assortment of fast-food restaurants, hotels, and discount stores he could have found anywhere. No hint of the dark side suggested by the billboard.

4

An old service station caught his eye. The shack of a building reflected the downhill slide of his afternoon, with its peeling, gray look of weathering and neglect, well beyond anything a paint job could save. He pulled in for gas.

But what was with that primo vintage gas pump at the island? The shiny relic stood like a one-armed man, proudly displaying GULF in black letters across its round, orange face. Any picker would kill to wander into an old garage and find *that* inside.

Brian got out to put the thing through its paces, but he couldn't find a slot for his debit card. He headed inside to pay.

He hurried past the open screen door before a rusty sign above could fall on him—*Hal's*—then paused at a soda machine with the same restored look as the pump outside. He opened it, lingered in the cool rush of air, and traced his initials across the condensation on an old-fashioned glass bottle of orange soda. According to the instructions, a mere nickel would release the drink. But the one in the illustration was no ordinary coin. It had a buffalo on its back instead of Monticello. Must have been a thousand years old.

Big whoop. Add root beer to the wildly overstocked collection of orange crush, and maybe he'd be more into museum pieces.

He turned from the sodas and took in the sights. The store was sick with nostalgia. A 1945 wall calendar. A roadmap tacked beside it showing U.S. highways, state and county roads, but no interstate. Vintage toys in a barrel—mostly tops and trucks made of metal. Wooden dolls.

And the comics! Batman and Superman for a dime apiece? In mint condition without plastic wrapping, even though they had to date back a zillion years. Okay, yeah. He was getting into it now.

A slim man with tufts of graying hair poking out from beneath his *Gulf* service cap—Hal, according to the name patch—came around the counter and flashed a gap-toothed smile. "What brings you to Sidney, son?"

"It's kind of a long story."

"Those are the best."

Not always. Initial boredom plus mean hitchhiker times angry mom equaled *skip to the punch line.* "That billboard was different."

Hal cocked his head and squinted at him as if trying to decipher a code. "Billboard, huh? What did it say?"

"Something about lynching."

"Ain't nothing worth seeing here now." Hal scowled out the station's sooty window at the shadowy landscape beyond. "Every July, the town hangs a rustler or two in the Wild West show, but you're too late for that. And Boot Hill's closed for renovations."

"They closed a cemetery?"

"Progress."

Hal opened the soda case and jimmied a bottle from its clutches with a pocketknife. "Coin thing's broken." He used the jaw-toothed opener on the side of the case to snap the metal cap off. "Want a swig?"

"No thanks." Brian eyed the exit. "So this town is just another dead end, huh?" The time had come to gas up and head on down the road.

"Huh. You made a joke there, didn't you?"

"Yeah, I suppose." Brian couldn't drum up enough enthusiasm to fake a laugh.

Hal gulped his drink, came up for air, eyed him. "Where you headed, son?"

"Wisconsin."

"Whew, that's a hike. What's waiting back there?"

"College."

"You look kinda young, son."

"I skipped a year." Two, actually, counting kindergarten. His parents had thrown him on the fast track from day one.

"In a hurry, huh?"

Not lately. High school had been okay, but college led to harder stuff. Brian cringed at the prospect of an eventual briefcase, two-point-three kids, and a mortgage in some ordinary suburb. How was it that because his dad had carved out a boring career in accounting, *he* was supposed to follow in those footsteps?

But just try arguing the point. Or—gasp—suggest taking a year or two off to sort things out. Bring up becoming a cop maybe, or a fireman. And duck. No way would his parents ever get how success was spelled out in the comic books back on that rack. Be the hero the girl in his nightmare needed, or *some girl* needed. Number crunching was more of a Clark Kent existence, without the great alter ego.

Hal drained the rest of his soda and set the bottle on the counter. "If you *ain't* in a hurry, the northern route's a lot more interesting."

"Yeah?" Spam emails would be more interesting. Shopping for socks would be more interesting. The I-80 experience had been like drinking sparkling grape juice. "If that means getting me off the interstate, sign me up."

"Off *what?*" Hal traced a leathery finger along a line on the old wall map. "This road here leads you up the western edge of the Sand Hills to the town of Chadron. Stay there overnight and take Highway 20 east tomorrow. The hills are full of legends. You might find a few ghost towns if you watch for the signs."

"Works for me."

"You'll wanna fill up here first, though, for the drive."

"Okay. I need about ten gallons." Brian pulled his wallet out.

"Couple bucks oughta cover it."

Not a bad deadpan delivery for such a lame joke. He did the polite thing by playing along. "I never heard of a sale on gas."

"You angling for a discount?"

"No, really, I'm almost on empty."

"Just two bucks."

Enough already. Brian handed over a couple dollars. "Okay. We can settle up the difference after the fill-up."

"The price ain't gonna change."

"Whatever."

Hal followed him outside and ran a hand along the hood of his car. "Ain't never seen one like this before. Can't be American."

"No, it's Korean."

"Korean." Hal stared at it for a long moment, as if trying to work something out in his head. "Huh."

How did a gas station attendant not know a Kia when he saw one? They were all over the highway. He got back in the car, waited, glanced at the meter on the pump. *Nineteen-point-nine cents per gallon?* The numbers must have been stuck in place for decades.

After a few minutes, Hal tapped on the window.

Brian rolled it down.

"She took about ten gallons. Here's your change." Hal dug in his pocket and came out with a nickel and three pennies. He just wouldn't quit with his comedy routine.

Brian fumbled the coins around in his hand. "Hey, that's a good one, but these are old. I bet they're valuable." He reached to give them back. "Seriously, how much do I owe you?"

"Have a good trip, son." Hal slapped the hood of the car and motioned him to pull away.

The station seemed too small, but, "Wait, are you setting this place up to be a theme park?"

*HONK!* The booming horn of a semi drowned out his voice.

Hal signaled the trucker toward the pump with one hand and again urged Brian away from it with a sweep of the other.

Okay. Somewhere along the line, lame humor had been blown away by skin-crawling creepiness. Come to think of it, maybe as far back as that girl in Wyoming. With random pop-ups now filling the screen, the world needed a malware sweep real bad.

Brian drove the hell out of there and didn't look back.

# CHAPTER TWO

REBECCA TRACED A SMILE on the pane of her cabin window. Across the glass, the sun cast her Nebraskan hills in bountiful light, bringing out the gold and green of scrub brush and the white hints of sand beneath.

She twirled away, lifted a book from her shelf, and basked in the scent of old leather. A pitcher beckoned. She sipped its cool water, then filled Simon's bowl.

The cat lapped the drink greedily.

Rebecca detected a hint of roses in the musty air. Prolonged absence from the waking world had sharpened her senses. And why not indulge them? She returned to the window. Those pink and blue wildflowers out there would add just the right dash of color to her parlor. She'd find a vase and—

The air turned sharply colder.

*Abigail.*

Not the indulgence she had in mind.

"Hello, Rebecca." The imp's voice came from behind, cutting into the silence like nails on a chalkboard. "Shouldn't you be hanging yourself by now?"

*Mean. Always so mean.* "Come to visit me, have you?"

"I've come to tell you I met Brian on the road."

"You bothered *Brian?*" Rebecca spun around to deal yet again with a scraggly-haired nuisance, now shaped to look…sixteen? Same as Rebecca, not counting time spent in places where a girl didn't age. Why the same?

To break through Brian's defenses and torture him with pranks, obviously.

The imp flashed the menacing grin of a most unfriendly girl. Older in appearance now, but no less a worry than the twelve-year-old version who'd started the troubles in Salem.

Yet Abigail had inadvertently provided confirmation just now. Brian *was* coming.

"You look happy to see me, Rebecca. I like that smile."

"Please. If you liked anything about me, we'd have found enough common ground to be friends by now."

A chilly breeze provided confirmation. The atmosphere had always been a slave to Abigail's moods. "I discouraged Brian from meeting you," she said.

"What?" *Restraint is best. Restraint is best. Restraint is—* Rebecca went for Abigail's hair. Thick, curly, easy to grab and pull. She closed her hand around…nothing.

Had Abigail slipped away? The icy air lingered. "Henry will never love you, Abigail."

Heavy silence met her comment. The stifling quiet choked her with guilt. She shouldn't have been unkind. "I'm sorry for saying that. Perhaps he'll come around."

Abigail reappeared, hands on hips, any hurt hidden behind scolding eyes. "What he ever saw in *you* is beyond me, Rebecca. An Irish girl living in Salem? You were ridiculous."

"Half-Irish. I passed for English stock, just like anyone else."

"With red hair?"

Rebecca turned her back on the imp. Shadows out the window, stretching to midafternoon length, sent queasy anticipation fluttering through her stomach. Her champion would soon arrive. Wouldn't he? "Abigail, you delight in pranks, not heartbreak, don't you?"

"Do you mean, did I really chase Brian away?"

Rebecca held her breath.

The air warmed. The imp must have left…without providing an answer.

Brian *would* arrive. Such a bright, sunshiny day could never bring sadness.

Rebecca headed out the door and nearly toppled over Henry Stoddard. "Oh!" The object of Abigail's unrequited infatuation sat on the step with an open book in his lap.

The sorcerer came disguised as an innocent farmer, dressed in overalls with a straw hat covering his dark hair. He might as well have owned the place the way he showed up unannounced and didn't even bother knocking. His Great Dane panted beside him without showing any inkling he and his master might belong somewhere else, anywhere but at her doorstep.

First Abigail's storm clouds and now this misguided genius for trickery. "Behold the rain man."

He turned the page without looking up at her. "That's a relatively modern term, Rebecca."

"I try my best to keep up."

"Ah, but you jumble the long forgotten with the recently coined." Henry set the book aside and smiled warmly enough to melt an iceberg. "One could go so far as to call your manner of speaking charming."

Rebecca could never fall for *his* charms, any more than a cat might love a dog. "Your friend came calling just now."

"Pest, you mean."

Rebecca couldn't agree more, but hostility toward Abigail had never solved anything. "Henry, do you think if we were extra-special nice to her, she might move on?"

The sorcerer stood and bowed, sweeping his arm with a flourish. "Try that on me some time."

"Be nice to you? We have a history, and not a good one."

He settled back down on the step. "Yet here I am, calling on you."

"May I ask why? Wherever you go, Abigail follows. And she torments me every chance she gets."

Henry took up his book again and paged through it, as if

searching for a suitable response. "I've arrived to help you on this momentous day."

"The prophecy doesn't mention a sorcerer providing assistance." *Go it alone.* Not only her mother but *any* witch would be mouthing those words at the moment.

More page flipping, a pause, and Stoddard grinned at his dog. "Hear that, Shorty? A great prophet forgot to add *my* name to the words she carved into stone. What's this world coming to?" But when he returned his gaze to Rebecca, he turned somber, without a hint of ridicule in his expression. "The days of following some old hag's misguided message to the letter are long gone, dear girl."

"Please don't mock my religion, Henry."

"Perish the thought, young lady. I'm merely an old fool arriving on your doorstep to provide some assistance. Prophecies never come with user's manuals."

She knew that all too well. She'd already started improvising, bending time to string acquaintances together—Brian, Hal—but hopefully not fitting square pegs into round holes. Still, a lifetime of warnings from her mother and other witches to never trust sorcerers died hard. And Henry had tripped her up in the past. "This prophecy is clear. You are not in it."

"Foretelling or not, what makes you think a single white knight remains in the world, Rebecca? Have you looked around lately?"

"My ability to travel is somewhat limited, but I know the world hasn't come this far to end in darkness."

"Then do something about your worries. They're spilling onto your sleeves."

No, they weren't. She had no worries. Rebecca pulled her hands apart. She hadn't been wringing them.

Henry returned to his book, turned another page, moved his lips as he read. He seemed to forget her, until, "What are your plans for your visitor?"

"This and that."

He shot a sharp glance at her. "Give me a hint."

They stared at each other forever and a day. Rebecca tried to hold out, but Henry wore her down. "I'll court him," she said.

"The old way?"

"Where I come from, courting wasn't the old way."

The sorcerer guffawed. "It is in the twenty-first century! Riddles, half-truths, misdirection, and peek-a-boo. That's about the size of it, eh? It's a wonder any of you old-school witches could keep a young man from running for the hills halfway through the process."

Rebecca shifted a hand to her mouth but stopped herself before chewing yet another nail to the quick. She had prophecy on her side, and the happy endings of every romance novel she'd ever read. She'd court Brian, he'd follow her clues and learn his destiny, and everything would fall into place. Imp or no imp. Sorcerer or no sorcerer. She bit into the nail.

"Come along, Shorty." Henry got off the step and headed away, the dog at his heels. But he paused and glanced over his shoulder before he'd reached the nearest hill. "Do chase those worries out the kitchen window," he called. "Things will go best if you seem somewhat in control when you meet the boy."

The sorcerer and his dog disappeared. Good riddance.

He'd left his novel on the stair. *Wuthering Heights*. The old book had more dog-eared pages than clean ones, and it carried the curl-on-the-couch scent of rainy days. A treasure. For her? "I'll never understand you," she whispered.

She brought the book into the cabin and found a spot for it on her shelf. "The best collections are built from forgotten odds and ends, no matter the source, Simon." She scooped the cat into her arms and carried him to the kitchen.

Simon purred all the way but meowed in annoyance when she set him down to crank the window open.

"What's the matter?" she asked. "Don't any of your worries need chasing?"

The cat hunkered down on his haunches. He seemed content enough.

"Very well, then, I have plenty for the both of us." She

cupped her hands and held them six inches from her face, as was the custom for speaking one's worries and casting them away.

"What if Hal grows confused by the modern-day world and points Brian in the wrong direction?

"And if he does arrive…no, not if. *When* Brian arrives, Abigail will torment us with her pranks. She could ruin everything."

She hesitated, but she couldn't leave unspoken the most haunting worry of all. "Will Brian love me? He touched my heart when we met so long ago, but what if…maybe…oh, suppose I'm wrong about my role in this." She shuddered.

Those were enough worries. Try chasing too many, and they come back all the quicker. She blew on her hands until her troubles floated out the window toward the hills, little bubbles glittering like sparklers, then popping as loud as firecrackers until they all disappeared. She headed out of the cabin.

She walked through the hills with concerns still heavy on her mind. Abigail, misinterpreted prophecies, *a hanging.* Then, five furlongs out, an old piece of torn fabric caught in a bush reminded her. If what she planned left a mark on her neck, she'd need to hide it.

She ran back to fetch her scarf and then resumed her journey along the old footpath with as brisk a pace as she could manage without getting a stitch in her side. But when she reached the tree, her twenty-furlong marker, a little blue car already approached on the county road.

*Brian!* Her heart pounded. She was about to miss him by half a mile. If she didn't do something, he'd drive right past the place she hoped they'd meet. She needed to improvise and keep him occupied until she got there.

Rebecca focused on the horizon and found a spot of gray where one puffy cloud cast its shadow on another in an otherwise clear blue sky. She stared at that point until it stretched into a line, then a rectangle, wider and wider, casting its pall toward the approaching car. Shadows and illusions. What more fitting way to burst into Brian's life? With luck, her magic would distract him for a while.

So much for fun and games. She shifted her gaze to the oak tree until a thick limb grew a rope. Strands of twine twisted together, stretching downward until her creation stopped ten feet off the ground. A noose shaped itself.

She swallowed. Straying beyond twenty furlongs required a great sacrifice. A ritual hanging as part of a bargain struck long ago. Having done this once before and come out unscathed made the act no less dreadful.

She'd choke and writhe.

She'd experience terrible visions.

Surely Abigail hid somewhere watching.

And laughing.

Rebecca levitated, floating high enough to fit the noose around her neck. She dropped to spend a symbolic life.

She gagged.

Blackness.

She floated.

Rebecca opened her eyes and beheld unfamiliar trappings, deep inside the World of Mortal Dreams. No longer constrained by waking boundaries, she ignored the rope and flew high above the landscape to get her bearings.

Down below, time had lurched backward. Long before such a thing as a blue car. Or a paved road. Judging by the pristine landscape, she might have drifted all the way to the pioneering days when she and her mum were just getting started in Nebraska. Had she fallen into one of her mum's old dreams?

Could be. Dreams live on for centuries. Well beyond the era the dreamer might have walked the earth.

But, in this case, a dark void extinguished half of the hilly landscape.

She swallowed a sob. Her mum's dreams were disintegrating. The World of Mortal Dreams had begun a slow decay into a checkerboard of good places and bad, wonder and emptiness, just as prophesied. The fantasyland visited at night by every man, woman, and child might eventually disappear altogether.

And then what? Nothing good.

The rope returned and tightened around her neck. She choked but fought to keep her eyes open as the scene beneath her changed.

A group of people dressed in tatters staggered about like zombies, with outstretched arms and vacant stares. No, not zombies. Refugees. A sprawling city, modern, *futuristic,* cast angry flames into a midnight sky.

She wasn't in Nebraska anymore. This city was on a coast.

And it was on fire. Almost consumed.

Precognition?

Or a warning of what might be?

Having read *A Christmas Carol,* she latched onto the hope the future had some malleability. Like a baking dough yet to be shaped.

She'd do everything in her powers to help Brian find his destiny. The waking world hinged on his ability to stop the void from swallowing its secret cousin. Otherwise, without the nourishment provided by the World of Mortal Dreams, everyone's spirit would shrivel and die.

*Enough.*

The rope evaporated, and her feet touched the ground.

Rebecca fastened the scarf to hide her throat. The lynching self-illusion had been so intense she'd surely marked her own skin.

With the stench of smoke clinging to her, she hurried toward the road. How would she ever convince Brian to join her quest? Riddles, illusions, and dreams could only take a girl so far, but the Witches Code was explicit about how courting should be conducted.

She should have cast more worries out the window.

# CHAPTER THREE

**A THIN, DARK LINE** looming on the horizon hinted at an approaching storm. Brian rounded a curve and lost sight of it. Ghost towns. That's what he wanted to find, not rain. He crested a rise, came around again, and...the line exploded into an elongated rectangle, blotting out miles of hilly prairie. He hit the brakes.

The shadow closed the distance to his car with ridiculous speed. Massive weather front? Dust storm? *End of days?*

*Get real.* He'd been watching too many disaster movies. This had to be a solar eclipse. How cool was that?

Car met shadow. The headlights kicked on, and the dashboard brightened to nighttime mode.

Brian pulled to the shoulder for a better look. A burst of returning sunlight blinded him as he rolled to a stop. He hurried outside.

The air had cooled enough for a jacket. From an eclipse? The line where darkness swallowed daylight shrank to the south, fast. Weirdly fast. He whipped his phone out of his pocket, took a couple quick pictures for Facebook, and hit send.

Nothing happened. The phone didn't show a single signal bar. And why should it? Nobody would bother to plant a cell tower sixty miles north of the interstate in the loneliest region of an underpopulated state.

17

A scary thought emerged, initially as a prickle in the back of his neck before making itself heard in his head. *Shouldn't solar eclipses move from west to east?* This one had raced from north to south.

While a small cosmic ripple such as a blue dandelion or a Friday-night movie without a waiting line might have edged him closer for a better look, this massive, sun-dimming crack in reality had him turning to his car. For all he knew, he might have wandered into an army weapons-testing field.

Empty hills.

Sand.

Weird, racing shadows.

It all added up to *hit the road, Jack.*

He should have listened to the hitchhiker in Wyoming. She warned him to ignore the damn billboard.

He got back in the car and turned the ignition key. The engine sputtered, belched, shook, and stopped. Three grinding attempts at restarting it failed.

And still no cell-phone signal.

This couldn't be happening. Any help was at least a half-marathon away. He'd passed the tiny town of Angora over a dozen miles back. Alliance lay ahead, but not much closer, according to the road signs. In between, at ground zero for wrong-way eclipses and stalled Kias, irrigated fields had given way to scrubby hills in all directions. A railroad track and an endless line of wind-beaten telephone poles ran along the east side of the road. Barren, sandy mounds lurked to the west. Closer in, on either side, barbed-wire fencing separated the pavement from the wilderness.

He eased sweaty palms off the steering wheel and tried to think.

First, the government didn't test its weapons along backcountry roads. So check that threat off the list.

And wrong-way shadows? Maybe when the sun and moon were positioned a certain way, eclipses moved in odd directions.

He had a problem with his car to deal with, nothing more. So his tongue needed to stop buzzing like he'd licked the hot points of a D-cell battery. Panic wouldn't get him anywhere.

As for the car, the tank couldn't have gone empty. He'd just filled up in Sidney an hour ago. Some kind of mechanical problem had to be the culprit.

He got out and opened the hood. A burst of shimmering heat bathed his face. He turned away, waited for it to dissipate, came back, poked around in there, and knocked a hose loose. *Why not make things worse than they already are?* He reconnected it, hopefully to the right pipe, and closed the hood before he could do any more damage.

Nothing to do but wait for help. If not from some random driver, then a patrol car.

A crow cawed. Gnats swarmed. The sun beat down on his brains. He wiped sweat from his forehead.

Not a single car or truck came along. Meanwhile, another shadow, this one his own, stretched to cartoonish proportions across the pavement. Unless he managed to stop someone, he'd be stuck there after dark. All night, maybe?

Without a tent.

Or food.

Wi-Fi.

TV.

Forget the basic necessities, what sort of critters wandered these hills? Snakes? Wolves? Wild boars?

His heart thumped in his ears.

He went back into the car, shifted it to neutral, got back out, and went behind to shove it onto the shoulder. Otherwise somebody would come around the curve and take him out, sooner or later.

"Mmmfff." The car wouldn't budge.

Kias were light. He'd moved this one before with no problem.

He cleared some chunks of shoulder gravel away from the tires and tried again. "Mmmfff."

Two sparkly things blinked and fluttered past his eyes. Overcharged electricity from another approaching shadow-storm?

He couldn't tell. The sky above was clear blue, but the surrounding hills shortened the horizon quite a bit. The ground did seem somewhat shaded though. Maybe—

The road shimmered in concentric circles, like ripples in a pool. He lost his balance and reeled forward, slapping his hands on the car trunk to break his fall.

Screeching birds racing skyward from the scrubby fields shook him out of the initial daze. Stinging palms, racing heart, and rapid breathing welcomed him back to earth. And the car's metal trembled beneath his palms.

No, the other way around. His fried nerves made his hands buzzy.

He shifted upright. Opened and closed his fists. Earthquake? No. Far weirder than that. Whatever just happened had been visual, not physical. He was pretty sure he hadn't *felt* the ground shake at all, only seen it. Yet the asphalt pavement, flat a minute earlier, now sloped sharply toward the shoulder.

Brian squared his shoulders. He was *not* going to let panic take over. Move the car and flag down a driver. Then head somewhere, *anywhere,* that didn't make his skin crawl. *That* was the plan. Use logic, leverage, science, and whatever the hell else he'd need to get the job done.

He squatted and studied the slope the way he might have lined up a putt for mini golf. As far as he could judge, his car was positioned to drag to the right if shoved forward, rolling down the incline onto the shoulder. Perfect.

He got back up and pushed again. Hard.

Unlike the world at large lately, the car followed the basic rules of physics, shifting down the incline as he shoved, and curving off the road. He leaned against the trunk and looked down at his asphalt putting green. It had gone flat again.

This had to be some sort of optical illusion.

Time to grasp at straws. The impossible eclipse and shifting road must have been proof he was asleep, dreaming in a nice, warm bed somewhere. Best way to get back where he belonged? He shut his eyes.

A warm breeze ruffled his hair. The land carried the damp earthy smell a passing shower might leave. *Real.* Very undreamlike.

Birds sang. Grasshoppers chirped. Louder. And louder. The sound roared like an engine.

He opened his eyes and waved both arms at the approaching car. "Wait!"

The driver sped by, spitting loose gravel in his wake.

Swell.

A punch line from the classic *Young Frankenstein* popped into his head. *Could be worse. Could be raining!*

No.

Nothing could be worse than this.

"Try lifting your hood again. That's the universal symbol for drivers in distress, isn't it?"

Brian spun around. Blinked.

The prairie gods sent a pretty girl to the rescue?

The best kind of pretty, too. Unconventional. Red hair brushed to a shine, freckles on her cheeks, and a long, washed-out blue dress all said farm girl. But her bright turquoise scarf made a cool *hand-me-down meets The Gap* fashion statement.

Wait.

He'd met her before. Once he got past the dizzying scarf, she looked just like…

*No way.*

The castaway girl in his nightmares had escaped the waves, the noose, and the glowing-eyed man to grin at him, right there in the wilderness.

*Earth to Brian. She was a dream. This girl is real.*

He tried to unfreeze his hanging-open mouth enough to smile back.

"Do you need help?" The girl spoke in a breathless accent. Something like…a brogue? The cherry on top of a chocolate sundae. Clearly, he'd won the cosmic lottery.

But he wasn't big on looking for help from anyone but himself. Never had been. "No, I've got this."

"You've got a broken car by the looks of it, and *I've* got a place down there." She pointed toward a bluff standing taller than the others.

Okay, so maybe he could use a *little* help. He held up his phone. "This doesn't work."

"Why would it?"

"Exactly. Do you have a landline at your place?"

She stared at him as if he'd asked the question in Greek. What was it about people who lived in Nebraska? Finally, "I could *never* let a stranger in my home."

"Oh. Well, that's easy. I'm Brian." He held out his hand. "See? I'm not a stranger anymore. Strange maybe, but not *er*." He was babbling. Unexpected help. Cute girl. Mostly the girl. Yeah, babbling.

"You're Brian...?"

"Danahey."

"And *I'm* Rebecca Church." She took his hand, shook it, let it go. "A fine Brian you are. I've known a few, but I do prefer the dark-haired, handsome type, such as you."

Rebecca's incredible appearance out of nowhere offered the possibility of rescue, the source of a phone, a way to avoid walking at least a dozen miles in the dusk and then darkness to the nearest town. The most important thing though, as he basked in the compliment, wading through the pools of her pale-green, probing eyes, was remembering how to talk.

Because?

The dream. How amazing to somehow *imagine* someone who turned out to be real.

"I never thought of myself as part of a Brian collection," he said...and he gave himself a secret high five for a halfway decent comeback.

"Oh, but you are." She touched his forearm, and the spark buzzed his tongue, this time in a good way. "Perhaps I'll cast a shrinking spell on you. I can keep you on my bookshelf and find others."

A girl who strung her words together like out of a Dickens

novel, *and* with a sense of humor. Always a plus when dreams came alive. He reached deep in the well to come up with another good line. "Lucky for me only witches can do that."

Rebecca looked past him toward the bluff. "If I am a witch, you must hope I'm a good one. I might disappoint you." Her eyes grew distant.

"I doubt that."

"Time will tell."

A cloud drifted across the sun, and a gust of wind set a tumbleweed into motion. It skittered past them and bounded over the road with long legs curled into a ball, like a giant dead spider. Brian would have pulled a hoody over his head if he had one. "Okay, that's just one more strange thing in a long list of weirdness."

She grinned in a sheepish manner as if she'd been the cause of the local insanity. "You mean you saw the shadow?"

"Uh-huh. What was with that?"

She swept an arm at their surroundings. "Hot sun, dry air, static electricity, and too many identical round hills. They all combine to trick the mind."

"And you choose to *live* out here?"

She shrugged. "I'm cabin-sitting for now."

"In the middle of a strange kind of nowhere."

"I'm used to it. Anyway, I have a cat, and we best go feed him. We wouldn't want to starve one of his nine lives away."

"Good one."

Except Rebecca didn't have the look of someone who'd just cracked a joke. Not much of a smile there. She gave off a funny vibe. As if unsure whether to laugh or cry. Maybe she was in a bigger jam than he was, even without a broken car to worry about. Rebecca wouldn't have been the first runaway who busted into an abandoned cabin looking for a place to stay. Imagine the sense of desperation. And here he thought he had it bad because some hitchhiker on the highway hated him, and his mom probably wanted to ground him. As if these were big deals. Like they were anything at all.

"I'll admit most people think this is the middle of nowhere and speed past," she said.

"Almost did, but I think my tank went empty."

"Wouldn't you know one way or the other?"

"Well, I did fill up in Sidney."

Rebecca's burst of laughter rivaled the best songs in the world. Brian knew he'd be a millionaire if he could bottle the sound. And the twinkle in her eyes? Priceless.

"Are you sure they didn't trick you down there?" she asked. "The town has a history of lawlessness."

"I think it's safe to say I got my money's worth." A buck ninety-two for gas. What did the old guy do, put a gallon in the tank and fill the rest with air?

"So now you'll be walking. With me." She turned on her heel and headed away, stepping over a section of barbed-wire fence flattened by time.

Brian hurried to lock the car before she wandered out of sight.

"One can't be too careful," she called. "Car bandits lurk behind every tree." Her voice trailed into giggles. "Come along now. The real villains come out in force after dark."

He rushed after her, got over the fence, caught up. "How far is it?"

"Twenty-four furlongs."

When did that term bite the dust, a century ago? No, he remembered where he'd last heard it. "My dad took my sister and me to the horse races last summer. Ever been?"

"Can't say I have."

"How far is twenty-four furlongs in miles?"

She looked down at her hands and wriggled her fingers, one at a time, as if counting the answer out. "Three."

This Rebecca was a riot. "You're a little crazy, aren't you?"

"You mean *eccentric*?" She grinned. "See? Furlong isn't the only old word I like to use."

"That's cool." Their hands brushed. Spark would be too mild a word for the charge he received. Shock, maybe. No, more than that. Burst, flare…destiny? He needed to get hold of himself. *The other girl was a dream. This one is real. No connection.* "So when you aren't cabin-sitting with your cat, where do you live?"

"I don't want to bore you with the details, Brian. Think of me as an Irish gypsy."

Fine with him. Connection with the girl in his dream or not, if this *eccentric* speaker of old words wanted a traveling companion for the next century or two, he was ready to go all in. "I'm Irish, too."

Her gleaming eyes took on a hint of emerald. "Aren't we a pair, then?"

They continued side by side in silence. Brian opened and closed his hand, still enjoying a slight tingling sensation from when he touched her.

The sandy hills turned gray, and the sun melted into a golden shadow. He and Rebecca kicked up powdery dust.

An oak tree came into sight as they rounded a hill. The hulking giant extended leafless arms upward from a gnarled trunk. Its lowest branches, still covered with greenery, almost masked the top of a rope. Brian's stomach flipped as he followed the thing down, to the rope's stopping point, some ten feet off the ground, *where it ended in a noose.* "Look at that!"

Rebecca muttered *Abigail* almost quietly enough to miss. She kicked dirt at the oak.

"Seriously?" Toilet-papering tree branches during Junior/Senior wars was one thing, but whoever did this had gone way over the top. "Friend of yours?"

"Not hardly." She crossed her arms and stalked away.

"Wait, Rebecca." He caught up with her. "Hey, we all live to be bullied, don't we? Somebody elbowed me into a pool a couple weeks ago."

She looked down at her feet, lower lip trembling, eyes welling. "You…were bullied, Brian?"

"Who hasn't been? It's always a question of toughing it out or kicking some serious butt."

"I suppose the consequences can be dire either way," she said.

"Exactly." He flexed his fingers. No more soreness at the knuckles. Punching the guy in retaliation had hurt like hell.

Rebecca took his hand and gave it a little squeeze. "You'd kick some serious butt to defend *me*, wouldn't you?"

"In a heartbeat."

"Or we could tough it out," she said. "Let's put the tree twenty furlongs behind us."

The warm softness of her hand, the fit, the casual way they intertwined their fingers all trumped the fact they'd only just met.

However far they walked, time passed in an instant. And she hummed all the way. Way too soon, a small cabin came into view. There'd be a phone, then a tow truck, his parents' wrath when they saw the bill, and that would be the end of it. He took a stab at small talk to stop a stifling sense of closure from choking the air out of his lungs. "What made you wander all the way to the road so late in the day?"

"I won't find my destiny sitting alone in a cabin."

*Destiny.* Great minds thought alike. "Were you planning to hitch somewhere?"

"No, Brian. You'll never find me with my thumb out. I'm not so needy I'd ever ask for anything."

"Then I don't get it."

Rebecca stopped walking. "What are we without our hopes and dreams?"

"What if we don't have any?"

"Then you haven't been challenged enough."

He turned to her without a clue what words of wisdom she could possibly use to stave off his ordinary future. How could he avoid putting on a Clark Kent suit instead of the superhero outfit anyone would want to wear instead?

"We want those things hardest earned. They're the very source of our hopes and dreams." The wistfulness in her voice chased the last of the sunlight behind the hills.

Rebecca rammed her shoulder against the cabin door. "This jams at times." *Abigail!*

Brian came up beside her and grabbed the handle. "Let me try."

"Not yet. I just need to kick it right here like this…ungh… and again here…oh!"

The door flew open. Rebecca's momentum nearly pitched her to the floor, but Brian caught her arm. She drowned in his eyes as he steadied her. Such a deep blue! She saw great strength in his steady gaze.

But did he have tenacity? She'd be teasing him for the longest time. The courting rules left no room for misinterpretation. Riddles, illusions, and dreams *only.* So said the Witches Code. Abigail would take delight in her struggles. And do her best to double the challenge.

*Thank you, Henry Stoddard.* He'd brought the mean imp to the cabin.

No matter. She'd prevail. The great prophet Aislinn had written *Rebecca* when carving her prophecy into stone…the girl who'd court a champion the witches' way.

Sadly, the witches' way meant following their code. Besides, she'd promised her mother to be a pure witch, *and pure witches followed that damnable set of rules.*

Enough. Any self-respecting witch should only want a boy so tenacious and loving he'd struggle past her illusions and misdirection, learn the best and worst of her, and still claim her as his bride at the end of it.

But what if he didn't? Could her heart take such a blow after she'd waited so long for Brian? Rebecca clenched her fists until her nails bit into the skin. She had no right to let some silly infatuation *from centuries ago* cloud her thoughts at this critical moment.

"So about that phone," he said.

"Phone?" She drifted in Brian's gaze like a rudderless boat, despite her need to control the game.

# CHAPTER FOUR

**THE DOOR SWUNG CLOSED** behind them, snuffing the twilight outside to total darkness within the cabin. Brian's eyes were slow to adjust. He groped the wall for a light switch. "Hey, where'd you go?"

A giggle. Rushing footsteps. Then, "Welcome to my parlor!" Rebecca struck a match.

Her face came alive in the shadows. Cute, funny, gorgeous, mischievous, glowing, ridiculous, and definitely in need of an invented word. *Fanhauntingtabulous!* The world might have turned a little strange, but overall, this version 2.1 upgrade was pretty cool.

She lit an oil lamp. Unfinished log walls, worn-out furniture, and scuffed slats of a hardwood floor came into view. With the scent of pine needles permeating the air, the only things missing were a rifle rack and a moose's head over the mantel.

A black cat crept out of the shadows while Rebecca hustled around the room lighting candles. "Simon will act shy until he knows you." She settled into an overstuffed chair, and the cat pounced onto her lap.

Man, who wouldn't kick back and stay a while?

Somebody with strict parents, that's who. Somebody with a road trip to finish and college to start. Brian needed to call for the tow truck.

The impending closure dimmed the candles, closed the walls, and lowered the ceiling. He already missed holding Rebecca's hand, missed wandering through the endless hills with her, missed whatever Irish ballad she'd been humming outside. And that upgrade of the world? The clunky beta version would soon become his reality again. Yeah, maybe she'd swap email addresses and phone numbers with him before he left, but more likely than not, they'd reached their control-alt-delete.

*Plenty of other fish in the sea,* his dad would say.

Yeah. Uh-huh. About that...

He backed into the couch across from her. The soft cushions pulled him in as though even the furniture didn't want to see him track down a wrecker for his car. But he couldn't torture himself by dragging out the inevitable good-bye. His cell phone still didn't show any service, so, "Where's your phone, Rebecca?"

"I haven't one."

He couldn't even think about allowing himself to believe he'd heard that right. Of course she had a phone. "Seriously?"

"Who would I need to call?" Rebecca shooed the cat away, sprang from her chair, and headed into the next room. "Are you hungry? I have bread and cheese."

He stared after her. She didn't have a phone. *Duh. How could she have a landline with no electricity?*

The immediate future reshaped itself into a rainbow now that he had an excuse for not hitting the road. Not to mention the fact Rebecca had led him to her cabin with the obvious idea he might stay over.

*But she's somebody's daughter,* his dad would say.

Or somebody's sister. And not the annoyingly older kind, like Kara, either.

So he hurried after her like...a big brother, maybe...cursing his conscience for killing the party mood. Followed her into a kitchen from a thousand years ago. A big open fireplace filled one wall, with blackened cooking utensils hanging above and on either side of the stonework. Shelves lined the rest of the room, holding spices and preserves in glass jars with hand-scrawled labels and metal mugs and little photos in oval frames. A long wooden table took up most of the floor space. No appliances. No indication electricity had ever been invented.

Oh hell, who needed Thomas Edison, anyway? Rebecca lit up the room with her smile.

"What are you waiting for?" She motioned to the plates on the table, the round loaf of homemade bread with its mouth-watering bakery aroma, the sliced cheese.

"Wow. Were you expecting company?"

"I *have* company."

That didn't come close to explaining the spread, but who cared? Eat first and ask questions later. He sat next to her on a bench at the table.

Rebecca poured cider from a clay pitcher. "A farmer made this from apples in his orchard."

He peered out an old-fashioned casement window cranked open enough to allow a refreshing breeze into the kitchen, but nightfall hid every feature outside. "You mean, somebody actually found trees out there?"

"Or planted them," she said. "He's quite capable. I'm sure he can help with your car in the morning."

*In the morning?* Music to his ears.

Nuh-uh. *Big brother, big brother, big brother.*

But she looked to be the same age.

Brian swiped the devil off his shoulder by focusing on the food. He devoured a cheddar-cheese sandwich and washed it down with cider tasting like liquid gold.

Rebecca ate quietly beside him. When she finished, she turned to him with an eye-twinkling grin.

"What?" He glanced down at his shirt for crumbs.

"Nothing. I just thought since we've finished eating, I might read to you in the parlor."

"Read?" No way. Maybe the big-brother concept ruled out anything hot and heavy, but they didn't need to go pilgrim, either. Plenty of better things to do. They could play games on his phone for as long as the battery lasted. He didn't need reception for that.

Or they could go outside, sit on the step catching fireflies and shooting the breeze. When they got bored, maybe they'd look for a creek to dip their toes into. "Yeah, you could read, or—"

"Don't you *want* me to read to you?" Judging by the tremble in Rebecca's voice and her suddenly downcast eyes, one might think he'd threatened to throw the last of the cheese on the floor and stomp on it.

What could he say? "Sweet. Let's do it."

"Sweet?" Rebecca furrowed her brows as if she'd strayed into the extra-credit section of an algebra test.

The girl needed an urban dictionary for sure. This had to be what living alone in Nebraska could do to a person. No sweat. He was happy to translate. So far, doing *anything* with her had been a kick-ass experience. "Reading sounds perfect."

The storm clouds lifted. A bright smile returned to her face. She fished a pencil stub and tiny notebook from her dress pocket and scribbled something down. "*Sweet.* I strive to be modern."

"Awesome."

"That one I know."

They finished eating and headed back into the living room.

Rebecca ran her fingertips across the spines of several books on a shelf—every one of them a girly romance.

Catching fireflies was looking better by the minute. Brian sank deep into the couch.

"Jane Austen wrote *Pride and Prejudice, Sense and Sensibility,* and *Emma,*" she said. "I know this sounds silly, but her stories flutter my heart."

"Adult fairy tales are your thing, huh?"

"Nothing's wrong with happy endings, Brian." She turned toward a corner of the room where an old wooden broom leaned against the wall. "I hope to have somebody to sweep after, one day." Her eyes moistened.

*Uh-oh.* Crying killed him. They'd already had one close call outside when they found that noose. "Well, if it's a choice between maid duty and listening to a Jane Austen reading, I'm thinking where's the mop?"

Rebecca shook her head. A slow smile chased the threat of tears away. She grabbed a leather-bound book from the shelf. "Okay, smarty, I'll read some of *my own* work to you."

That had to be better.

She came over with the book, but before she reached the couch, his shirt started puffing out, as if the seemingly innocent antique mirror a few feet away had gone into suction mode. He pressed the fabric back down with his hand. "Weird."

She stopped. "What's wrong?"

The suction slackened. "I don't know." He went over to the mirror and frisked it, touching the glass, running his hands down its oval wooden frame, tapping the stand with his foot. Seemed normal.

A cold gust ruffled his hair. He leapt back. And his shirt puffed toward the mirror again.

"Brian?"

"You've got gremlins, Rebecca."

"Or imps." She had a wary edge to her voice.

"It's cool. Who wouldn't want their very own poltergeists?" Not that he'd *ever* want to be alone with that mirror. But the two of them had strength in numbers. They could laugh it off. Or throw a blanket over the thing and then laugh it off.

He glanced around. She did have an old quilt on a chair.

Now he was being ridiculous. He looked at the mirror again. Faced it down. Wood and glass. Nothing more. And his reflection. And hers. And—*he became a young boy again, wandering between two mirrors across from each other in the bathroom of a train. They created an endless series of reflections, one against the other, smaller and smaller until too tiny to make out.*

*The mirrors pulled him by the hair and arms, dragging him into their vortex.*

*He cried out.*

*"Black magic," his mom said, coming to the rescue. She led him away.*

"Brian?" Rebecca closed a hand around his wrist.

He shuddered.

Rebecca's forehead was wrinkled. His random zombie fit must have done that to her.

But everything truly was okay. Wasn't it? Strength in numbers, right?

His hands were trembling. *Change the subject. Make some small talk. Anything.* "Hey." He motioned to their reflection. She stood shorter than him by a head, light-skinned, freckled. She wore an old-fashioned, neck-to-ankle dress. Their walk through the dry, windy hills had sprinkled both of them with dust and scattered their hair. "We look like pioneers."

The worry wrinkles disappeared. She smiled. "Perhaps we are."

"Fits pretty well here, log cabin and all."

Rebecca giggled. "Poltergeists, too."

But Wild West and horror didn't mesh. He glanced at the mirror, suppressed another shudder. "Honestly, how can you stay here alone? One creaky floorboard and I'd be racing out the door."

"No, you wouldn't." She brushed his face with the back of her hand. "I know a prophecy about someone named Brian. He'd never let a mere noise scare him."

Her voice came to him from a thousand miles away, barely whispering over her dizzying touch.

She dropped her hand away.

"I, uh, I haven't heard that one," he said.

"The prophecy says he'll be heading toward the challenge of his life."

"Worse than letting you read to me?"

"Ha ha."

He turned to the mirror again, made a face, smoothed his hair.

She touched his arm. "Brian, do you have a girlfriend?"

That came out of nowhere. And fit like a key in a lock. She'd had a hold on him from the minute they met. Hell, he'd been *dreaming* about her even before that. Beyond the intoxicating feel of her touch just now, or earlier when they walked together hand-in-hand, beyond the Irish brogue he'd been able to detect even when she hummed a ditty, beyond the way her dimples showed when she smiled and how wide that smile got when he devoured the simple meal she'd prepared...beyond all that, an undeniable sense of destiny had him ready to give the world a high five.

Step one on the road to herohood in every comic book he'd ever read was for the guy to find a girl who was special and who saw *him* in a special light. Superman had Lois Lane. Spiderman had Mary Jane. Both women were always in danger. Both needed to be rescued over and over again. Both inspired an ordinary guy to rise up and be something more than a newspaper reporter or a photographer *or an accountant with a briefcase and two-point-three kids.*

Take Rebecca, for example. Hints of darkness closed in on her from all directions. Shirt-sucking mirrors. Nooses in trees. Even the eclipse earlier. And she seemed unaware, innocent, needing a—

"I shouldn't have been so forward," she said.

"No, it's just you're too good to be true."

She broke eye contact and stared at her shoes. "That's the test of your feelings. Will you miss me when we're parted?"

He couldn't answer. The reminder he'd be leaving the very next day choked him.

"We shouldn't talk about farewells." Rebecca pulled away and crossed to the couch.

*Tomorrow is a million years away.* Brian sat next to her, and the cushions slanted them shoulder to shoulder. She could have read a thousand Jane Austen novels to him for all he cared, as long as they stayed together like that.

"I've written a collection of short stories in verse," she said.

"Poetry?" Okay, now that was a whole different thing.

"Don't look so scared. I have a nice story in here about someone who can't quite get where he wants to be. Sound familiar?" She cracked the book open.

Brian gaped at a page full of symbols. Poetry in code? He

couldn't get a fix on the alphabet she'd used. *Greek? Hebrew? Arabic?* Something else entirely. Handwritten vertical lines, diagonal hash marks, and other markings had been lined up row by row. Clumped together and spaced apart, they formed what must have been words and sentences.

A scene from *The Shining* popped into his head where the woman learned her husband had been writing the identical sentence over and over for hundreds of pages. The moment she realized he'd gone mad.

But this wasn't craziness. Rebecca had created something amazing. And not just the meticulous hieroglyphics. She'd decorated the margins with tiny stars, flowers, and fairies in a clean-line style and colors that put Disney artwork to shame. "Did you do all of this?"

"Every bit." Her eyes gleamed. "This is a language my mother taught me before I learned a single word of English. She was taught by my grandmother, my grandmother by my great-grandmother, and so on all the way back to my family tree's earliest roots in Ireland."

"And you can read it?"

"I wrote it, didn't I?"

# CHAPTER FIVE

**BRIAN'S POCKET VIBRATED. HOURS** earlier, his everyday life had faded into the background. Now, with a book of hieroglyphics about to be deciphered by a quirky, self-sufficient, *amazing* dream of a girl, now of all times…

"Wait a sec, Rebecca." He pulled out the cell phone. One message, from home. And a bar of service. He could call a tow truck now if he wanted.

*No way.*

He called home. Got the machine. "Hey, it's me. I found a place to spend the night. Talk to you tomorrow." Best he could do. His battery light flashed orange in a cabin short on sockets.

Rebecca gaped at him as if he'd invented wireless.

"They do sell smartphones in Nebraska, right?" he said.

She touched the display with a fingertip, snatched her hand away as if she'd burned herself, giggled. "Who would possibly want such a thing?"

"Me." He wriggled the phone at her.

She shrieked and shrank away.

Her crazy act cracked him up. So realistic he almost believed she'd never seen one before. "My parents worry over nothing. So that was me calling them."

"You're sweet, Brian." She rubbed her shoulder against his.

"You asked whether I had a girlfriend," he said.

"And?"

"I do now."

"You do now what?"

"Have a girlfriend." And who would have thought a single word rolling off his tongue might taste so good?

Rebecca beamed. "You know how being my boyfriend works, Brian?"

"Like maple syrup soaking into pancakes?"

"No, silly." She flipped the pages of her book to a sketch of a scruffy man dressed in rags. "Like I read a story about gallantry, misdirection, and dreams, and you humor me by listening with rapt attention, whether you think it's an adult fairy tale or not."

"Got it."

"I call this poem 'The Vagrant.'" She looked down at the open page.

*"Sunlight bathes his face from blue skies overhead.*
*He blinks*
*and sleep fades from his eyes.*
*Rising now amid the leaves which formed his bed,*
*he stands*
*as morning dew drops dry."*

Rebecca glanced up from the book. "All of my verses have the same meter as the opening stanza. Eleven beats, then two, six, eleven, two and six. The rhythm keeps the words in your head like a favorite song."

Could be, but hieroglyphics in verse? He couldn't get past that. She *had* to be pulling his leg.

Rebecca went for the Academy Award by wetting her finger against her tongue for ease in turning the page, but he refused to buy it. Most likely, she memorized the poem, and the rest was world-class pantomime.

Brian couldn't resist pulling her chain at least a little bit. "Wait. Teach me how to read some of that."

She pressed her lips together, shook her head.

"Top secret, huh? You'd have to kill me if you told me?"

She grinned. "Or turn you into a toad, Brian."

"Nah. Toads eat flies. I'll stick with bread and cheese." And anyway, why not indulge in the cool fantasy that Rebecca could read and write a stick-figure language? He leaned his shoulder against hers and listened.

*"Kneeling by a brook, he washes shaves and drinks.*
*Light beard,*
*blue eyes stare back at him.*
*Combing long blond hair, 'adventure' he now thinks.*
*'A day*
*of magic is my whim.'*
*"As he walks through town a voice from shadows cries,*
*'Go in,*
*your fortune she will tell.'*
*'No.' The vagrant laughs. 'The future care not I!'*
*'Go in!'*
*The voice a magic spell.*
*"Spreading beads apart through candlelight he peers*
*at her,*
*a gypsy beckoning.*
*Turquoise dress, green eyes, gold bracelets, auburn hair.*
*'Sit down,*
*for we must speak of dreams.'"*

Simon jumped up and wedged himself between them, purring like he'd eaten Tweety Bird after years of trying. Rebecca dragged her fingers through the cat's sleek coat. "The fortune-teller sends the beggar away, promising he'll meet a beautiful maiden."

A simple tale with a Hollywood finish, but Brian needed more. He'd been pulled into the gypsy's lair to the point he could smell the candles. "Don't tell me we're closing in on the happily ever after already."

"Not quite yet, Brian. Oracles are vague about the future. The fortune-teller hasn't told him how things will turn out when he meets this maiden."

"Great. Bring it on." Who would have thought a poetry recital could be awesome? A fig bar of a listening experience had magically transformed into two scoops of vanilla fudge in one of those oversized waffle cones with sprinkles melted into the chocolate coating. Whether Rebecca had been reading hieroglyphics—*no way*—or pretending to be, he was all over this concoction.

She took one of his hands. "First, let's see what the future holds in store for *you*, Brian."

Even better. Not that he wanted to know his future. How boring would life be if he knew the outcome in advance? Still, her hand in his was poetry in its own right, enhancing his sprinkle-cone metaphor by throwing alliteration into the mix—try saying *extra ice-cream scoop* fast—not to mention the wow factor.

She traced a fingertip along his palm. "This is your lifeline. It's long, like mine." She slid her finger sideways. "This other line says you'll have a great adventure and try to save the world. I hope you're clever enough to succeed."

"Me, too. Any suggestions?"

But she released his hand and returned to her story.

Before sending the vagrant away, the gypsy used her magic to tattoo his wrist with the likeness of a red-haired maiden. Thinking the marking would lead him to the love of his life, the vagrant headed off to find his promised one.

At nightfall, he stopped at an inn for shelter. The owner beckoned him inside, having interpreted the tattoo as a sign the vagrant had been chosen to fight a dragon. When the vagrant refused to go along with this ridiculous conclusion, the innkeeper and his cronies locked him in a basement dungeon.

Rebecca turned the page to a sketch on the left of renaissance partiers gathered around a feast. On the right, the vagrant cooled his heels behind bars. "Look at the poor man."

"Yeah. Tell me more."

The vagrant relented and agreed to slay the dragon. He soon battled the monster, barely escaped with his life, and ran for the hills. On the way back to town, he stumbled upon the woman of his dreams.

*"Ready now to kiss her lips, her nose, her hair.*
*But no.*
*She fades with plaintive cries.*
*Sunlight bathes his face, he smells the morning air.*
*He blinks.*
*Away from him she flies.*
*" 'Has this dove of mine been just another dream?*
*Good lord,*
*a fantasy I loved!*
*Shannon was my moon and stars aflickering.'*
*Just then,*
*a beast flies past, above."*

Rebecca shut the book, startling Simon to the floor and pulling Brian out of the story before they'd reached the punch line.

"Hold on, Rebecca. I don't get it. Did he dream everything, or what?"

"Who can say?" She got off the couch and stretched her arms. "People *always* think they're awake, even when they're sleeping."

That idea had nothing but downside. Brian teetered at the edge of its slippery slope. "I'd hate to open my eyes and be back on the highway."

She giggled. "Should I be flattered you're enjoying my company? You've earned a gift!" She fished a coin out of her dress pocket and gave it to him.

Brian rolled it from front to back in his hand. Each side showed the face of some hag whose hair flared out behind her as if caught in the wind.

"Once upon a time, a young man stole a lass's heart when he appeared at her window and gave her a coin as well as a promise."

"Is that from another poem?"

She shrugged. "Or a romance. Use this one to buy something, Brian, first chance you get."

What to buy? He glanced around the cabin. Books, candles, old furniture, the cat. He turned to her, and he knew.

"No, not a kiss," she said.

"I wasn't..." Sure he was. The little-sister idea wouldn't hold him at bay much longer. First, she wasn't his sister. And second, she was so... Best not to go there. He slipped the coin into his pocket and glanced at the book. "I should jot some of those symbols down and look them up on the Internet."

"On the..." Rebecca crinkled her forehead, giving the impression she wanted to try her unaware-of-technology joke again. She even reached in her pocket as if going for her little notebook. But she quit the game, motioning to the door, instead. "Come with me. You can't say you visited Nebraska unless you breathe the night air."

They headed outside, sat on the step, caught fireflies, chatted. Rebecca wouldn't answer any questions about herself, steering their talk instead to the local geography. Apparently the sandy hills had been formed by ancient rivers and glaciers. "Or maybe an inland sea," she said. She pulled a tiny shell out of her pocket. "Look what I found behind the cabin one day."

"I'll definitely buy me one of those." He held up the two-faced coin.

She laughed, they traded, and he became the proud owner of a Sand Hills seashell.

Later, they found a creek and dipped their toes into the rushing water. A shooting star shot over the roof of the cabin. She kissed him then, quick, on the cheek, and he wrapped an arm around her. They sat together on a rock and listened to the crickets until she yawned.

"I've got overnight stuff in my car," he said, "and a sleeping bag."

"Too far to walk in the dark, Brian."

They went back inside. Rebecca led him into a tiny room where two simple beds sat a few feet apart from each other. She fished a faded nightgown from a dresser wedged in a corner of the room. "You'll have to sleep in your clothes unless you want one of these."

"Ha ha."

"Turn around, Brian."

"Wait. I'll go in the kitchen while you change."

"The food's all gone," she said. "Stay here. I trust you not to look."

Rebecca must have come straight out of the comic books. Lois Lane would have trusted. Mary Jane would have trusted. Who else? *Nobody.*

Maintaining her trust became more important than breathing. So he turned. He waited. He dared not to look. He hoped not to blush.

"Now back."

Although dressed in an ordinary nightgown, Rebecca stole the oxygen out of the room. Her red hair threatened to ignite the simple white fabric into flames.

His heart pounded. Had to be because she'd changed right behind him. Had to be because they stood so close together.

She settled onto the edge of a bed. "I wondered something."

With head spinning from a bullet blend of desire mixed with emotions less defined, Brian almost didn't hear her. He collapsed onto the opposite bed. "What?"

"You had an odd look on your face when we met, almost as if you'd seen a ghost. What was wrong?"

He hesitated. That moment he first laid eyes on Rebecca had destiny written all over it. He'd seen her earlier in his dreams! But would she buy a ridiculous story anyone else would laugh off? "You startled me, coming out of nowhere the way you did."

"I almost had the impression you knew me." Rebecca leveled him with a razor-sharp stare she must have stolen from his parents. They had B.S. detection down to a science.

He squirmed.

She waited.

He swallowed. "Okay, don't laugh. I've been having nightmares about a girl who looks like you. She's stranded on a rock in the ocean, and there's this hangman or whatever after her. A guy with glowing eyes."

"Oh." Rebecca broke eye contact. She grabbed a corner of the bedsheet in her hand, bunched it up, released it, then crumpled it again. "Is there an imp in your dream?"

"A what?"

"An *imp*." Her voice had gotten edgy, and not in a good way.

"Not unless imps look like tall dudes with glowing eyes."

Rebecca shut her eyes and worked the sheet in her hand like a stress ball.

*Silent vow time. Nix on any dream talk ever again.* Brian looked past Rebecca and counted the wall. Twelve, thirteen, fourteen, fifteen planks. He started in on the floorboards. One, two, three—

"I'm glad we met today." She'd opened her eyes again. And she was smiling at him. The storm clouds had passed.

He breathed. "Same here."

Rebecca came off the bed, kissed his cheek, and skipped to an oil lamp hanging from the wall, blowing out the flame. "Sweet dreams, Brian."

"You, too." He shut his eyes, but the idea of getting any sleep was ridiculous. Rebecca's odd mood shift triggered a parade of disturbing images through his mind—the creepy hitchhiker, the wrong-way eclipse, the impossibly shifting road surface, *the noose*. Some local bully, Abigail, had been punking Rebecca. He clenched his fists.

A better image came waltzing in. A pretty girl coming up behind him on the side of the road. The same girl he'd seen in his dreams. *Rebecca.* She'd kissed him. Twice.

He opened his fists.

Rebecca had read that story about the vagrant for a good half hour, maybe longer. No one could have memorized so many stanzas. *She knew magic.* How else could he explain it? And not only because she translated hieroglyphics. Where did the food come from? How about that funhouse mirror in the next room?

Rebecca knew magic. Rebecca *was* magic. And she liked him. But mysterious storm clouds darkened her mood at times. She needed a hero.

A guy could build his plans around being there for her.

*Yeah?* What kind of plans? How did a girl living in Nebraska fit in with a guy going to college in Wisconsin? A girl without a phone, or a computer.

He clenched his fists again and tried to fight off reality. Rebecca knew magic, Rebecca was magic, and Rebecca liked him. *Almost as much as he'd fallen for her?* One could only hope they'd find a way.

Sometime later—minutes? hours?—he opened his eyes.

The room had gone pitch-black. Judging by the steady breathing coming from the other bed, Rebecca had fallen asleep. Hopefully no glowing-eyed man ever messed with *her* dreams.

Brian closed his eyes again.

More time passed. Dreams became nightmares. An empty gallows. A snarling black cat. Maggots spilling out of the bread and cheese in the kitchen. Brian shot his eyes open. His heart pounded.

A muffled moan came from the next bed.

He was up in an instant.

But Rebecca had simply rolled over in her sleep. The bottom of her sheet slipped to the floor, leaving her legs bare against a chilly draft humming like a harmonica through cracks in the cabin's window frames.

House-sitting for friends? Squatting? Either way, she'd picked one creepy cabin to stay in.

He pulled the sheet over her again.

A sliver of moonlight sifting through the window revealed a door on the opposite wall. Brian stared at it, demanding himself to man up.

He opened the door and stepped back, fast.

Just a closet. What did he think he'd find on the other side, zombies? He grabbed a blanket from a shelf.

Something rubbed against his ankle. "Huh!"

Simon meowed. The black cat would have blended into the darkened room if not for a pair of bright eyes offering no apology for scaring the daylights out of him.

Brian reached down.

The cat didn't shy away.

So he lifted the little guy and put him next to Rebecca. "Keep her warm."

She slept like an angel. A tangle of red hair splaying across the pillow framed her peaceful face.

Rebecca snuck an eye open again, as she had when Brian covered her with the sheet and blanket and made the clamor with Simon. What wonderful qualities he had, just as she remembered from so long ago. Protectiveness, kindness, gallantry. She lay beneath a blanket and had a purring cat at her side as evidence. And Brian had been quick to console her earlier when Abigail's tree-noose prank nearly broke her into tears.

Rebecca and Brian had met before, of course, and she'd briefly prayed he remembered—impossible a notion as that might be. She'd been fooled by the dim recognition in his eyes when she approached him and his silly car, only to have her spirits later dashed when he told her about the nightmares. *Abigail* or *Henry* had surely planted her image in his mind. Pranks, always pranks, especially from Abigail.

Rebecca gazed down at her hands. She'd balled them into fists yet again.

*Good.* She clung to the anger like an extra blanket. If in too soft a mood, she'd never be able to leave.

She got up, knelt beside Brian's bed, and ran her fingers into his hair.

He didn't stir.

"I'm sorry, but courting can't be rushed. I have to follow the Witches Code."

Rebecca hurried out of the cabin.

# CHAPTER SIX

**BRIAN SPED PAST THE** snarky hitchhiker without giving her a second glance, slowed at the billboard, gaped at two nooses this time, and swerved toward the sun. A solar flare shot into his eyes. He gasped, hit the brakes.

Car became bed. Daylight streamed in from the window. Not as bad as in the dream. Not blinding. But still annoying.

He grabbed for his pillow.

It slipped to the floor.

Where was he?

*Nebraska.* Yeah, in a cabin with…

With anyone? Something didn't feel right. Like he'd awakened in a place with about as much life as an empty storage shed.

He cracked his eyes open. The bed across from his was deserted. "Rebecca?"

Not a word in reply. Or a meow. Or the sound of anything but an occasional wind gust humming through the cabin.

He crawled out of bed. Empty drawers hanging halfway out of her dresser sent him reeling. A closet stripped to the hangers dealt another body blow, and a bare Jane Austen shelf in the living room delivered the knockout.

He had trouble inhaling the heavy air. Or maybe he didn't feel like breathing. How had he slept over the noise Rebecca must have made when leaving? And why would she pack up and take off without a word of explanation?

He sank onto the couch and stared into a mirror that had showcased them the night before, not as pioneers really, but as boyfriend and girlfriend. Yeah, that idea had been rushed and ridiculous and the kind of thing they might have joked about later, but now he had nobody to laugh with.

The still air smelled as stale as an attic. Sunlight leaking through dull windows barely illuminated the dust motes caught in its halfhearted rays. Rebecca hadn't merely taken her things. She'd stripped her magic out of the cabin.

He couldn't allow himself to wallow in this gloom. He had to open the front door, let in some fresh air, and—

A pulse of brighter daylight came at him from the side. He glanced through the kitchen doorway and found so sharp a contrast he blinked to be sure. Yep. The sunshiny room beckoned him like a strobe light. A ray of hope. "Rebecca?"

Still no answer.

Off the couch to check it out, he paused at the kitchen doorway and caught his breath. The change in atmosphere was like flying in Oz's balloon from the grayness of Kansas to a land alive with 3-D color images. A yellow brick road, only without the Munchkins. *She'd left echoes of herself,* starting with pink and blue wildflowers bursting out of a vase on the table. Even from a distance, their fragrance overcame the cabin's stifling mustiness with a whiff of summer.

His next step into the kitchen brought the bakery aroma he'd relished the day before. She'd made more bread. And a smiley face grinned up from a plate beside the loaf, formed by curved slices of cheese, a matchstick nose, and two eyes made of sugar cubes.

A small, folded piece of paper poked out from beneath the plate. She must have torn it from that little notebook she kept in her pocket. The question of what she might have written stirred more anticipation than a thousand un-cracked fortune cookies. He snatched it up.

*Enjoy a hearty breakfast! You'll find cider in the jug by the window. Also, I left something important in the cupboard above the spice rack. Keep it for me, and please be clever. You must figure everything out on your own.*

*R*

Brian hurried to the cabinet. Cups, dishes, salt and pepper shakers on the lower shelf. He stretched onto tiptoe.

Her book sat on the upper shelf. She'd tied it closed with a blue ribbon.

How did a girl several inches shorter than he was get it up there? Whatever. Good at jump and toss, maybe. He stretched on tiptoes, grabbed it, and got it down. Then opened the thing and flipped through the pages. Same Greek script on steroids. Same sketches of vagrants, dungeons, dragons. An upright oval mirror like the one in the living room but with a spiral where the glass should be. A black cat. A half-empty hourglass.

What did she mean by clever? Were these drawings supposed to be clues to a riddle?

He flicked the tied ribbon with a finger. It twanged back down like a rubber band, and a sensation of wild genius washed over him. Like what he might have gotten from gobbling an extra slice of pie or by scarfing down half a bag of glazed donuts. Like he could solve the secrets of the universe if only he'd stop bouncing up and down.

But he still couldn't decipher the hieroglyphics, and he didn't see a pattern in the sketches. He set the book on the table and tied it closed again.

The sugar buzz lingered. Twitchy now, he went to the window, took in the vast expanse of hills and prairie, and figured Rebecca out. She'd been escaping this lonely chunk of nowhere when he met her at the road. He'd acted as her pause button, tripping her up for a few hours. But not long enough. Not nearly long enough.

She moved on.

The future dimmed to a zombie-like existence where he'd drag himself from moment to moment, place to place. He didn't even have the energy for *that*. Maybe he'd just crawl back in bed and sleep for a few days.

But wait. Her note hinted at a possible reunion. *Keep it for me,* she'd said. This wasn't the end, then, was it?

What would Spiderman do if Mary Jane bolted before they'd gotten the chance to kick their friendship out of low gear? What would he do if, instead of buildings to swing from, he found nothing but scrubby bushes?

He'd *run* out the door and head for the road, where Rebecca had gone yesterday.

A gas can on the doorstep nearly sent him sprawling.

He found a second note tied to the handle with a string.

*This is from the farmer. Don't look for me. I'll come after you when I can.*

Yeah? How? He fished a pen out of his pocket and scribbled his contact information on the other side of the note. Address. Phone number. Email? *Good luck with that.* Social media wasn't Rebecca's strong suit.

No way would a note work. She'd already left. He crumpled the thing and almost tossed it, but he didn't have any other straws to grasp at. He took the note into the kitchen and left it on the table for her. Just in case she did come back. Maybe. Hopefully.

Of course she would. Otherwise, what was the point of exploding into his life in the first place?

Now what? There had to be a better plan than the Nebraska version of a message in a bottle. Maybe her farmer friend would have a clue where she went. Or he could shoot back to the road and look for her there.

Oh, to be a thousand feet up, scanning the countryside for redheaded angels.

*Farmer first.* He headed back outside. The trail he and Rebecca had taken from the road to the cabin yesterday forked out back, with one prong leading to the creek where they'd soaked their feet. The memory of watching a shooting star with her ached as bad as the empty drawers in the bedroom. He wouldn't find any farms by the creek, only hopeless longing.

He chose the other path and followed it through a narrow gap between two small rises. The trail spilled into a field of undulating hills on the opposite side.

Off in the distance, someone walked alone—not on the path, but angling instead through the scrub. Someone in a dress.

He blinked, shaded his eyes, and still saw her in the fantastic, golden rays of a beautiful, sunny day. "Rebecca!"

He hurried after her, got closer, shouted again.

She didn't turn.

Closer still, the sunlight took on a sinister edge. His eyes had tricked him. This girl had different hair. Darker. Scraggly. She wasn't Rebecca, but he'd seen her before. *Hitchhiking.*

Okay, now he was leaping to crazy conclusions. The crabby hitchhiker in Wyoming didn't have a monopoly on the farm-girl look.

The girl sped her pace. He quickened his. She broke into a run.

Did he make her do that? He stopped chasing. "Sorry," he said to the wind and the bushes, the hills. He hadn't meant to scare anyone.

He'd lost the path. Where had the girl led him? To that farm in the near distance.

He hurried over.

No sign of the apple orchard Rebecca mentioned. Just a low wooden fence separating Brian from some animals gathered alongside an off-kilter barn more gray than red. Chickens clucked and flapped their wings. A couple cows munched on whatever cows eat. The wind didn't do him any favors, gusting their stench in his direction.

A German shepherd charged out from around the side of the barn, barking, snarling, then settling on its haunches near the gate. A gate that wasn't closed all the way.

*Oops.* Brian eased sideways alongside the fence, away from the open gate and the dog's direct line of fire.

The sound of hammering rose from inside the barn.

"Hello?" he shouted.

The pounding stopped. An old man in worn overalls and a straw hat came out. The source of the gas can?

Twitchy again, Brian shifted from one foot to the other. Hot on the trail. Closing in. But what would he say when he found her? She'd chosen to leave, hadn't she? *Don't look for me,* she said. Indecision froze him.

The farmer waited, staring at him with barely a hint of mild interest, as if they had all the time in the world.

But they didn't. "Hi," Brian said, "I'm looking for Rebecca."

"Fixin' to rain later, I reckon."

"What?"

The farmer squinted up at the cloudless sky.

Who cared about small talk at a moment like this? Let it rain. He'd swim though raging floodwaters just to say, *Hey, I get it, Rebecca. You couldn't spend another day out here. But let's stay in touch and—*

He needed to stop zoning out and stay focused. "Did Rebecca tell you where she was headed when she came by for the gas?"

"Who?"

*"Rebecca."*

No reaction, just the patient stare of a man who probably spent his days counting the same hills over and over again.

"You know her, right? She's my age, red hair, about five foot six. She has a thing for plain dresses and loud scarves."

The man spat on the ground and ran a heavy work boot over the splotch until it turned from mud to dust. All…the time…in the world. "Ain't nobody named Rebecca or anyone else around here."

"Sure there is." Brian had gone from twitchy to screechy, but he couldn't slow down. He swept an arm toward the hills behind him. "She's been staying in the cabin up that way."

"Ain't no cabin, neither."

Wrong guy. Brian needed a *sane* farmer. He bunched his fists. "Which way is the next farm?"

The man cackled. Like this was a joke. "You're in rangeland, son. The soil ain't suited for much of anything else. I've been hanging on to this plot way too long. You won't find another farming fool between here and Alliance."

The dog snarled again, and the farmer's calm demeanor dissolved into the weary, pressed-lip expression so common in adults when they've been asked too many questions. Clearly, this man hadn't built his day plan around talking to Brian. He had random hammering to do. "Watcha doing out here? You're way off the main road."

"My car broke down." Brian fished the phone out of his pocket. A blank screen. The battery had died. Not that he expected to find any service bars on it anyway. "I sure could use a landline."

"It's down." The man pointed to the farmhouse. Wooden telephone poles as gray as the barn tumbled along nearby, but nothing connected house to pole. No wires hung loose, either. The line might have been down for years.

More cosmic malware. Brian suppressed a shudder. Another eclipse could sweep through any minute. And Rebecca was out alone somewhere in this godforsaken place.

The farmer turned and walked off. The dog followed him into the barn. A moment later, hammering resumed.

*Now what?* The road. He should have headed that way to begin with.

Brian hurried the way he'd come, but he couldn't find the trail. Identical sandy hills surrounded him in all directions. The prospect of being stranded in this wilderness did an even better job of making his heart pound than the crazy farmer had.

He hated to go back to Old McDonald, but that stupid place with its dumb cows, clucking chickens, and insane weather reports would probably be the best vantage point to get his bearings and start over. He turned around and—

No farm in the distance. Only hills.

He climbed a rise for a wider view.

More hills.

He came back down and found a path of trampled twigs and grass. It led him in a circle.

Brian fought the panic gurgling in his ears by constructing a list. *Find Rebecca. Wish her well. Get the car fixed. Finish the road trip.*

He'd missed some steps. *Find the road. That's where she'll be. No. Stop at the cabin first for the gas can.*

The sun beat down on his brains. The list simplified. *Walk faster. Look around that big hill over there.*

He did.

On the other side, a familiar pair of hills separated by a narrow gap beckoned him.

Maybe. *Please.* He hurried between them.

And saw the cabin.

"Yes!" Brian punched his fist in the air. His shout stirred a few birds into flight, over the cabin roof, and across the sky.

As he approached from behind, he noticed a wooden cross he hadn't seen earlier when chasing down some scraggly-haired girl. A girl who'd done a pretty good job of getting him lost and costing him what little time he had before Rebecca's trail got cold.

Nah, he'd done that to himself by wandering off the path without taking note of any landmarks.

The cross lurched out of the ground, ringed by a circle of red and blue flowers. Not wildflowers like in the kitchen vase. These had been planted and cared for. He bent close but couldn't make out much of the weathered inscription on the cross, just a portion of the date—seventeen hundred and something. No, that had to be a faded nine, not a seven.

He headed to the front of the cabin and went inside.

She hadn't returned.

If only he could talk to her for a few more minutes. *Are you okay? Here, take my phone. I'll get a new one, and I'll call you so we can talk when you're ready to talk.* But she'd left without talking. And what could she have done with a dead phone anyway?

*Please be clever,* she'd said. *You must figure everything out on your own.*

Figure what out? How?

She wanted him to take her book. He went inside and got it, came back out, grabbed the can of gas, and headed for the road. This time he stuck to the path and didn't get lost.

When he reached the oak tree, the noose was gone. Did Rebecca come this way and take it down? She'd been bullied by someone. A girl named Abigail. Maybe Rebecca had done the best thing by getting away.

But they'd held hands. She'd hummed. They'd been pioneers.

He trudged past the noose-less tree.

Furlong count. What else to do when a morning turned stale? She'd told him two distances. Road to cabin was twenty-four furlongs. *Tree* to cabin was twenty. So tree to road was four. A half mile. A thousand more steps. The sun was getting hot already. He wiped his brow. Shouldn't have left his White Sox cap in the trunk. He walked, counted, tried not to think. Six hundred. Eight hundred. Nine hundred. He looked up—

Brian gaped at a Kia on the wrong side of the road. He and Rebecca hadn't crossed the asphalt on the way to her cabin the night before, but he *would* need to walk over it to reach his car now.

A second impossibility sent his stomach into a dive. The late-morning sun, behind him at the cabin, somehow had gotten ahead of him at the road, traveling way too far for the forty-five minutes or so he'd been walking. He glanced at his watch.

The numbers blurred.

A wave of dizziness sent him into a slow, circular spin, as if a gigantic merry-go-round dragged him and everything in sight along the same round path.

He looked up. Now the sky twirled while he stood motionless beneath it.

Brian staggered into the car and shut his eyes. The hike from cabin to road shimmered like a fuzzy dream. But he had that gas can as proof he'd been awake, didn't he? He got out and poured the fuel into the tank.

Back behind the wheel, Brian turned the key in the ignition.

The engine roared to life.

So he *had* run out of gas, Sidney fill-up or not. *A buck ninety-two.* That practical joke had started him on one insane adventure. He had a hole in his heart now to prove it.

Still, Rebecca's notes had been cheerful. And she'd brought flowers into the kitchen. Maybe he'd made her happier in some small way.

Her scribbled words carried an oracle's vague promises of a better future. *Keep it for me… I'll come after you when I can.*

This couldn't be the end of the Brian-and-Rebecca super team. For sure he'd find her walking along the road.

# Chapter Seven

REBECCA STOOD A STONE'S throw from the end of the world. The darkest cloud conceivable stretched for miles in each direction and all the way from ground to sky. Biting cold radiating out of this void chilled her like a winter wind.

In the waking world, she could have hurried to the warmth and safety of her cabin a short distance to the west.

Even here, in the World of Mortal Dreams—the vast dimension created by the collective imagination of everyone who ever lived—she wouldn't normally worry over finding her home. This place had always contained a fairly reliable duplicate of the waking world in addition to the fantasyland its dreamers constructed.

Until recently.

A tear tickled her cheek. The prophecy foretold a period of creeping decay before full apocalypse arrived, but a dear piece of real estate had already fallen. Her mother's most vivid dreams took place in this hilly wilderness of northwest Nebraska where she'd spent many years in exile. Yet the last time Rebecca came looking, much of the region had been swallowed by the darkness.

Did she now have reason to hope? The void had shifted to the north and east. The thriving prairie grass at her feet had been hidden a week earlier. Perhaps she'd find the cabin now. She hurried west along the edge of nothing.

A mile later, just beyond the westernmost side of the suffocating gloom, the ramshackle structure came into view. Would the void return? *Of course it would. Eventually. Just as foretold.* Tears blurred Rebecca's vision.

Once at the cabin, she settled onto the doorstep and tried to steel herself for the confrontation sure to come. Her mother wouldn't be happy to see her. Not when she realized Rebecca had traveled back through time from the twenty-first century. *"Leave thy dead kin in thy fondest memories, where they belong,"* she'd scolded many times.

No matter. Despite the wooden cross rising from the sand behind her waking-world cabin, she knew she'd find her mother alive in this one. Everyone's dreams lingered beyond the grave. Interacting with her mother was simply a matter of stepping into those resonating dreams from the past. She still clung to these echoes of her mother's life, pretending with all her heart they were real, pretending a woman's life could last forever, at least in this netherworld.

Rebecca found her mother slicing potatoes in the kitchen. She stood in the doorway and watched, savored, before stepping forward to make her presence known. "Hello." The word nearly caught in her throat. They'd never gotten along well in the days when they prepared their meals together, so why did the sight of her mother working alone at the table now threaten to melt her heart?

Her mother beamed at her. She dried her hands on her apron, reached out, and swept a bang out of Rebecca's eyes. "Why the sadness?"

"No, it's happiness! I haven't seen you in so long."

"Nonsense. Art thou not sleeping in that very room?"

She followed her mother's gaze to the lump beneath the sheets visible through the doorway to the bedroom...and shuddered. Time travel always brought the surreal possibility of encountering one's earlier self.

Her mother narrowed her eyes. "Thy father is long dead, but my grief still bubbles to the surface whenever I visit *his* dreams. Do not torture thyself in the same way."

Another tear warmed Rebecca's cheek.

"Store my dreams in the purse of thy mind, but stay out of them, Rebecca."

"But Mum, the void might keep me away from them forever."

"What void?"

Rebecca held her tongue. How could she worry her mother over such things?

"Hast thou found the lad?"

At last, a happier topic. She nodded, smiled.

"But why must I capture his heart, Mum? Is this not cruel for both of us?"

Her mother clucked her tongue. "I see the lad has captured yours already, child. And so he should. Does the prophecy not call for Rebecca and Brian to face the darkness *hand in hand?*"

But would they succeed in defeating the void? Rebecca didn't see how they could.

"Follow the code in courting him." Her mother motioned to the thick, leather-bound book resting at one end of a spice shelf, a work handed down from generation to generation and one Rebecca had spent many hours studying in her younger childhood. This book was now a source of frustration, if not outright misery, because of its strict rules for communication between suitors, which it termed a *celebratory dance of misdirection.*

Rebecca wrung her hands. *Poor Brian. Poor me.*

Her mother had spoken of the book with a note of pride in her voice. And why shouldn't she? She'd used the Witches Code when landing a husband, raising a daughter, making a life in the wilderness, and any number of other notable accomplishments.

"Yes, Mum." But what if Brian forgot about her during the mandatory separation required by the code? What if he found some other girlfriend? Boys did that sort of thing, didn't they?

All the time.

# CHAPTER EIGHT

**WITH KNEES PRESSED AGAINST** the hard pavement of some random Madison street, Brian ran his hand along the tread of his flat tire. He cut a finger on a shard of glass. "Damn it!" He pulled away, sat on the curb, and daubed a drop of blood against the bottom of his shirt.

Time for a self-intervention. He belonged on his campus here in Wisconsin, so why keep trying to head out of town where broken beer bottles might be easy to find, but missing girls? Not so much.

Two-weeks earlier, the day he lost Rebecca, he'd searched up and down the dusty roads of northwest Nebraska for a whole afternoon. He didn't find her. She was history, and he had a life. So he limped to Wisconsin, started school, found a part-time job, made new friends. He built the same wall between past and future everyone did when they entered college. Who looked back? Who clung to old girlfriends? Especially girls they'd only known for a single day.

No one.

Except him.

The urge to drop everything and return to Nebraska, the mad impulse to *look for Rebecca,* just wouldn't quit. He thought about her, dreamed about her, and even suffered through dreams aimed at keeping them apart. A recurring one, starring the scraggly-haired Wyoming hitchhiker with a brand-new message. *"You'll never find her. I'll stop you."*

No, she wouldn't. Not if he set his mind on going back.

But his car wouldn't rise to the occasion. His starter broke a few days earlier when he skipped a class and started driving west. Now a tire had gone flat.

"Brian?"

He jumped at the sound and swung around.

No scraggly-haired villain, that was for sure. Long blonde hair, friendly smile, loud Badgers jacket. This girl seemed familiar. She knew his name...

"It's me, Sharon, from the video store?"

Oh. His part-time job. Remembering all the new people in his world had been a problem at school, too, especially with the girls, unless they looked like Rebecca. This one didn't. "Hey. Yeah. I didn't recognize you."

Sharon lowered her gaze to her jacket and played with the zipper. "I'm not always memorable."

Great. He'd hurt her feelings. "Sure you are. But I'm living the dream at a hundred miles an hour. New city, new school, new job. I'm surprised I can remember my own name."

"No, I totally get that." She gave up on the zipper, glanced into his eyes, looked past him, then at him again. "Anyway, Abigail told me you aren't in the dorms. You're living with your aunt, right?"

"Yeah, it's free and I get more than half a room." They'd lapsed into small talk, and he needed to deal with his tire. But something didn't fit just now. "Who's Abigail?"

"My roommate. She knows you."

"She does?"

"Sure. And she suggested I take you for ice cream tomorrow night. After two weeks alone off campus, it's time you mingled, right?"

Mingle. Yeah, in Nebraska, maybe. With Rebecca. He glanced at his flat. Did he have a real spare buried in the trunk or one of those stupid donuts? "You mean, like hanging out? Sorry, I'm kinda—"

"I mean, like friends." Sharon shifted around to the trunk. "Come on. I'll help you put the spare on."

They changed the tire together, like friends. Then he went his way and she went hers.

A few hours later, back in his aunt's condo, Brian gave up on the textbook in his lap. Supply and demand, market fluctuations, Keynesian theory—seriously? He turned his attention to the PC on his desk and logged on to Google maps.

*Nebraska.* For a couple weeks now, he'd been reliving an amazing day by staring at roads and setting his mind on wander. *There.* He and Rebecca met on Highway 385, a little south of Alliance. The map didn't show much. No other paved roads. A lonely area littered with random hills. And somewhere in those hills, one very important cabin.

He had to drive back. But only after he slogged through an upcoming ice-cream date with Sharon in a couple nights, a heavy load of classes the day after, and two eight-hour shifts at the video store over the weekend.

*I'll find a way.*

He glanced back down at the economics book and fought to keep his eyes open.

Brian's ear ached. His pillow had gone lumpy. The air changed, too, from the scent of the flowers Aunt April left in vases everywhere to...pine?

"It's me," Rebecca whispered from above.

He almost shot up. He almost shouted with joy. But Rebecca's voice left a hollow echo. If he opened his eyes, would he see her standing over his bed? No. He'd been dreaming and probably still was. The merest whisper on his part might fade her into the night.

He kept his eyes shut. He held his tongue. He listened.

She breathed above him, steadily, reassuringly.

Brian ignored his pounding heart and counted to ten, just to be sure.

More breathing. The pine scent grew stronger.

"Rebecca?"

"Yes."

His happiness meter shot from zero to sixty. Like the DJ at a rave, he set his mind on loop, replaying the awesome ring of her voice. *It's me. It's me It's me.* He pushed the needle, scratched the record, played the chorus. *Yessss.* After a fruitless search along the roadside in Nebraska, after his failed attempts to drop everything and look again, and after two disappointing weeks of college because one half of a super team wasn't super at all, now, at last, he'd found her.

Or she'd found him.

A sense of weightlessness floated him to an upright position. He opened his eyes.

Rebecca perched on the edge of the bed. The glow of early dawn, or maybe twilight, filtered through the window, allowing him to make out her dimples, an almost smile, and the grayish green of her eyes. She came dressed in the same nightgown she'd worn in the cabin that night. Or *this* night? He glanced around.

*Wow.* He might have gone to sleep in Aunt April's condo, but he'd awakened in a cabin hundreds of miles to the west. They were in her tiny bedroom, the rustic one with four walls made of plank and harmonica gusts of wind humming through the cracks. "Tell me I had a weird dream about starting school and spending a couple weeks there, but I'm actually still at your place."

Her smile wavered. She looked down at her hands. "I can't say that."

Of course she couldn't. Because he'd gone to sleep in his clothes that night in Nebraska, and now he wore a ridiculous pair of Superman pajamas his mom had bought for a joke, the ones he only put on after every last item in his drawer found its way into the laundry basket. He reached for the sheet to cover himself. *Wait. Why bother?* "*This* is the dream then, isn't it, Rebecca?"

She nodded, solemn-faced.

He slumped back down to the lumpy pillow.

Looking up at her, he could swear her eyes became mirror-like, reflecting through welling tears the loneliness and longing he'd been dragging around like a shadow since she left him.

Her smile crept back. "We witches know when we're dreaming. We have a sixth sense for that sort of thing."

"Wait. You only have six senses?"

She poked his arm. "I have a coin you can use, funny man, so you'll always know whether you're asleep or awake. I tried giving it to you before, but you bought a shell from me with it, remember?"

He tried not to remember. Memories stung. "Either way, this isn't real, Rebecca. You're only in my head."

"Dreams *are* real, Brian. You have to believe that." She faded. The wall behind her became vaguely visible, as if she'd turned into a veil. "I miss you, Brian."

"Wow. Do I *ever* miss you." He groped for her hand, grabbed nothing.

"I'll leave proof how real this is," she said.

*Bip, bip, bip, bip, beeeeeeeeep!*

Brian jerked his head up. He'd crashed at his open laptop, settling his face on the keyboard.

He rubbed his ear. Another dream about Rebecca. She might have hit the escape key out of his life, but his subconscious kept booting her back online. Even just now.

Brian tried to remember what they'd said to each other, but the harder he focused on the dream, the vaguer its details became. No matter. He'd been with her. That was enough.

But where was this Rebecca fixation going? Did it really

make sense for him to keep his hopes alive by driving to Nebraska at the next opportunity? Why not lose himself in school, new friends, or whatever, and give up the fight? He needed to get over his obsession. He needed a distraction.

Not much of that here in the condo, though. His aunt worked the late shift at a local diner and usually headed to her boyfriend's apartment after work. Days and nights often passed without any sign of her. Some mornings she'd show up and greet him with a warm breakfast and friendly banter, but she never stayed long. *A young man needs space,* she'd told him, an initially awesome concept now gone flat.

"April?"

No answer.

He glanced at his computer screen through bleary eyes, blinked, stared more closely.

*Sunlight dances past glass beads in doorway strung.*
*She frowns*
*then combs her auburn hair.*
*"Tell me crystal ball another day begun,*
*who now*
*will tread upon my stairs?"*

"Oh. My. God." A poem. On his computer. Where Google maps should have been.

*Gazing in the ball her eyes flash emerald green.*
*She stands,*
*slips on a simple dress.*
*Every day the same, she rises, dresses, preens,*
*then writes*
*of princes and their quests.*

Rebecca told him something that night in the cabin. "All of my verses have the same meter as that opening stanza. Eleven, then two, six, eleven, two, and six."

He took a deep breath. Counted the beats per line. Eleven, two, six, eleven, two, six. *This had to be her writing.*

"The rhythm keeps the words in your head like a favorite song," she'd said.

Yeah, but these weren't stanzas Rebecca recited that night. So where did they come from? *He* wouldn't have burst into a poetry-writing fit. Or if he did, whatever he might have come up with would have been to poetry what stick figures were to art. He couldn't have done anything this good.

*Haze turns sun to gloom, but candles quell the dark.*
*Gold flames*
*reflect within her eyes.*
*Other than a couch and mirror the room is stark.*
*She sighs.*
*She sits. She starts to write.*
*Words flow through her pen directly from her heart*
*to feed*
*her fiery fairy tales.*
*Gallant knights, fair maids, true lovers torn apart,*
*her dreams*
*like ships begin to sail.*

Rebecca had told him something in the dream he'd just had. What did she say? The few remaining fragments of their conversation had sunk into the muck of misplaced memories where all dreams go to die.

*Minutes turn to hours she scribbles restlessly,*
*her tale*
*of wizard's evil spell,*
*cloistering a maid so she can never flee*
*beyond*
*a glass-surrounded shell.*

End of poem.

What did she tell him in the dream? He closed his eyes. He let his mind wander. Then he focused quickly, trying a surprise attack to dredge her words out of the muck.

*I'll leave proof this is real.*

"Oh. My. God." She'd left proof, all right.

A draft blew in from a half-open window, and he caught a whiff of a pine tree outside. Just like an old song on the radio bringing memories to life, the scent ushered the feel of her into the condo. He could almost hear her voice. If he closed his eyes, he'd see her in her cabin.

He printed the poem and took it into the kitchen. Rebecca's book sat beside the microwave, still tied closed by the ribbon she left. He'd been treating this spot like a shrine. All he had left of her.

As he set her verses on top of the book, his hand brushed the ribbon.

What a rush! Like he'd plugged his mind into a power outlet. A parade of ideas popped into his head but raced away before he could grab hold of one. They looped around and came at him again. He tried to slow them down.

What if he and Rebecca had bonded so tightly during their brief time together she was now able to *hack into his dreams with her mind,* delivering a poem, which he'd pounded into his computer in an epic fit of sleep-typing?

Suppose Rebecca was way beyond ordinary. *"If I am a witch, you must hope I'm a good one."* She'd said that. He'd taken it as a joke. But what if it hadn't been?

That old guy in Sidney pointed him north, leading to a breakdown farther up the road, complete with wrong-way eclipse and shifting pavement. The cause and effect had supernatural manipulation written all over it.

The sequence of impossible events later accelerated, from the cheese and cider she came up with out of nothing to the suction-like tug of her mirror, and later her recital from a book of hieroglyphics—not to mention a full can of gas waiting on the doorstep the following day and a farmer claiming the cabin didn't exist.

*I hope you're a clever boy. This line says you'll have a great adventure and try to save someone.* What had she meant by that? The sensation of her fingertips dancing along his lifeline had been too dizzying for him to ask.

And who was he supposed to save? This latest poem had to be about her. The fortune-teller had green eyes. The description of her simple home sounded like the cabin. But what danger could possibly threaten a witch whose powers could blot out the sun, manipulate a car, bend the road, and create food, drink, *and fuel* out of thin air? Someone that amazing couldn't be in trouble, could she?

Wrong question. If Rebecca *was* in trouble, what was he going to do about it? This was his call to action. Spiderman would be swinging from the buildings by now.

Brian moved his hand from the ribbon, and the flood of ideas abated.

He touched it again.

Nothing.

Had he drained it of its power?

Now he was thinking goofy again.

But the poem said otherwise. The poem served as *proof* something big was going on. He hurried back to his computer. Had to find a way of contacting her directly. He hit the return key. He tried the escape. "Where are you? How do I track you down?"

# CHAPTER NINE

**THE GIRL IN A** wall poster across from Brian and Sharon's booth must have been sipping liquid gold through a straw, judging by the rapturous lift of her eyes to the heavens. She did a great job of selling Crazy Bob's Soda. Sharon was on her second.

The ad proved to be the perfect icebreaker, too. Rotating lights aimed from the ceiling changed the poster girl's hair from blue to red, yellow, green, and colors with designer names like turquoise, magenta, amber, taupe. Her eye color, too. And her lips. Brian and Sharon joked about the combinations during what might have been an awkward beginning to their ice-cream date when they would have otherwise had to watch each other and talk about themselves.

That would have been tough, because Brian didn't have much to say. He never would have agreed to the date if he'd known the sleep-writing poem was coming. Once he had proof he and Rebecca were linked through an impossible wireless signal *right into his mind,* the idea of dating or mingling or whatever Sharon had in mind didn't shine with a whole lot of luster.

He'd come close to canceling. Almost called her. Almost texted.

But Sharon helped him change his tire. He at least owed her a sundae.

So they'd gone to Crazy Bob's Concoctions, grabbed this

booth, and slowly, with the help of the poster, Brian began enjoying himself.

At first.

His milkshake went down smooth and chocolaty with a hint of peanut butter. Flavor of the week. Also, Sharon proved to be more than a blonde-haired, blue-eyed Badgers cheerleader, which would have been plenty for most guys. She was a movie buff, a Mumford and Sons fan, a reader of Spiderman comics.

But after they'd kicked around the latest DiCaprio movie and raved about a Marvel phone app, their conversation sagged. Brian glanced again at the soda ad, and Sharon faded into the background. The poster girl's hair had turned red, her eyes pale green. Her resemblance to Rebecca pulled him right into the frame. She might as well have shouted the words now echoing through his head. *Go to Nebraska and find her.*

How? He had classes. He had a part-time job. He had a car that broke down all the time. He had an aunt who'd never understand his reasons for taking off. She'd call his parents, and they'd ground him for life.

*Excuses.*

Would Rebecca even be there if he looked? She'd left the cabin and taken all her things.

*She typed a poem on your computer. She's longing for you.*

And he *ached* for her.

"Why aren't you paying attention to me, Brian?" Sharon set her milkshake down and eyed him as if she were studying a new species of fern in the biology lab.

How long had he been gaping at the ad? Why had the lights gotten stuck on those colors? He forced his gaze back to Sharon. "Sorry, I've been out of it lately."

She reached across the table, took his hand. "Something's on your mind."

No spark. Not even when touching. *She isn't Rebecca.*

He couldn't explain that to her. Discussing a different girl during a date went against all wisdom. That's how guys ended up getting splattered with milkshakes.

"Maybe *somebody's* on your mind," she said.

Great. His thoughts were leaching into the airwaves. Consolation time. "Listen, Sharon, you're fantastic."

She yanked her hand away. "Let's not go there. We're friends having milkshakes. And *this friend* wants to hear why we won't become anything more than that."

"Because I fell on my head when I was a little boy?"

Sharon looked past him. And why not? He'd given her reason to write him off as inattentive at best, if not outright rude. She'd have no problem finding worthier ice-cream companions.

Could he say the same for himself? Blasting out of high school early had its disadvantages, and living off campus made it worse. He'd just started college where *everybody* was at least two years older than he was. So far, people hadn't been waiting in line to help him fix his tire or have ice cream at Crazy Bob's. If he wanted a friend, the time had come to open up. "I met somebody before the semester started."

"Knew it!" Sharon beamed like she'd won the lottery. Clearly, she lived for boy-meets-girl stories. "So what happened? You went to college and she joined the army?"

"Nope. That would be different. This was *weird*."

"I'm all over weird!" She shifted her elbows to the table and settled her chin in her hands. "Tell me everything."

*Everything?* Maybe just a watered-down version that wouldn't send her running for saner ice-cream pals. He took a deep breath. "I was driving home from a wedding in Wyoming. The trip got old, so I let somebody at a gas station talk me into taking a detour. He filled my tank, only he didn't fill it, and I ran out of gas in some wilderness area called the Sand Hills."

"Wait. You lost me at the tank."

"I can't explain. The whole first part of this thing was like wandering into a psychology experiment. After that, the *entire world* morphed into the final exam of Insanity 101."

"In English?"

"Like I saw an eclipse, but the pictures I took didn't show it." He pulled out his phone and opened the photo icon for her.

She scrolled through the pics, turned the phone sideways, flipped it upside down. "Looks sunny."

"Right. And try finding a story about the eclipse online. Anyway, that's where I met Rebecca for the first time. *But I knew her!* I'm sure I saw her earlier in a dream."

Sharon clicked through more of his pics. "Where is she?"

Good question. He took a gulp of his milkshake, but not even chocolate laced with peanut butter could ease the sting. "Feel free to call me an idiot for not snapping her picture."

She passed the phone back across the table. "I should. You dreamed about Rebecca before you ever met? She must be your destiny."

Yeah. Exactly. "But how could I dream about somebody I didn't know yet? You don't find the concept a little crazy?"

"Not in the slightest." Sharon pulled her own phone out of her purse and opened the notes icon for him. She scrolled through dozens of entries such as *Saturday, June 1: Banshees,* and *Thursday, July 25: Endless hallway.* "You're talking to a girl who writes all of her dreams down and looks for hidden messages."

That sounded like a great idea.

She shoved her phone back into her purse. "So you met the girl of your dreams. *Literally.* Then what?"

"She took me to this old cabin where she'd been staying. The place didn't have electricity, so we spent the evening in candlelight."

Sharon's smile widened to dreamy. "Romantic."

"Uh-huh. You'll probably love she's a Jane Austen fan." But he couldn't laugh it off. He would have been willing to read every romance novel in the world to buy one more day in that cabin with Rebecca. Maybe if he hadn't slept like a log when she left, he could have slowed her long enough to make sure they had a way to stay in touch.

Still, they *were* in touch now, weren't they? Through dreams. And poetry.

Sharon stirred the remnants of her milkshake with a straw, as if trying to dredge up a storyteller who didn't zone out every ten seconds.

"Okay, here's the weird part, Sharon. She read a poem from a book written in some foreign language. Way foreign. We're talking a different alphabet. She translated so fast you'd think she was reading English."

Sharon kept stirring, glanced up at him, shrugged. "You mean like Chinese? So what? I have a friend who took Chinese in high school. Not everyone signs up for Spanish."

"I mean like Sanskrit. No, not even. Different combinations of lines and hash marks."

She stopped stirring.

"Rebecca read *hieroglyphics* with no problem."

"Shut up." Sharon had her chin in her hands again.

"Yeah, that's what I mean! Anyway, Rebecca hit the road while I was sleeping. She took everything she had except the book. She did leave a couple notes with hints she'd come looking for me, but—"

The waitress came over with their check in the nick of time. He'd been ready to babble about mind-melded poetry written in his sleep, dream visits by Rebecca, failed attempts to go after her, a hitchhiker haunting his dreams and saying no at every turn. A story line Sharon wouldn't buy in a million years whether she took notes about her own dreams or not. Nobody would buy this.

"Can I see the book?" she asked.

"I don't know. I—"

"You're in love with a ghost."

"A what?"

"A girl started haunting your dreams." Sharon ticked the point off on a finger. "Then she appeared out of nowhere." Another tick. "No pictures." Another. "She read to you from a fairy book." A handful now. "Then, she disappeared in the middle of the night."

She grabbed her purse. "Don't you think this sounds like a ghost story? Let's go check out that book."

An hour later, Brian and Sharon soaked up the Indian summer atmosphere from the top step of his aunt's porch. The warm weather fooled all manner of insects into swarming out of their hiding places. Fireflies flashed on and off—odd little ones darting so fast he couldn't grab one. Chirping crickets reminded him of his early-evening walk to the cabin with Rebecca. No gnats, though, and for that he was grateful. Only a cluster of moths dancing around the porch lamp.

The door opened, and Aunt April burst out, sporting a tight leather skirt and studded jacket. Long hair brushed to a shine tumbled down her shoulders. Date night.

She came bearing smoothies in glasses cold as ice. Although at least twice their age, April hadn't lost touch with the modern world. She was a One Republic fan, a serial text-messager, and, above all, a blender ninja.

Brian slurped at least a third of the chocolaty-banana delight in the few seconds it took April to step around them and hurry down the stairs.

"Don't wait up," she shouted.

Sharon sipped quietly in her own little corner of smoothie heaven—must have been the hint of rum that pulled her in— until April clicked her four-inch heels all the way down the block. "There goes your hall monitor."

"I'm living the dream."

Sharon finished her drink, set the glass on the step, and looked up at an awesome sky boasting ten thousand stars plus a full moon. But she sighed. "This street's awfully quiet, Brian. You should reconsider the dorms."

"And share ten feet of space with somebody annoying? Like maybe a Cubs fan?"

"Abigail's neither. She's cool."

The roommate, who supposedly knew him. "Hey, I still can't place her, Sharon."

"Really? I'll ask how she knows you." Sharon grabbed the book and held it up to the light. She tried to undo the ribbon holding it closed, but a spark shot out of it. "Oh!"

The book went flying. He caught the thing before it could do a nosedive down the stairs.

Sharon inched her finger back to the ribbon and gave it a flick. "I've been getting sparked a lot lately."

"Don't shuffle your feet when you walk."

"Thanks, Mom." She took the book back, opened it, and fit the ribbon between the pages. "You're supposed to use this as a marker, see?"

A mere glimpse at the weird alphabet brought Rebecca right onto the porch. Brian closed his eyes and breathed the strawberry scent of her hair, felt the warmth of her hand in his, heard the laughter he wanted to bottle.

"Brian?" Sharon's voice came at him from a thousand miles away.

Strawberries soured to street exhaust. Rebecca's hand hardened to the cement of the porch beneath his palm. The sound of her laughter became his own heavy breathing and pounding heart. Brian tightened his eyelids, thought about the hills, the sand, the cabin, her eyes, but Rebecca didn't come back.

"Brian?"

"What?"

"This is a book of witchcraft."

He motioned to Sharon's empty glass. "How much rum did April pour into that thing?"

"I'm serious." She tapped her finger on a circled pentagon in the margin of a page. "This little guy is a pentacle. Wiccans use them to invoke spirits during their rituals."

A carload of shouting students raced down the street. One of them flung something out the window. It clattered along until coming to rest against the streetlamp while the jubilant cries faded into the distance. Brian stared at the banged-up beer can left behind. Once in a while a speeding car and discarded can might disrupt the monotony of a quiet street, but how often does a girl in a dream appear in the flesh or a poem write itself on a computer or the same girl get accused of... "One little symbol and she's a witch?"

Sharon pointed at a tiny circle sketched in the margin. "How about this one? Ever hear of the druids?"

"You mean the Pixar movie about cave people?"

"Very funny. The druids were a class of priests in ancient Celtic society, and this wheel with six spokes was one of their signs."

"So they were witches, huh?"

"Even worse. Supposedly, they practiced human sacrifice."

The smell of burning leaves drifted across the porch. Halloween lurked just around the corner. People in the neighborhood would start decorating their porches and yards pretty soon, preparing to celebrate a mood, a fantasy, not anything real. "You don't believe in witchcraft, do you, Sharon?"

"I kinda do, actually." She fished a pen out of her purse and jotted some of the markings on a sticky note. "I'll ask my anthropology professor whether he recognizes this language."

"You mean Sociology, right?"

"No, Brian. This alphabet is primitive. It's like something you'd see in a cave painting."

As ridiculous as the notion sounded, it sent a flutter through his stomach.

"Anyway, it's getting late. Tell your aunt I'll kill for another smoothie." Sharon scribbled something on another sticky and stuck it in the book. "My dorm room number. Come over sometime, and I'll sketch your portrait."

"You draw?"

"Not as well as this missing witch of yours." She stood, started down the steps, but stopped halfway down.

"What?" he said.

"Be careful, Brian. Witches are dangerous."

No, they weren't. He closed his eyes when Sharon left, trying to summon Rebecca again. He looked for the awesome girl in a country dress. Not some warty witch on a broomstick. The poet, the translator of strange languages, the *girlfriend* whose laughter brightened the sun.

He lifted the book, touched the ribbon. *Where did you go?*

# CHAPTER TEN

**PROFESSOR SLOAN USED HIS** laser pointer to flash a red dot on a map of Brazil. "Thirty miles from civilization, yet this Amazon tribe still lives in the stone age."

Brian stifled a yawn. Stone age loomed in *his* future, too. The monotonous lecture didn't merely slow time, it threatened to turn the clocks backward. Try as he might, the tousle-haired, wrinkled-shirt professor couldn't bring South American jungles alive the way an Indiana Jones might. Not even a floppy hat would have helped.

Most students lucky enough to sit in the back of the lecture hall had either slipped out the exit, escaped to their cell-phone apps, or fallen into hushed conversations with their friends.

But Brian had an agenda, supposedly. He leaned toward Sharon. "*This* is your language expert?"

"Shh, he's learned." She whispered the word in two distinct syllables. Who could blame her for overselling? Students had been sneaking away right and left.

The idea of escape crossed Brian's mind, too. Not over boredom. School had always been famous for that. More because uneasiness had been gnawing the pit of his stomach from the minute he sat down.

According to Sharon, the professor had news about Rebecca's hieroglyphics.

What kind of news? Something best left for Rebecca to reveal on her own in the next dream? A secret meant for him alone? Brian slumped in his seat. He shouldn't have let Sharon untie the ribbon and open that book. Rebecca's wishes might have been vague, but she didn't say he should turn her writing over to science. That was probably the last thing she would have wanted.

*Finally,* the lecture ended. Everyone gathered their stuff, hustled out of their chairs, and hurried down the aisle toward the double doors in back. Sharon pushed past them, heading upstream, to the front of the hall.

Brian fought the urge to swim away with her classmates. He lagged behind.

"Come on," she hissed.

By then, Professor Sloan had left the podium and hustled toward them. "Ah, Miss Spencer and Mr.... Danahey?"

Uh-oh. The professor had life in his voice now, and in his eyes. This same man who recently rafted down a dangerous stretch of Amazon and told *that* story without a pulse. Now, he had *news.*

Brian stopped walking.

The professor waved Sharon's scrap of notepaper over his head like he'd won a prize.

Double uh-oh.

"This is Ogham!" the professor exclaimed.

*Ogham?*

Brian couldn't maintain eye contact. He'd caused the worst possible scenario, allowing all magic to be stripped from Rebecca's book. Professor Sloan had just categorized, classified, defined, pigeon-holed, boxed, and labeled her slashes and hash marks as a known language. Yes, Rebecca learned the alphabet in a weirdly old-fashioned way. She'd gotten it from her mom, her mom from her grandma, and so on. Yet apparently anyone could have hopped online and nailed it on their own.

*Ogham.* So what else? Did she really conjure the bread and cheese in her kitchen, or did she order carryout from a store he hadn't noticed just over the next hill? Did she meld into his mind to type a poem through his fingers, or did *he* download it before falling asleep?

*No, I'd remember that.*

"Brian!" Sharon's voice was unaccountably shrill. "Did you hear what the professor just said?"

*Yeah. He slapped the kind of name on Rebecca's language you'd find on a gourmet cheese.*

Sharon shook her head like a girl scolding a bad puppy. "How can you not be listening?" She turned to the man with the answers. "Sorry, Professor, I'm working with Brian to help correct his *attention problem.* Would you say that again?"

The professor folded the paper and pressed it into Brian's hands. "Ogham fell out of use after the sixth century. No one can translate it."

"Huh?" Brian would have elaborated his grunt into something resembling a question, but the sudden resurrection of magic caught in his throat, preventing any coherent words from escaping his mouth.

"The alphabet you found predates medieval times. Some scholars think the symbols formed a hidden language used by the Celts for keeping the Romans in the dark regarding military plans."

The professor slipped into lecturer overdrive, pacing back and forth, waving his hands. "The only Ogham inscriptions remaining are thought to be names and dates, not meaningful sentences. They're etched into stone monuments throughout Britain and Ireland."

Brian caught his breath. Not meaningful sentences? Or poems about medieval derelicts shanghaied to fight dragons? He reached deep to find his missing voice. "Wait. That can't be right." Not much better than *huh,* but the best he could come up with while fighting off a seizure.

The professor clutched his arm. "Until this morning, the world thought of Ogham as dead and buried, but Sharon says you have an entire volume of it."

"I do, but—"

"Bring it in. You might have the key for translating a dead language!"

Brian pulled away. "I get why you want the book, but it isn't mine to give." He turned to Sharon. "Or show."

The professor and Sharon reacted in slow motion, first staring with widening eyes as the news sank in, then gasping, and finally, in Sharon's case, exploding into sound. "What?" She seemed fully capable of blasting death rays out of her eyeballs.

The professor spread his arms—a sad, rumpled shepherd hoping to pull one lost clown of a sheep back into the fold. "Your book could be groundbreaking."

"I'm sorry." Brian hurried down the aisle before they figured out how to turn him to stone.

"Wait!" Sharon caught up with him in the back of the hall. "What's wrong with you, Brian?"

He pushed through the double doors and stepped outside. "When Rebecca left that book behind, it was a *for your eyes only* kind of thing."

Sharon gaped at him like he'd confessed to a triple murder. Storm clouds gathered. Birds dove for cover.

He cringed.

But instead of pummeling him, she let out a long, stifling sigh. "You might have a CNN story. Don't you get it?"

Boy, did he ever. Rebecca's talents didn't start and stop with the ability to conjure a meal out of thin air or beam herself into his nighttime dreams.

Where *did* they start and stop?

# CHAPTER ELEVEN

AFTER THE PROFESSOR SLOAN debacle, Brian fell off Sharon's list of peeps. She gave him the cold shoulder at the video store and steered clear of him on campus. Even worse, Rebecca went silent, too. Not one single dream about her or with her or whatever they'd been doing.

Dead silence. For days.

He couldn't sleep. Or when he did, he couldn't remember his dreams. School became a blur of half-heard lectures, sloppy homework, and tortured daydreams about his amazing Ogham-speaking girlfriend and what he might have done to chase her away. The list was short.

*I let Sharon look at her book.*

Then, a week after the Ogham incident, Sharon texted him.

*Can you meet me at Grainger Hall right away? I've been helping Abigail with a research paper on American myths, and you won't believe what we found! First study room upstairs. Don't bring anyone.*

No chance. He'd already messed up by letting a secret see the light of day. Best to keep his distance now. He texted back.

*Can't make it.*

Fifteen seconds later:

*Don't make me kill you, Brian.*

Okay, so this was big enough to prompt death threats. But his lips were sealed. No more book showings or other Rebecca info of any kind.

He headed to the appointed meeting place and opened the door.

"Quick! Close it behind you!" Sharon stood before a table so cluttered with documents and news clippings, some had fallen to the floor.

She flashed a sunny smile, chasing away whatever cloud of ill will had been hovering between them before. Wider than she'd been smiling when lights turned a poster girl's lips from blue to yellow to purple during their ice-cream date a thousand years earlier. "Look who I found!"

Not the cleaning crew. They would have swept the mess away. But seriously, only a surprise of massive proportions would have anyone this ready to jump onto the table and tap-dance.

Surprises hadn't been his friend lately. He almost didn't ask the question begging to be asked. "Who did you find?"

"Rebecca!"

Geez. He should have ignored the death threat and stayed away.

Sharon thrust a copy from some old journal page into his hands. "Remember the research I was doing for Abigail? Well, did I ever find a smoking witch! Her legend dates back to the days when the first trappers traveled across the Great American Desert."

This conversation could only be heading toward the revelation Rebecca's cabin sat on the gravesite of some mythical witch. He'd seen the marker. And now, he groped for the doorknob behind him.

"Don't even think about bolting." One after another, Sharon held up copies of maps, beginning with one so old it didn't define anything west of the Mississippi, to another segregating the Nebraska and Kansas territories, and finally to a map showing all forty-eight contiguous states. The same general area had been circled in orange on each. "The Witch of the Hills has been haunting the region *you visited* for centuries!"

He had to humor her. Sharon was too jacked with insane enthusiasm to let him out of the room without a fight. So he took a closer look at the highlighted sections of each map. Yes, his car had stalled *somewhere* in there, but the circles were big. Maybe fifty miles across. Besides, did she say centuries? "Rebecca's our age, Sharon."

"Who says witches show their warts and wrinkles?" She gestured to a pile of newspaper clippings. "Those accounts date back two hundred years, and they all describe a *teenage girl*. She provides food and shelter to anyone who finds her cabin. Sound familiar?"

*Right.* If he'd met Rebecca in Oregon, Sharon would have called her Bigfoot. Other than the mild coincidence that Rebecca had been in the same general area as this mythical witch, he probably wouldn't find a single thing on the table linking her to the legend.

He grabbed the nearest clipping to prove his point. "Okay, Sharon, I'll read this one and you tell me how—"

A single word jumped out at him. *Furlongs.*

His voice caught in his throat.

Sharon's eyes widened. "What's the matter? You look like you saw a ghost."

Yeah, something like that. He had two choices. Turn and run or peer down into the chasm. Option one was awfully tempting but, "Can you...read this? I got something in my eye."

"Sure." She took the clipping, read in silence, looked up. "Okay, listen. *According to the legend, the witch camouflages her cabin, spins compasses in the wrong directions, and shifts landmarks from place to place. We haven't found a single report mentioning multiple sightings by the same person.*"

The room swam—just as the sky had that day in Nebraska. After he'd had an impossible time trying to find the cabin from the farm. He reached for the back of a chair to hold steady. "No, Sharon, lower down."

"Oh. *Twenty furlongs but never more, the circle at the edge and the cabin at the core.*"

*Furlongs.* Rebecca used the same term. His hands tingled.

She looked up at him. "Rebecca can't step outside the circle."

"Don't say Rebecca, Sharon. This is some myth about—"

"About a random girl who just happens to write a dead language in her book and sketch Wiccan symbols in the margins?"

Somebody knocked on the door.

Brian swung around…and caught his breath.

The scraggily-haired girl in the prairie dress stood in the doorway.

No, not *that* girl. Had he totally lost it? *This* girl did look vaguely similar, but she wore a skirt and blouse. And her hair was curly, not scraggily. Same brunette color, but was today the day for taking wildly circumstantial evidence as gospel? This girl stood *here*, a thousand miles and a whole different world away from *the other girl*, the crazy hitchhiker he'd met on the side of the highway in Wyoming.

Right?

"Come on in, Abigail," Sharon said. "This is Brian."

He tried to speak. Swallowed. Tried again. "Um, have we met? Sharon said you know me."

Abigail looked him up and down, blank-faced. She glanced at Sharon, shrugged. "Maybe you're a friend of a friend on Facebook?"

Not likely. Sharon had implied far more than a vague connection the day she helped him with his tire. "Didn't you tell Sharon you knew I was staying with my aunt?"

She shrugged again. "I must have read your profile."

*Dreaming.* He had to be. Too much weirdness had been packed into the last ten minutes. "Listen, I've gotta run. Good luck with your paper, Abigail." He headed out the door. "See you at work, Sharon."

He should have headed for his next class, but the urge to get in his car overpowered him. The time had come to drive into the sunset and not slow down until he reached the Sand Hills. Maybe the shared dreams had stalled out, but he could still head west and find the real deal. *Rebecca.* In the flesh.

He turned toward the hallway doors leading outside.

"Stay away from her, Brian."

Abigail's voice cut right through him. A nasally tone he'd definitely heard before, on the side of the Interstate in Wyoming. He stumbled, caught himself, and turned to face…who?

A friend of a friend on Facebook who'd taken stalker to a whole new level, tracking him halfway across the country?

*No.* He'd driven away that day. The hitchhiker had faded into the background in his rearview mirror. She wouldn't have known how to find him.

*But she did find him.*

License plate?

Abigail closed in, staring with the same dead-eyed expression she'd used when she warned him about the billboard. "Witches are dangerous, Brian. Let her be."

He bunched his fists. "What's your game?"

She smiled. First time he'd seen her do that, and the difference was night and day. No longer the cult type he'd met on the highway, she came across as the friendly, innocent girl next door. "My game is *dots.*"

"What?"

"You have to connect them." Abigail turned on her heel, walked to the end of the hall, opened the door, and stepped out of his life.

He hoped.

Brian's legs were jelly. He wobbled one foot in front of the other, heading in the opposite direction. He reached the door, grabbed the bar handle with both hands, and…a few dots came together. He remembered exactly what Rebecca had said about distances that day in the hills. "Let's put the tree *twenty furlongs* behind us."

But the road had been farther. Rebecca walked a good half mile beyond the circle to meet him by his car. She wasn't some mythical witch. She was a fantastic *girlfriend* he'd soon find.

He pushed the bar…and remembered something so creepy a chill ran down his back. When they found the noose, Rebecca muttered the name of her bully.

*Abigail.*

The dots didn't come close to connecting. His encounter with the hitchhiker had been random. Same with his detour north into the Sand Hills. What were the odds the same Abigail had been in both places?

What were the odds she'd track him to Wisconsin?

And why would she?

He shuddered. Hurried to his car.

All four tires were flat.

# CHAPTER TWELVE

**REBECCA APPROACHED A BARN-SHAPED** mailbox resting handsomely on its pole at the edge of the street. She matched the address of Brian's parents with the note in her hand. A rush of giddy relief watered her eyes, and the mailbox swam like a mirage.

Traveling to and from the World of Mortal Dreams had always been a breeze for her. Just a matter of wishing where she wanted to be. But she did need the general coordinates of her destination. The thought she might never have gotten them, might never have found this house sent a tingle down her spine. She wrapped her arms around the mailbox and hugged it.

Since dreams were a mixture of fantasy and reality, the World of Mortal Dreams varied from the surreal to the specific. Only within the district where every place on earth was duplicated could she find people and places she hadn't visited before *if given an address*. Thank heavens Brian left contact information behind in the cabin. Despite spending an entire evening with him, she'd been too schoolgirl-smitten to probe for specifics about where his parents might live.

She turned to a white fence, opened the gate, and paused to enjoy the sweet scent of hollyhocks vining up a trellis. Then she followed a tidy sidewalk to the front porch of the Cape Cod—a little brick castle, as if in a fairy tale come to life. How fitting! After all, Brian was her knight in shining armor.

*Knight in shining armor.* She'd been resorting to breathless clichés when thinking about him. She was supposed to be the one wielding magic, yet *he'd* been the spell caster from the beginning—first in a long-ago meeting he didn't remember yet. He'd given her a nickel that day and made her a promise. More recently, he'd been there for her, as prophesied. Ever since, for fourteen lonely days, she longed to study the stars with him again while they cooled their feet in the creek. Or share another poem. Or walk hand in hand through the hills.

Abigail was wise to keep her distance during the maddening wait mandated by the Witches Code. Rebecca might have throttled the imp if she'd shown her mean face and made one of her many snide comments. But where had Abigail gone? What mischief was she planning now? A noose hanging from an oak tree came to mind. Rebecca clenched her fists at the memory of the prank she and Brian stumbled across during their walk from the road to the cabin that day.

The little home fluttered like a leaf on a tree in the face of a stiff breeze.

*No! Don't flit away.* She shifted her focus to the house. Remaining long at any one site here in the World of Mortal Dreams required concentration. Otherwise, she might slip into the fantasy realm, where no image could be trusted and an address for locating Brian's mother would be useless.

"You won't find anyone there. I already knocked." Whomever the speaker was, the ring of her voice firmed the house on its foundation. Dreamers added substance to this realm. In a city neighborhood as thick with people as this one, the dream-eating void kept its distance. But the day would come when even *this* home got swallowed. Perhaps soon.

*No. Not with Brian and me fighting back.*

Rebecca turned to the woman who'd spoken, a middle-aged neighbor peering over the fence at her. The woman wore only a nightgown, but she'd slung a sizeable purse over her shoulder.

Rebecca couldn't help but smile. One might dream without a dress code, but accessories were always a must.

"Are you calling on Cassandra or Joe?" the woman asked.

Rather than shout across the lawn, Rebecca came back to the gate. "I'm looking for Brian's mother."

"That would be Cassie. She uses a lighthouse for her quiet place. Maybe she went there tonight."

*A lighthouse?* Rebecca loved the way people took incongruities in stride during their dreams. Within the waking world, everyone clung to constants and science and cold, hard facts far too readily. By stifling spontaneity, they encouraged the void. "Where is this lighthouse?"

"You shouldn't bother people who want to be alone." The woman lost substance, shimmering to the translucence of a silk scarf.

One more wrong move and Rebecca might frighten her awake. Then what? Sit on the doorstep and wait for Brian's mother to come home? When would that be? After two long weeks, a single extra minute would be more than she could bear. Her heart pounded. She didn't have a clue what to say other than the truth. "I'm looking for Cassandra so I can ask permission to spend more time with Brian."

The woman paled even more, turning so sheer that a blooming peony bush behind her showed through as a pink shadow. She pressed her lips tight. She crinkled her forehead.

Rebecca held her breath. Perhaps she should have made something up. Now, instead of frightening this neighbor awake, she'd *confused* her into the same condition.

But the woman came back. Solid. Opaque. She must have found sense in Rebecca's explanation. *What did Henry Stoddard know?* He'd warned her how foolish a witch's method of courting might seem to most people. Yet this woman's eyes brightened with understanding.

"How sweet!" the neighbor said. "Is this Sadie Hawkins day? No, that doesn't fit. You'd be asking the *boy* for permission, not his mother."

Rebecca barely followed, except that last part. "Where I come from, this is how things are done."

"Where you come from? Is it a place with more girls as precocious and polite as you? I have a son your age if you have a twin sister." The woman opened her purse and rummaged through it. She came out with a wondrous device. Something Brian owned, too. A *smartphone.* "The lighthouse is on Lake Michigan. Let's see if we can find the address in here."

Wishing to be at the lighthouse brought Rebecca to the entrance at its base. From there, she climbed up the winding staircase within.

Eighty, ninety, one hundred stairs. Brian's mother certainly didn't make the going easy for anyone wanting to visit. Rebecca leaned against the banister and waited for her heart to stop thumping in her ears.

She resumed the climb. Ten more stairs, twenty, thirty. She reached the top landing and opened the door. "Hello?"

A dark-haired woman in a floral dress sat in a rattan chair, the only stick of furniture the little round room had to offer. That and a cuckoo clock on the wall were the sum total of adornments in an otherwise empty space.

The woman gazed through a picture window at a sweeping view of an angry lake. Row after row of white-capped waves marched to the shore.

*Brian's mother at last!* Rebecca's heart raced, and this time not from climbing that impossible stairway. But she had rules to follow. She lingered in the doorway, waiting for permission to enter.

Cassandra didn't favor her with the slightest glance. "I come here when I want to be alone. Go away."

*What?* Rebecca's temples throbbed. She hadn't come this far to be dismissed like an unwanted servant. The room took on a magenta hue, as though her rising anger had painted the walls a matching shade.

Yet this woman, Cassandra, was *Brian's mother!* Rebecca looked down at her hands. She closed one into a fist. Slowly. Then the other. She took a deep breath. She reopened her hands. *There.* This meeting was too important for her to let her temper take over.

She stepped into the room. "I can't leave. I have an important matter to discuss with you."

"Fine. Pull up a chair and speak in a softer voice. I was enjoying the moment before you banged your way into my room."

Another challenge. Pull up a chair in a room that had no extras. Very well. Cassandra was dreaming, and dreamers never took note of impossibilities. Rebecca conjured a second chair next to her reluctant hostess.

Cassandra glanced over her shoulder. "Well, that settles that. I pegged you as a witch. What other wisp of a girl would have the fortitude to climb so many stairs?"

Rebecca gasped. She shouldn't have been *pegged* as anything. Dreams were supposed to be *her* turf. With *her* in control. No surprises.

Now what? *Regain control.* She went to the chair and sat. She rested her hands apart, one on each arm of the chair, so as not to fidget. She took a deep breath and turned to a surprisingly formidable woman. "You're just having a dream, that's all."

"Whether I'm sleeping or not, you just produced an entire chair. Mortals don't conjure in my dreams."

Rebecca gripped the chair arms. Mortals didn't refer to others as mortals. *Witches did.* But how could Cassandra be one? Witches didn't have sons. They only had daughters, like in the nursery rhyme she'd learned as a child. *Marry a mortal and bear a girl. She'll help cook the meals, and you'll iron her curls.*

She never heard of a boy being borne by a witch. *No one had.*

The implication burst into Rebecca's heart like fireworks. What better sign Brian was a chosen one than to be a *boy* borne by a witch? She restrained herself from leaping off her chair and pirouetting across the room. She had the code to follow. Dancing could come later.

What powers did Brian have? She fought the urge to pepper Cassandra with questions. Instead, she loosened her grip on the chair arms, took another deep breath, and tried to think of the best way to make the request she'd come to ask.

Cassandra leveled a steady gaze on her. Friendly? Hostile? Perhaps a little of both. "You travel from dreams to reality and back, always knowing the difference. You conjure illusions so real you can sit in them." Cassandra reached over and touched the arm of Rebecca's chair. "I know what you are. A witch. So why don't you tell me *who* you are, young lady, and why you're here."

Rebecca swallowed. "My name is Rebecca Church. I met your son, and—"

"You're seeing my son?"

"No, we met and spent some time together in my cabin. The Witches Code is clear on the matter of courting. A fortnight must be waited between the first meeting and the second."

Cassandra lifted a mirror and brush from her lap. She began primping her hair. "Let me get this straight. You *like* my son, but you're keeping your distance because of an archaic code?"

Rebecca's stomach quivered. She turned away in case worry showed in her eyes. Had she truly followed the code? That question had been weighing her down like a ship's anchor for days. She tried to find her voice. "I'm *technically* following the code, but I missed Brian so much that I did visit him, ever so briefly, in a dream or two."

Cassandra clucked her tongue. The universal damning tsk of annoyance.

"Please don't say I violated the code." Rebecca barely managed to choke the words past the lump in her throat.

Cassandra dragged the brush the length of her straight black hair, once, twice, three times before speaking. "I suppose a pure witch does her best, following the spirit of the law if not the letter."

No sweeter words had ever been spoken. Rebecca would have basked in their echo, but even *the spirit* of the code still mandated that permission be obtained from the mother before a witch dated the son. "I want to see Brian again—more than once, actually. I'd like to start—"

"Are you asking permission to see a boy perfectly capable of choosing girlfriends without his mother's help?"

"Yes. The Witches Code requires—"

"Again with the code." Cassandra returned her things to her lap and folded her arms. "Tell me, Rebecca. What word does the code use to describe this first meeting between a witch such as you and a mother such as...*me*?"

Rebecca's head swam. How could she remember the precise words from a thousand-page book? She hadn't prepared for a quiz. She would have steeled herself if she expected this meeting would be such a challenge, such a contest of wills, such a... "Trial! The code calls it a trial." Obviously for good reason.

Cassandra left her chair, stepped to the window, and pressed a hand against the glass. The foaming waves below whipped higher, into a frenzy of whitecaps. "You'd date him no matter what I say."

"Date?"

"No one calls it courting anymore."

Rebecca fell back on her deep-breathing exercise, but neither that nor the slow closing of her fists could fend off the red anger clouding her sight. "How dare you suggest I'd violate the code, Cassandra? I will not *court* Brian without permission. You can be sure, though, I'll come up here asking, every single night, until you say yes. You can't imagine how patient and purposeful *a pure witch* can be."

Cassandra turned from the window. Her eyes flashed with the fires of a hundred foundries. "Are you implying I am *not* a pure witch? And who allowed you to speak my given name?"

"No one, *Mrs. Danahey.*" Rebecca stomped to the door.

Cassandra's own footfalls beat just as loudly from behind. "You are a stubborn, willful, and mean young lady."

Rebecca grabbed the door handle and wrenched it down. "Pure witches don't have mean bones, *Cassandra*."

"Argumentative and rude, too."

She tightened her grip on the handle. "I stand up for myself. Get used to it."

Two hands came down on her shoulders. Not heavily. Soft as a mother's touch. So unexpectedly gentle the anger drained out of Rebecca in an instant, leaving her spent and wobbly.

"My son does need a challenge," Cassandra said. "He moped around the house all summer, and he's been in a daze since he started school. Thinking about you, perhaps?"

If only half as much as she'd been thinking about him. Rebecca kept her grip on the door handle to keep from falling.

"Yes, you may court him."

She couldn't have heard that right. She swung around on shaky legs.

Cassandra stood tall with head held high. Yes, a formidable figure but far less intimidating with the smile now spreading across her face. "As you said, the code required you to have a trial. So I gave you one."

Rebecca's knees buckled.

Cassandra took her arm. "Come and sit with me before you leave."

She scarcely felt her feet hit the floor as she walked to the window and again sat with Cassandra. Her hands trembled. She settled them on her knees and gazed at the bluest, calmest lake she'd ever seen.

"Brian has been seeing someone who works at a shop with him."

"What?" Rebecca hadn't detected any sign of another girl in Brian's dreams. Did the parade of surprises never end?

"He claims she's just a friend. I'm sure you'll shoo her away once you step in and take control of the relationship. This Sharon isn't the real problem."

Rebecca caught her breath. If a *rival* wasn't the real problem, what was?

Cassandra lapsed into silence.

The cuckoo clock marked time. *Tick, tick, tick.* A flock of seagulls arced across the water from north to south. The birds circled twice, dove low, and resumed their journey.

Rebecca was in no hurry for bad news. She didn't say a word. The other shoe could take its time falling.

Cassandra sighed. "At first I thought Brian was dealing with gremlins. He's been reporting the most ridiculous problems with his car. Lately, though, I've been thinking an *imp* might be the cause. You wouldn't know anything about that, would you?"

*Abigail.* One loathsome shoe. Rebecca's cheeks burned. She couldn't speak. The ringing in her ears would have drowned out whatever she said.

"Just as I thought." Cassandra stood and paced the floor. "Rebecca, I don't understand why a young witch would appear out of nowhere and take an interest in my son. What are the odds? We witches are few. We don't grow on trees. Yet of all possible girls, a witch comes along. And she sends an imp as an advance scout?"

Rebecca bunched her fists. "It isn't like that."

"Tell me what it *is* like, then."

*Torture. By an imp who hates me for no good reason.* Or an imp with a larger scheme? An imp in league with the void? No. The Abigails of the world were simple, foolish, clumsy creatures. Most fell into servitude for sorcerers. Some even served witches. She'd never heard of an imp who—

*She'd never heard of a boy born to a witch, either.* Maybe the world had more secrets than she'd ever imagined. Perhaps she was no more than a grain of sand trying to fend off a boulder. Or in this case, trying to fend off an imagination-eating void threatening to swallow the World of Mortal Dreams whole.

*And she'd fend it off, by trusting a prophecy and following the code.* But Rebecca didn't know whether Brian's mother took stock in the prophecy. So few ever had. Perhaps if she danced around the edges... "Mrs. Danahey, have you seen the growing darkness in this world?"

"You mean politically? Socioeconomically? Who wouldn't?"

So Cassandra hadn't seen it. Perhaps no one had.

The lake had gone wild again. Rebecca had nothing to fall back on for comfort except her own resolve. "The code says I can only reveal information through riddles, illusions, and dreams when courting. I'm not sure whether that restriction extends from Brian to you, but—"

Cassandra held up a hand. "I like you, Rebecca. You'll be good for Brian. But if some imp has taken such a dislike to you she's now treating *him* to her mischief out of spite or whatever, I do expect you to resolve the matter. And soon."

"I'll try."

Rebecca swallowed. A grain of sand gaping up at a boulder.

# CHAPTER THIRTEEN

**THE WORLD RESUMED ITS** normal spin. No flat tires. No Wyoming-to-Wisconsin stalkers. An uneventful day of classes. Then another.

Brian's initial relief faded into boredom. Anxiety followed fast on its heels. He needed to make things happen, tie loose ends, *find Rebecca.*

Then he met her in one more dream.

"I'm coming for you," she said, "*soon.*" The promise quelled the burning urge to head west and find her. At least for the moment.

Ever since a music appreciation class in his senior year, he'd been a Beatles fan. The old *Abbey Road* album was a favorite of his. And so the morning after the dream, a verse played in his head. *Woke up, got out of bed, dragged a comb across my head.* The guy in that song fell into a dream—a great concept if Rebecca was waiting inside. But Brian had classes until noon and work right after. No time for falling into dreams or confronting crazy stalkers who might have let the air out of his tires a few days earlier. He barely had ten minutes to spare for reading the news today and saying *oh boy,* like John Lennon in the song.

Aunt April poked her head out of the kitchen, dragging a comb through *her* hair. "I forgot to grab the mail yesterday."

"That's not one of the verses," he said.

She looked at him and smiled, not missing a beat, although she couldn't have had a clue what he was talking about. "Let's improvise."

So he headed into the main entranceway of the condo complex, where everyone's mailboxes held up a wall. He counted five across and three down, then opened his and April's with a little key he was sure he'd lose sooner or later.

Bills, brochures, no letters, of course—who ever got those anymore?—magazines, junk mail. He cracked open a pink flyer wedged between April's latest copy of *Cosmo* and the cable bill.

*Rebecca Church, femme fatale at Club Intrigue's grand opening! Tonight at eight p.m.*

Everything spilled from his hands to the floor.

He fell into a dream for the rest of the day, pulling the flyer out of his pocket again and again, not to reread the printed words but the promise between the lines—a reboot of the Brian/Rebecca super team. He counted the hours to the appointed time, oblivious to the chaos of lectures, study groups, elbows by friends who wondered why his brain had locked down, and the raised voice of a supervisor later at work wanting to know the same thing, only with greater urgency.

How could he explain? Other guys' girlfriends texted, tweeted, liked, instant messaged, called, or simply came knocking with the numbing regularity of a metronome. Their girlfriends didn't turn the sun off by disappearing, until they later parceled out a few rays with a dream, a poem, another dream, before bursting back into their lives in one massive flare of a flyer.

Scented with pine, no less.

Nobody else had gotten one. He'd peered through the little windows of the other mailboxes. Rebecca's flyer had been no mass-mailing coincidence, no random announcement by a wandering Irish gypsy. He'd gotten a waking-world poke from an amazing girl who finally managed to track him down.

The tide had turned. Everyone else lived the first day of

school. He now lived the last. They were stuck in Monday morning. He'd found Friday night.

But shortly after work, Brian tried and failed to find a Club Intrigue on the Internet.

No sweat. Just a new place without a website yet.

Hey, that rhymed. Rebecca brought out the poet in him.

Anyway, website or no website, the universe had *not* started hiccupping again.

He wanted to rush to the club early, get there first, but April slowed him down.

"I *cooked* for us." Her voice held a note of triumph. Neither of them was good with an oven, or even the microwave, for that matter. They typically fell back on carry-out, the greatest invention since the spoked wheel.

Truly out of it, Brian hadn't even noticed the mouth-watering aroma of roast chicken until she said those words. He grabbed a seat at the kitchen table and tried to listen between bites while April asked why his brain was locked down, why he wasn't holding up his end of the conversation, and why he actually scarfed down those beets she'd ladled onto his plate as a joke.

"What do you mean, *beets*?" He almost gagged. Not even a chocolate-banana smoothie could kill *that* aftertaste.

An hour later, the bitter taste of doubt picked up where the beets left off. Brian stood beside his car in the parking lot of an old warehouse. Red neon letters sizzled, blinked, stuttered, came to life—*Club Intrigue*—then staggered again, barely holding their own above the canopied entranceway. Every window in the upper floor was broken.

He shoved his hands into his pockets, headed over, tried the door. Locked. He peered through the glass at an empty cashier's cage, a concessions counter without attendants, a few sawhorses scattered about.

A placard on an easel summed up the situation. *Opening night?*

Okay, so Rebecca's performance announcement was her little joke. She just wanted to meet him here. But where was she? And why pick a half-renovated club in a bad part of town?

He glanced around the lot. A few drivers waited in their cars with engines running, as if maybe the place would open if they idled long enough. The glow of cigarettes and low murmur of conversation at a corner of the building revealed some hardier souls who'd gotten out of their vehicles.

He walked over to three spikey-haired guys in leather jackets and a girl who'd gone too heavy on the black mascara, all puffing away.

"Hey," he said.

The girl grunted. Two of the guys nodded. The third dropped his cigarette butt and ground it out with a shoe.

"No show tonight?" he asked.

"And to think, we've been living for one," the girl with overly darkened eyes said.

He turned from one unfriendly face to another but didn't give up. Rebecca *had to be* on the grounds somewhere. "Have you seen another girl out here?"

One of the guys tilted his head to where an asphalt path broke away from the driveway and snaked around the building. "Some chick headed that way," he said.

"No, she didn't," dark eyes said. "You're a liar."

A half-broken, flickering streetlamp halfway down the path perfectly summed up the odds of finding Rebecca behind the building, but Brian had nowhere else to turn. He followed the trail until it ended at a weedy area of broken glass, discarded wooden crates, and a pile of old tires. Just beyond, the gloom of night took hold with staggering density. A black void stretched high enough to snuff out the stars. It swallowed the moon.

Dark eyes' voice rose softly in the distance, "You're such a liar, Dave."

"I call 'em how I see 'em," the guy said.

"Rebecca?" Brian stepped toward what had to be a thick patch of fog. Maybe she'd walked through it to the other side.

Something at his feet glimmered in the reluctant light cast by the nearby streetlamp. A brownish coin, but too large to be a penny. He would have stepped over it and looked for Rebecca behind the fog, but the coin changed color briefly, from gold to silver and back. *Weird lighting.* He picked the thing up and flipped it over in his hand, almost dropping it at the sight of a familiar engraving on either side—a hag whose long hair billowed in the wind.

*Use it to buy something, Brian, first chance you get.* That's what Rebecca had said back at the cabin when she'd given the very same coin to him. His heart pounded.

The thing was as warm in his hand as if she'd just been holding it seconds earlier. "Rebecca?"

No answer.

A cold gust of wind blew through the lot, bringing worry as dark and thick as the blanket of fog looming ahead. Suppose Rebecca wasn't anywhere within a thousand miles of this place. *Suppose she hadn't been the one to send the flyer or hold this coin.* He tightened his jacket.

A footfall on the gravel sounded behind him. Every nerve in his body twitched. He swung around.

Dark, scraggly hair, downturned mouth. Of all people to find out here. *Abigail.*

"I warned you to stay away from her." The crazy stalker crossed her arms and stared him down with mean eyes.

This girl had to hit the road, and fast. "Why are you in my face at all the wrong times, Abigail?"

She brushed past him, walking straight up to the fog. "Suppose you did something so terrible you couldn't live with yourself. What would you do?"

"I wouldn't stalk someone."

"*I'd* embrace the darkness," she said.

"Knock yourself out." He turned his back on her.

A banjo sounded through an open window of the warehouse. A fiddler joined in, then a trumpet, and a drummer, all combining into the signature chaos of a band doing warm-ups. The best sound he'd ever heard. A show after all.

Brian hurried around to the front. Spotlights from the top of the building bathed the driveway. More cars had parked. A short line of people filed through the open door of the place.

He went inside and stepped up to the cashier's cage.

"The cover charge is two bits," a girl said from behind the bars.

The hair on the back of his neck prickled. Hadn't *bits* gone the way of *furlongs* in the parade of forgotten words?

"Come again?" he asked.

"Twenty-five cents," she said.

A quarter to get into a night spot? And what did *that* remind him of?

*How much for gas?*

*Couple bucks oughta cover it.*

The time had arrived for a return to the mother ship before this weird, alternate universe devoured his brains.

But Rebecca was here. Somewhere. He had her coin in his pocket to prove it.

*Or did Abigail bring the coin here and drop it?*

No way.

He glanced at his watch. Almost the eight p.m. show time. "Do you have a performer named Rebecca Church?"

"I haven't seen the program," the cashier said. "Maybe she's doing one of the poetry readings."

"Now you're talking." Poetry and Rebecca went hand in hand. He fished in his pocket for a coin—*no, not that one*— found a quarter, and nearly fumbled it to the floor before handing it over. Hard to hold steady when landing in the last day of school, Friday night, and Christmas all at once.

A silent hostess led him down a saw-horse-cordoned pathway across an unfinished, plaster-strewn hall so cavernous their footfalls echoed.

He tried to keep up with her, bouncing questions off her back as they walked. "Is Rebecca Church reciting here?"

No answer.

"Red hair, about your height, likes to dress retro?"

The hostess ignored him.

*Awesome dimples when she smiles? Reader of hieroglyphics? Sharer of coins? Visitor of dreams?* He held his tongue. No point spilling his heart out.

They reached a small section way in the back. Just a dozen or so cocktail tables and a little stage. Unlike the larger area, this one was finished, up to a point. Murals on a wall depicted knights, maidens, and dragons in medieval settings. They brought Rebecca's sketches to mind, until the resemblance faded three-quarters of the way to the ceiling. Pipes and catwalks hanging down from above dragged him back to the real world. The contrast between fantasy and urban ugliness must have been meant as a statement, like one of those modern paintings he'd seen in the Art Institute—brick buildings under construction reaching for the sky right next to old tenements crumbling to the ground.

The hostess brought him to a table right by the stage. Couldn't have been better, *if* Rebecca was actually here, waiting to perform, or doing her rendition of gotcha, planning to catch him from behind like when they first met on the side of the road.

"I didn't get a program," he said.

The hostess walked away.

*Thanks for all the info.* At least he had a good line of sight to both the front door and the stage. Rebecca had to show up in one spot or the other. He pulled up a chair.

A waitress hurried by, balancing a tray of drinks in her hand, wearing the deer-in-the-headlights look of someone with too many orders to fill.

"Wait, I have a quick question."

She slowed but didn't stop. "Yeah?"

"Rebecca Church is performing, right?"

"Is she the redhead who set this up?"

Brian's heart raced. He tried to thank her, but she got away before he could form coherent words.

The lights dimmed and curtains parted, revealing a noose hanging above a wooden chair, *for a poetry reading and some songs?*

The others at their tables chattered away, laughed, shouted for waitresses.

Brian eyed the exit and started pushing his chair back. Creepy from the get-go, this place had now raised the hair on his arms.

Rebecca picked that moment to pad onstage from behind the rear curtain in bare feet, dressed in black. Their eyes met, and for a perfect moment, he shared a long-overdue smile with the girl who turned his heart to mush.

But she shifted her attention past him to the larger audience, giving them a long zombie stare before speaking.

*"Nineteen poor souls hanged in sixteen ninety-two.*
*The claims*
*against them were threadbare.*
*Witches on their broomsticks stoking fears anew.*
*The cause?*
*The girl with auburn hair."*

Rebecca climbed onto the chair, put the noose around her neck, tightened it, and jumped.

# CHAPTER FOURTEEN

**FOR THE BRIEFEST OF** moments, Brian couldn't process the image of Rebecca swinging at the end of the rope. He didn't accept that the gathered group offered some light applause and then continued chattering, laughing, and tinkling their ice-filled drinks. For that one tenth of a second, Rebecca's much-earlier words rang in his head.

*People always think they're awake, even when they're sleeping.*

No.

Not even in the darkest, craziest region of his subconscious mind could he conjure a nightmare this horrific. The scene was real.

He sprang out of his chair, overturning the table and sending his drink crashing to the floor. Somehow, the clatter of breaking glass accomplished what Rebecca's hanging failed to do. The audience quieted.

He rushed the stage.

Two hulking, shaved-headed bouncers grabbed his arms before he could get halfway up the stairs. "Are you crazy? You'll ruin the show," the bruiser on the left shouted.

"The recitals are about to start," his buddy on the right added.

They hustled him toward an exit.

Brian twisted, kicked, got an arm free, and lashed out with it. "She's hanging!"

"Who?"

He managed to break away and turn to the stage, but before he could take a step forward, Rebecca, the noose, and the chair shimmered.

*And faded away.*

The room swam. He collapsed into the waiting arms of the two bouncers.

A simple stage trick must have fooled him. Mirrors and lighting can work wonders.

He met the gazes of a few others in the club, but most looked away. The unspoken message couldn't have been clearer. *Beat it, and don't come back.*

A teenage girl took the stage, clutching a sheet of paper in her hands. She turned to the saner people still at their tables, people who didn't randomly go berserk over nothing. "I've written a poem about unrequited love."

The bouncers shoved Brian out a side door and slammed it behind him.

End of story? No. He'd messed up. Clearly. But he'd come looking for Rebecca, he'd seen her in there, and he wasn't leaving without a chance to talk to her.

He hurried around front and back into the club.

Another bouncer folded his beefy arms and blocked the way to the seating area. "There ain't no admittance after the show starts."

"Wait. I already was admitted." He pulled the ticket out of his pocket. "I'm just looking for one of the performers so I can—"

The man lifted Brian by the shirt and shoved him all the way back through the doorway. "The show ends in half an hour, pal. You wanna see one of the performers, go cool your heels in the parking lot till they come out."

The door slammed in his face. He pushed on it. Locked. He pounded on it.

Yeah, like that would work.

He snatched the cell phone out of his pocket. But who could he possibly call—the cops? *Officer, I imagined a suicide attempt, and the club invoked its discriminatory policy against hallucinating clowns.*

His breath came out in hazy puffs. A fat raindrop chilled the back of his neck. If he had to wait a half hour for Rebecca, sitting in an idling car with its heater on would beat standing outside and freezing.

Back at his Kia, wind flapped a flyer wedged under his wipers. He yanked it out.

*Poetry Readings, Songs and Comedy at Club Intrigue! Opening night!*

A shadow of handwriting bled through from the other side. He flipped it over.

*The world isn't what you think it is. Go home. I'll find you there, later tonight. R*

The wind caught the note and blew it out of his hands.

# CHAPTER FIFTEEN

**BRIAN LET HIMSELF INTO** the condo and hit the light switch, illuminating the ordinary contents in the immediate area. Couch, chair, TV, table, book.

*Book?*

Rebecca's Ogham poetry lay open on an end table—the book he always kept by the microwave in the kitchen. Somebody moved the thing, opened it, and angled the ribbon and Sharon's address card on either side, shaping the whole arrangement into a flower—the kind of decorative touch April lived for.

Only his aunt shouldn't have been home. She'd left for her shift at the diner just before he went out.

One of the kitchen drawers clattered shut.

He caught his breath, took a step back. "April?"

No answer.

The little umbrella stand by the door didn't offer much in the way of defense weaponry, although a parade baton did poke out, ready for action, with its red, white, and blue stripes and silvery tinsel. Ridiculous? Yeah. But it looked heavy. He grabbed it.

Light plastic. *Great.* Perfect choice, if whoever snuck into the condo came packing a Wiffle Bat instead of a gun.

More noise.

He clenched the useless weapon tight. "Who's in there?" Oh to know tae kwon do at a time like this.

"It's me, Brian."

He dropped the baton. "Rebecca?"

The most sensational girl in the universe stepped out of the kitchen. Tangled red hair fell down her shoulders and hung in clumps across her forehead, as if she'd gotten caught in a rainstorm and didn't quite finish drying in the wind. Bags under her eyes dampened a weak smile. And what were those marks around her neck? He wouldn't let his crazed imagination go there. No way had she actually *hanged herself.* That had been a stage trick.

"Don't look so worried," she said. "I'm fine."

"How did you get in here?" He looked past her, into the kitchen. The back door was supposed to be locked.

"Does it matter? I need a white knight, and here you are." She leaned forward, quick, kissed his cheek, backed off, smiled.

One little kiss and every one of the hundred questions bouncing around in his head took a back seat, leaving an echo up front. *White knight, white knight, white knight.* "I crashed a poetry reading trying to save you."

"That's what heroes do."

*Hero.* Like Spiderman and Mary Jane. Rebecca got it. But the questions came roaring back. What happened on that stage? How did she get into the condo? Where did she go when she left him, back in Nebraska? How did one of her poems write itself on his computer one night?

What *was* she?

"You're looking at me like I'm a ghost, Brian." She took his hand. "See? I'm solid."

Yep. Solid and soft with pale green eyes melting his shoes into the floor. *Kiss her, kiss her, kiss her, kiss her.* He leaned forward.

"Actually, I'm a witch, not a ghost."

*Kiss her, kiss her, kiss her*—Wait! "What?"

Rebecca crinkled her forehead. The lighting changed, tinting bluish. The air turned damp and warm as a greenhouse. The shoot of a plant sprang out of the floor, sprouting thin branches, growing green fronds, becoming a palm as it stretched to the ceiling.

He staggered back.

"I know how to take fantasies from the dream world and shape them into illusions here," she said. A smiling, gleaming-eyed girl who'd just turned the laws of horticulture—and time?—on their ear.

He blinked, and in the tiny fraction of a second between closing his eyes and reopening them, the palm disappeared, the air thinned, the lighting went back to normal. Not his heart, though. It beat the daylights out of him.

"See?" She grinned wide as a kid finishing off a card trick without a hitch, which, actually, she kinda was. "The code allows me to tell you *one thing* about myself, so there it is. I'm a witch."

"Um, there are *other* things about you?" He stared at the point in the floor where the plant had grown, a little afraid to take his eyes off it. "You can do more than *that?*"

"Let's see," she said. "I can cast illusions, write poetry,.." Her eyes gleamed with either pride or humor. Maybe both. "Oh, and dream hop."

Brian tried to take it all in. Tried to cram a massive balloon bursting with impossibility into the little shoebox people called science. Rebecca actually *had* been in his head. The mind-meld thing. Not because he'd been suffering from some crazy fit of illusions. "This is way different than Oz."

Rebecca stared at him, lost, as if she didn't get the reference. She shrugged. "Anyway, I'm a *pure* witch, so according to the code, you have to figure everything else out on your own."

"Code?"

"It's complicated."

"More complicated than growing a tree out of the floor?"

Her smile faded. "Much more."

"What's wrong?"

"You're supposed to guess at things. I've got riddles for you to solve. And if I don't do this right…"

Uh-oh. Did witches crinkle their foreheads that way just before guys turned into toads or melted into little puddles? "Should I be worried?"

The crinkles eased. Her eyes gleamed again. "You muddle me, Brian."

"Same here." He touched her face, she settled a warm hand over his, and they came together in an eyes-closed, tingly kiss.

The air warmed again. Birds sang, crickets chirped, and faeries giggled in an unmistakable, faerie-giggling way. Like from a cartoon…except real? He'd worry about that later. For now, mmmmm.

The kiss ended the way the greatest dreams did, with every detail rushing away, leaving a warm glow in their wake.

Rebecca wobbled into his shoulder. "My toes curled!"

"Same here." He tried to catch his breath. "Teach me how you do that stuff!"

"Illusions? Sorry. Only a witch can cast them." She headed into the kitchen. "Hot chocolate helps when I feel faint. It's mostly sugar."

"Slow down. We need to process this."

But she'd slipped away, humming some song until she stopped at the stove and fished a baggie of white powder from a pocket of her dress. "No, not flour." She pulled out another, light green. "Not this one, either."

She found a third and held it up with a grin. "Presto!"

"You carry baking supplies around in your pockets?"

Rebecca rummaged beneath the sink until she came out with a pot. "Where's your fireplace?"

"Right next to the door for my wine cellar."

"Oh. Where's that?"

"I'm joking. You have to use the stove."

She went up to it and examined one of the burners, poking beneath it with a spoon. "I don't see any pilot light."

"It's electric."

She jerked away. Stared it down with hands on hips.

This couldn't be happening. How could he even begin to process her smile, her magic, her crazy sense of humor all bursting back into his life? "I'm dreaming, right?"

"Do you have the coin I left for you, Brian?"

"You mean the one I found behind that warehouse?" He fished it out of a pocket, held it up. "Yeah. Why?"

"You'll need that. Now how do we make hot chocolate some *other* way?" She glared at the stove, turned to him, spread her arms.

Crazy funny. She had enough power to grow a tree out of the floor, but she was afraid to deal with a stove. "Use the sink faucet on the left. The water comes out plenty hot."

Rebecca gaped at him as if he'd told her pigs could fly.

"Trust me," he said.

She brushed her lips against his ear. "Modern devices defeat me," she whispered.

In what universe were hot and cold faucets modern?

Who cared? Rebecca's lips were there for the taking. He found them with his and savored the taste of peppermint. The kiss brought stars—two little ones wobbling around like drunken fireflies before fading out.

Rebecca staggered to the sink from that body blow of a kiss. "Wow."

"Yeah."

She ran water from the faucet until it steamed. "We need to take baby steps."

"Uh-huh." Otherwise, one more kiss and their heads would explode. Besides, he had a boatload of questions. If the hanging was a trick, why did she show up here with marks on her neck? The red splotches had faded away somewhere between kisses one and two, but he'd seen them for sure.

Illusions?

*Please don't let this be a dream.*

A black cat came out of nowhere and rubbed against his leg.

*Make it all real. I promise to be good forever.*

He followed Rebecca into the living room. They sat on the couch. The cat came over for more leg rubbing but darted away when Brian tried petting him.

Rebecca grabbed a pen from the coffee table and tossed it across the room. The cat ran after it, slapping at it with his paw until he zigzagged into the kitchen. "I wasn't sure my flyer would work."

"You could have just knocked."

"What fun would that be?" Crinkles of humor replaced the shadows beneath her eyes.

"Why did you leave in the first place, Rebecca?"

She lifted a hot-chocolate mug to soft, pale lips capable of transforming the world into a wonderland with each kiss. "This should be warmer. Why not make a fire out back for cooking?"

"Yeah, we could just toss some hot chocolate on the grill next time. Come on, Rebecca. Throw me a bone. What's been going on?"

She set the cup down, crossed her arms. "The rules won't let me tell."

"Okay, then how about explaining the rules."

"I can't. That's one of them. I'm following a sacred code."

*Bong, bong, bong*—a miniature pendulum clock that never worked before went off with enough gusto to almost shake itself off the mantel. He'd bought it for next to nothing at a garage sale and forgotten it even existed.

Rebecca looked up at it. "How smart! People think a clock should mark time, but yours *celebrates* it."

Give her credit. She had evasiveness down to a science. "Let's try going over this again," Brian said. "You can't tell me what's happening, because of some crazy rules."

She sipped her drink and eyed the clock, then him, weighing something, rolling it around in her head for so long he didn't expect a response. Finally, "I know other ways to communicate besides *telling.*"

"How?"

"Anytime something odd happens, consider it a clue."

"I'll keep that in mind next time you hang yourself."

She elbowed him. "Don't be sarcastic. This is about a prophecy."

"A *prophecy*?"

"More of an Irish fairy tale, but I believe it's true." She touched his cheek, drifted her fingers down the side of his neck, and walked them the length of his arm. "In the distant future, a maiden named Rebecca and a lad named Brian will stare down the darkness, hand in hand. Those words were set down many centuries ago. Then, one day years later, somebody showed up at a young maiden's window, proving the prophecy with a simple coin while winning her heart with a promise."

Rebecca's voice came at him from a distance, barely piercing through the fog of her touch. But he needed to wake up and focus on the questions. "A coin? A promise? *Darkness?* Where do we start? It's everywhere."

Her eyes lit up. "You mean you can see the void?"

"What void?"

"Oh." She frowned. Lowered her gaze. Dropped her fingers from his wrist.

*Me and my big mouth.* Every inch of his arm itched for her touch again. How to bring it back? "Rebecca, I saw something earlier. Like a black fog, behind Club Intrigue. Is that what you mean?"

She gripped him again. "The void will swallow every dream if we don't stop it. But the prophecy says we might prevail."

Okay, this was getting crazy. Or crazier? The whole night had been nuts from the beginning. But before he let himself descend with her into total insanity, he needed to at least make a token effort at chipping away at the weirdness. "Rebecca, I don't know about a prophecy, but I did hear a legend about the Witch of the Hills. She lives near your cabin, supposedly. Some relative?"

"Am I so famous I have a special name?"

"Nope. This witch has been around for centuries."

"I see." Rebecca had that cheek-puffed, lips-pressed look of someone about to explode into laughter.

No way could she be the Witch of the Hills. Yet what was impossible anymore? She'd already done plenty to prove the universe had gotten so far off-line even the hardest of reboots would be a waste of time. "Rebecca, how old *are* you?"

"Look and tell me what you see." She stood and struck a pose, a dead ringer for the girl on the cover of his sister's favorite book, *Anne of Green Gables.*

"You aren't the one I'd send into a 7-Eleven to buy the beer for me and my friends."

Her expression went blank.

"I'm guessing sixteen."

"There you go." Rebecca came back, sat beside him, and settled her hand on his knee.

Once again, mere physical contact threw his head into a spin cycle. He groped for the words to express the jumble of thoughts and emotions bouncing around up there, found one he'd used before. "Girlfriend."

"Boyfriend," she whispered.

What more could a guy want? Except... "Here's the thing, Rebecca. For all I know, you'll disappear on me again. It's hard to say something special knowing I'll feel like an idiot later if you go away and never come back."

She arched her brows. "Something special?"

"Yeah, I mean something like... I don't know."

"White knights take risks."

"Okay. I've been totally obsessed with you from day one."

Rebecca's smile couldn't have gotten any wider. "Have you now?"

"Uh-huh."

Those green eyes bored into his again. "I'm obsessed with you, too. But know I have a jealous heart, Brian."

What girl didn't? "Hey, we all have our flaws."

"I do try to be a good witch most of the time."

"So, your family. Are they all—?"

Rebecca's face fell. The humor washed out of her eyes. "I have no family."

Great. He'd blown it, turning an unbelievable moment into something three days past expiration. Heavy silence sucked the oxygen out of the room, because he was an idiot. What was he trying to accomplish, tricking her into spilling background info after she'd said she couldn't?

*Bong.*

The clock! He went to the mantel, grabbed the thing, brought it over. "We first met just about a month ago. Here's an anniversary present."

Rebecca cradled the clock in her hands, turning it around, up and down. She lifted it high with arms outstretched, a smile beaming from her lips to her eyes. She set it down. Leaned her head on his shoulder. "Thank you."

More silence, but plenty of oxygen this time. Enough to grow plants out of the floor for sure.

"This will be hard on us, Brian. Things have to be done a certain way."

"No problem. I'll back off the questions until you're ready to tell."

The lights dimmed. Rebecca's book of poetry popped onto her lap, and the clock shifted to the coffee table at their knees.

He lurched back. A world this full of magic needed to come at him in bits and pieces. Not like a bat across the side of the head.

Rebecca opened the book to a sketch of a faerie on one page and her hash-mark hieroglyphics on the other. "I love reading to you. Listen for the big clue about what I am."

*"In a distant town long centuries ago,*
*there lived*
*a gypsy all alone.*
*Fortunes she did tell and poetry she wrote.*
*Her tales*
*inscriptions set in stone.*
*"When this woman died at seventy and four*
*she left*
*not just her written words.*

*Faeries, goblins, witches, elves and many more*
*now live*
*within a netherworld.*
*"Dozing in the day and waking in the night,*
*the ones*
*who shadow in our dreams*
*come from fairy tales that story queens oft write.*
*They join*
*the exiles unredeemed."*

Brian racked his brain to find a clue in all of that. "You're not some sort of shadow."

"No, I'm as real as you are."

"And you're not seventy-four."

She gazed at him without a word.

"So you're an *exile unredeemed*?"

Rebecca kissed his cheek.

"Where, in your cabin?"

"No," she said. "That's my refuge. Where have you been seeing me lately?"

"In dreams."

She turned the page.

*"Stand with me to peek through beads in doorway strung,*
*we see*
*a vagrant sitting so.*
*This man isn't real. His dreaming self has come.*
*He died*
*three centuries ago.*
*"When this mortal sleeps his spirit walks the earth,*
*but time*
*is twisted inside out.*
*This one often roams outside the span of birth*
*and death*
*beyond his waking route.*
*"Fortune-teller thinks a beggar sits with her.*
*She strokes*
*the coarseness of his hand,*

*feeling his lifeline, his pulse steadfast and sure.*
*It beats*
*illusion of the man."*

Rebecca stopped reading.

More clues to process? "So, we're talking time travel, right?"

"Or dreams," she said. "They can be one and the same."

"In which universe?"

She clapped the book shut. "Exactly! We pass through the walls of time and space whenever we sleep. In one dream, you might get lost in the Amazon. In another, maybe you'll visit your early childhood again. Everyone leaves the here and now."

Rebecca spoke with enough bright-eyed sincerity to convince him. On the other hand, if their hips kept touching, she could probably get him to believe in the tooth fairy.

"That was a simple lesson in metaphysics," she said. "I haven't revealed a thing about myself." She sprang off the couch, twirled like a red-haired dream ballerina, finished with a flourish, and bowed. "Ask me about my world, not about me, and I'll answer if I can."

"Do you know a farmer near your cabin?"

"Maybe not."

"Where did you go after you left me?"

She twirled away.

"Where did the cider and cheese come from?"

"I conjured them!" Rebecca reached the mantel and traced her fingertips in a circle where the clock used to sit. For a moment it returned. Then it jumped back to the coffee table.

The overload of weirdness created a physical effect on Brian, like the tingly, metallic taste from touching his tongue to a battery. "Did you make the cabin, too?"

"My home is real."

"How about the shifting bluff I saw near it?"

Rebecca settled next to him on the couch again. "The wind blows dunes around."

"Right. Even when they're anchored down with prairie grass?"

"Let's talk about something else." She swung an arm in front of her, and a card fluttered in its wake, dipping, curving, then veering off course. It landed in his lap.

The card Sharon left with her phone number that night on the porch.

"Do you have another girl in your life, Brian?"

He flinched. This must have been what she meant by a jealous heart. "No, it isn't anything like that. Sharon's just a friend."

"No one else has taken a special interest in you?" Pale green eyes bored into his. Not angry eyes. Or jealous ones. Worried eyes. Scared even.

But who had he met that Rebecca would possibly know?

*Oh.*

"Do creepy stalkers count? Sharon's roommate, Abigail has been—"

*Poof.* Brian was all alone on the couch.

He blinked. Looked down. As if what—she slid underneath to hide?

Gone.

"Come along, Simon." Her voice almost shot him through the ceiling. "Brian has some research to do, and *I* need to handle a holy terror."

"Wait! What—"

The cat darted out of the bedroom, leapt toward where Rebecca had been sitting, and vanished.

"I'll cherish the gift, Brian."

The clock on the coffee table was gone.

He tried to get up, wobbled, sat back down.

# Chapter Sixteen

**BRIAN TOOK A QUICK** visual sweep of the condo from the couch—stained hot-chocolate mugs on the coffee table, a clump of cat fur on April's new area rug, an empty space on the mantel where the pendulum clock belonged. A Club Intrigue admission ticket still poked from the pocket of his shirt.

All genuine.

Real.

Rebecca even left a fragrance behind—a scent of pine lingering like leftover smoke, but in a good way. The aroma brought her cabin right into the room.

So he didn't fall asleep and dream the whole insane adventure. Or if he did, the universe upgraded to 2.2 anyway—the version including witches—bringing a whole different screen layout for him to navigate. He had to get used to it.

He opened a fist. Found the ribbon from Rebecca's book. No point even questioning how it got there.

His fingers tingled. A burst of amazing ideas flashed through his mind. Books he'd write, calculus problems he now knew how to solve, and dreams he might step out of. Like from one dimension to the next. Weird and ridiculous but possible.

Then his palm burned. *Hot.*

He flung the ribbon to the floor. Flexed his hand. Fine now.

The ideas shattered into a million fragments before he could hang on to the slightest bit of wisdom. Back to his old clueless self.

This had happened twice before. Once at the cabin when he first pulled the book from Rebecca's kitchen cabinet and touched the ribbon. Later, here in the condo, on the night a poem wrote itself on his computer.

He poked at the ribbon with his shoe.

Nothing happened.

He bent and touched it.

Nope.

He held his breath and *grabbed* it.

*Brian has research to do.* Rebecca's parting words.

But no mad rush of ideas.

He let the ribbon go. Counted to ten. Grabbed it again. Squeezed tight. Nothing.

Reality check. Did he believe in witches? Maybe. After all that had happened, he was definitely coming around. Magic ribbons? Not so much.

But *should* he believe in watching and listening for clues about what exactly was going on? Not a bad concept.

So here goes: *Brian has research to do.* Since Rebecca's comment was completely out of context to the situation, it could only be a clue, right?

Sooooo, research what? Witches? Teleportation? Abandonment?

Her vanishing act stung. If he'd struck a nerve by mentioning Abigail, why didn't Rebecca hang around and compare notes with him? Why skip out of his life *again?*

The whole evening didn't make sense, all the way back to the point she stepped onto a stage and...

*recited a poem about witches with a specific reference to the year 1692.*

He rushed to his computer and searched that year on the Internet. Numerous links to articles and stories covering the

Salem witch trials popped up. He dove into the Wikipedia version of the darkest episode in colonial history.

In the spring of 1692, eleven-year-old Abigail Williams and her nine-year-old cousin, Betty Parris, turned into exorcist fodder. They contorted their bodies in weird positions, bleated like farm animals, burst into fits of rage, shrieked in pain. Nobody ever figured out what caused their possession or why it spread like a virus to other girls in Salem.

Although the Puritans were supposed to be better-educated and more tolerant than the typical colonists, they embarked on the witch hunt to end all witch hunts. When the dust cleared, nearly two dozen of their own had been killed, mostly by hanging. A black-and-white sketch showed a bunch of them strung up in a row on Gallows Hill, where anyone could have stood to watch. *And what, order maize popcorn?*

Brian closed the page.

Sixteen ninety-two Salem. Hangings. Like Rebecca did to herself on stage.

Good theory: Rebecca wanted to be like a modern-day Poe, writing dark verses to send chills down spines.

Bad theory: She and Abigail weren't witches at all. They were the ghosts of two girls hanged in colonial Salem.

No way. He couldn't even begin to process *that* idea without melting his heart into water. He and Rebecca clicked. Boyfriend and girlfriend. A walk through the hills, a night in a cabin, dream visits, a reunion, kisses. She had to be real.

He stared at the search menu forever before swallowing and reopening the Wikipedia page. He looked for a Rebecca reference. Couldn't find one. Read about the girl named Abigail again. She was a player—kind of a weird coincidence with that name and all—but she wasn't a hanging victim.

He scanned some other articles. No Rebecca on the victim lists. Couldn't have been. Spirits don't have substance. They don't touch. Or kiss. Or leave things behind when they leave.

He turned to the window and stared into darkness almost as black as the fog he'd seen behind the club.

If they weren't ghosts, and Rebecca was a good witch and Abigail a bad one, or something else altogether, what did the poem mean?

Brian's phone went off with a deafening guitar riff. He dropped the mouse. Nearly fell off his chair. The ringtone needed to be lowered by about a thousand decibels.

He glanced at caller ID—*Sharon*—and he answered.

"Brian." Something was off with her tone. "Please ask your *witch* never to step foot in these dorms again."

Sharon *always* had a smile in her voice. Not this time. How to even respond? Was she talking about Rebecca? Had to be. Rebecca had gone after Abigail, *Sharon's roommate.* But what went down? "Um—"

No point in saying anything more. Sharon had already ended the call.

"I'm back, Brian." Rebecca's voice came at him from the kitchen doorway.

He leapt off the chair. Spun around.

"That didn't go well at all." She stood with arms lowered, water dripping from her hair.

# CHAPTER SEVENTEEN

"**I WENT TO THE** dorms and found Abigail with your friend Sharon, but she blinked away." These were the first words Rebecca had spoken in at least five minutes. She'd been sitting across the kitchen table from Brian in endless brooding silence, toweling her hair into a frizzy mess.

During the long wait, Brian distracted himself by watching squiggly raindrops race down the window beside her. He hadn't asked a single question. Not with angry death rays threatening to shoot out of Rebecca's eyes at any moment. But now she'd calmed and broken the silence. Maybe he could get some answers. "What do you mean, blinked away?"

Rebecca picked a cherry out of a bowl on the table. She closed her fist around it. Then opened her hand. Empty.

Cool trick. This illusion thing was great.

*Oh.* "You mean Abigail disappeared? As in *poof?*"

"Yes." Rebecca tossed her towel aside. "Do you have a brush?"

He got one, brought it back. "So Abigail's a witch, huh?"

"No, she's an imp. And they're supposed to be harmless." But the worry lines across Rebecca's forehead spoke volumes. She ran the brush through her hair, caught a snag, tried again. "Ow."

Brian had a dozen questions she probably wouldn't answer.

*What's an imp? How does somebody blink away?* And so on. But his best bet was to keep quiet and let her talk. "Can I help with that?" He took the brush.

"My hair is hopeless." Still, she shifted her chair sideways so she'd have her back to him, and she swept her hair over her shoulders, where he could get at it. Best of all, her frown curled into something almost resembling a smile.

What guy had experience brushing a girl's hair? He had nothing but instinct to go on. Why hadn't he offered a mug of hot chocolate to make her happy? An ice-cream cone from the freezer? A cold slice of pizza from the fridge?

He scooted his chair behind hers and went to work. Right away, he found a snag, held her hair tight near the scalp, closed his eyes, and *eased* the brush through. Slowly. But with purpose. The snag untangled.

*Yay.*

"We were outside the dorm room in the hallway. All three of us," Rebecca said. "Then two of us, after Abigail poofed away. I told Sharon I'm Rebecca, your girlfriend, and Abigail is *nobody's* friend. Sharon didn't hear any of that. She was too busy wringing her hands over the poofing incident."

Yeah. Who wouldn't be? He worked on another snag.

"Then I started burning some marks into their door."

"You what?"

"Ow! Be careful, Brian."

"Sorry." The pizza idea would have been so much better than combing a girl's hair during *this* crazy story.

"Sharon called my marks a curse."

"Burn marks kinda sound that way."

"Witches shouldn't curse people, Brian. Except in storybooks. I simply left a warning for Abigail to stay away."

"Got it. Burn marks in the door? Yeah, that would definitely make a good warning."

"And that's when Sharon doused me with a pitcher of water." Rebecca shifted around to eyeball him. "Why did you befriend such a mean girl?"

Brian wilted under the weight of her wounded gaze. Jealousy might have been part of that look, but not the largest share. "You're mad because you think my friendship with Sharon led to Abigail barging into our lives?"

Rebecca turned her attention to a loose thread poking from the sleeve of her dress, twisting it left, right, up, down. "I suppose that imp would have schemed her way in one way or the other."

"Yeah. You already knew her. Didn't Abigail hang the noose from that oak tree by your cabin?"

No answer.

"I had a run-in with her in Wyoming that day," he said.

Twist, twist, twist. The thread popped free. "Maybe she's gone for good now." Rebecca put her hand over his and eased the brush along the length of her hair. "I like your touch, Brian."

And he loved hers. Questions could wait. Except one. "Why do you keep vanishing?"

She snatched her hand away. "This last time, I went calling on your *friend*, hoping to get rid of a pest. Besides, I did come back."

Yeah, but each disappearance sucked the oxygen out of the world. Advance notice would have helped. Mutual planning. "How long can you stay?"

Rebecca turned to the window without answering. The rain had changed to sleet, pinging against the pane in windblown bursts.

He worked the brush through her hair, back in waiting mode again.

"Brian, do you know the machine that plays songs when you feed money into it?" Rebecca's tone was softer. Her shoulders had relaxed. "You're the song I drop a coin for, but the music stops when the needle reaches the end of the grooves. Even worse, I only have so many coins."

He almost didn't ask the obvious question for fear of the answer. "And then what?"

She swung around, grabbed his hands. "My poems are bursting

with clues! After you solve all the riddles, the song will play and play."

Rebecca's touch had the same dizzying effect as always, but he fought past it. He needed concrete answers before she vanished again. "Why not just come out and tell me everything without all the guessing?"

"I've told you. According to the Witches Code, I can only share information through riddles, illusions, and dreams."

"And you have to follow this code, because...?"

"That's what *pure* witches do." With lips pressed tight and eyes set on high gleam, Rebecca couldn't have looked more dedicated to her cause, whatever it was exactly. She was a girl on a mission.

What mission, he didn't know. He was supposed to guess. From clues. In poetry. "Suppose I don't solve your riddles."

"Open the window and I'll show you how to cast your worries away."

"No way. With my luck the wind would just blow them back in my face."

They shared a laugh. The world brightened. Rebecca leaned toward him like a co-conspirator. "Your mother is nice."

Wow. Talk about coming out of left field. "Say that again?"

"I called on her, Brian. A girl can't just go visiting a mother's son without permission, you know."

"According to your code?"

She nodded. Grinned. "You're catching on!"

"So you spent one of your few jukebox coins to visit my mom?"

"I went at night. Dream visits are free."

Brian's stomach roiled. "Did she kick your butt? My mom isn't the type who'd want somebody busting into her head."

Rebecca took up the brush and finished her hair. "I don't go into people's heads. I go where *they* go, to the common area everyone visits in their dreams. It's an exact replica of the waking world."

"Uh-huh." With all the other ridiculous cracks in the universe, who was he to question this one? "And she kicked your butt, right?"

"A little."

"She's touchy."

Rebecca yawned. She stood. "It's late."

"Don't go."

She cocked her head sideways like a startled bird.

Was she surprised at how needy he sounded? Disappointed? He stretched for a strong rebound. "Why not stay over? Here's the thing, though. My room has only one bed, and my Aunt April's room is…hers. So let's flip a coin to see who gets the couch."

As he fumbled in his pocket for a quarter, Rebecca's grin couldn't have stretched any wider.

"What's so funny?" he said.

"Brian, do you honestly believe a witch has ever been bested in a game of chance?"

Brian woke up, fell back asleep, drifted in and out. Couches didn't make the best beds.

Rebecca grabbed his wrist. He opened his eyes and looked up at her. "Is it morning already?"

"Shh, keep sleeping, Brian. I'm visiting your dreams."

He stood in the weeds behind Club Intrigue, watching Abigail interact with a thick black bank of fog. She plunged her arm into it, pulled out, stepped back. The darkness bulged after her, expanding in size.

Rebecca gasped.

"What's going on?" he said.

She grabbed his wrist. "So you *can* see the void!"

"Is that what it is?"

"Nobody else seems to know about it. I've asked."

"Did you ask Abigail?"

"No," she said. "Let's get away from here."

The scene swirled with dizzying speed. Bright flashes of color bombarded him. Wham! He landed on his feet in some kid's bedroom.

Winnie the Pooh wallpaper decorated the walls, and dozens of stuffed animals lay cluttered everywhere—on the floor, on a pint-sized yellow chair, on an orange bookcase and the top of a pink desk.

A little girl slept in bed, hugging a Raggedy Ann doll. Big rainbow letters spelled *Laura* in the headboard above her.

Rebecca gripped his wrist again. She'd gone pale. "I can't get away from it."

"What?" He whipped around to see what she saw. "I don't get it. There's nothing but a window."

"Look through it, Brian."

He couldn't. The blackness outside was all-consuming. No street lamps or stars or moon. Nothing. He shuddered.

Rebecca tugged him toward a pair of slatted doors filling half a wall. "We have to move Laura before she looks out there and gets frightened."

"Wait!" He'd seen enough horror movies to know bedroom closets should never be opened at night. "Don't pull—"

With her free hand, Rebecca yanked one of the doors open.

Another wild swirl of color blasted Brian. He cringed...then blinked at bright sunshine. He followed Rebecca through the doorway onto a bed of grass. The sun warmed his face, birds tweeted, and puffy clouds drifted across a blue canvas of sky. But when he glanced over his shoulder into the room, the black gloom still lurked at the window. "We can't leave her alone in there."

"We didn't." Rebecca motioned toward a bed of flowers where Laura lay sleeping. "Luckily, things are easy to fix here."

Brian stole another peek in the room. The bed was empty. *Because Laura had somehow beamed into the garden.* "Um, can I ask where *here* is?"

"We're in the land of a little girl's dreams. Shut the door, would you?"

"Gladly." He closed the door on the room, the window, and the nightmare beyond.

"Where should we go, Brian?" Rebecca's eyes sparkled, and the tremor in her voice was gone. They'd defeated the gloom. "I can take you anywhere."

"Anywhere?"

"Anywhere and any when. The laws of time and place are suspended in the World of Mortal Dreams. In fact, I'm not aware of any rules at all."

They'd stepped into an impossibly vibrant scene for a dream. A shimmering waterfall crashed down the side of a snow-capped mountain. A colorful flock of jungle birds cawed overhead. The green, dewy grass beneath Brian's feet dampened his shoes. "So this is all a figment of my imagination?"

"Not yours. We've stepped into Laura's dream. People do this sort of thing all the time, but they forget when they wake up." Rebecca opened her hand, revealing the golden two-sided coin he'd last seen in the lot behind Club Intrigue. She gave it to him. "*They* don't even know they're dreaming. With this compass, you will."

The gold coin was as warm as clothes pulled out of a dryer. He flipped it back and forth in his palm. "How does it work?"

"The temperature and color let you know you're in the World of Mortal Dreams."

"And when I'm not?"

"Cold silver." Rebecca closed her hand around his. "The image on both sides is Saint Brigit, the Irish patron saint of travelers. She'd want us to go exploring now, I think."

Rebecca led him though an endless grassy field. They walked and walked, basking in the sun, grooving to the chirp of crickets, until they reached an enormous redwood tree rising alone in the meadow.

She turned the knob of a wrought-iron door fitted into the bark. "A friend of mine dreamed her way into this tree once."

The door opened, revealing a youngish woman dressed in a roaring-twenties flapper costume. Thick blonde curls cascaded down her neck in a style that must have bitten the dust ages ago. Her short black dress came down to her hips, and dark, gartered stockings took over from there, creating the impression she'd been outfitted in a turn-back-the-clock line by *Victoria's Secret.* The room stayed true to the era, full of antique wooden furniture and with oval black-and-white portraits on the wall.

"Dreams linger," Rebecca whispered. "In a sense, we've gone back in time."

The scene wobbled. Brian reached into his pocket for the coin. It had cooled.

"Stay with me." Rebecca took his arm and led him inside.

The coin warmed, and the woman went into motion, stepping up to a museum piece—a wooden cabinet case with an ancient phonograph on top, complete with a horn-like speaker and a crank on the side. She turned the handle a few times. A record started spinning. Then she swiveled a mechanical arm and lowered it onto the disc, starting a scratchy piano tune.

"Scott Joplin," Rebecca whispered.

The woman swayed to the music, twirling around in their direction, and froze. She recovered with a smile. "Rebecca, how nice to see you again! Is this your boyfriend?"

"Yes, he is." Rebecca ran her hand down Brian's arm. The tone of pride in her voice dizzied him as much as her fingertips against his flesh.

The woman extended her hand. "I'm Agatha Christie."

Words caught in his throat.

The scene went purple, then orange, blue, yellow...green.

Brian wobbled on the lawn, next to Laura's garden. His heart beat like the lead drummer of a heavy-metal band. "What happened?"

"You woke up for a moment," Rebecca said, "and now you're dreaming in Laura's world again."

"How far back did we go?"

"Nineteen twenty-seven." Rebecca squeezed his hand. "You'll need to travel much further if you want to learn all there is to know about me. You'll figure out how to do that, won't you?"

"Huh!" Brian shot up from the couch. He glanced across at his bedroom.

Rebecca was gone.

"Not again." He sagged back down. Opened his hand. Found the coin.

Cold silver.

The waking world totally sucked.

# CHAPTER EIGHTEEN

TWO EMPTY WEEKS LATER, Brian pushed a cartload of DVDs down an aisle, rounded a corner a little too fast, and caught a quick blur of color—blue jeans, beige blouse, blonde ponytail—before nearly running Sharon down. She'd been kneeling on the floor to line the lower shelves of a display case with DVDs.

"Sorry," he said.

"No problem." She scooted away to let him pass.

He hadn't seen much of her since the burnt-door incident. They'd been working different shifts or she'd been avoiding him or both. "Is everything okay?"

"Peachy." But she sounded pruney. Cauliflowery. Weedy. Didn't *look* too happy, either. Her signature smile had gone dim. Not much eye contact, either.

He glanced at the DVDs on her shelf: *Pride and Prejudice, Titanic, The English Patient, The Hours*. He took a stab at humor. "Wait. I'll go find the *Saw* series to round out the field."

Sharon pulled a DVD out of a carton on the floor and stood it on the shelf. "These romance movies are my happy place, Brian. I've been having a little trouble coping."

Uh-oh. *Having trouble coping* was girl-to-girl language. Chicks didn't lay that sort of line on a guy unless they were (a) girlfriend and boyfriend, or (b) so messed up over something, they'd forgotten to speak in girl-to-guy language, such as *get out of my face*. He'd been ready to move on and wait for a time when Sharon was in a better mood or whatever, but would he ever hear a louder cry for help? Something was wrong. And he was supposed to be her friend. So he stayed rooted to the spot.

Sharon looked up at him. "Did Rebecca tell you what happened the day she came to our dorm? Did the two of you talk about it?"

"Not much." Looking back on it brought nothing but uncertainty. He hadn't seen Rebecca since then, except for visits in his sleep at night. The shared dreams faded to the dust of forgotten fantasies by the next morning *every time*. Were the visits even real? *Of course they were.* He couldn't give up hope. She'd show up in the flesh again, sooner or later.

"Abigail *disappeared*, Brian. And I don't mean she walked away. This was more like into thin air."

"Damn."

"She faded back in a few minutes later, didn't answer a single question about what happened, and then she said she was done with school. Just like that." Sharon turned her attention to the DVD carton, pulled one out, set it on her shelf. *The Twilight Zone.* "She went home. And that's fine. But what did I see happen?"

How could he have been so thoughtless not to realize an unexpected *poof* in Sharon's everyday world might cause collateral damage? He should have called her the next day rather than selfishly wallow in the misery of his own emotional damage when Rebecca skipped out on him. "Listen, Sharon, you're into the occult and all, and that means you're open to out-of-the box thinking, right?"

She fixed him with a deer-in-the-headlights stare. "I'm not sure anymore. I used to like my predictable world. Now I'm in a weird one."

"Well, work with me here, because what I'm gonna tell you fits right in with science." He reached into the box, riffled through some DVDs, and found *Inception*. He put it on her shelf.

"Can you buy the idea that during our dreams we cross into a different dimension and interact with everyone else who's dreaming?"

"Nice try." She fished in the box, pulled out *The Illusionist,* and smiled.

"Trust me. The more you think about it, the more it'll make sense. But here's the quantum leap. Maybe some people can jump from one dimension to the next at any time. With both feet. Back and forth. *Poof.*"

"Poof?"

"Uh-huh. And they can return from there to anyplace *here* they want. In warp speed. Abigail might be anywhere right now." He searched Sharon's face for a hint of acceptance. If he'd managed to reconcile the scientific world to this new, virus-infested beta version, maybe she could start coping again. God. She'd been obsessing for two weeks? He should have called her.

"Thanks, I think." Sharon held up another DVD. *Hope Floats.*

*Bbbbbrrrrrrinnnnnggggggggggggg.* The door chime rang much louder than usual and ended with a weird, tuning-fork resonance. Although Sharon usually shouted a greeting to any and all customers, she kept her gaze on him.

He turned to the front, but Charlie at the checkout counter seemed oblivious, too. Who could blame the guy? Ever since he'd made a name for himself as starting quarterback for the Badgers, girls had been using movie browsing as an excuse to corner him. In this case, a sultry brunette stood at the counter kneading his upper arm. Charlie lived for these moments.

*Bbbbbrrrrrrinnnnnggggggggggggg.* Again! Maybe gusts of wind wobbled the door back and forth just enough to keep the bell vibrating. Charlie would have known from his vantage point, if he could tear his gaze from his groupie for a second, whereas Brian couldn't see past a row of shelving near the entrance.

The chime lingered on, impossibly long. Doors just didn't vibrate that way, windy day or not. Brian reached into his pocket for the St. Brigit coin. Cold. He definitely wasn't dreaming.

"Do you hear that, Sharon?"

"Hear what?"

"The bell. It keeps—"

Rebecca stepped into view.

He blinked. He grabbed the coin again. Still cold. Meaning he was awake and Christmas had come early. The first day of school. The *last* day of school. His birthday, Easter, the Fourth of July. A burst of delight went off like a flare, painting his thoughts every shade of the rainbow. They took a joyride around the color wheel until settling on...yellow?

Rebecca's ridiculous scarf propelled his ponder reflex in a mach-four takeoff that kicked his celebrating heart to the curb.

Why would a girl whose fashion statements centered on faded dresses and, in this case, a gray overcoat, wear the one loud thing? She'd done it before, too, the day they met in Nebraska. Was she trying to tell him something? A clue maybe?

"Brian?"

The first bite of a chocolate-covered strawberry paled in comparison with the sound of Rebecca's voice. Questions about winter-wear choices could wait. He hurried toward her, and she to him, with so much abandon they could have starred in any of Sharon's favorite romances. He finally got why those movies were so popular. People lived for moments like this, and not only chicks.

He lifted Rebecca right off her feet with his hug.

"Did you miss me?" she asked.

Yeah, he did, enough for everything else to fade away. He looked her up and down, kissed her, smooched again, and one more time before he noticed an odd aspect of the fading-away thing. Stillness.

He peeked over her shoulder at the reflection in the window. The cashier, Sharon, and every customer in the store had gotten stuck in place. "Wow."

Rebecca stepped back. "You're as handsome as ever! I should have waited a bit longer before visiting you again, but I couldn't resist."

He tried comprehending what she'd just said, but the store proved too great a distraction. The scene looked as though someone had pressed the pause button in the middle of a reality show.

A girl had knocked a DVD from the shelf. The box hovered in the air while her mannequin mom reached a frozen arm to catch it. A man bent over the drinking fountain, the stream of water hanging midair like a gob of glue. Charlie had fumbled his groupie customer's change across the counter. Some of the coins stood on end at odd angles.

Rebecca took his chin in her hand. "I'm standing here, not over there. This is our moment."

"But what's happening?"

"I stopped your world for a few seconds."

Brian's mouth had gone dry. "You stopped…my world?"

But she wasn't paying attention to him anymore. She stared down the aisle at Sharon with anything but love in her eyes. "Why is *your friend* here, Brian?"

"Sharon? She works here and—"

Rebecca waved an arm.

The store came back to life. Everywhere. All around him. Including Rebecca, who clenched her fists and headed down the aisle.

He hurried after her. "Hey, wait up."

Sharon had her back to them, still busy with her movie display and showing no awareness she'd been frozen moments earlier. She turned when he spoke. "Brian, where'd you go? I—"

Rebecca cleared her throat.

Sharon's smile faded.

The two girls shifted hands to hips and stared each other down. The crackling animosity had the effect of a firestorm, sucking the air out of Brian's lungs.

Rebecca broke the silence. "I see you're still hanging around *my Brian!*"

Then Sharon. "I work with *your Brian*. Why don't you forget petty jealousy and worry about getting rid of the burn marks on my door?" Her voice was loud enough to carry to the far corners of the store.

"You don't need me for that," Rebecca shouted. "A pail of soapy water will do the trick."

"I wish I had one right now!"

"I'm sure you do! You take delight in drenching people, don't you?"

Brian dodged the girls' waving arms and made an attempt to step in the middle, but Rebecca stopped him with a hand to his chest, and Sharon shuttled him aside with a well-placed shift of her hip.

The two combatants glared at each other in dangerous silence until—

Rebecca cracked a smile. "You got me good with that pitcher of water."

"Yeah." Sharon said nothing more for a long moment. Then, "Sorry about that."

"Don't be." Rebecca spoke to the floor in barely more than a whisper. "I deserved it."

Brian breathed.

In some kind of instinctive bonding ritual, the two of them slumped to the floor at the same time and wrapped their arms around their knees.

"You and Abigail scared the hell out of me," Sharon said.

"I have a history with her," Rebecca said, "but we shouldn't have behaved like that in front of you."

Sharon arched her brows up at Brian. "You mean Abigail shouldn't have scared the hell out of me by disappearing?"

Rebecca nodded. "And I shouldn't have pretended to sizzle your door. That was just a trick. The marks do wash off."

They went on like that, back and forth, in quiet voices, until they'd reached something of a truce, if not outright friendship. They each stretched an arm up, and Brian pulled them to their feet.

Rebecca hugged Sharon. "Nice seeing you again, friend of Brian's."

"Ditto," Sharon said.

Brian went for the coin in his pocket. Still cold. Rebecca slipped a hand in his that wasn't. He staggered to the front of the store beside her.

The shouting portion of that love fest had flustered Charlie into head-down, pretend-to-be-busy mode. His groupie had moved on, and he didn't have a customer in sight, proving that even a brute of a varsity football star could be totally intimidated by a catfight.

Brian tried to catch his eye. "Hey, meet Rebecca."

The cashier, college jock, shift boss, but mostly chicken finished straightening some movie guides before looking up, first at Brian and then with a furtive glance toward Rebecca. "Hey."

"Mind if I leave a half hour early? We're gonna hang out."

"N-no prob. Sharon and I can hold the place down. Here, knock yourself out." He tossed a bag of popcorn to Brian.

Once outside, Rebecca grabbed the bag. "How sweet! Do we steam it?"

"No, we microwave it."

"Oh." She threw the bag into a garbage can, then turned to him, beaming the brightest eyes in the world. "Why don't I just cook for you tonight?"

He grinned. He was onto her. "You mean conjure, as in bread, cheese, and cider?"

"No, I mean cook. Do you like goose? With only two of us to eat it, you'll be taking leftover sandwiches to school for a week. Still, I think you'd love it. I can make mashed potatoes, cranberries, beets—"

"I don't like beets. Nobody does."

"No beets then. What kind of dessert would you like?" Rebecca prattled on about the dinner. Broccoli-cheese dip, buttered rolls, eggnog.

When she paused for breath, he settled his hands on the shoulders of the most captivating girl he could ever hope to meet. "I love you."

She gasped. "After the way I acted back there?"

"I pick odd times to blurt these things out."

"I love you, too, Brian. More than you can ever imagine."

"Even though you poof away without warning?"

She kissed his cheek, whispered in his ear. "I poof back, don't I?"

Yeah. And he'd figured out how, or thought he had. "You're using dreams, aren't you?"

She gaped at him, eyes twinkling more than ever. She didn't confirm or deny. Just took his hand, started walking with him, and swung her arm with his. She hummed.

He was in love with a hummingbird. "Rebecca, you're using dreams to come and go, just the same way I poofed into that girl Laura's room with you and then popped back at her later in the flower garden."

She stopped. He did, too. She moved her hands to his cheeks. "Don't think you'll figure out everything so easily, mister."

He hugged her. Tight enough to feel the beat of her heart.

"Look at you warming me like a fire, Brian. My heart is lumpy."

"Same here. Totally."

"Peas in a pod?"

"Uh-huh."

Another two weeks dragged by without her, except in dreams.

One afternoon, Brian joined a group of guys for a three-on-three game of basketball in the university gymnasium. One of them pointed at his shirt. "You're skins, dude."

Brian peeled it off and threw it toward the risers.

"That means you don't pass to the guys in shirts." A shaved-headed jerk in an oversized Milwaukee Bucks jersey hanging almost to his knees leered at him. The last time they played together, Brian got tricked by somebody calling his name from behind. He passed the ball to a guy on the wrong team. This idiot couldn't let it die. Brian would have liked nothing more than to dunk the basketball right in his face.

Right. Fat chance of jamming at five foot eight. He just needed to remember the basics, like not passing to the guys with shirts on.

They started a game to eleven, with one point awarded for each basket. The other team had the ball first. Brian fell into his usual playing style, hanging out near the half-court line. Defense wasn't his thing. Better to let his more capable teammates do the heavy lifting, being careful not to let them trip over him in the process.

Early on, the players on both teams passed the ball back and forth and took their shots without giving him a second glance. He tried to get his ass in gear and at least move on offense, but that only led to his fumbling the ball away the one time he got it in his hands.

His two fellow skins were nice enough not to say anything, but one of them glanced toward the risers, probably hoping a suitable replacement might come along before the next game started. If the universe did have a Scotty, Brian silently pleaded to get beamed up. Basketball wasn't his thing.

After the shirts built up a seven-to-two lead, Brian managed to grab a rebound when it deflected off two sets of taller hands. He started a clumsy dribble, nearly lost the ball, but kept going to the half-court line. He brought it back and eyed the hoop.

"Pass it to me!" The taunting goof, Mr. Dress-for-Success, pressed close. Brian glanced around, found nobody free, and tried a wild fadeaway shot over the guy's head.

The ball hit the rim, bounced on a sideways angle to the backboard, made an impossible return on *the same angle*, and fell through the basket. Seven to three. "Wicked spin!" one of his teammates shouted.

*Yes!*

On the next play, a shirt tripped and lost the ball. It bounced into Brian's hands at half court. He went into an out-of-control dribble toward the basket and flipped the ball up. The crazy thing spun a stubborn circle around the rim, refusing to let centrifugal force send it airborne. Laws of physics be damned! It dropped into the net. Seven to four.

All of a sudden, playing basketball was a lot more fun.

His teammates started looking at him differently. A shirt missed a shot, and a skin got the rebound. He actually passed the ball to Brian.

Intoxicated by his burst of luck, Brian lobbed the ball from the top of the key. The shot was beyond his range, and he regretted it the moment he let go, but the ball floated well past the point where gravity should have claimed it as a victim...and into the net. Seven to five.

"Awesome, dude!"

Heaven.

The moment he let himself bask in the glory, his flat-footedness returned, forcing his two pals to go up against the three shirts with little assistance on his part. He did his best to stay out of their way while they grunted, shoved, stole, shot, and rebounded until they tied the game ten to ten.

One more point. Had he ever been on the winning side? Coming this close, and better yet, having scored three actual points ranked this day no lower than the seventh best of his life—way below meeting Rebecca, but somewhere between his first kiss and the day he passed the road test for his driver's license.

Before he could walk off the court and retire from the game for good—why risk a letdown by playing out that final point?—the jerk on the other team came straight at him with the ball. Brian had no delusions he could ever defend against whatever fancy move was about to unfold. He should have gotten out while the getting was good.

But his right hand took on a life of its own, scooping low and deflecting the ball enough for him to knock it from the guy. He looked down at the thing. It was in his hands! He moved the ball to the half-court line and stopped.

"Pass it!"

"Over here!"

"Shoot it!" A girl's cry rose from the risers, and not just any girl.

*Rebecca.*

Adrenaline blasted through Brian's veins like a rocket ship. He dribbled toward two defenders and took a jump shot from a little behind the foul line. The ball hit the rim, went straight up, and came down.

Swish.

One of his teammates slapped his back. "Sweet!"

"That was epic, man!" the other said.

But who cared about a game of hoops anymore? Not with Rebecca returning to his life. She clapped like crazy from the risers.

"The dude has a fan," one of the guys said.

He rushed over to her.

Rebecca shot up and wrapped her arms around his neck, her loud pink scarf tickling his ear. "We sure showed them, didn't we?"

"*We?*"

Her eyes gleamed with mischief. "I love doting on you."

*The scarf. What was it about that scarf?*

He sat with Rebecca across an old kitchen table facing a poet from a forgotten era. A warm, gold Saint Brigit coin proved their little get-together went beyond the bounds of waking reality, but according to Rebecca, whatever went down would be genuine all the same.

"Your verses are clever, Rebecca, but you need to take greater risks!" Walt Whitman had the bald-headed, scraggly-bearded look of somebody's hippy grandfather. No, that wasn't it. His voice boomed like Santa Claus. Hearing *ho, ho, ho* out of this guy would have been no great surprise.

Rebecca slid her book of Ogham across the table. "Show me what you'd change."

Walt flipped through the pages and paused in the middle, moving his lips as he read. "Good alliteration here."

Wait. Walt had to be putting them on. Brian leaned forward and tried to read the page upside down. "How can you make that out? It's Ogham!"

"Ogham?" The poet pushed the book across the table. He'd opened it to a page showing a series of verses written in English.

"But I thought—"

"She's a handful, isn't she?"

Somebody knocked on the door.

Brian grabbed the book and paged through it. More English. Rebecca had hidden secrets in her poetry—clues—and now he could read them! He saw something about reflections. A mirror. Would he remember this when he woke up?

*Please. Let me remember mirrors.*

The pounding on the door grew louder, relentless. He cracked his eyes open.

"In a minute!" Oh man, of all the times to wake up. He'd been learning something. *But what?*

More pounding.

"Coming!" He dragged himself out of bed.

The tapered end of a Christmas tree pushed the front door open. And the girl at the other end? "Rebecca!"

A six-foot fir exploded into the room. He hurried around, brushed some needles out of her hair, and kissed the tip of her nose.

Rebecca touched his face, warming him from head to toe, while Simon darted by and started swatting branches with his paw. "I know it's early, being two days before Thanksgiving and all, but you're probably going home to your family, aren't you? I thought we could dress a tree before you leave."

"I don't have any ornaments."

"I've got that covered." She motioned beyond the doorway to two cardboard boxes on the porch. The first overflowed with the kinds of glass ornaments found only in dusty antique stores. Angels, Santa Clauses, snowflakes, teardrops, birds. All hand-painted in Christmas colors. The other spilled over with strings of red beads, gold garlands, and blue lights.

"Rebecca, tell me you didn't drag this stuff up to the door all by yourself."

She bounded into the kitchen, a stream of words trailing behind her. "I'll make hot chocolate. Do you have any Christmas music? Plant the tree in the stand, would you? And change out of those pajamas, Superman! It's ten in the morning!"

"Yeah, I'll get right on it."

He didn't want any of it to end—the dreams, Rebecca's wonderful, albeit rare and all too brief appearances, her bursts of childish glee. He'd follow her to the end of the earth and beyond. But beneath the elation, hidden in a corner of his mind he hated to visit, lurked the nagging worry she might disappear one day for good, and he'd never be able to find her.

What was that dream about? He'd seen something. A shelf. A table. A window. No, something else. He needed to pepper her with questions. Maybe she'd slip up and tell him what he'd seen, code or no code. He couldn't just ride along, hoping the merry-go-round would never stop.

Rebecca called from the kitchen. "I see you still keep my book in a cherished place, right next to the food sorcerer. Honestly, Brian."

*What did he dream?*

"Take my verses home to show your mother."

"What?" He headed into the kitchen. "Why?"

"Just do it, Brian." Rebecca stood balanced on a chair, fumbling in a cabinet above the stove. "I forgot my hot chocolate mix. Where's yours?"

She wobbled, and he reached up, catching her by the hips.

"Thank you, Brian."

"Uh, yeah. You bet." Only the thin fabric of her dress separated her warm flesh from his hands.

*What dream?*

# CHAPTER NINETEEN

**THE CRASH OF WAVES** faded to whispers by the time the sound reached Rebecca at the top of the cliff. She'd come to find peace in just such white noise, but a stone captured her attention instead. Lumpy and forgettable on one side, sparkling with jagged crystals on the other, it served as a reminder that all clouds do have silver linings.

She could almost forget her troubles here in this dream, on this rock, but not quite. "Too many visits have come and gone, Simon."

The cat clicked his teeth at a fly.

"But we're not here to worry." She ran her free hand through Simon's comforting coat.

A climber reached up from below. She started, but then recognized the crescent-shaped ring he wore. *Henry Stoddard.* Would this cretin never leave her alone? She shifted away.

Another hand joined the first one, then a mat of dark hair. In a moment, the entire sorcerer hauled his conniving self up and perched next to her. He wore a bright purple cloak and handsome pants instead of farmer's jeans this time, but her mother had always said a dandelion is still a weed, even when it blooms.

"Henry Stoddard! I told you once already your assistance isn't welcome. I have everything under control, thank you."

"And this is why you chose a brooding rock for a sitting stool?"

"Feel free to crawl under it."

The sorcerer winked. "Your skills as a hostess are lacking, dear. I noted the flaw on the day I first came courting."

"I didn't climb up here to take a walk down memory lane with you, Henry."

"Then let's talk about the present. Where's the handsome young man?"

The audacity of his question stole her breath away. She counted to ten. She listened to the foaming waves far below. She found her voice. "Where Brian might be is of no moment to you."

"Oh, but it is! I've taken a special interest in him."

Rebecca clenched her fists. Saying the wrong thing out of anger might provoke the sorcerer to escalate his interference into a mission rather than what she hoped would be a passing fancy. But she couldn't stop the rage from boiling out of her mouth, undistilled. "How *dare* you send Abigail to torment us! And now you ask where Brian is, as if you hadn't provided exact coordinates to her."

Stoddard tossed a small rock over the edge. It hit the side partway down and set a small avalanche of gravel into motion, tumbling, bounding, until the entire mess disappeared into the waves below. "I suppose thinking Abigail is on my leash would be less frightening for you than to imagine she's running wild on her own."

"You think I fear an imp?"

"I think we both should fear this one, *if* she's an imp at all."

She shuddered. "What are you suggesting?"

"Nothing. Let's focus on Brian. You've been in love with him all this time, from the day you first met him, haven't you?"

Rebecca didn't dare speak for fear the flood of emotion bringing tears to her eyes would also break her voice.

They sat in silence until he touched her hand. Gently. And he smiled. The sorcerer could be a disarmingly likeable sort to the unwary, thanks to those perpetual crinkles of humor at the corners of his eyes. "I didn't expect an answer. Still, I feel obligated to give a piece of advice."

Rebecca pulled her hand away. "No thank you."

"I took the trouble to do some research, Rebecca. This prophecy of yours says nothing about the witch falling in love. How many of your precious visits have you squandered prancing around with this boy?"

His worthless advice came a little too late.

"That isn't my advice," he said.

"You read minds now?"

"Your heart is on your sleeve. My advice is for you to take control and stop waiting for things to happen. How did you know the boy would arrive in Sidney on that August day?"

She'd been holding the half-plain, half-crystal stone in her palm until that moment. She dropped it now, or it fell on its own and disappeared into the foaming waves without anything close to the splash he'd sent through her stomach. "What do you know about Sidney?"

"Save your misdirection for the boy. Just tell me how you knew."

"An angel told me, a long time ago."

"Demons are always bent on telling *me* things, but I take their counsel with a grain of salt."

"You liken angels to demons?"

Stoddard's booming laugh cut across the sea in search of the nearest rock to bounce against. "They're both part of the ruling class, aren't they? Call me an anti-establishment type."

"It's not the first name comes to mind."

"Rebecca, I'm simply saying if an angel told me a young man would appear at a certain time and place, I'd do something to make sure it happened. Maybe I'd give him a nice dream and plant a billboard."

"A what?" Stoddard's maddening babble would surely drive her to distraction.

"Does this lad have a keen sense of direction?" he asked.

"Are you asking whether he's a schemer, like you?"

"No, here's what I'm asking. By showering the boy with love in that hypnotizing manner of yours, are you inspiring his curiosity or stifling it?"

"Go away."

Stoddard's laugh found a cliff several furlongs distant and echoed all the way back. His image faded, but his voice lingered. "Your love for Brian prevents whatever control you might have had over this situation, not that you knew how to run the game to begin with. I suppose things will just have to play out on their own, unless you choose to tell him everything."

"I won't violate the code! What makes you think you can come here and—"

Stoddard disappeared. He'd accomplished his obvious mission to set her heart pounding over the uncertainty of a random future.

"Henry, you've seen the void, haven't you? You know it's real. That means the prophecy is, too."

No answer.

How had Henry researched the prophecy? She'd learned about it from her mother, her mother from her grandmother, and so on through scores of generations. Suppose whatever source Stoddard came across provided greater detail? She should have asked him whether the prophecy foretold the champion would be a witch's son. Not that she needed further evidence. Brian had to be the chosen one. She felt it in her bones.

A fleeting thought of her mother renewed her worries. The void had started shifting west again, threatening to snuff out every old dream in its path. *And Abigail was helping it grow.*

How long would the cabin be safe from its clutches?

# CHAPTER TWENTY

BRIAN SAT SHOULDER TO shoulder with his dad at the basement worktable, sifting through mounds of plastic pieces. Shelves lined the walls, displaying models of houses, forts, Star Wars cruisers, and even the Eiffel Tower, all assembled brick by brick with painstaking care. They'd spent the better part of the afternoon preparing this latest project, a scale model of the Taj Mahal, by organizing its thousands of pieces by color and size into plastic containers.

"We're missing the girl with red hair," Dad said.

"We're what?" Brian hadn't broached the topic of Rebecca with anyone in his family. How could he? *I'm seeing this girl, but mostly in my dreams*—a relationship in dire need of progression beyond that obligatory modifying clause. Otherwise, his parents would interrogate him about drinking parties while his sister laughed her silly head off.

"There you are." His dad pulled the tiny figurine of a red-haired girl out from beneath a pile of bricks. "Thought you'd get away, did you?"

Brian breathed. He needed to get a grip. The first trip home from school was disorienting enough without misinterpreting random comments into impossible conclusions.

"Do you guys need any help?" Kara pulled a stool up to the

table. Home from college for Thanksgiving, his sister wore her finest black, as usual. She dyed her hair from blonde to midnight, too, bucking the trend set by legions of girls before her. Kara sometimes went so far as to gray her lips as well, but she'd spared them this time, going blood red for the Thanksgiving holiday.

Brian held a piece up. "We're short one of these, I think."

She went to work, rummaging through one of the piles. "I'll bet you accidentally mixed it in with these single-nozzle fireplug thingies." The missing piece did look like a tiny hydrant but with a nozzle on every side, unlike the set's dozens of one-nozzle pieces.

Kara served as their finder of lost things. She had a knack for locating anything from a misplaced article of clothing to a miniature brick. Often during these construction projects, she'd sit on the stool and read a book or hum to herself or both, until the inevitable cry for help propelled her into action. Kara loved her small role in transforming chaos into order.

*A finder of lost things.* Brian studied her in a new light. "Kara, if you were looking for someone who lived off the grid, where would you start?"

The question flew past her and smacked unimpeded into a far wall of the basement. She'd already turned her attention elsewhere. "Your hair has more pepper than salt, Dad. What's with that?"

Their dad flashed a Cheshire-cat grin. "It's called dye, Sweety. Call me Red."

"Oh. Too bad. I've been reading legends about people who never age." Kara shifted her focus again. She gazed directly into Brian's eyes, as if her words held a secret meaning just for him.

Brian didn't know what the hell she was talking about, but her stare was intense. *Knowing.* He fought off a reflexive squirm.

"Nope," Dad said. "The fountain of youth comes in a bottle."

"Maybe that's where Brian found his new girlfriend. Think she's a genie?"

Huh? How could she know about Rebecca? As usual when

confronted with something impossible—a recurring theme lately—Brian grabbed the Saint Brigit coin in his pocket. It was wide-awake cold. "Where did you come up with the girlfriend idea, Kara?"

"Maybe Mom told me."

"I never told *her* I had one."

Dad glanced at him over the top of his reading glasses. "I thought I noticed a spring in your step."

"He isn't moping around like he did all summer," Kara said.

"I wasn't moping."

"Do you have a girlfriend or not?" she asked.

"News flash, I've had them before." But how could his mom have told Kara about *Rebecca*?

*Because Rebecca said she visited her in a dream.* Except his mom shouldn't have mistaken a dream for something that really happened.

And yet what had he been doing lately?

"Nothing wrong with playing the field," Dad said. "Keep your options open."

"Or just pick the one you love and don't waste time with the bimbos," Kara added.

This was getting out of hand. "I don't hang out with bimbos."

"No? Remember Trudy? Or Marla?"

He groaned. "Come on. I was thirteen, and we were in a study group."

"Karen Steeplewood was a prize." Kara laughed so hard she almost fell off her stool.

He would have been happy to help her along with a little shove.

Hurried footsteps pounded down the stairs. "Quick! Where can I hide?" Tall, blonde, and sloppy, Kara's boyfriend, Brad, celebrated the holiday in his typical fashion, wearing a faded plaid shirt with tails hanging out over a pair of worn jeans.

"Brad?" Mom's call chased after him from the top of the stairs.

He glanced over his shoulder, hurried across the basement,

and hid behind some shelving. Kara giggled and followed him. "What does she want, Brad?"

"I don't know, but I know what *I* want."

"Oh, Brad!" Kara screeched with laughter.

"Get a room, you two," Dad said.

"Brad!" Mom's voice grew louder. "You come up here this minute and bring that silly girlfriend of yours with you. I need help setting the table and putting the food out."

They came from behind the shelves hand in hand. "Why do you two guys get off so easily?" Kara asked.

"She knows we're useless," Brian joked.

After they left, he and his dad began laying the foundation of the palace, mostly in silence but with an occasional probing question thrown in with the bricks. "Getting used to college, Brian? Your aunt says you've taken to it."

"Yeah, but I'm wondering what else is out there. Besides accounting, I mean. What do you think of journalism?"

"Stay the course."

"Got it."

"So what's this girlfriend of yours like?"

Brian fumbled a piece to the floor. The simple question stirred up so much emotion it showed in his face for sure. "Rebecca's great. Kinda mysterious. She gets stuck in my head a lot."

"Sounds like your mom when I first dated her. Does she live in Chicago?"

"No, she's pretty far from here."

Brian lifted a savory forkful of turkey and gravy to his mouth. A mouthwatering chaser of cranberries waited its turn on the plate before him. The cozy gathering had his dad on one end of the table, his mom on the other, with Kara and Brad sitting together, across from him. Looking past them through the dining room window, he could make out a light snowfall in the glow of a streetlamp. He'd fallen into a Norman Rockwell painting, Danahey style, but he kept forgetting how to smile. He would have traded the entire Thanksgiving feast for a plateful of beets if he could have had Rebecca at his side.

Mom was in one of her quiet, broody moods, but everyone else tag-teamed him with favorite pantomimes, jokes, and skirmishes that never grew old, as if they sensed his malaise and rallied their forces to turn it. And why not? He probably had *longing* written all over his forehead.

Kara did something to make Brad jump. Her foot must have snuck up his leg.

"We need to buy a clown table," Dad said. "You two can sit at it next time."

She curled her lower lip into a comic pout. "If we did, you wouldn't get to hear the things on my Christmas list, would you? Or my ideas for *yours*."

"How many things do you think you're getting?" Brian had gotten pulled into the banter. They'd recently decided on a thirty-dollar limit per person after haggling like Turkish rug merchants.

Dad speared some turkey, moved it to his mouth, but paused as if he'd come up with something better than food. He looked for it on the ceiling, then out the window, and finally around the table at each of them. "I've been thinking about that new scale model of the White House. Maybe we should raise the limit."

"No way," Kara said. "You're the one who keeps saying times are tough, remember?"

"The set has six thousand pieces. Think how many we'd lose! We're talking hours of fun for you, too." Judging by the exaggerated, wide-eyed expression on his face, Dad was putting her on. He lived for ridiculous arguments.

"Why don't you take your other models apart?" Kara asked.

Their dad dropped his fork. She might as well have debunked the dinosaurs.

A proven expert at playing this game, Kara took her time

before continuing. "That'd be hours of fun, wouldn't it? You can put them back in their boxes and sell them on eBay. Then you could buy the White House model and have money left over to get more Christmas presents for *us*."

"Point for Kara," Brad said.

Dad gestured to a magazine rack on top of the sideboard. "Where's the circus catalogue we were looking at, Brian? We can order the clown table and set it up by the window."

"My father used to whittle for a hobby." All heads turned. The out-of-sync comment by Mom went over like a blow horn at a church service.

She'd been mostly silent throughout the dinner, doing her best impression of Edgar Alan Poe's raven, sitting at the end of the table wearing a dress as black as her hair, and watching. Whenever Brian had taken his mind off his pining long enough to notice her, she'd had her eye on him. He couldn't imagine what he'd done wrong, but her steely gaze made him fidget anyway.

"Whittling costs a lot less than a White House scale model," she said. "And there's nothing wrong with being old-fashioned, is there, Brian?"

He nearly choked on a mouthful of turkey. He searched her face for signs of a double meaning, but she stared back at him like a world-class poker player.

"I had building blocks as a boy fifty years ago," Dad said. "They're just as old-fashioned as whittling."

Their dad might as well have tried talking to a tree. An argument over hobby preferences stood zero chance of interrupting Mom's unwavering gaze. Without breaking eye contact with Brian, she sipped some water and motioned to the hallway where her woman cave lurked. "Let's spend some time alone after dinner, Brian. I'd like to catch up on how college is going and what that new *girlfriend* of yours is like."

An invitation to the dungeon. Brian slumped in his chair.

The rest of the meal was a blur until dessert. Even under duress, Brian couldn't help but savor every warm, juicy bite of homemade apple pie. He dragged the dessert out, not only to prolong the taste but to delay an inquisition, although he still couldn't think of what he'd done.

But nobody ever got summoned to the den for pats on the back.

When the last crumbs were gone and Kara started clearing the dishes and Dad hurried downstairs with Brad, ostensibly to work on the Taj Mahal but more likely to lie low, Brian followed his mom down the hallway. The den served as her lair. Visits by anyone were rare and by *her* request only, for a scolding or a lecture.

Typically, his mom would leave the door open while she browbeat him, but she cornered him this time, not only closing the thing but locking it behind them when they walked into the room. He glanced out the window, a ridiculous escape route. The storm window behind and nighttime darkness beyond didn't offer any hope for such folly.

So he sat across from her at a table overflowing with newspaper clippings and magazines. A born hoarder, his mom never got rid of her old stuff. Brian cleared a space to keep some of it from spilling off the table onto his lap. Once settled in, and with the risk of an avalanche under control, he took a stab at controlling the conversation. "I'm thinking of changing majors."

No dice. Mom's pressed lips, the furrow in her forehead, and the scalding focus of her gray-green eyes trumped any diversion he'd ever come up with. "I had a visitor," she said. "Sometimes, when I dream, I relax in a nice, secluded lighthouse with a wonderful view. I don't appreciate anyone disturbing me when I'm resting in it."

*Dreams.* So, Rebecca's visit had triggered this little get-together, not the worn-out argument over career choices. But this made no sense. Mom shouldn't have interpreted a dreamed interaction as real.

"We have a nice home," she continued, "and the door is always open for a friend of yours to come over and say hello."

"Yeah. About that, see—"

"My personal space, on the other hand, is mine and mine alone. You know how I feel regarding privacy."

"Uh-huh." He would have loved to melt through the window, run around to the front door, sneak back inside, and head downstairs to work on models with Dad. He didn't follow how his mom could treat her dream encounter with Rebecca as if it were an everyday occurrence, only to be criticized for its rudeness. That suggested knowledge of a funhouse-mirror side of the world he himself never would have considered possible before meeting Rebecca. The line between reality and fantasy, once so sharp, had been wavering ever since his car broke down in Nebraska.

*And apparently Mom was in on the cosmic joke.*

A yellowing newspaper cupcake recipe on the table caught his eye. A distraction? New conversation piece? He slumped. Dessert wouldn't be the best topic to capture his mom's attention at the moment.

He could have argued people can't invade dreams. He'd be diplomatic, of course, avoiding the suggestion she would have to be crazy to think they could. But the knowing look in her eyes stopped him.

He could have told the truth—Rebecca had gone through a dream-crashing phase just after they'd met—but that wouldn't reflect well on her.

So he took one for the team. "It was my idea for her to say hello. She knows how to get into people's dreams, and we didn't think you'd remember."

Mom took her time processing that. He braced himself for an outburst, but she surprised him with a smile. "You're defending her!"

"No. I mean yeah, um—"

"Rebecca's bringing your gallantry out. I *will* say she's a lovely and assertive young woman. She has her flaws, but I'm touched she asked my approval to spend time with you."

*Rebecca.* Mom remembered her name. He jumped in with both feet. "I have a book in my backpack she wanted you to see."

Brian hurried to his bedroom, came back with the book, spread it open on the table. What to say? *My girlfriend who pops into dreams, reads weird, hieroglyphic languages, too.*

He said nothing.

His mom tried touching the ribbon nestled in the crease but pulled her hand back. "Oh!"

"What?"

"This is an enlightening rod," she said. "It takes the fragments of thought from the corners of your mind and merges them into wonderful ideas at the center. All you need to do is touch it. This one's charge feels weak, but it still has some power."

"It's a what?"

"You touch it and get smarter."

Well, yeah, he'd been suspicious of that ribbon from the beginning but, "How would *you* know?"

His mom traced a finger along the length of the ribbon and mumbled something. The fabric transformed into a glowing green rod, maybe six inches long. She touched it again, and it reshaped itself into a ribbon. "No ordinary paranormal girl would have ever been entrusted with such a prize. How did she get it? Why would she pass it on to you, Brian?"

He gripped the edge of the table with both hands. "You're asking me?" Things were moving too fast. If anything, *he* should have been the candidate for the national weirdness award, not his mom. "You just used ordinary and paranormal in the same sentence."

"They can go hand in hand, but we've traveled well beyond that with this girl, haven't we?"

His stomach lurched. How much did she know? What other info should he spill?

She flipped through the book, pausing here and there to gaze at a sketch or run her fingertips across the markings. Then she went back to the first page, pursed her lips, and looked up. "Well, I did learn this much when I met her." She glanced back down at the page.

*"When she finds her love she'll need to speak in code
or read
the verses she has penned.
For the Witches Code has muted her, we're told.
Cannot
reveal her tale to men."*

With memories of the Walt Whitman dream crashing through his head, Brian studied the page for an English paragraph or two, even a phrase, but he found nothing more than Rebecca's Ogham scrawl. "How did you read that? It's a dead language with no key."

Mom leaned back in her chair. "Ogham is a language my mother taught me before I learned a single letter of the conventional alphabet. She was taught by my grandmother, my grandmother by my great-grandmother, and so on all the way back to our family's earliest days in Ireland."

"So what are you saying?" Why ask? He knew. From the minute she did the ribbon-to-rod thing, he'd known. He couldn't process the bombshell in a thousand years, but he definitely knew.

A gust of wind hummed through cracks in the window frame, and branches of an overgrown bush scratched against the glass. His mom's long, black hair riffled as if blown by the same breeze, and her steady gaze bored into his soul. "I'm a witch, Brian, just like Rebecca."

# Chapter Twenty-One

**BRIAN AND HIS MOM** still sat at the cluttered round table in the den. A picture on the wall continued showing a sailboat race across a lake. The window on the opposite wall opened to the backyard—proven authentic by the shadowy branches of a familiar bush scratching against the glass in the darkness. Rebecca's book lay open to a sketch he'd seen before. Everything had to be real.

Except...

*Mom was a witch?* He thrust his hand into his pocket for the coin.

Cold as ice. He was awake. But he still had to take anything he now saw and everything he'd ever experienced with a grain of salt. He gaped at the former touchstone of his life, now redefined as a witch, and tried to keep his voice from coming out as a shriek. "Just like Rebecca?"

"Not so loud." His mom gestured toward the door she'd closed and locked. "Every girl in our family line has been blessed, all the way back to our earliest ancestors in Old Ireland. Rebecca's line has been blessed, too, apparently."

Brian tried to swallow, but his mouth had gone dry. "What about Kara? And Aunt April?"

"Shh." She acted impossibly calm about the matter, oblivious that he was in danger of falling to the ceiling in this newly upside-down world. "Your father knows, but your sister has been putting off telling Brad."

Dark, frizzy hair did give Mom the static-electricity-gone-wild look of a stereotypical witch. She must have forgotten to use conditioner that morning. But normally, she couldn't be singled out so easily in a lineup. For years, she'd represented herself as a PTA mom, dinner maker, homework assistant, sore throat curer, clothing buyer, and everything else a typical mom might be. She didn't poof in and out or freeze his world or conjure cheese.

*Or did she do all those things when he wasn't looking?*

And what about his sister and aunt? "I've never seen Kara or April do anything unusual."

"Their powers are weak."

"Are yours?" His voice came out screechy again.

"There's no need to be so agitated."

Her eyes were green, too. How had he missed all of these clues?

"We have little more power than the gift of illusion," Mom-turned-witch said. "We harness the magic of dreams and bring a tiny smidgen into the waking world."

"That's it, huh?"

"Pretty much. We aren't all that different than mortals."

He'd have to take that on faith. For the moment, she loomed larger than life, and escape out the window had great appeal.

"Think of me as a magician. That's closer to how a boy regards his mom, anyway, isn't it?"

"Maybe a six-year-old."

She turned the book to the opening page again, the one showing Rebecca's little poem about being muted by some code—a verse written in a language with a surprisingly large following, seeing how Ogham was supposed to be dead and all. "Witches ought to be old hat for you, Brian. You're dating a devout one, judging by the courting description I translated for you."

"The what?"

"The earliest witches in our line established a code of behavior, and one of their rules called for courtship to be a celebration of enchantment, teasing, and misdirection. That's what this passage is saying."

He struggled mightily to get past the *Mom-equals-witch* revelation and hear the words she'd spoken, but the news wasn't exactly encouraging. "So Rebecca *could* tell me everything, but she's torturing me, instead?"

His mom flipped to another page and read in silence. A moment passed before the question sifted through her dark, witchy hair and into her head. "Tell you everything about what?"

"About *anything!* She won't share a thing about herself, where she came from, why she disappears all the time, or where she goes. Nothing."

That got her face out of the book. She leaned back in her chair and grinned. "I knew the minute I laid eyes on Rebecca she'd be the one to challenge you right out of your funk."

"Oh, so this is funny, huh?"

The sparkle in her eyes sure said so. She might as well have been rubbing her hands together with glee. "Don't be angry with her. If the joke is on you, it's a good one. Rebecca's a prize. You have to understand how special she is."

"Yeah, she's a witch. So are you. I'm on top of it."

"She's a throwback to a better time. She came to me in her prairie dress and begged permission to date you."

"She did?" Despite his alarm or anger or whatever mixed-up emotions had triggered his knee to start bumping up and down, and regardless of the fact Rebecca's perceived need for permission still didn't make a whole lot of sense, the revelation she was so into him she'd *beg* to spend time together sent a tingle through his stomach.

Mom nodded. "That girl is following a code other witches have ignored for at least a century, Brian. You have no idea how much love and doting an old-fashioned witch is capable of doling out. She'll devote her life to your happiness!"

His knee stopped twitching, and his smile stretched to what had to be goofy proportions. But before he could get totally lost in the glory of what she'd said, something dawned on him. The breathtaking turns their little talk had taken were strikingly similar to the typical meandering—and unrevealing— conversations he'd been having with Rebecca herself. His head swam. They'd just gone from A to B to where exactly? "Wait. I thought you brought me in here to yell at me over the dream-invasion thing."

"Partly. But I have things to tell you."

Pay dirt! He leaned closer, but she turned toward the window and went quiet.

"Come on," he said. "You can't leave me hanging. What things?"

"How much can I say?"

He assumed the question rhetorical and waited.

"He didn't want me to reveal anything," she said.

"Who?"

"I met someone recently, a relative you've never seen…but forget him. Whatever my source, your girlfriend has a skeleton in her closet. She's an exile."

"You mean, like a prisoner?" The term struck a chord. Rebecca had implied as much when she read the poem about dream-world exiles the night she hanged herself on stage.

For a long moment, his mom stared out the window into a fog of newly falling snow. When she turned to him, her eyes had gone dreamy enough for him to wonder whether she'd had one too many glasses of the spiked eggnog. "In another dimension."

"Let's get real, Mom."

"The line between reality and fantasy is blurry at best. Surely you've learned that by now, haven't you?"

She had him there. He was the guy who carried a coin in his pocket so he could distinguish one realm from the next. Still, "If Rebecca was exiled to some fantasyland, she wouldn't be able to visit me."

"Does she stay long?"

"Define long."

His mom flashed her trademark knowing smile. "In other words, she doesn't."

Why not hit him over the head with it?

"You look thinner, Brian. If she's been conjuring food for you, keep in mind it has no substance."

"No way."

Mom returned her attention to the book. She turned to a page with drawings of a castle on one side and a jumble of Ogham lettering on the other, some scribbled upside down. "Did Rebecca say why she wanted me to see this?"

"No."

"She has issues with a sorcerer, you know. They're like male witches, only twenty times stronger. Think she might be in a bit of trouble?"

The news got better and better. "You're pulling my leg."

She sighed.

Nope. Definitely not kidding. She'd never been known as a prankster.

Brian clenched his fists. If Rebecca was in trouble, he'd find a way to get her out of it.

"Look at you! I love your chivalry." Mom flipped deeper into the book, pausing at a drawing Dante might have enjoyed, a battle among horned creatures in a flaming netherland. "The world hides more than mere witches in its shadows—angels, demons, sorcerers, not to mention monsters and dragons."

Great. But the thought *anyone or anything* might have it in for Rebecca started his heart pounding. He'd never let somebody mess with her.

His mom leaned closer and spoke in a soft, conspiratorial tone. "You can peg sorcerers at night by their luminescent eyes." Then she turned another page and mumbled something about fallen angels.

He lagged a step behind, stuck on his old recurring dream about Rebecca on a rock and the guy with glowing eyes pointing at her. "Wait. Are sorcerers the bad guys?"

"I wouldn't paint them all with that brush, but as a lot, they do tend to be shifty."

"Can they visit dreams?"

"With ease."

He slapped his hands on the table hard enough to sting his palms. His dreams hadn't been nightmares or precognitive, they were *visits* by some sorcerer. But why?

Mom got up and went to the window. She peered into the snowfall.

"What's wrong?" he asked.

"I've told you more than I should. You're supposed to figure things out on your own."

"You're killing me."

She came back to the table, settled into her chair. "Rebecca needs your help, Brian. I'll tell you that much."

"You've hardly told me anything!" His knee was getting twitchy again. "Can you translate more of her book?"

"Don't you think the code might frown on a witch's boyfriend asking his mother for help? Not that our ancestors imagined anything *that* ridiculous could ever happen. Honestly, Brian."

"Please." He stared at her, looked down at the book, glanced up again, caught her gaze, and held on for dear life.

She sighed. *And* she rolled her eyes. Favorable signs? Silence hung in the air as he debated whether hard-core pleading would help his cause. The best course might have been to hold his tongue and not even breathe. When it came to decisions by parents, the slightest shift of wind could blow the scales of justice the wrong way.

"One poem," she said.

Even then, he didn't risk a smile. But in some duplicate world, if not where Rebecca had supposedly been banished, then in a secret corner of his mind that didn't show in his face, he jumped for joy.

His mom riffled through the book and settled on the sketch of a mirror. "Looking glasses are full of magic, and they love conjuring the truth right in front of our eyes. I'll read this one."

*A mirror. He'd dreamed something about one recently.* He took a slow intake of breath and listened for all he was worth.

"*Lo the maiden fair, the man on bended knee,*
*the ring,*
*and promised wedded bliss.*
*She forsakes his plea and chooses prophecy.*
*then runs*
*and hides within the mist.*
*" 'Turn my offer down? Your heart is cold, my dear.'*
*Such scorn*
*and loathing in his look.*
*'Cloister you I will within a magic mirror,*
*your life*
*imprisoned in a nook.'*
*"With the scorned groom's words a pane of glass is formed*
*to block*
*her world from that outside.*
*As a prison wall the looking glass is born,*
*a mirror*
*as tall as it is wide."*

Mom looked up from the book. "Go ahead."

"What?"

"Touch the ribbon."

"Oh." He closed his fist around it, and a flood of ideas raced through his mind. They almost flitted away, but he managed to grab hold of a single fragment. A small one, but oh so important, and obvious. "Rebecca has a big mirror in her cabin. I bet it's a portal into dreams."

"You think?"

"Read another!"

"Whatever for?"

She was right. He'd heard plenty. He pushed out of his chair and stood.

"Where are you going?" she asked.

"If I tell you, you'll say I'm sixteen." She'd hardly spoken to him for days after his unapproved road trip back in August.

"Sixteen is nothing more than a number. Maybe I'll give you a hall pass this time."

"What?" This suggestion was almost as earth-shaking as her witch revelation. He grabbed the back of a chair to keep his balance. "You'll let me drive alone to—"

"Nebraska. That's where her cabin is, isn't it?"

"How do you know?"

"I just do, and I have a magical device to keep us in close contact all the way." She reached into a pocket of her dress.

More fantastic than an enlightening rod? He gripped the chair tighter.

She pulled something out and opened her hand to show it, a shiny silver miracle worker also known as a smartphone.

"Very funny."

"This is no joke. If you don't pull over and check in with me at every single rest area from here to Sidney, we'll be trading that Kia of yours for a bicycle when you get back."

"Got it." And what a rush! When he unlatched the door and cracked it open, his hand was shaking. But the everyday world lurked on the other side. The voices and laughter of Kara, Brad, and his dad wafted in from a distance. Maybe they were in the basement working on the Taj Mahal. Or they might have been in the living room watching movies. Kara had been talking up a *Harry Potter* marathon for the weekend.

All of a sudden, the mission to rescue Rebecca from a supposed exile fell into a little gift box on the floor, wrapped with the promise of certain homesickness. End of rush. "Look, Mom, obviously you know more than you're letting on. Why not just tell me everything? Even if Rebecca's following some code, you aren't bound by it."

She got up. Went to the window again. Didn't answer.

"What's out there?"

"Nothing." She brushed past him and stalked out of the room.

"Wait a second. I'm just—" His voice echoed back as if from a cavern. He hurried after her into an empty hallway.

"Find her, Brian." Her voice came from all around but left nothing in its wake. No Mom. No Dad. No Kara. No Brad. He rushed to the basement stairway. The lights were off down there.

The living room was just as empty. Silence pressed down on him. The air had gone stale.

The TV flicked on to a screen full of static. The walls wobbled in Jell-O-like ripples. The furniture glowed.

# Chapter Twenty-Two

**BRIAN CLOSED HIS EYES.** Reopened them. Same weird scene. Rippling walls. Glowing furniture.

He backed to the couch and came down on it, but the cushions didn't have the right amount of give. He glanced down…and found himself on an old, threadbare couch.

A wave of dizziness swept over him. He shut his eyes again. Opened them. "No way." Either he'd crazily transported into Rebecca's cabin or hallucinated the overstuffed chair over there and the collection of romance novels tumbling across the top row of her bookshelf. After only one stolen sip of the spiked eggnog?

"Brian." Her voice rang like church bells.

"Rebecca!" He turned to the antique mirror. There she was, in reflection.

A flash of light blinded him.

He refocused.

Shouldn't have.

End of fantasy. His parents' living room returned to its normal, stale, totally uninteresting state.

"Follow your destiny, boy!"

Brian jumped at the man's voice, shot a glance around the room, but didn't see a soul.

He collapsed onto the couch and tried to catch his breath.

Follow his destiny. Yeah. Those jukebox coins of Rebecca's were limited. She'd told him so. She couldn't keep coming after him. He needed to drive to Nebraska pronto and track her down. If the car failed him again, he'd hitch.

He'd make things happen *and find her*. Otherwise, suppose she ran out of chances to visit him and fell out of his life? He'd just become a regular guy then. Maybe he'd find an ordinary girlfriend, finish school, and eventually pursue a boring career. What a thrill.

Ordinary couldn't be the right destiny for the descendant of a long line of witches.

Ordinary didn't play well for someone attracting the interest of a glowing-eyed sorcerer.

What a ridiculously bad choice ordinary would be for someone who had a shot at Rebecca!

But he was thinking in selfish terms. This wasn't about him. This was about rescuing Rebecca from whatever. *From Abigail?* Could be. So he'd need to track down Little Miss Scraggily Hair, too, and find out what was going on between them.

Brian hurried to his room, stuffed his scattered things into his bag, came back down, grabbed the book from the den, and headed out of the house.

He bent against the fury of a snow squall and hurried into his car. Started it up. The wipers created two half-moons of visibility. Melting snow dripped down his forehead and into his eyes. He dried them with his jacket sleeve and started down the driveway.

Halfway to the street, the lamps and porch lights up and down the block blinked off. Even his headlights went out. He hit the brakes and groped for the light switch in pitch-blackness.

The brights kicked on before he got his hand on the switch, highlighting a hooded man and a dog in their glare. The guy's black coat and thick, dark head of hair steamed as if the driving snow thawed against him on impact. The Great Dane beside him glared through the windshield with reddish eyes, drops of melting snow oozing down its lean, muscular body.

The man hurried around and tapped on the glass of the driver's window.

Every horror movie Brian had ever seen screamed for him to drive away.

"Please," the man mouthed. The grooves in his forehead, tiny wrinkles by his eyes, and encouraging smile painted him as somebody's dad. Not a serial killer.

Brian cracked the window just enough to hear what the stranger wanted.

"I'm looking for someone. Perhaps you can provide directions."

*The man's eyes started glowing.*

Brian pushed the button to run the window back up.

It didn't budge.

The man leaned forward. "Solve this, wandering man, my riddle if you can. Tell me when a cat becomes just like a man."

"Wh— What?"

A gust of wind swirled the snow into a whiteout. Then the air cleared, revealing an empty driveway. No sign of man or dog.

The window got unstuck and ran back up. The neighborhood lights blinked back on.

Brian tried to remember how to breathe.

Who *was* that guy? A male witch? Another imp?

Nope. Glowing eyes equaled sorcerer. *They do tend to be shifty,* his mom had said. And they liked riddles, apparently.

He glanced in the rearview mirror and saw his mom standing at the den window. She held something up for him to see. Her cell phone. Ha ha. She waved and closed the blinds.

*Wandering man.* Rebecca's book resting on the seat was crammed with secrets disguised as fairy tales and written in a language supposedly only a witch could read. Yet that guy used a term from her poem about the vagrant. How could he know it?

Brian looked down at the ribbon poking out of the book. An enlightening rod, huh? He touched it and tried to gather his thoughts.

Brian had to be the vagrant in Rebecca's original poem, the wandering man, a hero singled out to rescue her. From what, a curse? Some spell had exiled her into a shadowy world reachable only in dreams. Yet sometimes she came out and visited him. If she'd committed a crime, what kind of weird sentence was she serving? She couldn't tell him other than through vague hints hidden in her verses. One of them implied a link to the Salem witch trials, and another suggested the importance of mirrors. Those clues, a vague prophecy, and this latest riddle were all he had to go on.

When *does* a cat become like a man? Brian had never been good at riddles. Both walk, but a man uses two legs and a cat uses four. Both eat, but one sticks its head in a bowl and the other uses a fork. Both sleep. Both grow old and die. So does any other living thing.

Something Rebecca said about Simon in their very first conversation teased the back of his mind, but he couldn't get hold of it, even with the ribbon in his hand.

He put the car in gear and drove away from the house. Within a mile, the snow on the ground thinned and the street dried. In the past, he would have guessed a localized lake-effect storm whitened his parents' neighborhood, and the brief blackout had been caused by its gusty winds knocking a power line down. That was before his world had changed into an unpredictable land where the real, the imagined, and the illusory could no longer be distinguished, except with a coin.

He checked in with Saint Brigit.

Still cold in his pocket.

He drove to the interstate and headed west.

# CHAPTER TWENTY-THREE

**WITHIN A SECRET MEADOW** surrounded by thick woods, Rebecca knelt before a weathered statue. She set a purple stone among the other gems adorning the ancient shrine and prayed for strength.

Aislinn, the witch honored by this shrine, carved a prophecy into rocks and scattered them across Ireland during the age of the Celts. Her Ogham scrawl foretold a girl named Rebecca and a boy named Brian who would save the world from darkness on the five thousandth anniversary of a much earlier witch's birth—Renin, the greatest of them all. Maddeningly, the date of birth hadn't been established with any degree of accuracy. But most guesses held the critical anniversary to be right about now, early in the twenty-first century.

Rebecca had been chasing this prophecy ever since a boy appeared in her cabin window back in the colonies with a promise and a modern-day nickel, proving he'd come from the future. A boy whose very presence convinced her that although ten thousand Brians and Rebeccas had probably lived and died in the many centuries after Aislinn's foretelling, she and *her Brian* were the chosen ones. On the day of this realization, her heart had lifted to the heavens.

Lately, though, a ton of worry pressed its heavy weight on her chest. The void was expanding. It had already swallowed wide swaths of dreamscape. How would she and Brian stop it? Yes, he might solve her riddles, learn everything there was to know about her, accept the worst she'd done, and still take her hand at the end of that journey. But what then?

"I can erase him, you know. Then where would your prophecy be?"

Rebecca spun around at Abigail's unexpected voice. She turned in time to see the imp swing a squirrel by the tail and fling it into a swirling column of blackness.

The squirrel screeched and disappeared into a portion of the void Abigail had somehow brought here to the waking world. *An illusion?* How could it be? An imp had as much ability to cast illusions as a fly had to recite poetry.

The column twisted like a tornado. It lifted from the ground and rose high above them, roaring in anger and spilling waves of cold air in its wake.

Rebecca wrapped her arms around herself. Something was so very, very wrong.

The cyclone vanished.

Abigail gazed up at where it used to be. "I can erase him just like that," she said.

Rebecca almost rushed her, but she thought better of it. Unexplained void illusions notwithstanding, imps weren't known to be terribly bright. An imp could be handled without a ridiculous spat of hair-pulling, slapping, and whatever else they might do to each other. She followed Abigail's gaze to the point in the sky where the twister had disappeared, and she feigned a gasp of terror. "Storms frighten me. Now you know my weakness."

"*Storms* frighten you?" Abigail dropped her arms and frowned at her. "Doesn't losing Brian scare you more?"

"No." Rebecca fixed Abigail with the most sincere look she could summon. "There's really no accounting for one's fears, is there?" She smiled the smile of a confidante, a comrade, a fellow victim of the universe's random treachery.

Abigail relaxed her shoulders and hinted at a smile. "With me, it's spiders."

"Spiders, you say?"

"Indeed."

"Oh my." Rebecca closed her eyes. She imagined arachnids in all colors and shapes. Black, oily ones. Thick, hairy, brown ones. Outdoor spiders with long, spindly legs. Tarantulas. Widows. She pictured spider eggs—disgusting white pods holding thousands of hatchlings.

Rebecca summoned ten million spiders out of the forest in a steady, purposeful march. So many the leaves crunched beneath their feet. So many they covered the ground in a thick, gray, roiling fog of spindly legs.

Abigail had her back to them. "You're lying, Rebecca. You fear losing Brian more than anything. This precious prophecy of yours hinges on—"

A tarantula dropped onto her shoulder.

She shrieked, brushed it off, and turned to the advancing horde of creepy, crawly, eight-legged nightmares. "Stop them!"

Rebecca spoke in her lowest, most menacing tone. "Abigail, if you ever so much as utter Brian's name again, let alone *threaten* him, I'll send spiders crawling up your skirts for the rest of your useless life."

Abigail shuddered. She sniffled. But then she did something Rebecca wouldn't have expected in a thousand years. She grinned. "Useless? *I* am serving someone important, Rebecca, while you chase a long-forgotten witch's misguided fantasy."

She stomped a foot down on the first of the advancing spiders and disappeared.

Rebecca stared after her. Her heart ticked the time away in fast beats, then slowed. Eventually, she stopped trembling.

Fear wouldn't win this game. Answers would. So she took one step, followed by another, out of the waking realm and into the World of Mortal Dreams. She plodded along until the grass scattered into weedy clumps. In time, greenery disappeared altogether in favor of shifting sands hot enough to warm her feet through the soles of her shoes. Calming heat. Purposeful heat.

She continued her trek, navigating around some dunes and over a few others when jagged rocks blocked her path. She forded a shallow river of flowing cinders and later used a scarf to protect her face from a windblown blizzard of glittering sand crystals.

Rebecca journeyed on foot all the way to Henry Stoddard's tower. She found him puttering in a flower garden at its base.

Stoddard's unusual height reminded her how short she was. The sorcerer always held the upper hand. Even his costume choice seemed designed to throw her off. He wore a bright orange cape, which, in combination with his curly black hair, brought to mind a pumpkin with a hardy stalk. She tried sarcasm to balance the scales. "I would have expected thorny weeds out here, not flowers, Henry."

"You prefer weeds? Well, here's a little beauty with a thorn." Always the showman, the sorcerer pulled a purple rose from his sleeve.

She closed her hand around the stem.

"Has nature ever created a more enchanting enigma, Rebecca? Behold the exquisite architecture of the petals. Take in the fragrance matched by no other flower. Then press your thumb against the angry thorn until it pierces your skin."

She did all those things, but the painful pinch proved no more effective in getting her mind off her troubles than the journey had. She moved her thumb to her lips.

"I have a name for your rose," he said.

She had trouble finding her voice. "What is it?"

"Rebecca."

"Don't play mind games with me, Henry. I've come to ask something important."

"Ask away, then." Stoddard sat on a bench and folded his arms.

Rebecca came down beside him. "Abigail was your ward once, yes?"

He nodded. "*And* her cousin Betty. A pair of more mischievous brats probably never existed. I brought them with me to Salem. But you know this all too well."

Rebecca wasn't sure how to pose the next question without sounding accusatory. She didn't want an angry sorcerer on her hands. But she had to ask. "What is Abigail to you now, Henry?"

Stoddard's scowl said it all. He stalked off the bench, muttering to himself.

She came up behind him and risked touching his arm ever so lightly.

He shrugged her off. "How dare you suggest I would have anything to do with this mess, Rebecca? I've extended the hand of friendship to you again and again, and instead of thanking me, you suggest I'm a villain."

"I'm sorry," she whispered.

"She's feeding the void, Rebecca."

Her heart leapt at the unexpected validation. "You know it exists then, don't you?"

The white background noise of singing birds and chirping insects died. A cloud blotted the sun. Henry Stoddard turned to her. His face held shadows deeper than the darkest corners. "For too many years, Abigail fooled me into thinking of her as a mere imp, Rebecca. An imp with a crush on me and fierce jealousy toward you. The ruse worked."

"If not an imp, what is she, Henry?"

Stoddard's booming guffaw scattered a flock of birds out of the nearest trees. Their screeches ushered sound back into the world, and the cloud moved past the sun. "If I were a gambling man, I'd bet she's a fallen angel's apprentice. You don't happen to know any fallen angels, do you?"

"What's so funny? Of course I don't—"

Henry disappeared in a cloud of purple smoke. Always the upper hand.

# CHAPTER TWENTY-FOUR

**TRAFFIC THINNED TO A** trickle. For long stretches of lonely highway, the porch lights of scattered farmhouses pierced the darkness, serving as random reminders of the glowing-eyed man Brian had seen in his parents' driveway. He tried to ignore them and focus on the center line. But he had to know.

He pulled into a rest area near some town called Wyanet and phoned his mom. "I'm assuming that guy outside the house was a sorcerer, right?"

"Who?"

"The man with the dog. You waved to me from the window after he left, remember?"

"Stay the course, Brian."

"Come on, Mom, I need more than that."

The line went dead. Out of service range. And *that* was almost as skin crawling as random encounters with sorcerers. His car had always been the absolute epitome of unreliability. Now, the distances between farmhouses in this wilderness of fallow fields looked to be a mile or more in the freezing cold. At such a late hour, most residents probably wouldn't answer his knock if he broke down and needed help.

He touched the window—frigid—and turned the heater up.

By the next way station, his phone had a couple bars. He called again.

"Where are you, Brian?"

"I don't know, Minooka?"

"Okay."

"The guy in the driveway had glowing eyes, Mom."

"He's a bit of a puzzle, that one."

She knew him? No way. "Could you, um…elaborate?"

The long pause on the other end gave him the answer he'd been getting used to. Nothing. But then, "He wouldn't hurt a fly, Brian. Just so you know."

"Okay, but who is he?"

"Let's respect Rebecca's desire for you to learn things on your own."

Right. And he was deadheading to Nebraska to do just that. Not without a shadow of regret, though. "What did Dad and Kara say about me taking off without saying good-bye?"

"I told them enough so they'd get the picture."

Probably way more than she'd tell *him*. This hide-everything-from-Brian game had gotten old.

"Your aunt is expecting you Sunday night, Brian. Don't forget you have classes on Monday."

About an hour farther west, the darkened countryside turned creepy. Giant wind turbines formed a *War of the Worlds* nightscape of hulking, mechanical monsters, hinting at their vast numbers each time their strobe lights blinked in unison. His imagination got legs, conjuring images of giant, red-eyed demons skulking in the darkness, ready to crush anyone who trespassed on their turf. He kept his eyes on the road and his grip tight on the wheel.

He drove across another sprawling wind farm sixty miles down the road. After the last tower in that group blinked good-bye in the gloom, only a few houses with lights on and an occasional barreling truck lingered to kept him company. He made two more calls home. His mom offered advice. *Stop somewhere and rest.* And encouragement. *We're here for you no matter what.* She wasn't half bad. Just twisted.

An Omaha station's top-forty countdown ushered Brian into Nebraska, and the orange glow of a rising sun reflected in his mirror a little past Lincoln. He'd defeated the night.

Music and a straight-as-an-arrow highway helped put him in a zone through the last long leg of frozen prairie. He daydreamed through York, Grand Island, Kearney—thinking random thoughts at first, then trying to process the bombshells his mom had dropped, later a chill remembering the man and dog in the driveway, before settling on Rebecca.

Witches had to be rare. They hadn't topped the charts since the Puritan days. The chances one witch would randomly cross paths with the son of another seemed slim at best, so maybe somebody set the whole thing up. After all, a glowing-eyed man had been pointing to Rebecca on the rock in his recurring nightmare, and his mom apparently had the same guy on her buddy list.

He pictured three circles connected by arrows—*Rebecca, Mom, sorcerer*. Somebody knew way more than they were willing to share.

So what else was new?

Brian pulled off the highway at the Sidney exit. The old gas station where he'd stopped seemingly a thousand years earlier was dark. He pressed on, blowing past a motel a little farther up the road without a second glance, even though he hadn't slept in over twenty-four hours. He wanted to find Rebecca in the waking world, not in a dream.

Seventy miles farther north, he reached the field of scrubby hills. While he didn't have a precise way to determine where his car had stalled, the distance from Angora was about right. He watched for a bluff rising above the knobby landscape and hopefully a glimpse of an oak tree. But the undulating wilderness smoothed into cultivated land near the town of Alliance without a sign of either. He'd gone too far north.

He whipped the car around and headed south. Brian hadn't paid much attention to his surroundings in August, other than noticing a big hill. Now, the voice of doubt rang in his head. He didn't know where the cabin was, and he couldn't be sure Rebecca would be inside, even if he found the place.

He slowed the car, careful not to miss anything, and he slammed on the brakes at the sight of a treetop poking up from behind the nearest rise. He got out and craned his neck only to see a scraggly birch where a thick oak needed to be.

At Angora, he made a U-turn and headed north again.

Brian drove back and forth several times, all the while refusing to let his worries take hold. He *would* find Rebecca.

Wouldn't he?

Somewhere between Alliance and capitulation, a plume of chimney smoke curled into the sky. He came to a gravel-spitting stop on the shoulder and hurried out of the car to gaze across the frosty landscape. The top of an oak tree did peek up from within the hills, and a higher bluff rose farther in the distance.

"Yes!" But when he considered the angles, the shadow of doubt grew longer.

He remembered the cabin being north of the bluff, yet the smoke now billowed from the south. Still, nothing else up and down the road had shown any promise at all. The old Witch-of-the-Hills journals Sharon dug up did mention shifting landmarks near the cabin. Yeah, he was grasping at straws, but what choice did he have?

Crisp air turned his breath to puffs of fog. He tightened his jacket and weighed the risks. Back in August, he'd almost gotten hopelessly lost looking outside for Rebecca—a bad idea now in cold weather. And this time around, an overcast sky eliminated the possible use of the sun as a compass. Frozen ground, bare of snow, didn't hold much promise for footprints, either. So how would he find his way back to the car if he didn't find her?

The oak tree was tall enough to serve as a marker. It would rise above the bumpy low hills for miles, most likely, if he needed it to find his way back. He grabbed his rucksack and Rebecca's book from the car. If he did get lost, an enlightening rod might come in handy.

He locked up and hiked to the tree.

Winter-bare limbs displayed little more than a couple bird nests and some decaying, leftover leaves. The absence of a rope sent the same tingle through his stomach its appearance had triggered three months earlier. Did Abigail take it away? She had amazing stalking abilities.

He stopped and glanced around. No sign of anyone. *I'm getting ridiculous now.* He moved on.

A new problem popped up a half mile later. The oak disappeared behind a hill far sooner than should have been possible, as if it sank into the ground. To walk any farther would be to risk getting lost. He pulled the ribbon out of Rebecca's book for whatever enlightenment the crazy thing might come up with.

*Leave a trail of breadcrumbs!* Thanks, Hansel. Like the birds wouldn't eat it. And who carries bread around, anyway?

But when he shoved the ribbon into his pocket, he found a handful of change. *Breadcrumbs.* Okay, got it.

He dropped a coin every fifty paces. That worked for a while, but eighty-seven cents later, he went broke. The smoke was close by then. He had to take a chance.

Brian continued beyond the point where he could glance over his shoulder and still see the last coin. A straight-line journey would have been the best idea from there—the most easily backtracked—but a hill got in the way after a few hundred yards. He took a key from his pocket, dropped it to the ground, and started rounding the hill. If he didn't see the cabin from the other side, he could come up with some other plan when he traveled full circle and returned to his starting point.

But halfway around…

The tiny log cottage poured smoke from its chimney with a vengeance.

"Woohoo!" He ran to the door—unlocked—and broke inside. "Rebecca?"

Although his cry went unanswered, he found plenty to cheer about. Rebecca had left a pair of woolen mittens on an end table, a bowl of water on the floor for her cat, and an assortment of romance novels tumbling from one end of her bookshelf to the other. The crackle of fire from the next room clinched the deal.

He headed into the kitchen and found Simon curled up by a roaring fire in the hearth. Better yet, Rebecca had set the table, leaving slices of cheese and homemade bread on a plate and a handwritten note beside a pitcher of cider. *My cabin will always welcome you, Brian.*

He collapsed onto a chair, stretched his legs out, threw his head back.

He'd found her.

Right?

He went into the living room, to the antique mirror resting on its stand in the middle of the floor. This was a portal. Had to be.

He tapped the glass, walked around it, moved the mirror up and down on its swivel, and fogged it with his breath.

Nothing happened.

"Rebecca?"

Dead silence.

He backed to the couch, sat, and stared into the mirror for all he was worth.

"Brian."

He shot up and blinked the sleep from his eyes. How long had he been out?

Wow. Night had fallen.

He groped around until he found matches on an end table. He lit one. And an oil lamp.

"Brian."

A blurry image formed inside the mirror.

"Rebecca?" He reached for her outstretched hand.

The glass dissolved into tiny beads tinkling like crystal wind chimes as they spilled across his shoes. The wooden frame transformed from polished antique to a splintered oval with cobwebs hanging where the mirror had been.

His shirt puffed out. And his slacks. Just a tug at first.

He jumped back.

*But if she waited on the other side, if this portal would lead him to her, not in a dream but for real...*

He leaned into it.

A sudden, powerful force sucked him through the empty frame.

# CHAPTER TWENTY-FIVE

**BRIAN TUMBLED FORWARD INTO** the mirror but spilled out backwards, skidding on his butt until he came to a head-banging stop against a windowsill. The room swam, then brightened impossibly, considering he'd lit only a single oil lamp earlier. A warm breeze carrying the dewy scent of spring through the window didn't fit, either.

He reached into his pocket and found a warm Saint Brigit coin in there.

Warm equaled dreaming.

*Damn.* If he learned anything in a dream, he'd probably forget the answers when he woke up. The mirror had to be a portal leading to some big answers, such as why Rebecca kept flitting away. Or whether his mom was right about her being exiled to another dimension. And if so, how was he supposed to rescue her?

Maybe his hand was too cold, and it made the coin *seem* warm. Grasping at straws for sure, but he pulled the thing out of his pocket to see whether he'd gotten a false reading.

Silver. *Yes!* She'd told him about the colors, too. Silver meant he was awake.

But the coin hadn't cooled one bit.

*Am I dreaming that I'm awake?*

He got up and turned to the window, shading his eyes against the glare of a scene that was so not Nebraska. Or November, for that matter. The previously barren, frosty hills had thickened with lush forest.

A pair of monarch butterflies darted into the cabin through the open window. They danced up to him, turned, and fluttered back out. Brian's heart raced after them. Coin or no coin, everything was too real for him to be dreaming. *It worked!* He'd fallen through a portal into an entirely different place.

Still a cabin, but not the same. Packed dirt instead of a finished floor. Smoke-stained hardwood planks where cedar walls used to be. A rustic bench and several high-backed wooden chairs filling the space where Rebecca's bookshelf and country furniture had been.

*Not just the furniture.*

The mirror had disappeared. He caught his breath. Getting answers was the plan for sure, but finding a way back home afterward was supposed to be a big part of it. *This* was like walking into a vault full of riches only to have the door close and lock behind him.

He bunched his fists. The coin heated in his closed hand even more.

Dreaming?

*No!* He needed answers he'd remember. He could worry about the missing mirror later. He dropped the coin.

Saint Brigit hit the dirt and bounced back up like a yoyo without a string.

He grabbed it again. *Cold.*

The coin went crazy, flashing colors and changing temperature, before settling on totally useless information— warm silver.

*I'm awake. Period.*

He could only hope so.

Voices rose from the kitchen.

He hurried over to the doorway. Stopped at the sight of an Amish scene. No, not Amish. *Colonial.*

A girl slicing beets at a table *might* have been Rebecca, but not quite. She was a little shorter and less filled out, like a younger sister, maybe. She and the woman standing beside her looked like they'd raided the early American racks of a costume store. They wore long black dresses puffed below the waist as if filled with air by a bicycle pump—hoop designs like the one Kara once bought for a Halloween party—and tight, renaissance-faire bodices. White aprons and matching bonnets covering their pinned-back red hair completed the outfits.

*Where the hell had he fallen?* He tried to speak. "Wha?"

The girl moved a finger to her lips. "Shh."

The woman had bent to a sack of potatoes on the floor. She glanced up. "What, Rebecca?"

"Nothing, Mum."

Brian took another stab at coherent speech. "Rebecca?"

She pressed her lips together, furrowed her forehead, motioned to the woman now rising, shook her head.

"I don't get it," he said. "Why—"

The power of a thousand vacuum cleaners sucked him backward through the cabin. The front door opened just in time to prevent him from bashing against it. He landed outside on his back, hard enough to see stars.

A V-shaped formation of geese honked their way across the sky above. He watched them till they disappeared behind a line of trees, and then caught the drift of a cloud moving in the opposite direction. This place seemed like earth, more or less, at least in some respects. Brian scrambled up and did a slow three-sixty.

The woods he'd noticed through the window surrounded a crescent-shaped cluster of log cabins. Farm animals came into view—random chickens clucking and flapping their wings, a pig tethered to a stake.

In the center of the little settlement, women dressed in more balloon-skirt-white-bonnet outfits took turns filling wooden buckets with water from a well. The combined aroma of chimney smoke, pine trees, and animals came at him like no dream ever could.

A man pulled a cart along a dirt pathway leading into the woods. He wore white stockings rising to meet dark pants that ended just below the knees, a white shirt, and a tall black hat. Other men in similar getup stacked wood, wielded axes, burned brush, or loitered on the steps of various cabins. One whittled. Another smoked a pipe. They all looked like they'd stepped out of a first Thanksgiving museum diorama.

Although Brian had made plenty of noise bursting out of the cabin—his scream still rang in his ears—no one noticed him. *Must be a dream after all, then.* Yet his palms stung from striking the ground, and who ever experienced pain in a dream?

He eased away from the land of Ichabod Crane until his back was up against the cabin door.

He grabbed the handle.

It wouldn't budge.

He turned and knocked.

Nobody answered.

Now what? He'd come to the mirror seeking answers, but he must have hit the wrong channel on the remote. Definitely a right-church-wrong-pew kind of moment. Time to try control-alt-delete for a quick reboot.

Enough clichés already. The mirror—*the portal!*—had to be inside that cabin somewhere.

He pounded on the door.

Still no response.

Brian rushed around to the window off to the side, almost tripping over something along the way. A panicky rabbit scrambled back and forth inside a small wooden cage. *Yeah, buddy, I know the feeling.*

He peered through the open window.

The youngish version of Rebecca sat on the bench in the living area of the little cabin. Her hooped dress puffed upward, but she managed to balance a sheaf of papers in her lap. A black cat slept at her feet. Colonial Simon? *Get real.*

"Pssst."

Rebecca ignored him. She reached without looking and groped her hand across a low table beside her. In doing so, she nearly spilled a small bottle of black liquid. Then she turned to the table and frowned. "Mother, what use is ink without a quill? Did you take it?"

The woman came into the room, wiping her hands on her apron. "Work aplenty I have for thee, Rebecca. Chores are more important than the nonsense in thy journal."

Brian couldn't imagine what weird, alternate universe he'd beamed into. The colonial costumes and Shakespearian language suggested a three-century trip backward, not the mere two or three years accounting for Rebecca's younger age.

Rebecca waved her mother off. "Leave me read what I set down when a quill *was* at hand. My *nonsense* is a discourse about the ancient foretellings."

"Mind thy tongue, child." The woman stalked back into the kitchen.

Alone again, Rebecca pushed her papers aside and rushed to the window like a little kid on an Easter-egg hunt.

Brian instinctively responded to her wide smile with one of his own despite the queasy feeling in his stomach.

"Be you demon or angel come to visit me in secret this day?" she asked.

"Huh?"

"Twice you appeared, and Mum made no note of you."

The people outside didn't, either. Popping through a portal had been like stepping into a 3-D holograph. No interaction, except for now. And she'd noticed him earlier, too. "I don't get it. You're Rebecca, right?"

She nodded. "And you are…?"

"You don't know?"

"Why would I?"

"I'm Brian."

Rebecca gasped, stared at him wide-eyed, then finally cracked a smile. "Oh! 'Tis a joke!"

"Rebecca!" the woman's shout rang out from the kitchen.

Rebecca grimaced at the sound. "Please don't leave, Brian. We must speak."

"Where would I go?"

The woman stormed out of the kitchen and looked through him as if he wasn't there. "I heard thy laughter, Rebecca. Pray close the window, lest thy pleasure fall upon unwelcome ears. Frivolity is not at home amongst these people."

Rather than shift her gaze to her mom, Rebecca kept her focus on him. "We should find a new district, then. Or perchance a suitor from another land will sweep me away instead of the dreadful man you invited for supper, Mum."

Brian kept a vise-like grip on the windowsill to avoid floating away. He'd become the actor who'd forgotten his lines, the butt of a joke gone over his head, a castaway on puzzle island.

"*Henry* shall sweep thee to a new district, Rebecca—out of Salem and into Albany."

*Salem?*

Duh. The poem she recited on stage. The research he'd done about the witch trials.

That crazy mirror hadn't transported him to some random place. It sent him to colonial times. Something important had happened here, something affecting Rebecca, and he was supposed to find out what it was.

He could have a panic attack over the lack of any return portal later.

Right?

His heart pounded anyway.

Rebecca's mom draped an arm over her shoulder and led her away. They settled onto the bench together. "Thy sharp tongue begs taming by an elder, Rebecca."

"*You* are an elder. I need no one else," she replied.

"A young witch could do far worse than marry a rich merchant from the fine town of Albany."

"Henry is older than you, Mum."

"Am I a hag now?"

Brian could only half listen. His thoughts raced in a circle from where he was to *when he was* to how old the modern-day Rebecca might actually be. Did she have some supernatural ability to age only a year or two every couple centuries?

Rebecca turned her back to her mother. "I will not marry money! A filched station brings no joy."

"Perchance not," her mother said, "but it does bring security. The man offers what he shall, and the maiden gives what she must—a bedmate and a child. Such bargains have brought men and lasses together since long before the days of Old Ireland."

"Speak not of bargains, Mum. You care only for the advance of our line."

The woman clucked her tongue. "Thou art fourteen and unwed, Rebecca. Shall I feed and shelter thee beyond the age when sensible maidens have taken a husband?"

Brian cringed. His mom had been sixteen when she married his dad, lying about her age or producing phony ID or whatever. The only consistent part of his parents' story was the punch line. *What happens in Vegas stays in Vegas.*

Fine. But expecting someone to marry at fourteen brought to mind the old joke, *this is a nice place to visit, but...*

The woman stormed into the kitchen. "An extra pair of hands would be a kindness."

"In a moment, Mum."

Rebecca hurried in the opposite direction, back to the window. Excitement gleamed in her eyes. "Where do you live?"

"When I'm not stuck on the wrong side of missing mirrors?"

Her bright expression dimmed to forehead-wrinkling confusion. Had mirrors been invented yet? Hopefully, a seventeenth-century girl would have heard of them. If not, he'd be diving into reflecting ponds in search of an escape hatch. He tried to keep his mind off *that* little wrinkle by sticking with the conversation at hand. "I grew up in Chicago, but I live in Wisconsin at the moment."

"Wis Con Sin?"

"You say it faster. It's west of here."

"And w*hen* do you live?"

Ah ha! So this younger Rebecca was already onto the time-travel angle. That would make the conversation a whole lot easier. "I live in the future, actually."

Rebecca grabbed one of his hands. "The twenty-first-century future?"

He reached into his pocket, found a nickel, and handed it over, showing her the date. "How did you guess?"

Rebecca stared at the nickel, glanced at him, then back at the coin. She beamed as though he'd handed her a million dollars. "'Tis prophecy," she murmured. "You are the Brian from the land of tomorrow."

"No. I mean, yeah, but we're sleeping. I've stepped into your dream, like with Agatha Christie that time in the tree or—"

"I am *not* dreaming, Brian."

Of course she was. A person in the present interacted with a person in the past by stepping into their lingering *dreams*. Rebecca had demonstrated this concept more than once. If she wasn't asleep now, she wouldn't have created a dream for him to step into.

Except...witches knew when they were asleep. She'd told him that. Meaning he'd fallen through the mirror *into the actual, waking past?* He took her hand and found a possible *yes* in the warm flesh and bones gripping back.

Brian backed from the window and looked up. Unassuming blue sky. Puffy white clouds. *From three hundred years ago?*

"Brian." Rebecca gazed at him with the rapt expression of someone watching the Red Sea part. "The foretelling is carved into stones all over Ireland. Brian and Rebecca shall face the darkness together!"

"Let me get this straight. You believe in a prophecy because I showed up from the future today?"

She moved her head slowly—up and down—snatching simple logic's false bottom away to reveal a spiraling hole beneath.

Brian needed to sit down before he fainted. "No, Rebecca. I wouldn't have fallen into this place if you hadn't met me in my world first."

"I've never journeyed to Wisc… Wisc—"

"Wisconsin." Not yet, anyway. But she would eventually. *Or did.* What came first, the chicken or the egg?

"How do we get from here to there, Brian?" Rebecca bored soft, gray-green eyes into his soul. "You must know a way. Else how could you come from there to here?"

The question lurched his stomach like one too many hot dogs. This version of Rebecca wasn't the girl with all the answers. She didn't have any more clues than he did for racing forward to the era of supersized French fries.

Slow seconds ticked by while he and Rebecca stared at each other. Colonial Salem, his new home, rang in his ears from behind—the voices of women in the square, the cluck of chickens, the bleat of a pig. He forgot how to swallow.

But logic hadn't totally spiraled into a black hole, had it? Rebecca *would* find a way to leap into the future. After all, they'd met in the twenty-first century. Her tomorrow was his today. Or something like that. And if she could figure out how to do it, so would he. He relaxed his tightened fists.

She tried to give the nickel back to him.

"No," he said. "Keep that as a reminder I'll always be there for you, even when you're…waiting maybe, for a really long time."

Because, seriously, that might have happened, right? Somehow, Rebecca came from this place and time to his, and not necessarily on the fast track.

"But I'm nothing. Who would wait for someone small?" Nevertheless, she kept the coin, slipping it into the pocket of her dress.

"Don't be silly, Rebecca. You're everything to me."

She smiled a mile wide but then looked down with a shyness he'd never seen in her modern-day rendition.

"Rebecca!" Her mother's sharp voice rose from the kitchen.

"Yes, Mum!" She grabbed his hand again. "A horrid man comes for supper this day. Please stay for me."

"Um. You mean, like, out here by the window?"

She hurried into the kitchen.

"Hey, wait, Rebecca! If we work together, maybe we can wrap our minds around this whole thing and—"

The sucking force of ten thousand vacuum cleaners grabbed him again and yanked him away.

# CHAPTER TWENTY-SIX

**BRIAN CARTWHEELED THROUGH THE** air, catching glimpses of a seventeenth-century settlement with each tumble.

Cabins.

Sky.

Women in dark dresses and white bonnets.

Sky.

Chickens.

A fir tree came at him. He gasped, scrunched his chin, pulled his arms and legs in, and missed splatting into the trunk by inches. A thick limb got him in the stomach. "Ooomph." He flailed at the branches. Grabbed hold. Lost his grip. Broke through layer after layer. Pine needles scratched. A scream caught in his throat.

The forest floor knocked the air out of his lungs—ten times worse than a belly flop from a high-dive board.

Brian rolled onto his back.

A swarm of bright specks flickered above, then blinked out, one by one.

He sucked in a deep breath of air, stood, and leaned against the trunk of the tree he'd ridden down. Pretty firm for a dream. But guys who *weren't* dreaming didn't typically get flung airborne or survive falls from the treetops.

He reached into his pocket. Not the one holding the coin. Silver, gold, warm, cold—Saint Brigit had picked up a bad dose of malware somewhere between the looking glass and Wonderland.

No, he shoved his hand into the other pocket and came up with the enlightening rod. He clamped his fist around it. Shut his eyes. *Am I awake?*

One of Rebecca's verses popped into his head.

*Fortune-teller thinks a beggar sits with her. She strokes the coarseness of his hand, feeling his lifeline, his pulse steadfast and sure. It beats illusion of the man.*

Meaning what—Brian had dreamed himself into Rebecca's waking past? If this *was* her past and twenty-first-century Nebraska her present, she might have recently remembered his long-ago appearance in the window fondly enough to write the poem about it.

He could almost buy that. But how could colonial Salem be part of her past?

Before he could squeeze a little more intelligence out of the ribbon, children's voices rose behind him.

He swung around.

Two scruffy girls knelt facing each other a few feet away. They wore mud-stained versions of the local fashion, except without the bonnets. Both girls had scraggily black hair.

They didn't notice him. No surprise there. Nobody but Rebecca had seen him so far. Yet here was something interesting—she had complained about losing a quill pen earlier, and these little munchkins had one on the ground between them.

The smaller of them, the one who faced him, wrapped the pen into a piece of dirty cloth and slid the package into the hollow of a fallen log. Her friend drew a pentagram and two names in the dirt with a stick. Betty and *Abigail*.

A chill iced the back of Brian's neck. He shifted around to get a better look at the girl with the stick.

A younger rendition of Abigail glanced up at him with her trademark mean pout.

Their eyes met. She narrowed hers.

*Recognition?*

He staggered back.

Abigail looked past him. She tossed a stone at a squirrel on a tree branch, then giggled and redirected her attention to her friend.

Did she follow him through the mirror? No way. This eleven- or twelve-year-old version looked like she belonged here. Same way the younger Rebecca fit in. They were part of the past he'd fallen into. The three-hundred-year-old past.

An enlightening rod wasn't enough. He'd need string theory to figure this one out.

The girls vanished.

Brian blinked.

He glanced around.

Nada.

He'd seen this movie before. So often now that his heart didn't skip this time. Back in the modern, somewhat-understandable world, Rebecca had told him Abigail was an imp. Apparently imps could pull the same disappearing act as witches, vanishing from one dimension into the next.

But would the Salem version of Rebecca know that this particular creature was also a creepy stalker with a thing for dark curtains of fog? Brian hurried out of the woods to find his funhouse reflection of a girlfriend and warn her to beware of scraggily-haired imps.

The settlement buzzed with activity. Brawny colonists split wood. Others threw brush into a bonfire. Somebody hammered on a rooftop. A few kids played a marble game in the dirt.

He cut through the throng, heading straight for Rebecca's cabin and passing so close to the women at the well that somebody's sleeve brushed against his hand. Oblivious, the woman waved to a man driving a horse-drawn wagon loaded with jugs and then busied herself pumping water into her bucket.

Brian might as well have been a ghost for all the notice he attracted.

*Maybe I am.*

*Uh-uh.* His leg still stung from his crash through a tree. The sun glared in his eyes. The aroma of sizzling bacon from inside a cabin almost had him drooling. *I'm not dead. Just stuck at the intersection of dreams and insanity, waiting for the light to change.*

Good line. He needed to write it down if he ever found his way out of this place.

Rebecca stepped out of her cabin with a bucket in her hand. The mere sight of her brightened the sky.

He rushed to her side.

She waved him off. "Go away, Brian. I asked you to wait by the window. Then you deserted me."

Right. Because he'd been thrown a hundred yards into the woods, and... Oh, why whine about it? The disappointment in her voice stung worse than the scratches he'd gotten on the way down that tree. "Don't worry, I'll stay right here with you. Something big is happening."

"You mean my destiny?" Rebecca spat out the word. She swept her arm toward a group of workers piling sacks of grain on the porch of a small warehouse. "See those lads? Each wants a wife to serve as seamstress, cook, and bed warmer. Mum insists I marry a merchant who cares no more for my thoughts and dreams than they do."

"Listen, Rebecca, there's a girl in the woods who—"

"Hush." She motioned to the well. "My mum couldn't see you. If these women can't, they'll mock me for talking to myself."

Would they notice? The women were knee-deep in a gossip fest when he and Rebecca got within earshot.

*"Chloe Barnes's husband beat her again for failing to sweep their cabin."*

*"The poor soul is frail. She won't survive the summer with that man."*

*"She brings it upon herself with her slovenly ways."*

Rebecca and Brian reached the well. She lifted her bucket to fill it.

A teenage girl sidled up to her. "Behold the wench expecting a caller. I shall brush the knots from thy hair before he comes." She touched a stray lock hanging out of Rebecca's bonnet.

Rebecca slapped the girl's hand away.

A woman grabbed her sleeve. "We respect others in this community. Pray Master Stoddard beats the devil out of you."

Rebecca went pale. She hurried toward the cabin.

Brian caught up with her at the step. They sat together. He took her hand.

"No." She tried to slide away, but her balloon of a dress slowed her to a series of shuffles and frustrated little grunts. "Leave me be or take me to your future *now*, Brian."

Gladly. But how? And even if he could, what would happen to the modern-day Rebecca already there? He slid closer. "Let's say I can't at the moment. Meanwhile, there's this kid you need to watch out for. Do you know an Abigail?"

She scooted to the end of the step. Pouted. Said nothing.

"Rebecca?" her mother's voice rose from inside the cabin.

She glanced over her shoulder at the door, then back at him. "You can't or *won't*, Brian?"

"Can't."

Rebecca scuffed her shoe back and forth across the ground. She looked up, caught his eye, and stared forever. A dare-you-to-blink-first contest.

He held steady. "Can't."

She broke eye contact. "The merchant Mum insists I marry is named Henry Stoddard. He brought Abigail and her cousin to our district. "

"They poofed out on me, Rebecca. Did you know they could do that?"

She crinkled her forehead. "Poofed?"

"Disappeared."

Rebecca narrowed her eyes. "Yes, I knew. What honest merchant brings *imps* in tow? I do not trust Stoddard. But as for Abigail Williams and Betty Parris, these silly servants of his are no more dangerous than field mice."

*Abigail Williams and Betty Parris?* Brian almost fell off the step. They were the girls he'd read about during his Internet search of 1692 Salem. Their possession ignited the Salem witch hysteria, the trials, *and nineteen hangings.*

He tried to slow his pounding heart by considering the possibility he'd been deposited in Salem *after* the witch trials, when things calmed down. "What year is this?"

"'Tis the year of our Lord 1692."

*Oh crap.*

The wind picked up, carrying the women's voices from the well. The gossipy bunch glared at them with enough hostility to chill the air.

Rebecca clutched at his sleeve. "Pray take me to your tomorrow."

*How?* Although he'd probably bust out of his dream sooner or later, the most he could do for this wide-awake, in-the-flesh Rebecca was help get her out of the village. And then what? Expect her to live off the land? Go make nice with the local Native Americans? They'd been dissed by white settlers from day one. What if they scalped first and asked questions later?

He clenched his fists. "We'll come up with something."

"Rebecca!"

"Yes, Mum." Rebecca stood. "Soon, Brian?" Her pleading eyes searched for guarantees he didn't know how to provide.

*Wait.* Of course he did. Rebecca must have gotten out of this jam. Otherwise, she never would have burst into his life in the twenty-first century.

"Rebecca, I told you before I'll always be here for you. You're in my heart."

She crinkled her forehead. "Already? We only just met."

"It's complicated. But you might need to wait a bit for things to fall into place."

"How long am I to wait?"

"I can't lie. This might take a while. But you can *always* rely on me being there when you finally do come looking."

"You men are all the same with your vague promises." She

turned her back on him and went inside, but he did catch a smile and twinkle of the eye she couldn't quite hide before stalking away.

Rebecca and her mom roasted three plump birds in the hearth while Brian watched from just outside the kitchen doorway. His stomach growled from the enticing aroma of what he hoped were unusually small chickens...pigeons being the far less appealing possibility.

After the birds browned, mother and daughter put them on a platter and set it on the table. Plates of yams, beets, and sliced bread rounded out the feast, along with a jug of cider.

"Master Stoddard expects proper manners," Rebecca's mom said. "Remove the man's boots and tend to him when he arrives."

"I'll do no such—"

A loud rap on the front door drowned out her words. Her mom hurried out of the kitchen.

"Look at her," Rebecca muttered. "Hell-bent on marrying me out of her life. Stoddard would take me to his estate in Albany."

Brian didn't know what to say. Did the mirror pull him here to steer Rebecca in some way? The idea of this Stoddard guy whisking her to a place *not* famous for its witch trials had its appeal, but she obviously didn't want anything to do with him. "Your mom can't make you marry anyone, Rebecca. It's your life."

*There.* But what if, by speaking out, he'd just created a butterfly effect with all kinds of weird consequences? Things might turn out worse, according to Murphy's Law or whatever.

So what? Having somebody's back meant taking the occasional risk. He flashed a reassuring smile.

Rebecca's mom opened the front door. "Hello, Mister Stoddard!"

"Good morrow, milady." The chillingly familiar man removed his top hat, sweeping it down in a theatrical gesture. He'd spoken in the same gravelly voice he'd used in a snowy driveway when delivering a different message. *"Solve this, wandering man, my riddle if you can. Tell me when a cat becomes just like a man."*

Brian cringed. Stoddard's eyes weren't glowing. He wasn't giving himself away. Would Rebecca know she was dealing with a sorcerer? Doubtful. She'd referred to him as a merchant.

Brian slipped into the shadows, biding his time until the opportunity arose for a surprise attack and rescue.

*Right. Like I'm a Navy SEAL or something.*

A big mirror would have come in handy. He could have grabbed Rebecca by the hand and—

Rebecca's mom stepped away from the door. "Do come in, Master Stoddard."

"As you wish." Stoddard played the part of a wealthy merchant to perfection. Polite. Beaming smile. He'd dressed like an aristocrat, wearing a fur overcoat, lacy white shirt, and a curly wig. Younger than he'd been in the driveway, too. No age lines crinkled his forehead anymore. Of course, he would have been three centuries older in Chicago.

That was when, a day and a half ago? The paradox of time travel made Brian's head spin.

Rebecca's mom helped Stoddard with his coat. "Henry has boots, Rebecca! Have thy manners left thee?"

Rebecca called from the kitchen, "I fear they loiter at the well gossiping with the wenches."

Her mom chuckled. She pointed to a cane resting against the wall in a corner of the room, thankfully opposite where Brian lurked. "Perchance yonder stick shall serve as a dowry."

"Every man needs a challenge." Stoddard's eyes shined with humor. He removed his own boots and headed for the kitchen. "Rebecca," he boomed. "I bring a gift to replace thy pout with a smile. Thou wilt soon see a fair maiden reflected back upon thee."

"You speak in riddles," Rebecca said.

Boy, did he ever. Brian crept closer.

Stoddard grinned. "The mystery shall soon be solved. My servants will deliver the wonder whilst we sup."

The sorcerer settled down with Rebecca and her mom at the kitchen table. Rebecca muttered a halfhearted blessing, and they started in on the food. Their conversation drifted from one ordinary topic to another—weather, planting, canning, a recent sermon—until her mom brought up a battle in some place called York between settlers and savages.

"Mine own husband traveled to York to visit his sister that day. Rebecca was but an infant. 'Twas God's will I became widowed." Her voice broke.

Stoddard reached across the table and patted her hand. "Cruel fate. My two young servants lost their parents in such a skirmish. I took charge of them and—"

Rebecca laughed. "Do *imps* have parents now?"

Her mother dropped her fork. "Imps, Rebecca?"

"Have you not seen them, Mum?"

"My word!" Stoddard glanced appraisingly from mother to daughter. He lifted his napkin. Dabbed his mouth. Sipped some ale. "Imps are rumored to be common in these hills, but only a witch or sorcerer would recognize one as such, is this not so?"

Rebecca reddened. Giving away that she and her mom were witches wasn't just a bad mistake. In Salem, it might have been deadly.

Brian crept closer. Almost to the doorway. The idea of hurrying Rebecca out of town had a whole lot more appeal, living off the land or not.

But Stoddard slapped the table and burst into laughter. "You say this in jest, Rebecca! Imps, indeed." He leaned forward, lowered his voice. "The older of the two has taken quite a fancy to me. And she's a jealous brat. If Abigail is an imp, she'll confound you with her mischief."

Stoddard's guffaws broke the tension. Brian unclenched his fists and eased back into the shadows.

"Not to worry," Rebecca said. "I have a sorcerer to protect me now."

"What is this you say?" The humor washed out of Stoddard's eyes in an instant.

"I've met a lad named Brian." Rebecca's church-soft voice carried enough raspy passion to give anyone within a hundred yards a bad case of goose bumps.

Forget the shadows. Brian shifted forward, readying to lunge into the kitchen, wrap her in his arms, stare Stoddard down and—

"Brian is a *sorcerer* from the future," she added.

*A what?* No. He was just a bumbling clown who'd fallen into Salem at the whim of a whacky mirror. What now? Run in there and explain the whole thing? The story was so ridiculous maybe *he'd* be the one strung up as a witch. He edged back a few steps, almost to the front door, eyeballing the surrounding area for a golden key, a button he might push, an anagram waiting to be solved. There had to be some way of advancing to the next level of this insane video game.

Voices at the table grew sharper. "Pray tell who this Brian may be, Rebecca," her mom growled. "Dost thou keep secrets from me?"

"I know of no sorcerers named Brian in these parts," Stoddard said.

Rebecca gasped. "How would you know any sorcerers at all, sir? Are you not a simple merchant?"

Stoddard reddened. He cleared his throat. Started to speak. Stopped. She'd dealt a pretty good body blow with *that* question. "Rebecca, things are not always as they—"

The front door burst open, nearly leveling Brian with its backswing. Two burly men marched in. "Ho! Delivery for Master Stoddard!" They set a full-length, wood-framed mirror in the middle of the room.

And not just any mirror.

*The* mirror.

The glass began spinning. Fast. Quicker still. Teasing Brian's mind like an enlightening rod on steroids. It brought connections. Answers. New questions. No answers.

The mirror in Rebecca's cabin had once been *this mirror,* a gift from Henry Stoddard. Therefore, she and the sorcerer had a history. An impossibly long one. And for some reason, this history brought Stoddard to a snowy, modern-day driveway hundreds of years later, offering a riddle to be solved.

Why?

And when *does* a cat become just like a man?

Rebecca's history with Abigail stretched at least as long. Why did Abigail tell Brian in the lot behind Club Intrigue she'd done something so wrong she now embraced darkness in order to live with herself?

Because she'd stolen Rebecca's quill pen?

No way. *Something else was going to happen.* Abigail and her cousin would somehow become triggers of the Salem witch hysteria and trials.

The spinning mirror tugged his sleeves. Gently at first. Then stronger. Harder.

*Not yet. Not without her.* He lurched out of its grip. "Rebecca!"

She raced out of the kitchen but stopped at the sight of the portal. Her jaw dropped. Eyes grew wide. "Get away from it, Brian!"

"No!" He stretched an arm to her. "Take my hand. It's your only way out of here."

Rebecca reached. Their fingertips touched.

The vortex yanked him into its darkness.

# Chapter Twenty-Seven

"SO THAT'S MY TALE." Rebecca's throat had gone dry from the telling. She stopped twisting the loose thread of a button on her sleeve and glanced across the kitchen table to read the impact of her saga in Agatha Christie's eyes.

After a slow sip of tea, the writer met her gaze and winked.

*Thank goodness.* Rebecca leaned back in her chair. She hadn't lost her World-of-Mortal-Dreams friend despite revealing a chain of events that hadn't always reflected well on her—the history of intrigue, betrayal, compromise, and fierce commitment from the day Brian somehow appeared in old Salem to their reunion in the hills of present-day Nebraska. Apparently the whole overcame one or two regrettable parts.

"I loved the storybook beginning," Agatha said.

A moment Rebecca would cherish forever. She closed her eyes and flipped through the photo album of her mind, pausing at an image she once sketched for her poetry book—Brian leaning into her Salem cabin window on the day he changed her life. She'd torn it out before their far more recent evening in Nebraska. Otherwise, his skin would have crawled had he found his perfect likeness sketched in a book drawn by someone who supposedly never met him before. He might have thought her a stalker, like crazy Abigail. "I think Brian fell into Salem during a dream he hasn't had yet. Otherwise, he would have recognized me in Nebraska."

Agatha left the table and rummaged in a cabinet. "But you were a real, waking person in this dream of his? Living in the colonies?"

"It's complicated."

"That word is the story of your life." Agatha returned with a silver decanter and two crystal goblets. She uncorked the bottle and poured for both of them, then settled back into her chair.

Rebecca studied the amber liquid inside her goblet. The fragrance hinted at vanilla, raisins, and caramel. "What is this?"

"Brandy."

"No, not for me." She shied away from spirits as a rule, even in the World of Mortal Dreams.

"A nip won't kill you."

In no hurry to find out, Rebecca ignored the drink and motioned to the window over the sink. A covered wagon lumbered by, scattering a swarm of monarch butterflies from a grassy field dotted with dandelions. The wagon rambled over a rise and continued into the forest beyond. "Look outside, Agatha. You've dreamed yourself into the past."

Agatha hurried from the table to peer out the window. "Early America? I'd have no reason to come here."

"Perhaps this is somebody else's fantasy, and you've been drawn into it. Such happenings are common here."

Agatha sighed. "If only I could share one of Shakespeare's dreams, instead."

"You can up to a point, if you think about him before falling asleep. But someone like Brian would be able to step into the bard's *waking* world."

"Can you?"

"No." In fact, she wasn't entirely sure how *anyone* managed to jump off the carousel of shared fantasy. The illusions Brian brought with him in his travels rivaled the conjuring ability of the most powerful witches. He'd come to Salem wearing clothes. She'd felt his hand when he touched her. "I didn't realize he was dream-walking at first. His image was as sharp as a knife."

Rebecca lifted her goblet. She sloshed the brandy in a circle, then brought the drink to her lips and gulped some down. A rich, fruity, liquid flame burned her throat and watered her eyes. She gasped.

"You're supposed to sip it."

"Will brandy help me feel more in control?"

Agatha giggled. "You should have asked before you drank it."

Rebecca pondered another sip of the horrid drink but went for her teacup instead. The smooth blend helped chase the aftertaste away. "Later, I met others like Brian. They can't pick their destinations very well, but they'll follow my suggestion if the place is one they wouldn't mind visiting."

Such as the service attendant, Hal, in Sidney. But thinking of her 1940s friend dampened her mood. Stoddard's comment about not doing enough still rankled. She'd done plenty when she asked Hal to steer Brian north toward her cabin in August rather than letting events play out on their own. Perhaps the prophecy had anticipated a different series of events entirely. What if she broke a predestined chain?

Agatha sipped her brandy with such a show of relish one might almost imagine the drink a pleasant one. She paused to fit a cigarette into a holder, struck a match, lit up, and soon sent smoke rings drifting toward the ceiling. "Why are you so cagey with your young man? You must be bursting to tell him everything." She set her cigarette onto a crystal ashtray.

Wisps of smoke began finding their way across the table. Rebecca slid her goblet in their path hoping the flavoring might do the drink some good. "Pure witches celebrate evasiveness when courting."

"And you say the prophesied Rebecca is a pure witch?"

"Yes. So the chosen one can only be me if *I* am pure, you see? Besides, I promised my mother on her dying day everything would be done a witch's way."

Agatha stood. "Did I mention we have a visitor? She's been waiting in the sunroom."

Rebecca nearly choked on the smoke. A visitor had been here all this time? And since when did Agatha's tree house have a sunroom? Stoddard had warned she might lose control, but she never imagined her powers of observation would jump ship, too. Had she somehow become a pawn in somebody else's game?

She suspected whose game it might be.

*Abigail's.*

She followed the writer through a doorway into a bright, flowery room furnished by two wicker chairs and... "What in the world is my couch doing here?"

Agatha trailed her fingertips across its threadbare arm. "She arrived just before you. Didn't you send her?"

"No, and my furnishings don't usually follow me around like lonesome puppies."

The cushion on the right side compressed.

Rebecca couldn't make sense of the vague message. "You're getting saggy."

The couch didn't respond.

"I need to dust you."

Still no answer.

"Someone is sitting on you?"

The couch rocked back on its legs, then returned to its proper position.

Why had events careened so far from a predictable course? "What else?"

The left cushion compressed in sympathy with the one on the right.

"Somebody is *lying* on you?"

The couch rocked back again.

"Who is this someone?"

Nothing.

Rebecca had to know more. A bandit might have strayed across her cabin and broken in! "A ragged, old love seat has so little to tell. Why didn't you bring my chatty mirror with you?"

The foolish couch turned its back on her.

"I think you hurt the poor thing's feelings," Agatha said.

"She's moodier than I am." Rebecca stroked a cushion. "I'm sorry."

The couch held firm.

"Don't make me beg, couch." Most likely, Abigail broke in. Who else could her visitor be? Not Brian. He'd never be able to find the cabin on his own. Besides, she hadn't sensed his arrival.

On the other hand, she hadn't sensed *anyone's* arrival! "Agatha, you've been such a wonderful hostess and good listener, but I need to—"

"Run along," her friend said. "I have a party to attend."

# CHAPTER TWENTY-EIGHT

*TICK, TOCK, TICK, TOCK.* The steady beat of a pendulum clock welcomed him to wherever he'd landed. He'd been sleeping too deeply. Lost his bearings.

*Crreeeccchh.* A floorboard squeaked.

*Bdrbdrbdrbdrd.* An electric razor low on its battery?

A small, soft paw tapped his right temple. Once. And again. *Oh. A purring cat.*

Claws snagged his hair. He shot his arm up and glimpsed a sleek blur of black fur leaping away.

He closed his eyes again. Tried to remember…

His name—Brian.

The cat—Simon.

Where he was.

No clue.

Something new touched the side of his head. Not a cat. Fingers combed through his hair.

He opened his eyes. *Rebecca.* No bonnet. No Puritan dress. *The* Rebecca.

But before he could reach out and touch her to be sure, two images from a truly sick adventure stomped through his memory—Abigail and her cousin lurking in the woods, and a sorcerer pretending to be a merchant.

Brian's pulse shot into overdrive. "I need to get you out of there."

"Shh. Wake up." Rebecca's words came soft and easy, a near whisper so close to his ear that the warmth of her breath puffed every bad thought out of his head.

He shifted up and glanced around. Candlelight flickered against the upright mirror in the center of the room, lighting the bookshelf and the overstuffed chair and sending shadows dancing across the cozy walls of a Nebraskan cabin nowhere near Salem, whether measured by distance or time. He took a slow breath of sweet, non-colonial air. Leaned into the cushions of a familiar old couch.

One stubborn little worry still throbbed in his head, though. What happened to the younger Rebecca he'd left behind? "You didn't end up marrying a sorcerer, did you?"

She opened her mouth to speak. Stopped. Studied him. Weighing something. "This was no ordinary dream, was it?"

"Not even close."

A slow smile spread from Rebecca's lips to her eyes. "Then this will wake you up." She pushed a cup and saucer at him. "I made herbal tea for you."

Tea wasn't his thing, especially with a fruity aroma, but she'd made it for him. He risked a sip.

*Gagggg.* His throat burned. Steam nearly blew out of his ears. "Did you spike this?"

"I added a dash of brandy. Do you like it?" Judging by the gleam in her eye, she sure wanted him to.

"It's...it's...good?"

Rebecca exploded into laughter. She took the cup and set it on an end table, sloshing some of the awful stuff into the saucer from her shoulder-shaking chortles. "I wasn't nearly as gallant as you when I tried some earlier."

"Very funny. Maybe you should give it another try and—"

The mirror caught his eye. He needed to stay on point, save the humor for later, talk through everything he'd experienced.

But Rebecca leaned forward, coming so nose-to-nose close she threw him *off point* by a billion miles. "Welcome back."

He gave in to the soft, warm magic of her lips. He touched her face. Closed his eyes. Oh, to get lost in the moment, freeze time, freeze the world—she could do that—but he had so many...questions.

Eyes wide open now, he stared into hers. The kiss ended.

Rebecca settled onto the couch beside him.

He fished the Saint Brigit coin out of his pocket. Cold silver, for what it was worth. "So I'm awake?"

"Mm-hmmm." She rested her head on his shoulder.

"What day is it?"

"Friday night."

"Yesterday was Thanksgiving?"

"And you came looking for my cabin." She took his hand and threaded her fingers into his.

*Bong, bong, bong, bong, bong, bong, bong.* The little pendulum clock pounded the hour from its new home on top of the bookcase. The gift he'd given her back in Madison now held the left side of her romance collection steady. But the chime stopped way too soon. "It can't be only seven, Rebecca. I was in Salem for hours."

"Salem, you say?" She flashed a smile as wide as a kid's on Christmas day. "I wondered when you'd go there."

Good. Now they could get at it. He opened his palm. "This coin didn't know whether I was asleep or awake. What's your theory?"

"Saint Brigit becomes confused when dreams and reality converge."

"So I was asleep and you were awake, like in your poem." He left the couch and went up to a mirror shrouded by over three hundred years of mystery. He tapped the glass. Solid. Slid a hand along the wooden frame. Real wood. "I thought this was a portal."

Rebecca came up beside him. "Did my looking glass make you sleepy?" Her eyes sparkled.

"Or you did, somehow."

She shrugged. Intertwined her fingers with his again.

"Forget how I got there. What were *you* doing in Salem, Rebecca?"

"Barely existing until I met you."

He tried not to get lost in her awesome eyes. He had too much more to learn. "Soooo, you were *existing* in colonial Salem when I popped into your life, and now you're over here, where you can tell me all about it."

Rebecca leaned into him and whispered in his ear. Her warm, intoxicating breath snuffed ordinary sound out of the world, leaving only a faint echo that had to be listened for twice. "Study my poetry, Brian. Find every clue."

"Clues?" He'd been down that road, but he kept wiping out at the blind curves. "You mean like your aversion to appliances? Did you honestly think I'd be smart enough to guess you lived in Salem over three hundred years ago based on the fact you don't own a toaster?"

"You were clever enough to find my cabin today, and that's no simple task."

Simon bounded out of a corner, meowing for all he was worth. Rebecca headed into the kitchen with him.

"Finding it was no big deal," Brian called. "I saw the chimney smoke." Actually, the deal had been a lot bigger than that, starting with a poetry reading from his mom, followed by a sorcerer in the driveway, an endless drive, a nearly hopeless search for the cabin...

Brian's trip down memory lane veered east to Chicago, where he'd promised his mom he'd stay in contact. He grabbed the phone out of his pocket.

She'd texted him, and the message managed to sift through the local dead-signal zone. *Good-bye, Kia, hello, bicycle.*

*Wait,* he typed, *I'm with Rebecca and everything's cool. I'll call when I head back.*

The cat's cries grew louder. Rebecca clattered around in the kitchen. Sounded like she opened a can and scooped food into a dish. "You couldn't have seen any smoke," she called. "I lit the fire after you were already here."

"No way. It was already going strong. And why are you surprised I found the cabin? Weren't you expecting me?"

She returned to the doorway, wiping her hands in a towel. "What are you talking about?"

"You left food and a note on the table."

"No I didn't." Rebecca's wide-eyed bewilderment sent Brian's stomach into a roller-coaster dive. She was supposed to be the one with a handle on all the mystery.

But this particular riddle had a simple solution—the same stalker who'd been dogging them for months. "Don't tell me we're dealing with Abigail again."

Rebecca settled onto the couch. "No, I don't think this fits her scheme. She's bent on defeating the prophecy, not feeding visitors."

He sat beside her. "Can you at least tell me what this prophecy's about?"

She didn't. Not right away. She stared into the mirror instead, no doubt trying to figure out whether her code would allow the tiniest sliver of information to be shared. Maybe he'd need to find a prophecy poem.

He nudged her with his elbow. "Come on. Throw me a bone."

Rebecca turned to him and focused her gray-green eyes into his soul.

He stared her down, cracked a smile.

She did, too. "Very well. A witch named Aislinn made a prediction a thousand years before Nostradamus. Her followers carved her words into stones scattered across Ireland. Aislinn foretold brief shadows like Salem, and much greater darkness later—plagues, famines, wars—all leading to the collapse of the World of Mortal Dreams right about now."

"That's bad, huh?"

Rebecca sighed. "I had trouble finding my mum's dreams recently. I can't tell you how much that hurt, Brian."

"Oh. Your mom is—"

"Long dead. But dreams are supposed to last forever." Rebecca's sad expression rallied into steely resolve, from pressed lips to laser-sharp eyes. "I found hers, finally, but do you see how selfish I was to think only of her? Mankind won't survive if the void sweeps *all* the dreams away. Without the refuge of our dreams, we'd be zombies."

"What void?"

She shrugged. "I can't say."

"The black fog I saw that night behind Club Intrigue?"

Zipped lips.

Great. Back to square one. "Which is it? You know the answers and aren't telling me or you don't know?"

Rebecca found a loose thread on the sleeve of her dress and began twisting away on it. "The prophecy is scant on details, Brian, other than saying I will court you the witches' way, you will learn my secrets, and together we'll defeat the darkness."

"This secret-learning is coming real slow, Rebecca."

She grinned. "You've been to Salem. Perhaps you'll go back to learn more."

His first instinct was to grab a fistful of couch cushion and hang on for dear life.

"Not yet, Brian. Don't you know by now we witches love to drag out the mystery?" She leapt off the couch and went to the window. Stared into the darkness. "You asked me something when you awakened just now."

He followed over beside her. "About marrying a sorcerer?"

"He's not a bad man, Brian." She held up her left hand. A hand with no rings on her fingers. Probably the closest she could come to giving a straight answer. "I chose a more difficult path."

Brian wrapped an arm around her waist. "My mom told me the score. You're stuck in the World of Mortal Dreams or wobbling in and out of it or something. I've been busting my butt to figure out how to rescue you."

"Rescue me?"

"Yeah. You know, coins in the jukebox, getting the record to play and play."

A slew of emotions paraded across Rebecca's face. She pursed her lips together and gazed into his eyes long and hard. "You came all the way to Nebraska to rescue me and keep the music going?"

"Yeah."

"What made you think you could possibly find me?"

"Everything was falling into place." Brian fought through his pre-Salem, hazy memory and went over the chain of events leading him to come looking for her—the Taj Mahal project with his dad, the family dinner, his mom giving him a hall pass to Nebraska. But wait. Before that. Or during... "I had a vision in my parents' living room. You called me from inside your mirror."

Wide eyes now. "I didn't give you a vision."

"Then who did? Abigail?"

"Not likely. Sending you to Salem works in our favor. You're learning things about my past. Abigail would never help us."

They stared at each other, then out the window together. The moon and ten thousand stars cast enough dim light to reveal shadowy images of the hills. Rebecca took his hand and squeezed. "You had a vision of me in trouble and went looking for my cabin."

"Uh-huh."

"A white knight would do that."

"A confused one. Something doesn't fit. You already knew me when my car broke down in August, didn't you?"

She nodded. "We'd met in Salem, as you now know."

"But I wouldn't have gone to Salem if I hadn't met you here, first."

"It's a paradox, you mean."

"Yeah." He needed a moment. Weirdness of this magnitude made his ears buzz. Nothing on earth could have looped him and Rebecca together through three centuries. He gazed at the sky and tried to single out the magical star.

"You've got a silly smile on your face, Brian."

"I guess I'm buying the prophecy angle now. Do you think

Stoddard is in on it? He came up to me outside my parents' place and hit me up with a riddle."

"A what?"

"When does a cat become like a man?"

The astonishment in Rebecca's expression topped the charts. "He asked *that*?"

"I'm guessing you know the answer."

"It's a big one, Brian, and I wasn't expecting his assistance providing clues."

"Hey, I need all the help I can get. Your enlightening rod hasn't been much use with this."

"My what?" Astonishment squared. *Cubed.* He'd hit the flabbergast trifecta. Rebecca seemed ready to keel over.

The floor threatened to open, spilling them into a pit of snakes, each one a riddle neither of them would know how to solve. "I'm talking about the ribbon you tied around your book of poems."

She shook her head. "That ribbon is a common, ordinary thing."

"But my mom says it has powers."

"Show it to me."

Brian went to an end table where he'd left the book, pulled the ribbon out, and brought it over.

The ribbon fizzed in Rebecca's hand like fresh soda. "Oh!" She nearly fumbled it to the floor. When she caught it, the crazy thing briefly transformed into a thin green rod, like it had in his mom's den, but just for a second. She pressed the ribbon into his hand. "Someone must have switched ribbons."

"You mean after you left the cabin that night in August?"

"Or later. When did you first notice anything unusual about it?"

"About a week later at my aunt's condo, I guess." The idea somebody might have broken into the place prickled the hair on the back of his neck.

But a smile eased its way back onto Rebecca's face. "An enlightening rod isn't bestowed lightly. You see? You *are* special. You're prophesied."

"An old prophesy, huh?"

She nodded.

Time to get at the main mystery of the day. "Older than you, Rebecca?"

She turned to the window. Stared into the darkness.

"Don't worry. I won't run screaming into the night if you say you're *ten thousand* years old."

"My white knight." Rebecca fogged the windowpane and made a row of dots with her fingertip. "Suppose you cross a brook by using stepping stones along the way."

"Okay."

She drew an X off to the side. "Something catches your eye, and you wade a mile upstream to look at it.

She traced another X back at the dots. "Later, you return to finish your short journey across the water. How far have you traveled?"

"So you're saying you waded three hundred years upstream?"

"Nobody ever ages when in the dream world. Please don't say I'm old." Those pale eyes of hers had gone misty.

"You're only sixteen, Rebecca. It's cool."

A smile crossed her lips again. "Thank you."

"I just don't know why the math is so goofy. Way back in Salem, you were fourteen."

"I get older when I'm in this cabin."

"So what are you saying, you've only left the dream world a few days each year?"

He let the question fade into the night. Silence usually meant yes with her. He'd learned another secret. "Same story with Stoddard?"

She turned to him, did the *let me weigh whether I can answer stare,* then shook her head. "Some sorcerers live longer than redwood trees."

"And you say he's cool?"

"Not as cool as you, Brian."

A shooting star traced a white line across the sky. They watched it together, holding hands.

# Chapter Twenty-Nine

**REBECCA'S PENDULUM CLOCK CHIMED** the midnight hour with a dozen hearty bongs. She left the window where she'd been standing and checked the gingerbread cookies.

Golden brown and giving off the most delightful Christmas aroma.

She pulled on her cooking mittens, grabbed the tray out of the hearth, and soon nibbled away at a single cookie...only one...or maybe just two. But these were for Brian.

The third went down in a couple bites.

*Enough!* She carried the plate into the bedroom.

Brian snored away.

Rebecca held the plate near his nose. Giggled.

Nothing but snores.

He had dark shadows beneath his eyes. Who wouldn't be worn out after dreaming his way three centuries into the past?

*Fine.* She'd let him sleep.

Meanwhile, the cookies, with their bulging candy eyes, extra sugar, and little smiley faces, begged to be eaten.

*Just one more.* She took her time with it, making it last.

*Oh, maybe another.*

*No.* She hurried the survivors to the kitchen table and turned her back on them.

*But you love us,* they whispered.

She needed a diversion.

Anything.

A book!

She went to the bookshelf in her parlor and gazed at a tired collection of novels she'd read over and over again, except for one—Henry Stoddard's copy of *Wuthering Heights.* She pulled the book out, basked in its old, leathery scent, and— "Oh!"

A scribbled-upon piece of paper poked out from within the pages.

How had she missed this when shelving the book the day he left it behind?

She couldn't have missed it. Henry must have slipped the note in the book recently.

*Or Abigail?*

She clenched her fists. A bolted door wouldn't do any good against either one of them.

Rebecca slid the paper out of the book and found it to be a hand-drawn map with notes scribbled in Henry's script. His series of arrows and prompts traced a convoluted course through the World of Mortal dreams, ending at a graveyard labeled *Sacred Heart Cemetery, Kenosha, Wisconsin.* He'd marked a plot near the back of the cemetery with an X.

Buried treasure? An important grave? The pot of gold at the end of a rainbow? Her heart raced. And he'd made the hunt so easy for her! While she couldn't afford to spend one of her few remaining coins to visit a graveyard in the waking world, this map provided the obvious solution. She could travel to a region within the World of Mortal Dreams, where every location on earth was replicated.

Still…cemeteries tended to be unlucky places when visited alone. Dark. Threatening. The air thick with foreboding.

She headed to the bedroom.

Brian slept with a smile on his lips. His chest slowly rose and fell. He'd wrapped his arms around a pillow as if it were a favorite pet.

Rebecca tried her best to ignore a twinge of guilt over disturbing the dreams of anyone enjoying so peaceful a rest. White knights must act when called upon.

She took his hand, closed her eyes, and eased her mind into the pool of calming images needed for crossing from one realm into the other. *A dove, puffy clouds, blue sky, an eagle, a crescent moon, a waterfall.*

The floor vibrated.

*A smile, butterflies, cupcakes.*

The walls hummed.

*Fireflies.*

The cabin spun like a top, careened against a barrier, bounced twice, wobbled, and righted itself.

"Open your eyes, Brian."

He did...and smiled at her. He glanced around. "What are we doing here?"

"I'm not entirely sure." She led him through the wrought-iron gateway of a country cemetery. They walked past row upon tidy row of headstones, the snow squeaking beneath their feet as it does on the coldest days.

A wooden fence blocked their way, but she climbed over a low section and beckoned for Brian to follow. Together, they stepped into a neglected section of the graveyard. The wind rustled through a cluster of trees, scattering dead leaves across the frozen ground and up against some of the cracked stones. She wrapped her arms around herself.

If *he* was as cold, he hid it well. Always the white knight.

Time had weathered many of the markers smooth. Others displayed no more than a few legible words of their epitaphs. Any indication visitors bothered to brave the cold and approach these desolate plots had been swept away by wind and snow, except in one case where a bouquet of roses provided a burst of color beside a gray stone.

Rebecca bent to a flower so deeply purple it could have passed for black. *I have a name for this rose,* Stoddard had said weeks earlier. *Rebecca.*

"Hello again, little friend." She pulled the flower out of the clay vase holding it. The fragrance intoxicated her, just as it had outside Henry's castle, and the prick of a thorn against her thumb brought no more pain than the kiss of a hummingbird.

Brian brushed snow from the gravestone. "Sarah Chance. But I can't make out the dates."

The name took a long moment to register—Henry's Salem-era wife. "Oh my. He's been visiting her grave all this time?"

"Who was she?"

Rebecca studied the name of an old friend from a long-ago time. A heroine. "She was a princess in someone else's fairy tale."

A dog's distant bark cut through the crisp air.

What now, confront Henry and ask why he discreetly invited her to intrude on his homage to the centuries-ago love of his life? *No.* Sorcerers lived for their riddles. He'd left a book behind. He'd later hidden a note in it. This was not a game of direct confrontation.

"We should hide." She grabbed Brian's hand and ran with him to a nearby clump of trees, glancing behind when they reached the sanctuary and erasing their footprints with a wave of her arm. A thrill tickled her tummy. Rebecca lived for riddles, too.

The incessant barking grew louder until Stoddard brought his dog around a hill and approached the grave.

Brian shifted in front of her like the bravest of knights. "What's *he* doing here, Rebecca?"

"Shh. I love you," she whispered. She'd make him a nice breakfast in the morning for protecting her in the face of perceived danger. She'd coddle him.

Stoddard and his panting dog fogged the icy air with their breath.

Rebecca watched and waited.

Soon, the sorcerer motioned to the roses at the gravestone. They burst into flames, burned quickly, and disappeared, leaving a puff of green smoke in their wake. He pulled a fresh bouquet from within his coat and placed it in the vase.

He turned and fixed his gaze in their direction, staring right at them for a moment, before shifting ninety degrees to the left and pointing toward a low hill in the distance.

But Rebecca couldn't see anything of interest that way.

Henry led his dog away. Message delivered, or so it would seem.

Brian stepped out of their hiding place.

"Not yet." She tugged his hand and brought him back into the trees.

A minute or two passed.

The neigh of a horse cut through the icy silence, and a black filly appeared at the top of the rise. The horse trotted to the grave, stopped, and kicked backward, shattering the vase of flowers. The filly snorted angry steam out of its nostrils as it turned its attention to the gravestone, perhaps considering whether a harder kick might shatter that, as well.

Dark fog appeared at the rise and poured downhill, painting everything in its path an inky black.

*The void.*

Rebecca shrank deeper into the trees, pulling Brian along.

Soon, the horse and grave disappeared into the shadow. A moment later, the fog lifted, revealing a girl, not a filly.

"That's Abigail," Brian hissed.

"Yes." *And now Rebecca knew what the "imp" truly was.* "She's a phooka."

"A what?"

"They're related to goblins in Irish lore," she whispered, "only meaner. I didn't know these shapeshifters even existed!"

The black fog washed over Abigail again, replacing her with a beautiful, winged faerie with long, golden hair flowing down her shoulders.

Rebecca caught her breath. Was Abigail a half-breed? Faeries had control over the elements. *And over the void?* But faeries were supposed to be benevolent, were they not?

She shuddered. "The combination of a phooka and a dark faerie could have frightening power."

"A dark what?" Brian's grip on Rebecca's hand tightened.

In the blink of an eye, faerie became filly. The horse lifted its front legs, whinnied, and galloped away.

Rebecca's heart fluttered despite what she'd seen. Henry Stoddard's motives had always been questionable at best. Yet he'd earlier given Brian a clue for solving one of her riddles, and now... "So, he's an ally after all."

"Who?"

"Henry. He just revealed the nature of the creature we're supposed to defeat."

Brian walked over to the gravestone. He touched his shoe against a shard of broken vase. Then he bent to a flower, picked it up, and rolled the stem in his fingers. "Why doesn't he beat her himself?"

"He can't."

"Or won't?"

"Can't. Sorcerers may be stronger than witches, and they certainly enjoy longer lives, but their powers are no different. We need more than the mere illusions Henry or I might cast to stop a dream-killing void and this...monster."

Rebecca's thoughts went back to Salem and all the torment a seemingly innocent imp had caused once already. *A phooka-faerie toying with the void could do worse by ten thousandfold.*

A cold wind chilled her to the bone.

# CHAPTER THIRTY

*"WHAT ART THOU GAZING AT?"*

*" 'Tis a looking glass!"*

The voices pulled Brian out of the cemetery and spilled him onto a lumpy mattress. He bolted out of bed, but utter disorientation stopped him cold. He had no idea where he'd awakened, let alone when.

He squinted into the harsh sunlight pouring through the window. *Don't be Salem on the other side. Don't be Salem. Don't be...*

Whew.

No woods.

No cabins.

No gossipy women by the well.

The bare hills were definitely Nebraskan, and even better, they'd been painted white by an overnight snowstorm.

High above, an airplane's contrail nailed the setting as modern day.

Couldn't improve on this if he tried, right?

Oh yeah, baby, maybe he could. The mouth-watering aroma of bacon wafted in from the kitchen. She'd made breakfast.

"Rebecca?"

No answer. Only the flat echo of his voice.

She must have left already. She never stayed for long.

Bacon or not, her absence turned the air stale. All of a sudden, crawling back into bed had far greater appeal than a single step toward an obviously empty kitchen.

*"'Tis vanity to gaze upon it."*

Brian caught his breath.

Her voice. Had to be. But the cabin *felt* empty. "Rebecca?"

One of her games? He scrambled into his clothes and went looking for her hiding place. Under the bed, in the closet, in the living area…all deserted. In the kitchen? Nothing. Not even breakfast. But he'd heard her voice. He'd smelled the food.

Brian stopped and listened hard.

Nope.

Back in the living area and time for a reality check. He reached inside his pocket but found the coin to be cold as ice. So he was awake, not dreaming.

*Or am I?*

He pulled the thing out.

Gold.

*So I'm asleep?*

Last time Saint Brigit got twitchy, he dream-walked into the early colonies. Yet he had his feet planted in the right time and place now—twenty-first-century Nebraska, as far as he could tell.

Imagined voices or not.

Bacon, toast, eggs…the aroma of a hot breakfast returned. Brian headed into the kitchen and found the food waiting on a plate for him. Utensils, a napkin, a glass of juice. Right there on a table that had been empty two minutes earlier.

So a game, then.

To prove the point, Simon meowed from a hiding place in a corner of the room.

"Boo! Now where's your owner?"

The cat sat and cleaned a paw.

Fine. He'd wait her out.

He grabbed a chair and dug into his breakfast.

*Screech, screech, screech.* The nails-on-a-chalkboard sound of something scraping against glass came at him…

Brian dropped his fork and bolted to the kitchen window. He didn't see a soul out there. Just snow and hills.

He hurried into the bedroom and looked outside. Same story.

*Screech.*

That sound had to be coming from somewhere. He glanced around.

*Screech.*

In the living room?

He raced over.

*Screech*—behind him.

Uh-oh. Brian's alert level escalated from orange to red. His heart thumped in his ears like a garage band. Only her mirror was behind him.

*Let's do this.* He spun around to the antique, full-length oval, squared his shoulders, inched forward, and tapped the wooden frame.

Nothing happened.

He went for the glass. First with a fingertip. Then with his palm. Up, down, sideways, and…he found a hot spot.

The glass shimmered like a mirage.

Simon, who'd sidled up against his leg by then and batted at the glass with his paw, let out a screech and scrambled away with his tail as puffy as a furniture duster.

And there she was, standing on the opposite side of a window between centuries. The Salem version of Rebecca. The girl who'd nearly been in the clutches of a sorcerer when Brian got pulled back to the present. But this guy was an ally supposedly? Hard to buy.

"Hey," Brian said. "Are you okay?"

She didn't give a sign of seeing him. Instead, she wet a finger against her tongue and touched the glass…then followed that up by rubbing the smudge with a cloth. *Screech.*

Ha. Well, that little mystery was solved. Honestly, when this gal wasn't drowning him in the pools of her awesome eyes, she had a knack for cracking him up.

"'Tis no time for cleaning," her mom said.

"Ah, but the lass has an eye for perfection." Henry Stoddard towered between mom and daughter, still disguised as a colonial merchant, white wig and all. "My looking glass pleases thee?"

Rebecca took a few red curls creeping out from beneath her bonnet and slid them back and forth across her forehead, striking a pose each time. She turned sideways and frowned at her profile.

Brian had spotted his sister doing the same thing a zillion times. Who needed TV, video games, computers, or phones? Mirrors were the greatest self-entertainment devices the world had ever known.

But Rebecca narrowed her eyes. "Gifts shan't buy me."

Fantastic. She wouldn't give Stoddard an inch, cool gift or not.

She stormed away, followed by her mom. Their voices soon rose in argument.

But Stoddard stayed put, gazing into the glass.

Brian felt a sneeze coming on. His eyes watered. He sniffled.

The sorcerer's focus sharpened.

Brian backed toward the door.

"You must be an angel, stranger. I know every demon in these parts." The sorcerer pressed a hand against the mirror.

The glass bubbled and melted into a steaming puddle across the floor, soaking the soles of Brian's shoes. Cobwebs formed around the mirror frame as they had a day earlier when he fell into Salem. This time, a seventeenth-century menace stood poised to cross into the modern-day side just as easily.

But no problem, right? The modern-day Rebecca labeled Stoddard a good man, and she had over three hundred years of history to go by.

Brian closed in on him. "Neither one of us is a demon. Let's start with that."

"Yet we are connected, you and I," Stoddard said.

"How so? Look, if you can shed any light on all of this, I'd—"

The doorknob creaked from behind. Brian turned. Saw nothing.

The queasy sense of having missed something swept through his stomach. He swiveled back.

Sure enough, during that brief moment, the window to Salem disappeared as if he'd tripped over the power cord. He gaped at his altered reflection in the mirror—no jeans, no shirt, only the pajamas he'd changed out of an hour earlier.

The door banged open, and there she stood—the modern-day Rebecca—looking like a snow-blasted version of Red Riding Hood. She motioned to the kitchen with a mittened hand. "You should eat the breakfast I made before it gets cold."

He followed her gaze to a plate of bacon and eggs waiting *untouched* on the table, then shoved a hand into his pocket, where an icy coin welcomed him back to the waking world. The time had come to laugh, cry, or break into the liquor cabinet and get seriously wasted.

Rebecca fitted her coat onto a wall peg. "You look pale. Are you all right?"

"You bet, now that you're here. Am I dreaming?"

"No."

But how could he not be? She held a fresh bouquet of white flowers in her hand. "Where did you find those? There's a foot of snow on the ground."

"How fitting, then. These are called snow drops. I have a winter garden." Rebecca skipped past him into the kitchen.

He headed into the bedroom. A change of clothes waited in his night bag—the same flannel shirt and jeans he'd been wearing in the dream. He couldn't decide whether to put them on again or just imagine he did and save the trouble.

"What are you doing in there?" Rebecca called.

"I'm figuring out what's real and what isn't."

"These eggs are real. Do you have any idea how tricky it was to fry them over an open hearth? I went out of my way."

"I'm on it." He got dressed again and found her sitting at the kitchen table, chin in hands, admiring a vase brimming with impossible November flowers. He grabbed the chair beside her. "How do you do it?"

"Do what?" She looked up at him, the picture of red-haired innocence, the girl he loved—amazing, beautiful, and completely comfortable with a universe turned on its head.

"How do you go back and forth between fantasy and reality, taking everything in stride?"

"I'm not going back and forth. It's all real."

"Dreams, too?"

Her eyes sparkled. "Especially dreams."

"Then how do you keep your balance?"

"Never look down."

Rebecca might have been a great tightrope walker, but he imagined a bottomless pit of illusion lurking just beneath her balancing act. "Are you causing this stuff?"

"What stuff?"

"My trips to Salem."

Judging by her widening eyes, probably not. "*Trips* as in two?"

"Sort of. I didn't actually fall through a looking glass this second time."

"That doesn't count," she said.

"You mean I'll be going back *again*?"

She grinned. "I remember two *visits* by my champion from the future."

Brian glanced through the doorway at the mirror—the portal to a settlement on the verge of witch-hunting hysteria, the portal to a younger Abigail—the dangerous stalker turned *phooka*—but most of all, the portal to an earlier Rebecca in need of a champion. "Bring it on."

# CHAPTER THIRTY-ONE

**SCRAMBLED EGGS. TOAST. CEREAL.** This time for real, if the cold, silvery Saint Brigit coin had any say in the matter.

Brian popped a slice of bacon into his mouth. He closed his eyes and turned off his ears to savor the smoky flavor without distraction.

He wasn't alone, though. Rebecca sat close enough to steal a piece of toast from his plate.

She giggled.

He tried to laugh, but...

He set his fork down. "How much longer till you poof away?"

Rebecca's smile drooped.

*Soon then. Had to be.* A code of conduct served as the playbook for her life, dictating how long she might stay. When she must leave.

"I'm never allowed to remain in this cabin for long, Brian."

"I figured as much."

She reached for his hand.

He squeezed hers.

"I'll walk you to your car," she said.

But they stared into each other's eyes first, exchanging a silent vow that things would turn better for them. Destiny couldn't have looped them together only to break them apart on a regular basis.

They grabbed their jackets, left the cabin, and headed toward the road. The snowdrifts slowed them until they came across a windswept stretch of bare ground where the sun glinted against a coin. Not a magical one, just a small token of Brian's eighty-seven-cent breadcrumb trail from a million years ago.

The thrill of the earlier cabin hunt was history.

He trudged now.

She walked beside him, matching his reluctant pace step by step.

Soon they reached the oak tree, a half mile from adios.

Rebecca stretched but couldn't quite reach the lowest limb. "We should hang a swing here." The cold air brought a blush of pink to her cheeks and a sparkle to her eyes. Or maybe she'd cheered up. Unhappiness had never been a signature mood for her, even though he suspected she'd been through a lot.

If she could lift her spirits, so could he. After all, the good always followed the bad. They'd hook up again. Soon. He grinned at her.

She rushed up and stole a kiss but stepped back before he could gather her in his arms. "Don't give up on me, Brian."

"You know I'd never—"

She vanished.

*Gone.*

Brian sank to his knees.

Minutes passed.

Hours.

Years.

Something creaked behind him.

He turned.

An old tire hung from the tree limb.

He laughed out loud. Rebecca must have conjured this makeshift swing when he wasn't looking. A parting gift of magic, beckoning to him on this bright, clear, beautiful winter day. He hurried over.

Brian touched the tire. She made it out of thin air. Definitely not real, right? But solid so…why not?

He grabbed a seat and put the swing through its paces. He pumped his legs, moving back and forth in a steepening arc. The illusion created so deeply personal a sensation he doubted the swing would be visible to anyone else. Maybe the weird scene to some random passerby would be Brian floating up and down with no apparent means of support.

Who knew? What if most of the world's mysteries represented lingering echoes of magic like this one? UFOs, Stonehenge, broccoli.

He'd found amazing cracks in the world, with one surprise after another lurking on the other side. Brian swung himself into a happy space wedged somewhere between reality and illusion.

Something bright flashed below. One more coin?

No. He'd left his night bag in the snow, and the rope tying it closed had loosened. Rebecca's book spilled partway out. Its ribbon blinked in bursts of green luminescence like a supernatural strobe light.

A swarm of vague ideas teased him, like little notes posted on a bulletin board a foot or two beyond his visual range. He took a mental step closer and focused on...

*Something.*

This thick oak's existence in the barren Sand Hills might have been a random mistake of nature, like a bush clinging to a mountainside high above the tree line. Yet the unlikelihood of finding a hardy tree springing out of otherwise unfertile ground suggested an awesome possibility. *Maybe Rebecca's conjuring went well beyond a simple tire swing.*

He glanced around for hints.

Last night's storm should have spray-painted only the downwind side of the oak's trunk. Yet this tree was white on all sides.

And the ground beneath had a uniform snow cover, even in the shadow of the trunk, where shallows would normally form.

*This thing isn't real.*

*Is it?*

How to prove it one way or the other?

*By jumping.*

Brian pumped his legs harder. His arc increased, and the tire strained against the rope as he rose above a horizontal plane.

Then he let go.

For a millionth of a second, he flew like a bird.

An eye-blink later, he stood on wobbly legs.

*Rebecca conjured an entire tree.*

Unreal.

For some crazy reason, she'd planted the thing months ago, in a spot he managed to stumble upon over and over.

But why?

Because she'd wanted a direction marker for her cabin?

No.

His thoughts careened down an alpine slide into a dark pool of dread lurking at the bottom.

Back in August, a billboard lured him off the highway into Sidney, *Lynching Capital* of Nebraska. He found a noose hanging from the oak that day—a tree Rebecca said was twenty furlongs from her cabin. And what did the Witch-of-the-Hills legend have to say about that distance?

*She couldn't travel any farther.*

Apparently she could, but her probable method sent icicles down his spine.

Rebecca hanged herself on a stage the night she crashed back into his life at Club Intrigue, and she wore a scarf around her neck every other time she came calling. Those bursts of color had been more than mere fashion statements. She probably had rope burns to hide, like the one he noticed when she came to the condo after her little stage show.

Brian knew without a doubt what the coins she'd been spending really were.

*Hangings.*

He shuddered.

How many more times would she do something so unthinkable to be with him?

*How many times would he let her?*

As if he had a choice.

Sure he did. There had to be a way of stopping this madness. Brian scrambled over to Rebecca's book of Ogham and closed his fist around the ribbon. The image of a rundown, old gas station popped into his head.

Back in August, the goofy attendant of that turn-back-the-clock place pointed him north, and the rest was history.

Good old Hal had to have some answers.

An hour and a half later, Brian tightened his jacket against a chill in his bones.

Overgrown bushes at the service island covered the spot where the antique pump should have been.

And Hal's shack of a store was boarded up.

Traffic noise from the nearby interstate provided some comfort he hadn't slept his way into a time warp again. Just to be sure, he grabbed the Saint Brigit coin out of his pocket.

Cold silver. He was awake.

*But what about back in August?*

He hurried to the building. A weathered poster nailed into the plywood advertised a county fair *dated ten years ago.* The faded depiction of hot-air balloons, hot dogs, and carnival rides peeled at the corners from age. And here was a church bake-sale announcement nailed just beneath it. Same year a month earlier.

Brian's hands trembled, and not from the cold.

He couldn't have met a station attendant in August. The place had been locked down for a decade.

A broken padlock on the door raised a knee-knocking question. Did he sleepwalk right into a condemned building that day?

"It's closed."

The unexpected voice shot through his nerves like a jolt of electricity. He swung around.

A girl bundled up in a down coat looked up at him. Eleven or twelve years old. Smiley. "I'm Gabriella," she said. A blonde ponytail poked out from beneath her snow hat.

He tried to smile back. "I'm Brian."

"Where are you heading?"

At this point, he didn't have a clue.

The girl gazed at him with keenly probing eyes, hinting at scary wisdom way out of sync with the rest of her appearance. Brian had to fight the ridiculous urge to make a run for his car.

"You must be heading somewhere," she said.

"Okay, yeah. I guess I'm driving to Madison. There's nothing here for me, obviously."

"Exactly." Gabriella pulled one of her mittens off and touched his bare wrist with her hand.

Brian's head buzzed. He couldn't feel the ground beneath his feet. A stream of confusion babbled out of his mouth. "I don't get it. I never would have met Rebecca if the old guy hadn't sent me north. He started everything."

Gabriella shook her head. "Some things don't have a beginning. They just are."

No beginning. No end. An eternity of questions? "So where does it all lead?"

"You mean the fairy tale of Brian and Rebecca? Perhaps it ends badly."

Brian flinched. He had to be dealing with another witch—and not a good one. Or another phooka maybe?

"I'm far more than that," she said.

*She could read minds?* He yanked his arm out of Gabriella's grip. Backed a step away. Eyed his car.

"Go on back to Wisconsin and consider this, Brian. Shouldn't you forget about Rebecca and help Abigail instead? She might be the one on a righteous path."

He couldn't even begin to process *that* twisted suggestion.

Gabriella closed in on him, all innocent smile and hypnotizing eyes. She said something that got lost in the whistling wind.

He wobbled. Steadied himself. Caught the echo of her words.

"The world's a terribly violent place, Brian. I never should have brought you and Rebecca together."

"Huh?"

"Dark-minded people gravitate to the most evil corners of the World of Mortal Dreams. They hatch despicable plans together." Gabriella wrinkled her forehead. "I believe the earliest ideas leading to the atomic bomb were born in the World of Mortal Dreams."

Poof.

She was gone.

*Another dream?*

No way. The silver Saint Brigit coin was cold to the touch.

But he wasn't in the lot anymore.

Or in Nebraska, for that matter.

Brian collapsed onto the porch stairs of his aunt's condo in Madison.

Rebecca sat on a fallen log at a favorite spot, where a vast meadow gave way to a grove of orange trees. But this time, the chatter of birds, scent of fresh citrus, and gurgle of a nearby creek did nothing to cheer her. She wept.

"I've noticed something." Henry Stoddard's booming voice startled her mushy heart into her throat.

She wiped her eyes in her sleeve. "Do you take pride in stalking me? Sometimes a person wants to be alone."

"Maybe you only think you do." The sorcerer settled down beside her. For whatever reason, he'd dressed in a dark, heavy cloak even though she'd fled to a summery scene in the World of Mortal Dreams, hoping to wash her sadness away with warm rays of sunshine.

"I've dressed symbolically," he said.

She scooted as far away as she could get without falling off the log. "We'll never get along well if you try picking thoughts out of my head."

He chuckled. "Are you saying we'll get along if I don't?"

She didn't see any point in responding to his babble. Perhaps if she ignored him, he'd go away.

"I won't stay long." Stoddard pointed toward the horizon, the sleeve of his cloak hanging low like that of the grim reaper.

She followed his motion, gazing all the way to the point where grassy field met hazy sky. The mystery hung heavy in the air for so long she finally relented and spoke. "What am I looking for?"

"You'll notice the tiniest speck a little right of center."

She found it. A gray smudge marring an otherwise perfect horizon.

Henry swung his arm, and the smudge disappeared. "I erase what little I can, but the void scatters and reforms every time."

Another wave of sobs overcame her. "My mother's dreams could get swept away again at any moment." She could only choke out her words between gasps.

"Let that serve as your motivation, Rebecca. Don't the words carved in stone hold that everything lost might be recovered?"

"You believe in the prophecy I've been chasing?"

Henry boomed his laugh across the empty field. "Maybe I do, and maybe I don't. But here's something to chew on. Word has it, only the prophesied girl, Rebecca, will have visions of the coming apocalypse. You wouldn't happen to know such a girl, would you?"

"Are you saying you believe…in me?"

"I'm just an old fool. What I believe is of little moment, except as a straw for a young woman with faltering resolve to grasp."

He was right. A vote of confidence, even from a scoundrel, made the air somewhat easier to breathe. "You've done me a service, sir. May I ask why?"

"Perhaps I'm making up for earlier transgressions. The world turns best when everyone is in harmony."

Even after all these years, the reminder of what Henry had caused in Salem stirred her anger like a hornets' nest. "Certain transgressions are so unforgivable as to never be erased."

The sorcerer stood. He towered over her with folded arms and a harsh glare. "Harden your heart the same way whenever you and Brian must part. You'll find the sailing smoother."

Rebecca bunched her fists. "How would you know we just parted unless you've been playing the Peeping Tom?"

"One need only look at your red eyes, dear. I haven't been spying, and I surely don't need an enlightening rod to figure things out."

*Enlightening rod.* Rebecca had gone years without hearing the term until Brian showed her the one he'd found. And here was Henry mentioning an enlightening rod as well. She'd never believed in coincidences and wasn't about to start now. "What do you know of such things?"

"I know the stories passed from mouth to mouth. An angel—some say a demon—created them over a thousand years ago. Most rods lost their power, and those still working are fickle. The holders must have the right blood coursing through their veins to get any use out of them."

She should have known he wouldn't say anything useful.

"Well, I suppose you came here for solitude." Stoddard began walking away.

"Good. Find someone else to stalk."

But he stopped and turned to her. "Oh, I just remembered one other thing. Aislinn is the one who set this prophecy of yours in stone, is she not?"

"What of it?"

"Supposedly she fashioned an enlightening rod to be used by the chosen one. They say she used a spell to disguise it as a ribbon."

*Brian's ribbon!* She started off the log.

The sorcerer vanished.

# Chapter Thirty-Two

"YOU'LL LOVE MY WITCH'S special." Aunt April plunged a spatula into her mixing bowl and stirred with a vengeance until she'd created a horrific pink mush with streaks of yellow. The individual elements were fine on their own—hamburger, mashed potatoes, peaches, catsup, mustard. But all mixed together?

Her concoction did smell like pizza. Props to her for creating the right aroma, but Brian couldn't get past the visual. He eased his chair from the kitchen table. "I'm not eating any."

"Stay put." She continued her frenzied attack on the food pyramid, frowning when the mess turned orange. So she grabbed the catsup bottle and squirted another liberal dose into the bowl, presumably for better coloring although the pukey result hardly bolstered his appetite.

"Seriously, April."

"You did ask me to conjure something, didn't you?"

"Not exactly." A week had passed since a demon/imp/phooka or whatever deposited him on the doorstep of the condo. End of road trip. Gabriella had even sent his Kia along for the ride, leaving it at the curb. April claimed he'd driven back, saying she saw him pull up, sit in the car endlessly, and then wobble over to the steps. Thought he'd been out drinking. Yeah, right.

Since then, he'd seen no sign of Rebecca other than dreams fading to dust every morning. She'd started rationing her waking-world visits like a squirrel down to her last few acorns. How many did she have left? What would happen when she used them all up?

He needed another go at Nebraska without missing his upcoming midterms. Just a quick in and out long enough for him to get at that mirror, go back to Salem, figure out the secrets he was still supposed to learn, and free Rebecca from whatever spell was keeping her from establishing permanent residence in his waking life.

If Gabriella could send him careening hundreds of miles east in the blink of an eye and Rebecca could pop from one place to another like a flickering light bulb, there had to be a way for an ordinary guy to do the same. "I need a World of Mortal Dreams bus pass, April."

"And I'm supposed to help?" She set the spatula down, rummaged in a drawer, and came out with an ice-cream scoop, eyeballing him like a drill sergeant in the process. Lecture time. But how seriously could he take a woman wearing a short leather skirt and a T-shirt listing the ten fairy tales most in need of the f word?

*#8: Who are you, and what have you done with my f\*\*\*ing grandmother?—Red Riding Hood.*

"Picture a chessboard," she said.

"Okay."

"Do you think the queen wants the rook badgering her for information he should figure out on his own?"

"Huh?"

"Exactly." She scooped a few orange blobs out of the bowl and piled them onto his plate. "Next time, maybe I'll try whipping something up that makes you smarter."

He poked at the mush with a fork. "I've got a ribbon for that."

"Really? Then how come you don't know the world has more mirrors than the one you found in Nebraska?"

Well, duh. Good question. "You mean—"

"I'm late for my shift at the diner." April headed out of the kitchen, grabbed her jacket off a chair, and made a beeline to the front door.

He raced after her. "Are we talking *any* mirror?"

"Think duets."

Before he could get another word in, she was out the door, ushering in a cold draft tempered by a winter scent best described as chestnuts roasting in an open fire. Conjured or real? The witches in Brian's life might have been stingy with their answers to simple questions, but they sure were good at spicing up the atmosphere.

Grainger Hall, a masterpiece of contemporary architecture, had been reduced to a hulking shadow even from a distance of a few hundred feet. A swirling curtain of snow hid the curved atrium entryway, the checkerboard pattern of beige and gray facing, the stark, rectangular windows—every modern touch that had defeated Brian's previous attempts to think of the vast, winged, vaguely medieval complex as a castle. Now the blizzard played into his fantasy, transforming Grainger and its grounds into the sort of winter-wonderland scene where fairy tales happened.

*But midterms were about to happen, too.* He had a study-group meeting—a last-minute stab at readying himself for a macroeconomics test in the company of several students as bewildered by the textbook as he was. Why had he skipped all those classes?

He hurried toward the entrance, fighting the bitter wind with every step.

A hooded girl caught up with him. The bangs poking down from her hood were red. She stood a head shorter.

He tried to speak. To say her name.

His mouth wouldn't work.

The girl veered away. Rebecca? A look-alike? A fantasy? A

dream? She headed around the side of the building and disappeared into the storm.

But wait. Did she sweep her arm toward something just before fading from his vision?

Those two buildings across the street. Positioned so close together the walls almost touched.

*Think duets.*

Thanks for the idea, random Rebecca look-alike! Brian turned from the hall and hurried back to the condo.

Mirrors.

They had one in the bathroom over the sink and another attached to April's dressing table. Brian went into her bedroom to check that one out. A wooden frame rising from the table encased the mirror. Eight wood screws held it in place.

He ran to the kitchen. Rummaged through a drawer overflowing with batteries, clipped coupons, tape dispensers, and...a Phillips screwdriver.

He hurried back to the dresser and went to work, managing to unscrew the frame without destroying the thing. He lugged it into the bathroom. Eyed the mirror already hanging on the wall above the sink basin.

Now what?

*Make a duet.*

Yeah. Two mirrors across from each other, creating an endless loop of reflections just waiting to pull him into a different dimension.

He got a stool from the kitchen and propped the dresser mirror on it, leaning it almost upright against the wall so it faced the sink mirror head on. The reflections were truly endless, becoming smaller and smaller, like fractals in a chaos experiment.

Alrighty then. He wanted a portal, didn't he?

Brian took a deep breath and stepped between the mirrors.

# CHAPTER THIRTY-THREE

**BRIAN TURNED FROM THE** medicine-cabinet mirror on his right to April's dresser mirror on his left. A light above the cabinet flickered from one reflection to the next in an endless series of blinks. Other than that, nothing special happened.

He closed his eyes. Opened them.

Nope.

He stood in the same ordinary bathroom as before.

What did he expect would happen? If teleportation were as easy as standing between two mirrors, nobody would have bothered inventing the spoked wheel.

The floor trembled.

*Yeah, right.* His imagination wanted him to believe this crazy idea so much he thought he'd just noticed—

The floor *shook.*

Brian lost his balance and fell against April's mirror.

A flash. The light of a thousand suns.

He clamped his eyes shut. Afterimages glowed green, yellow, red.

The colors faded to gray.

A mild breeze ruffled his hair. Crickets chirped.

*Yes!* Dueling mirrors rocked! He'd been delivered to her cabin.

A chicken clucked.

Huh?

He reopened his eyes to a full moon, casting just enough grudging light to reveal a semicircle of rustic cabins at the edge of a forest.

*Salem,* not Nebraska.

He staggered backward into something hard, then groped his hand across the rough wooden top of the well—smack dab in the village center.

Somebody's heavy palm came down on his shoulder, igniting every nerve in his body. He nearly fell into the well.

"I ain't no ghost, son." *Mr. Buck-Ninety-Two himself,* the gas station attendant from Sidney, stood grinning at his side. The man came to the party in jeans, a flannel shirt, and his Gulf cap, as if he'd slipped out the back of his store, straight into colonial Salem. "Why are you gaping at me?"

"Because your business has been boarded up for years."

The news flash wiped the smile off the man's face. He lifted his head to the sky. Spread his arms. "Did I ask to learn the future?"

No answer boomed down.

The man shrugged, found his grin again, extended a hand. "Name's Hal."

"I'm Brian."

Hal shook with a crushing grip and a sharp gleam in his eye. "My store seemed fine ten minutes ago when I closed my eyes for a spell."

"When was that?"

"June 3, 1945."

*No way.* Another Agatha Christie moment.

Or Walt Whitman.

But who was dreaming this time?

Brian whipped the reality meter out of his pocket. The Saint Brigit coin warmed, then cooled, switching from gold to silver and back in the process. That could only mean one thing. "So I'm asleep, and everyone here is awake?"

"This ain't my time and place neither, son." Hal opened his fist, revealing his own matching coin.

"What? Where did you—"

"Breathe, son. You're turning blue."

Brian inhaled. Cabin smoke. Barn animals.

He exhaled. "That's Rebecca's coin, right? You talked me into driving north. Then you filled my tank with just enough gas to—"

"Think of me as a tour guide." Hal motioned to one of the cabins. Torchlight cast an orange glow over the porch, where three bonneted girls huddled in conversation under a blanket. "You'll know the one on the right," he said. "Left one, too, I reckon, but they're both younger here."

*Both*, as in Rebecca and...? Brian started forward but stopped, weighted down by a thousand questions. "How much can you tell me about all of this?"

"Where would I start?"

"How about Rebecca?"

Hal moved his hand to his chin and rubbed. Like he didn't know her. "The name sounds familiar, but a lot of folks wander through my station. Anything special about the girl?"

"*Everything's* special about her. Come on, man, what's going—"

*Poof.* One second Hal stood at his side, and the next...

Brian gaped into the empty space the station attendant left behind.

A colonial woman approached from the cabins. She walked past Brian as if he wasn't there. The woman filled her bucket and headed back without giving him a second glance.

He'd been down this path before. Rebecca was the only one who noticed him when he fell into Salem the last time. And she had to be one of the three on the porch now, right?

He hurried over. "Rebecca?"

Somebody hit the mute button on the cosmic remote. His voice barely reached his own ears.

Meanwhile, the tone of the girls on the stairs climbed the anger scale, from snappy to annoyed to ticked off to s*hrill.*

He got close enough to recognize all three of them.

*Close enough to shudder.*

Rebecca and Abigail were at war over something, with Betty Parris cowering in the middle. No good could come of this. Not only was Abigail the definition of malevolence, history remembered both her and her cousin in a bad way. Their possession triggered the Salem witch hysteria.

*Or would trigger it soon?*

Brian plowed forward. "Oomph." He bumped into what felt like a wall of balloons. Invisible, squeaky, but unrelenting. They pushed him back.

Not ten feet away, Rebecca leveled a take-no-prisoners glare across the blanket at Abigail. "You stole my quill pen and hid it in a log."

"So what?" The phooka, stalker, goblin, or whatever met Rebecca's angry glance with narrowing eyes. "You want to steal my Henry."

Rebecca flicked a hand, as if batting a fly away. "I'll have nothing to do with the man."

"Lured him here, you did," Abigail growled.

"I did not. Besides, you're too young for Henry, you silly sot."

"Liar."

The fight had to stop before girls started getting twitchy, Puritans panicked, and the hangings began. Brian threw himself against the barrier.

It swatted him back, like a giant ping-pong paddle.

He came down hard on one knee.

*And Abigail noticed.* She caught his eye, sneered, waved.

Wham. The barrier knocked him on his back. He banged his head. Saw stars.

"Please don't tell Master Stoddard we filched the pen." Betty's voice squeaked out from deep beneath the blanket, where she'd been shrinking. "He'll take the switch to us."

"Stop whining," Abigail said.

Brian staggered to his feet.

Thick, menacing silence radiated from the porch.

Angry eyes glared back and forth.

Abigail broke into the world's most malicious smile. She mouthed something.

Rebecca arched her brows. "A nightmare you're wanting instead of a switching from Henry?"

"Art thou not a *witch* who can cast one?" Abigail said.

If nostril's could flare fire, Rebecca's were ready. "Who dares call me a witch?"

"All of Salem will when I spread the word. Unless...you give Betty a nightmare."

"A what?" Betty's eyes had gotten wide as saucers.

"Hush, girl," Abigail growled.

Rebecca crossed her arms. "Even if I *were* a witch, I would never try such a thing. A coven banishes any member who attempts an unauthorized curse."

Abigail laughed, and not in a good way. "A settlement *hangs* any exposed witch, no matter what she does."

Betty started to rise from the step. "We'd never tell a soul about you, would we, Abby?"

"Says who?" Abigail clamped a hand on the girl's shoulder and shoved her back down.

This nightmare idea had a real bad feel to it. Like downloading an email file attachment from Nigerian scammers, only a thousand time worse. If the moment had ever come to hit control-alt-delete, this was it. Brian shouted through the barrier. "Don't do it, Rebecca!"

But no one in Salem could hear him this time, not even her.

Rebecca lifted her gaze to the starlit sky and moved her lips in silence. Then she turned to the two girls beside her. "Hear this poem, and let thy dreams take ye where they may."

*"Burning twigs and leaves, a bonfire in the square,*
*the smoke*
*swirled high into the sky.*
*'Twas a dark-haired lass who saw a presence there,*
*a wraith*
*with menace in his eyes.*

*"Orbs as black as coal, a creature with no soul,*
*gray shroud,*
*the specter dark and grim,*
*followed not his will but that of one so old,*
*the beast*
*who had control of him."*

Betty shuddered. "Hold my hand?"

"Enough," Rebecca said. "I'll cast no nightmares on you."

"Yes, you will." Abigail's teeth and eyes gleamed white in the darkness. "Or shall all of Salem learn thy true nature?"

Another staring contest. Betty shrank even deeper into the blanket.

Rebecca broke eye contact with Abigail. She took Betty's hand and looked up at the sky again.

*"Rising from the flames he floated high above,*
*the wraith*
*searched for a fallen one.*
*Catching sight of her, a lass who scorned all love,*
*he pounced.*
*And she began to run.*
*"'This has just begun, from me you'll never hide,'*
*he warned*
*when he had cornered her.*
*Gazing at this ghost, this shadow of the night,*
*she begged,*
*'I'm innocent, please, sir.'*
*"'Black your soul is, lass, and dark shall be your fate,'*
*he growled,*
*cold eyes engulfing hers.*
*'Feeling pricks of pins, you'll scream and twitches make*
*then crawl*
*beneath the furniture.'"*

That last verse was a body blow. Rebecca had just described the exact signs of possession triggering the Salem witch hysteria.

Brian followed her gaze to a moon gone blood-red. It darted across the sky—first up, then down on an angle, up again, and over—leaving an incandescent green pentacle in its wake. On the porch beneath, Abigail and Betty had closed their eyes. Sleeping, *or worse?*

"What did you do?" he shouted.

Rebecca looked across at him. "Ah, 'tis Brian!"

Great. His voice pierced the barrier. *But too late.* "How could you curse them like that? You don't know what you started."

"I didn't curse them." She ran a hand through Betty's hair, then moved the girl off her lap, setting her next to Abigail. "This little dove will dream without a care in the world. As for *the imp*, 'tis a well-deserved nightmare she'll suffer, nothing more. For one hour."

Bile burned the back of Brian's throat. "The hysteria lasted for weeks, not an hour."

"Hysteria?" Rebecca scrunched her forehead as if he'd thrown the square root of negative one at her. "'Tis a simple, harmless spell."

"On who, Rebecca? *Abigail* isn't crawling around bellowing."

She shook her head. "The imp shall *dream* about crawling. Do you think me so cruel I would curse her waking life?"

"She isn't an imp, Rebecca. She's a—"

*Flash.*

"No, not yet!" Brian tried to grab something.

Anything.

To keep from being swept.

Away.

# CHAPTER THIRTY-FOUR

**A LIGHT BREEZE CARESSED** Brian's face like a gentle hand.

The wind whispered his name. "Brian."

He moaned.

A gust ruffled his hair and tweaked his nose. "Wake up, sleepyhead."

He cracked an eye open.

Rebecca's smile warmed him like a blazing sun.

Over her shoulder, the antique full-length mirror, the bookshelf, and a view of the snow-covered hills out the window had the proper coordinates stamped all over them. The dueling mirrors in the condo must have finally figured out where to deposit him.

*Nebraska.*

Brian shot off the couch and went for a bear hug. By dropping in on Rebecca rather than the other way around, he spared her the price of a visit—a noose around her neck.

His throat got scratchy just from the thought of a hanging. He eased his grip around her. Let his arms fall to his sides. "Next time I find Salem, I'm doing whatever I can to change the past."

"You can't."

"Why not?"

Rebecca turned to the window. Her boundary line cut across

the hills out there. *Twenty furlongs but never more, the circle at the edge and the cabin at the core.* One foot farther meant a hanging. The pendulum clock on the bookshelf ticked for all it was worth. Time kept moving forward. More than three centuries had come and gone. But whatever happened in Salem still cast a shadow over her.

"I'm taking the nooses out of your life, Rebecca."

"That's impossible."

"No, it isn't. Your poem in Salem started all of this, right?"

She started to speak. Stopped. Tears welled in her eyes. "You've gone back to Salem?"

"Uh-huh. And next time I'll show up early enough to keep you away from any and all clowns."

She averted her gaze to the floor. "Always the white knight, aren't you?"

"Think of me as a malware sweeper."

"A…?"

"Trouble stopper."

"Oh, Brian." A tear stained a path down her cheek. "Anyone who tries changing the past discovers he's been part of it all along."

"*No way.* I didn't do a thing over there. That's the whole problem."

"Yes, you did. Don't you see?" Rebecca took his hands, then broke away, pacing from the window to the mirror and back. She paused and retraced the circuit, stopping to stare out at the snowy hills. "By bursting into my life, you proved the prophecy to me. Then you made a promise you'd always be there for me when I finally came looking. So I figured things out and I made certain choices…" Her voice trailed off.

Brian's stomach clenched. How could he protect Rebecca from a mystery he still didn't understand? Time had dragged something forward—something that happened in colonial Salem—copying the collective sadness of a creepy settlement and pasting it into her eyes.

Did her downcast stare reveal an element of guilt, too?

"Rebecca, an hour after you finished reciting the poem, those two girls woke up normal like you promised, right?"

"Fit as a fiddle." She turned from the window and stood with hands at her sides. "Or so I thought…at first."

Outside, in the snowy landscape, the wind blew the branches of a tree from north to south. A tree that should have been blocked by Rebecca, who stood right in front of him. The image still showed in shadowy form, as if incompletely hidden behind a thin white veil.

"What's happening?" he said.

"You're fading out of sight, Brian."

No. *She* was the one who'd started shimmering like a mirage. He snatched the coin out of his pocket.

Warm.

Gold.

"Am I sleeping?"

"I think you might be." Rebecca came close. Touched his cheek. "Do you feel that?"

"Uh-huh." He placed his hand over hers.

She'd have to fight him to get it back.

"I almost can't feel you, Brian. You're bouncing from one reality to the next."

"Bouncing?"

Rebecca nodded. Eyes solemn. "Dream-walking. You might disappear at any moment."

Brian grabbed her hand. "Fine. Bounce with me, then."

"I don't think I can. Not without spending a coin."

He cringed at the thought of dipping into Rebecca's store of metaphorical coins. How many had she used already? Six? Eight? He tried counting backward from her most recent visit but got stuck in the math. "The night you hanged yourself on the stage at that weird club, visited me at the condo, mixed it up with Sharon, and then came back to me…were we talking *four nooses*?"

"I was muddled that night." Rebecca fixed him with a thousand-mile stare. "Four coins would be too high a price to pay. Let's call it three."

"Wait. You're under a spell or something, but you get to define its limits?"

Rebecca flinched. "Not now I don't. You're fading worse than ever, Brian. Try to focus."

A flash of light swept her out of his arms.

Brian wobbled and almost fell to the asphalt pavement at his feet.

Weathered fencing off to the side stretched in an endless line from one horizon to the other. A nearby railroad ran parallel to the road, and a tumbling line of telephone poles hugged the gravel of the track bed.

The season had changed from winter to summer. A mosquito buzzed his ear. Blue and white wildflowers sprouted in clumps amid the scrub brush on the side of a hill.

*He knew this time and place. Back in August, his Kia stalled right here.*

Beyond the first hill lay another one.

And another after that.

A taller bluff loomed in the distance.

Somewhere just out of sight, an oak tree stretched its gnarled limbs to the sky.

He got off the road and took a step toward the hills. The cosmos could bounce him around all it wanted. He'd never stop boomeranging back to Rebecca's cabin.

"Wait." A girl's sudden voice spurred a small flock of sparrows into hasty flight.

Brian's heart almost leapt out of his throat and took to the sky with the birds. He turned to the same ponytailed, dark-eyed terror he'd seen outside Hal's boarded-up gas station. *Abigail's ally.*

The girl flashed a smile. "I'm Gabriella, remember?"

"Yep. Go away."

If only. She didn't move. "You don't belong here, Brian."

He balled his fists. Started to head for the cabin.

Behind him, an engine roared.

Gabriella gasped. "Not *him* now, too."

"Who?" Brian swung around. He followed her gaze to a vintage pickup truck approaching from the south.

Gabriella faded.

*Dimmed.*

And disappeared.

The truck slowed to a stop beside him.

Didn't matter who he'd find inside.

The enemy of an enemy had to be his friend.

# CHAPTER THIRTY-FIVE

**AN OLD-TIMEY PICKUP TRUCK** rattled to the side of the road, kicking gravel and dust onto Brian's shoes. All soft curves, shiny chrome, and bright paint, the handsomely crafted, red-and-black machine bore no resemblance to the squared clones clogging the modern-day highways. This vehicle had a personality. The hood tapered to a snout, and the headlamps resembled beady eyes.

A wave of déjà vu sent Brian backtracking to an early childhood moment when he recognized the carved clawed feet of a dining-room table for what they were. He ran to his mom with the breathtaking news he'd found a petrified lion in the house.

She must have laughed. He couldn't remember. But her words now leapt out of his deepest store of memory. *"Take your surroundings with a grain of salt. Reality, illusions, and dreams are different shades of the same color."*

Wow. He should have picked up on her little hints from the beginning. Even in his earliest years, she'd been trying to tell him the waking world was only one part of the universe.

She never came out and said so directly, of course. Witches followed a code. They celebrated misdirection.

*They turned him upside down.*

The ache for Rebecca had never been stronger. Brian started toward the hills.

"Hey, son." A familiar voice graveled out of the truck. "You need a ride?"

"Huh?" Something was going down here. Gabriella had vanished the instant she saw this guy coming. Brian peered into the cab. The enemy of an enemy lurked inside.

But who would be afraid of *this* guy? "Hal?"

The Sidney gas jockey came dressed in his dorky duck-blind best this time, throwing Gulf cap and jeans aside in favor of a winter hat with flaps hanging over his ears, a plaid hunter's vest, and suspender overalls. He looked Brian up and down. Nodded. Flashed a grin. "Hop aboard, son."

Brian barely registered the man's words. That long-forgotten claw-footed table triggered the weirdest association. He'd mistaken a heavy piece of mahogany furniture for a petrified lion that day, but the carving could just as easily have represented the paw of a cat.

A cat with nine lives.

*So when does a cat become just like a man?*

Brian gasped.

He knew the solution to the sorcerer's riddle.

After a cat spends its first eight lives, it become just like a man, *each having only one life remaining.*

The ugly math buckled his knees. His vision swam. He grabbed the door handle to keep from falling.

Back in August, when all of this started, Rebecca had *only nine coins* in that imaginary purse of hers. Nine opportunities to stray beyond the oak tree and visit him. Why else would Stoddard pop up in the middle of the snowstorm to throw this massive clue at him?

How many times had she strayed beyond the twenty-furlong marker of her cabin already? Six? Seven? She might have no more than two visits left. What then? They'd only meet in dreams?

His eyes watered.

"Go ahead and cry, son. Ain't nobody gonna know but these silent hills."

Brian averted his face. "I *never* cry."

"Speck of dust in your eye then?" The old guy leaned over and extended his hand toward the open passenger window.

Brian reached inside and shook.

Hal gripped tight, eyed him, winked. "You and I oughta deadhead to Sidney now, son."

"No way. I'm staying."

"Fine by me." Hal released his grip and roared the engine. "Just one thing, though. You been on the side of this here road before, ain'tcha?"

"What of it?"

"You'll find it again, I reckon. So come on. I found something *down* the road she'll want you to see."

*She?* Brian wasn't sure he and Hal were speaking the same language anymore. "Who are you talking about?"

"Rebecca." Hal revved the engine again. "Let's go."

Brian couldn't get inside fast enough.

The truck roared to life, throwing him against the seatback. The g-forces, a fresh, new-car aroma, and the glint of shiny chrome on the polished-wood dashboard were almost enough to fool him. But not quite. He grabbed the coin out of his pocket for verification.

Saint Brigit was warm.

And gold.

He was dreaming. "Stop the truck."

"Whatever for?" Hal took a curve too fast, lurching Brian against the passenger door.

Dream versus reality...who could tell the difference? Better yet, who'd remember? "Hal, what's the point in seeing whatever you want to show? I'll forget it when I wake up."

Hal clucked his tongue and shook his head like he was dealing with the village idiot. "Ain't you learned nothing yet? Forgetting don't make a thing less real, son."

He took another curve on two wheels, then steadied the truck down the open road. "Besides, maybe you're special, boy. Could be you recollect things no one else can."

Could he? Brian had shared dozens of dreams with Rebecca since August. He *did* remember some details. Not all, but *some.* A smile. A kiss. A glimpse at the void in a graveyard. A whispered suggestion to look for mirrors. "You know Rebecca, don't you?"

"Yup. Met a girl goes by that name a month ago. I got caught in a blizzard up in them hills back there. She put me up for the night. Right fine girl, that Rebecca."

"Did she talk about anything weird, like a prophecy?"

Hal rubbed his chin for a moment. "Nope. Can't say she did."

"Did she read a poem to you?"

"I can read to myself, I reckon. Fell upon her place a little late for that, anyway. We chewed the fat some and turned in. I headed out at daybreak."

Brian racked his brains for a reason Rebecca would have hooked up with Hal. Came up empty. "What year are we talking about. Nineteen forty-five?"

"There it is!" Hal slammed the brakes and pulled the truck onto the shoulder.

A snow-covered field separated the road from a forest. Something flashed at the tree line, like sun reflecting against metal.

Brian held his breath. Bursts of light had been volleying him from one reality to the next lately.

"You're looking kinda pale, son." Hal opened his door and started out of the truck. "It ain't hunting season. We won't get shot at."

"How do you know? Seriously, do you even know what year it is?"

"Depends which side of the trees you're on."

*Yeah. Like that made a lot of sense.* Brian followed Hal, trudging all the way across the snowy field with him until they reached a gap cutting into the woods. The narrow path funneled wide about a hundred yards in, spilling into a broader clearing, where Salem's crescent-shaped cluster of cabins lurked in the distance, illuminated by a full moon.

Oh.

No flash of light, but they'd been transported all the same.

Hal let out a low whistle. "Ain't that something?"

Brian's heart pounded. The way time had been bouncing around, this Salem visit might have happened *before* Stoddard, Abigail, and Betsy came to town. If so, he'd have a chance to lead Rebecca away, over to the next village or wherever, before the local scene turned witch-hangy.

He tried to hurry with Hal, but every step got heavier, like a climb up a steep hill. The forest canopy twirled above. The ground wobbled below. Or did his knees wobble? Didn't matter. No way was he going to stop.

Halfway through, Hal doubled over, breathing hard. "Go on. I'll catch up."

Brian took another painstaking step. And one more. His legs gave out. He braced his hand against a tree trunk, dragged himself up from his knees, staggered forward, and—

Thick greenery bulged out of the woods on either side of the path, closing off the settlement.

He pushed the scratchy branches aside and lunged forward.

More branches sprang out, blocking his way.

Brian bunched his fists. Glanced around. Maybe if he ditched the path and cut through the forest…

Hal caught up and grabbed his elbow. "Look into the trees over there."

About twenty feet to his right, in a small clearing, a group of girls sat around a campfire. Abigail lorded over them like the queen bee.

Brian caught her eye. She flashed a malicious grin, held up a hand, and started reciting in a singsong voice.

" 'All the maidens fair will suffer thy black fate,'
he growled,
dark eyes engulfing hers,
'feeling pricks of pins, they'll scream and twitches make
then crawl
beneath the furniture.'"

"Owweeeooohhhhhh." A bellowing girl dropped to her stomach and slithered like a snake.

"Ungawaaaaaaa." Another stood, twirled, and fell.

Three girls twitched where they sat.

"Aighhhhhh!" A girl's shrieks pierced Brian straight through the heart.

He ran forward, swatting branches away, dodging trees, tripping, recovering, and coming face-to-face with the worst menace he'd ever met. "Make it stop, Abigail. *Now.*"

She eyed him up and down, this colonial urchin, stalker, phooka, *hypnotizer,* and God knew whatever else. She laughed. She waved an arm.

The trees disappeared. The settlement came into view. A murmur rose from a few women clustered in the shadows by the well.

"I can always count on gossipers," Abigail said. "They'll think Rebecca cast this spell."

"No, they won't. I'll set them straight."

Abigail touched his cheek. "Your name is Brian, yes?"

Her hand sent a chill racing down his spine. He pulled back.

"How can you tell them anything, *Brian*? You aren't even here."

A green flash blinded him.

*No.* He couldn't let this dream end. Not now.

# CHAPTER THIRTY-SIX

**BRIAN OPENED HIS EYES** and gaped at the medicine-cabinet mirror over the sink. He'd looped back to the beginning. His aunt's bedroom mirror reflected from behind, continuing the vortex that earlier swept him to Nebraska.

And on to Salem.

*Take me there again.*

He waited. Shifted from one foot to the other. Waited. Eased away from the sink.

Folded his arms.

Nothing.

He leaned forward. Thumped his forehead against the glass. He had to tell the settlers what Abigail had done. The mass hysteria of those girls in the woods had been the work of a malicious creature. A phooka. Nothing to do with Rebecca's harmless spell.

He'd set things straight and change the past.

No witch hunt.

No hangings.

But the mirrors weren't cooperating anymore, and…

He fumbled into his pocket for the coin. Pulled it out.

Cold silver.

*He wasn't dreaming anymore.*

The bathroom walls had gotten too tight for a guy to breathe. He escaped to the living room.

A roaring blizzard frosted the windows opaque, leaving him shut inside.

Alone.

Without Rebecca.

He grabbed the front door by the handle, yanked it open, gasped for air.

The storm lowered a white curtain over everything more than twenty feet away. Snow whispered like sugar through a sifter and drifted over every upright object, including his half-buried Kia at the curb.

He slumped against the doorframe.

"Brian?" His black-cloaked sister fought her way out of the whiteout.

"Kara!" He wrapped his arms around her and held on for dear life.

Kara puffed her cheeks and bulged her eyes. "Not *too* lonely, are we? Mom sent me to check on you."

"What for? Everything's fine."

"Really?" She brushed past him and into the condo, shedding her snow-covered ski cap, mittens, and coat on the floor. "If life is so peachy, why are you standing in the doorway like a lonely puppy?"

Brian followed her in. Closed the door behind them.

She dropped her purse. Lost her scarf. Kicked off her boots. Turned to fix a laser gaze on him.

Game over. Brian lost his brave front. How could he stare into those probing eyes and not tell the truth? "Okay, Kara. My world is in meltdown mode. Happy?"

"Not really." She headed into the kitchen. Clattered through April's stuff. Drawers opened and closed. A cabinet door creaked on its hinges. "It's time for some heavy drinking. You do have hot chocolate, don't you?"

"I'm trying to cut back. Twelve-step program."

"Here it is." Mugs clinked. Sink water whooshed out of the faucet. A spoon stirred. *Beep beep beep...* the microwave. "Hey, is this her book of poetry?"

Brian flinched. *Her?* The use of that pronoun suggested far more knowledge than Kara should have had. He hadn't told his sister anything. "Have you been talking to Mom?"

"She and I do live in the same house, Brian."

Kara came out of the kitchen holding two steaming mugs. "Let's cut to the chase. I know everything you know and more. I can't share the *more* part, though."

"Story of my life lately." Brian collapsed onto the couch.

"Yeah, it sucks being you, I guess." She flopped down beside him, offered a mug, then grabbed his phone from the coffee table and opened the picture gallery. She flipped from image to image and stopped at a recent one of Rebecca—all red hair, smiles, and dimples. "Pretty thing. How many visits does she have left?"

Brian burned his tongue. "What? How much do you know?"

"Not quite everything."

"You couldn't have gotten all of this from Mom."

"I didn't." Kara pressed her lips tight. Her gaze was unyielding. "How many visits?"

"*One,* I think. Two, tops." The admission turned the taste of chocolate sour in his mouth. He shifted up from the couch and paced the room. "I need to hit the road. If I can't dream my way to Salem, I'll drive to her cabin and take it from there."

"Salem? What are you talking about?" Kara's dark-shadowed eyes filled with confusion. "If you mean *Nebraska,* doesn't legend say Rebecca's cabin can't be found?"

"Been there. Done that." He grabbed his jacket from the back of a chair.

"Maybe you won't be so lucky next time."

"I'll chance it."

"Wait." Kara rummaged through her purse until she came up with a snow globe and a little wooden stand. She set it up on the coffee table. "Tell me what you see."

"Flying monkeys? I saw the movie."

She elbowed him in the side. "Very funny. Now look into the globe."

"Fine." Brian leaned close enough to peer inside. The globe encased a miniature cabin in a field of scrubby hills.

Something moved.

He jumped back.

Shadows shifted within, as if driven by unseen clouds drifting across the sky. A breeze rippled tiny bushes and shrubs. "Wow!"

"Isn't it?" Kara said something under her breath, and a puff of smoke curled out of the cabin's chimney.

The flood of magic and mystery pouring out of his previously normal, if somewhat annoying, big sister was more than Brian could handle standing up. He slumped onto the couch beside her. "Could you slow down a little and fill me in on what operating system we're looking at here? You lost me at Windows 14.0."

"Can't say. Somebody gave this to me."

*"Somebody?"*

"Uh-huh." She grabbed the globe and held it up with outstretched arms. "Think of this as a remote control for Rebecca's cabin. Like back on Thanksgiving."

"Slow down even *slower*, Kara."

She smiled from ear to ear. "I made smoke come out of this cabin's chimney so you'd see it coming out of *Rebecca's* when you drove out there. *Comprende?*"

"You...helped me find her?"

His sister had the same delighted gleam in her eye he'd seen in Rebecca's whenever she bowled him over. "I left a snack on the table, too."

"How in the world..."

"Like I said. Somebody helped." She set the globe back on its stand.

"I don't suppose this helper has a name."

"Not one I'd care to divulge. Anyway, we couldn't be sure you'd notice the smoke that day. We got lucky."

"Clearly not an all-powerful helper then, huh? Are we talking Mom?"

"Nope. Now pay attention. I'm going to use the magic word." She lifted the globe again. "Cratchmunkin." Smoke poured out of the chimney.

Did that mean smoke signals were now billowing out of Rebecca's *real* cabin chimney in Nebraska? The idea made his head swim. This went way beyond what little he'd learned about witchcraft. Illusions plus dreams equals telekinesis? "*No way.*"

"Your mouth is hanging open, Brian. Look, I need to go." Kara grabbed her coat from the floor. "I'll tell Mom you're fine, Aunt April is doing a *wonderful* job of taking care of you, and so on."

"That's it?"

"I promised Brad I'd be home by nine. We're going bowling."

"But it's blizzarding out. Why not stay here and drive home tomorrow?"

She slid an arm into her coat. "Don't worry. I came in Mom's SUV."

"Hold on." He hustled into the kitchen and hurried back with the book of Ogham. "Can you read this?"

"Please." She bent for her scarf. "Why would I interfere with a courting ritual your girlfriend is following so religiously?"

He touched the ribbon for a good answer. Came up empty. "Because you're my loving sister? Come on. This book is full of clues."

"Clues for what?"

"How to make your head explode."

She grabbed her mittens.

Brian wedged himself between her and the door. "I'm begging you."

But she made a zipping motion across her lips. "What fairy tale did you ever read where a boy's *sister* rescues the fair maiden?"

"This isn't about rescuing maidens. Well, partly, but there's this void-like black fog, too, and there's—"

"A prophecy." Kara eased around him. Turned the door handle. "Didn't somebody carve into stone that this is for you and Rebecca to handle?"

He dropped his arms to his sides. Racked his brain for the argument that might convince her to *read every clue in that book to him.* "Her visits are running dry."

Kara hugged him. Warm, snug, sisterly. But she pulled away and looked out into the storm. "Stop trying to peek at the last page of your fairy tale."

"But—"

"Ask anything more, and that globe's coming home with me."

"Fine." Witches lived for their secrets. He got that. Even Rebecca relished the game despite her obvious desperate need to be rescued. He was the ball of string, and she was the cat.

A cat with only two remaining lives at most.

Brian glanced over his shoulder at the globe on the coffee table. "Can you puff some smoke out of Salem so I'll find that, too?"

A gust of wind blew a cold burst of snow into the condo. Kara stepped into the blizzard. "You can't change the past, Brian. Worry about the future, instead."

# CHAPTER THIRTY-SEVEN

**THE COBBLESTONE PATH CRESTED** a hill, revealing a tapestry of pastoral beauty in the countryside below. Shared imagination by a thousand dreamers had nestled a thick meadow between a forest on one side and the bluest of lakes on the other. Rebecca paused to savor the pine-fresh air, bent to pick a wildflower for behind her ear, then continued walking into the rich fantasy.

But the sky darkened when she reached the field. The scene shimmered. The forest melted into wasteland.

She shuddered. The World of Mortal Dreams had always been a fickle place. Calm moments could collapse into nightmares from one breath to the next.

Yet the scene remained idyllic to her right. The path curved into a park where picnickers lounged in the sun, watching their children race back and forth with kites in tow.

Rebecca sighed from deepest longing—for a peaceful existence without any threat, where she and Brian might settle onto a blanket and share a basket lunch.

*That will never happen.* She choked back a sob.

She still had almost two centuries left to serve from her original five-hundred-year sentence. When her ninth visit had ended, she'd only be able to call on Brian in his dreams.

Surely, he'd lose interest in her. Inevitably, he'd age and she wouldn't.

Rebecca squared her shoulders. This was no time for self-pity. A key question needed answering. How would Brian defeat Abigail and the void? Did the unexpected appearance of an enlightening rod in his hands mean they had a sponsor? Someone with the power to help them do the impossible?

She had to know. The prophecy hadn't provided the slightest hint how she and Brian might triumph on their own. *And the answers wouldn't be found in a pleasant park.* She turned her back on the greenery and followed a forbidding trail of crushed glass across a blackened lava field. Only the few white skeletons of long-forgotten trees decorated the harsh landscape.

A fearsome sound, like a thousand out-of-tune trumpets, bellowed from a marsh to her right.

She hurried behind a rock and crouched down.

*Clomp.*

*Clomp.*

*Clomp.*

A massive dragon's footfalls shook the ground. White-hot flames shooting out of its leathery nostrils heated the air to its boiling point. She cringed and crouched lower, trembling at the sight of the scaly beast from her woefully inadequate hiding place.

*Nothing is real here.* Small comfort when caught in the throes of a fearful fantasy capable of driving any witch mad—as the scariest nightmares were rumored to do.

The dragon moved on.

She breathed. But she waited for a count of twenty before resuming her trek, just to be sure.

The burnt earth soon gave way to a hilly area dotted with lava pits and bordered by steep cliffs.

*Aaaaiiiiiiiiii!*

The shriek pierced her heart. A banshee? Or perhaps another witch like her, unwisely setting foot on this loathsome trail.

Rebecca turned to the direction of the park, miles behind her now but not out of reach if she wanted to head back.

*A refuge for cowards.*

She bit her lip. The guardians designed this forbidding land well, bent as they were on screening out all but the most tenacious, fearless women. Only the bravest of witches were welcome in the Gallery of Secrets.

Such as her.

Mere illusions couldn't stop her.

She pressed forward, mile after mile, until she reached the gate of a sprawling, stone-walled fort. A thick spider web blocked her passage. *Enough of this.* She lunged forward, breaking through the gooey strands to find herself at the edge of a magnificent interior garden.

She paused to catch her breath and slow her racing heart.

A rectangular pool of water, flower beds bursting with rainbow colors, and a maze of shrubs beckoned for her to linger, forget her troubles, then head on home once she'd replenished her spirit.

She turned her back on the fantasy, found a stairway beside a pile of bones, and headed into the gloom below.

Five hundred and three steps spiraled into the darkness. The symbolic descent honored the year the great prophet, Aislinn, had been laid to rest. At the bottom, Rebecca pushed through a door into a vast, torch-lit study.

Goblin librarians skulked about, distinguishable by their ancient faces, spindly fingers, and bare, hairy feet. One of them greeted her with a scowl. He took her arm with an icy hand and led her to a giant mushroom serving as a reading table.

He'd picked a spot off to the side, away from any other visitors, clearly understanding that witches were like feral cats, preferring not to mingle with their own kind except at a safe distance.

"Thank you." She settled onto a stool and used a quill pen to write her request in Ogham on a weathered parchment. With the note in hand, the goblin scurried off, only to return with a troll a moment later. The beast growled at her, shaking a thick, menacing club in a gnarled fist the size of a ham.

These caretakers guarded their moldy books as if they were made of gold and silver! She'd have none of their intimidating tactics. "I told you what I want."

A staring match ensued—fiercely determined eyes refusing to blink on either side.

At last, the goblin and troll shook their heads, muttered something to each other in a strange dialect, and stalked off. They opened a door at the far end of the study and disappeared down a passageway.

"The book you requested contains a secret only to be shown to a chosen one." The voice came from behind. A girl's voice. A soothing voice. A voice she hadn't heard in many years.

Rebecca turned to the blonde-haired, ponytailed Gabriella.

What protocol to follow when visited by an angel? She'd knelt the only other time they met, but perhaps she hadn't looked into Gabriella's eyes carefully that time. Now she found something unsettling in those ancient orbs—a hint of darkness completely in contrast with the angel's child-like appearance and pure white dress.

Gabriella resolved the impasse by making the first move. She climbed onto the stool beside her. "You want the book, because...?"

"I've come across an enlightening rod shaped as a ribbon, and I want to research its origins."

"What do you think the origins might be?"

Rebecca lowered her gaze, partly out of respect but mostly because her earlier glance into those eyes left her light-headed. What manner of angel hypnotized people? "Perhaps I've come to the wrong place for answers." She shifted off the stool.

Gabriella seized her wrist.

That mere touch sapped what little strength Rebecca possessed after her harsh journey through the nightmares, but she rallied herself by embracing a boiling sense of outrage. "Why would an *angel* need to grab someone and force—"

"You've had no assistance during your years since Salem, have you, Rebecca?"

"I've asked for none."

"Have you been a good witch? One who follows the code in all matters?" Something resembling kindness gleamed out of the darkness in Gabriella's eyes.

"I'm not sure." Tears warmed Rebecca's cheeks, bringing the taste of salt to her lips. "I've tried so very hard, but—"

"Let's just say for now you've done well enough to earn a bit of knowledge." Gabriella levitated, floating off the stool to hover above her...and disappeared.

Rebecca's wrist throbbed. She looked at the welt. *Would an angel do this? What is she?*

The door at the end of the study banged open. The troll lumbered in, holding an oversized, leather-bound book with outstretched arms, as if it were the Holy Grail. The goblins closest to the monster shrank back, and so did she. But the troll was at her side in an instant, slamming the book onto her table in a thundering cloud of dust. He muttered something in his odd dialect and stalked away.

Silence gave way to the resumed arguments between patrons and goblins elsewhere in the room. No books were ever provided without a fuss.

But she'd gotten hers. She eased back onto the stool and eyed the prize.

Rebecca needed both hands to turn the massive pages of a volume covering the entire table. As torches dimmed and shadows lengthened, she skimmed through the illustrated passages, searching from chapter to chapter for some mention of the unusual enlightening rod. Did Aislinn truly create the ribbon? And how had it fallen into Brian's hands?

Near the end of the book, a sketch depicted the white-haired prophet handing a ribbon to a young boy. She took a deep breath and studied the Ogham caption beneath.

*The witch bestowed an enlightening rod upon her grandson. "Find Brian in the distant future and pass this rod's wisdom on to him."*

*Aislinn considered her grandson unworthy of such a task, given the lad's dark nature. Yet she had no better choice. Henry harbored more than a witch's blood in his veins. He carried the blood of a sorcerer. As such, the lad would live many centuries, long enough to find the chosen one. Thus, the greatest of all witches trusted fate to decide whether or not he would carry out her wish.*

Connecting the dots took no great leap.

*Henry Stoddard.*

The conniving sorcerer had been Aislinn's grandson all along. He must have passed the rod on to Brian, *having identified him as the chosen one.*

What had Henry told her on the rock, just before Thanksgiving? *I've taken a special interest in him.*

Rebecca shook her head. Over the years, she'd thought Henry a scoundrel, a meddler, a cad. But he showed himself to be a possible ally that night in the cemetery, and this book confirmed that he was.

# Chapter Thirty-Eight

**THE MOON AND STARS** beamed their light from the sky, down through the window, and into the cabin. Rebecca basked in the glow of constellations large and small, many with names, some with legends. Could the heavens have blessed the world with a finer show than this?

Yet certain stars forsook the order to veer out on their own. Renegades. Mavericks.

A shadow of worry dampened her mood. She'd seen darkness in Gabriella's eyes earlier today. And she'd endured pain. The welt left by the angel's harsh grip couldn't be ignored.

*Have I been wrong about her nature all this time?*

She needed to reexamine her first and only other meeting with Gabriella, the day she thought she'd been visited by an angel. Back when *she* was an impressionable child.

Only by dreaming could she chip away centuries of rust, peel back the deceptions, and study the event with wiser eyes.

She turned to her mirror. "Hypnotize me."

The glass shimmered.

Rebecca paced the cabin floor, pressing hands over ears to mute the terrible sound echoing in her head. Two days earlier, an innocent woman's desperate screams of denial had gone unheeded by the angry Puritans. The gallows floor fell from beneath Bridget Bishop's feet, snapping her neck with an audible crack.

Rebecca had watched. And heard.

And cried.

Somehow, her harmless spell on Abigail and Betty ignited a firestorm.

Her own neck would snap just as horribly any day now. The coven queen, who had learned about the spell from Abigail, would surely serve Rebecca up to the magistrate in the hope of protecting the other witches from the rampaging settlers.

*Good.* How could she go on living with this guilt?

Her stomach heaved.

A sound like wooden wind chimes tinkled from behind. Rebecca swung around. "Who sneaks up on me like a brigand?"

"My name is Gabriella." The disembodied voice took on a shape, at first blurry and translucent, then becoming sharper—a girl in a white veiled dress. A halo of light hovered over her head.

Rebecca dropped to her knees. "An avenging angel you are, come to punish me for casting a spell."

"You have not caused these horrors, child."

"Yes, I have."

"Do you doubt my word?" Gabriella spread her arms and smiled with bright-eyed sincerity no one could question.

"No, it's just that I…" Fleeting hope almost silenced the echo of Bridget Bishop's broken neck. Rebecca cringed at her own selfishness. Confirmation of *her* innocence would do nothing to save the dozens of others soon to face the gallows.

Gabriella's smile faded. "Perhaps you can join a great battle, one day, Rebecca, and choose which side to save."

For an unsettling moment, Rebecca wondered whether a thought had been picked from her brain and expanded upon. She studied the angel's expression for signs of mischief but found only ambiguity. "What do you mean?"

"Child, do you know from your studies the *Pogrom of a Thousand Tears?* Sixteen centuries exactly after that horror, on the twenty-fifth day of August, a lad named Brian will arrive in Sidney, Nebraska. He'll be a hero. Or a villain. Who can say?"

Sixteen centuries from an event in the past—Rebecca worked out the sums in her head. "You mean three centuries hence?"

"Yes, Rebecca. You can only find Brian *in the future.*"

Rebecca gasped. "Do you speak of the prophesied Brian?" The lad from tomorrow visited twice but left without a word each time.

Gabriella's earthly form began to fade. "You must find your own answers, Rebecca." The wall behind became visible through her vanishing face.

"Wait! Where is this land of Sidney? How shall I find passage to such a distant time?"

"Scheme, Rebecca. Use your wits. Decide who to save and who to destroy."

*Bang, bang, bang.* Someone pounded the door.

"Go away!" Rebecca shouted.

The angel disappeared.

"No, not you, Gabriella. I didn't mean you."

The thumping grew fiercer.

"Leave me be!"

*Bang. Bang.* More thuds…relentless.

Rebecca sucked in her breath. Had they come for her? Her head throbbed. Her vision swam. *So be it.* She staggered to the door and opened it.

Henry Stoddard stood on the doorstep, hat in hand. His white wig tilted to the side of his head, revealing dark curls beneath. He hadn't shaved. The man reeked of spirits.

She glared at him in disgust. "You have been drinking, sir."

"Aye. And so should thee." He motioned behind him to a group of women at the well in the village square. "Rumors are beginning to circulate, Rebecca." He brushed past her into the cabin.

She followed after him. "You haven't heard *rumors*. I've already confessed to the coven queen about the curse I cast."

Henry lowered his head. "Nay, Rebecca. 'Twas I who copied thy curse and set these horrors into motion."

The weight of his revelation took her breath away. Her agony of guilt had been caused by this man? Even worse, a string of hangings had started and might never end, all because of him? She slapped his face as hard as she could—fiercely enough to bring a sharp sting to her palm.

Henry took the blow without defending himself. He stood hangdog before her with arms steady at his sides.

"Why?" she asked.

Stoddard stepped to the mirror and glared at his own reflection. "Foolish pride? Anger over your rejection of me as suitor? What does it matter? I've come to make amends. An angel advised me to help you now, Rebecca."

She clasped her hands together so as not to grab the man's throat and throttle him. "Any counselor of yours would more likely be a demon."

"Demon, angel, one is little different than the other."

"What? Take your heresy and leave my cabin this moment!"

"Very well." Henry marched to the door and grabbed the handle, but he stopped and turned to face her. "Five centuries in the World of Mortal Dreams. A prisoner would ne'er age in such a place. In fact, one might consider the land a portal to the future."

*A road through time to Brian?* Rebecca backed to a chair and fell into it.

Stoddard grinned. "Thy coven shall sentence thee for casting a spell."

The angel told her to look three centuries in the future, not five. Could she bargain for a shorter sentence? "Who spoke to you of this?"

"Word is bandied about. 'Tis no matter. I'll admit my involvement and end this farce."

"Nay." Rebecca barely lifted her voice above the hammer beats of her heart. "Tell nothing of this to anyone."

Rebecca blinked the dream away, turned from the mirror, and shook her head.

How could she have failed to recognize the blatant manipulation of an angel who advised her to *scheme?* As for Henry, the way he'd characterized the proposed sentence as a portal, he might as well have led her into exile by the nose.

*No.* Exile had never been the end game. He'd pointed out the path for fulfilling a prophecy.

From three centuries in the past, the snap of an innocent woman's neck reverberated in Rebecca's head, sending a chill down her spine.

She wrapped her arms around herself. So many deaths caused by a spell. But not Henry's, despite his admission so many years ago. That rake had always been a trickster, but she'd never found him to be an evil man.

She hurried into the World of Mortal Dreams.

"Ah, Rebecca!" The sorcerer glanced up from a bush he'd been pruning outside his castle. "For someone who loathes the ground I walk on, you do come to visit quite often." Eyes crinkling with good humor, he grabbed a pitcher from a workbench. "Care for some lemonade?"

"No. I have something to say to you."

He filled a glass and pushed it into her hands anyway. "Old family recipe…lemons, sugar, water, ice. Can't beat it."

"Henry, I know you didn't—"

"From your mouth to God's ears, Rebecca. You called me

Henry, not *sir* or *you*. How long has it been since you actually addressed me by name?"

"Probably never." She collapsed into one of the wrought-iron chairs scattered about the garden and sipped her drink before he could browbeat her for ignoring his hospitality. "*Henry,* I see how you got me to where I am. And I realize you're itching to help convince Brian he's the chosen one to stand with me against Abigail and the void."

"And this is a bad thing?"

"The prophecy doesn't mention a *sorcerer* helping Brian and his pure witch, Rebecca."

Stoddard let her words hang in the air. He bent to pick a bouquet of flowers—blue, red, orange, yellow—a hodgepodge having no business growing off the same bush. He arranged them in a vase, one by one. "What gives you reason to think I'd interfere?"

"I know you." How to get through to this tinkerer? She tried staring him down, but he only smiled wider. "There's no call for a sorcerer's interference. The prophesied Rebecca is foretold to court Brian *a witch's way*, with riddles, illusions, and dreams."

Henry set the vase aside, picked one last flower—a purple rose—and slid it behind her ear. "How very obedient of you to follow a prophet's ancient words in meticulous detail. Now tell me the real reason." The look in his eyes had changed, humor replaced by cold perception.

She shrank away as if the troll from the Gallery of Secrets had returned to smack a great book against her face. Henry seemed capable of guessing things she didn't want to admit even to herself. "Tend to your flowers. I shouldn't have bothered you here."

"You're in love with him, as I told you before. And now you recognize how manipulative love can make someone, don't you? There's no place for such a feeling in this game we play."

She clenched her eyes shut to stem the tears.

"You've always been in love with him, and you want to

know he's equally drawn to you. If so, he'll prove his feelings by going out of his way to figure everything out on his own. Otherwise, you'd never be sure whether he joined you in this prophecy quest simply because some old fool of a sorcerer talked him into it."

"Wrong, *old fool*. What good is being in love with someone I can only visit one more time? She snatched the rose from her ear and worried it in her hands. "And yes, I do see how selfish this makes me. The prophecy is real. I've had visions. But I may be putting my love for Brian ahead of the goal to help him save mankind."

"Rebecca?"

"Wait, there's more." She twisted and turned the rose in her hand, twisted and turned, willing it to somehow hold her tears at bay. "My mother knew I'd be going after Brian. She made me promise on the day she died that everything would be done a witch's way. I'm doubly selfish, putting all of this ahead of the greater picture."

"Rebecca."

She had trouble finding her voice anymore. "What?"

"Do you think you might find a way to regard me as a friend one day?"

The kindness in Stoddard's tone unleashed the flood of tears she'd been trying to stave off...followed by great, heaving sobs. What was wrong with her? The prophesied Rebecca had to be stronger than this. "What really happened in Salem, Henry?"

The sorcerer pulled up a chair facing hers and waited out her cry. When at last her tears eased, he spoke in the same tender voice he'd used before. "Three centuries ago a simple lie seemed the recipe to ease your troubled heart. So I told you that I cursed the girls."

"Truly?"

He nodded. "No more lies. Ask me anything you feel that wretched code of yours would allow, and I'll answer honestly."

"If not you, then who?"

"The usual suspect."

*Abigail.* Rebecca clenched her fists.

Henry grimaced. "I thought her an imp, not a phooka, but either way, she was in my charge. It happened on my watch, so I took responsibility for her actions."

"You enabled her. Now she runs rampant." Rebecca slammed her glass down, sloshing lemonade over her hand. She dried it with a napkin, weighing whether to ask anything more. Would he mock her? Speak only in riddles? "I found you and your dog on my doorstep the day Brian arrived from Sidney. How did you know he'd be coming?"

"The same way you knew. An angel whispered in my ear."

"*Is* Gabriella an angel?"

Henry stood and paced the garden. Back and forth. Back and forth. The creases in his forehead deepened. The crinkles of humor at his eyes disappeared. "She's been a meddler whispering in ears for centuries. *Henry, travel to Salem, where the witch stock is plentiful. Perhaps one will share your bed.*"

"No." In all her imagined motives behind Henry's actions, Rebecca had never thought… "Gabriella brought you to Salem?"

"With Abigail and Betty in tow. I doubt that was her first stab at worming her way into this prophecy of yours. You don't think an ignorant, sixth-century witch could have predicted the future on her own, do you?"

"Now you're trampling a sacred legend. If you don't believe any of this, why did you follow your *grandmother's* wish and pass the enlightening rod on to Brian?"

A rare expression of surprise came over Henry's face. "Someone's been boning up on history." He settled into his chair and stared at his garden with thousand-mile eyes.

Rebecca waited.

And waited.

At last, the sorcerer shrugged. "Regardless of whether my grandmother got the message from a scheming angel, a demon, or a twelve-year-old girl with the cutest little ponytail, everything came true. Floods, famines, wars, genocide…just as predicted. So who was I to deny Aislinn's wish?"

"But you're suggesting this was all Gabriella's wish, aren't you, Henry?"

"Saving the world?" Stoddard laughed. "No. I think that little blonde menace changed her mind."

# CHAPTER THIRTY-NINE

BRIAN CUT THROUGH THE frosty Nebraska countryside at ten over the limit, aiming his car in the general direction of a cabin he didn't have much hope of finding. He'd been lucky the last time. According to the Witch-of-the-Hills legend, Rebecca's home was impossible to locate, hidden in a region of shifting landscapes and useless compasses.

For the millionth time, he glanced down at the snow globe wedged into the console between seats. Ordinary people might have kept an actual GPS there, but Kara's gift was supposed to be a thousand times better. At the proper time and place, smoke puffing out of Rebecca's miniature cabin inside the globe would trigger a billowing plume from her real chimney.

*He'd see it from a distance and find her.*

Or so the story went.

Except the stupid cabin locator conked out when he wasn't looking, somewhere west of Kearney, Nebraska.

He'd tested Kara's magic word earlier without a problem, puffing smoke within the tiny scene at various milestones…the barn with a smiley face painted on its roof early on, the windmill farms a little later, the Missouri river at the halfway point, and the long arch of a frontier museum stretching across the highway just a few hours from the finish line.

He banged the side of the console with his fist. The globe bounced up, came back down, but still showed a pale blue, cabin-less interior screaming for a hard reboot.

*But how?* It wasn't like he could unplug the thing and pull out the battery.

He grabbed his cell phone and called Kara.

"Hey, Brian, how did the finals go?"

"Great, but here's the thing. I'm near Sidney, and the cabin finder isn't working."

"Sydney, Australia?"

"Yeah, maybe I'll stop in Perth while I'm at it. Come on, Kara, this is no time for jokes."

Someone in the background shouted her name. The phone went silent for a moment. Then... "Brian." Her voice had fallen to a whisper. "You won't believe this."

He pressed the phone against his ear.

"I have a seven-letter word if Brad leaves an E open. Hang on a minute."

"What? Wait! This is serious."

He was the one to wait, listening to his sister's annoying squeals of laughter from somewhere away from the phone.

"Kara!"

Like she'd hear his shout. The clown probably got so caught up in the wild excitement of a Scrabble game she forgot the call entirely.

He grabbed the globe. Stared into the blue fog.

His right wheel hit the shoulder, kicking gravel. He righted it. Put the globe back. Focused on the road.

What could he do but keep driving? He passed a truck, blew by a cluster of cars, and groped for answers that didn't involve strangling his sister. Maybe if he shook the globe harder it'd start working. *Yeah, or set seismograph needles jumping all across western Nebraska.* He kept his hands to himself.

Finally, long minutes later... "Sorry, Brian! So what's the problem?"

"The cabin's gone."

"That's what the crystal ball is for."

"No, I'm talking about the little one inside of it!"

Someone called her name again. "I better run, Brian. We're playing with a timer. Just say the magic word, and the globe will lead you wherever you need to go."

"But I—"

The phone went dead.

*Magic word.* Like he hadn't tried that already. He pulled off at the Lexington exit and stopped on the side of a frontage road. "Cratchmunkin?"

The globe clouded over, and...

A new scene appeared.

Brian blinked.

Two identical, old-fashioned motels faced each other on either side of a country road. *Mirror reflections.*

But what did they mean?

He snatched the coin out of his pocket—cold silver. He wasn't dreaming. Rebecca's cabin was *gone.*

At the Sidney exit, Brian cruised past Hal's boarded-up service station and headed north. He spotted an aging relic of a motel just out of town, a dive so old the flickering vacancy sign with its burned-out letter C advertised *Air Conditioning* in icy blue letters. Like that was a big deal. Forget about Wi-Fi or cable.

A cartoon penguin smiled down at him.

Early winter darkness had already descended, so stopping to spend the night made a whole lot more sense than pressing on. Even if the crystal ball eventually did show Rebecca's cabin, he wouldn't be able to see any chimney smoke until morning.

He parked by the chain-link fence surrounding a snowed-over outdoor swimming pool, stole another quick peek in the globe for the cabin...and gasped.

The two miniature motels inside were perfect copies of the one he'd driven up to. Even the tiny signs matched—*Air Conditioning* and the penguin.

Kara hadn't said a thing about her magical GPS having the creepy ability to mimic a roadside scene *before he'd even driven there*...or spawn a duplicate like an amoeba. In reality, only one motel existed. The lot across the road lay vacant.

Rebecca's words of wisdom popped into his mind. *Anytime something odd happens, consider it a clue.*

He'd already made some great discoveries following the vaguest of hints—the mirror, her scarves—not enough to free her from whatever warp in the universe held her in its vise-like grip, but plenty of stuff about her background and current predicament. So when a snow globe hit him upside the head, screeching *clue* at him, he needed to check the scene out.

He left his car and headed to the lobby. Squinted at the handwritten sign taped on the glass of the entrance door.

*Closed for the winter. See you in March!*

He sighed deeply enough to scare a bird into flight.

Back in his car, he tried calling Kara but couldn't get a signal. Seriously, his parents needed to find a more reliable cell service provider.

A flickering light on the other side of the road caught the corner of his eye. He swung to look out the passenger-side window and saw...nothing in the darkness.

*Bzzzzzzzzzzzzzz.* The crystal ball hummed like a high-tension power line. He grabbed the thing.

*Zzzzinnnggggg.* A sharp jolt of electricity buzzed his hand.

He dropped the globe to the passenger seat, flexed his fingers—still working, but tingly—waited for his heart to stop beating in his throat, and glared at the culprit.

The globe brightened. The miniature motel on the left now glowed with tiny lights like a Christmas tree.

Something across the road blinked again.

This time, he turned fast enough to catch it—a flashlight, maybe—beaming dimly at first but then brighter and brighter until it *exploded* like a supernova. He clamped his eyes shut and saw spots.

The dashboard started clicking.

He reopened his eyes.

The left turn signal blinked its arrow on and off, on and off, pointing toward the vacant lot.

This was getting way too creepy. If an arrow pointed like that in a horror movie, anybody dumb enough to head in the general direction would get chain-sawed, axed, or stabbed at the very least.

But Rebecca needed help, didn't she? She was trapped in some kind of weird dream dimension. She'd been framed by a phooka. She believed in a prophecy. Her allowance of visits was running out. And every single weird event he encountered might be a clue how to save her, regardless of whether he might have driven straight into a *Saw* sequel.

He took a deep breath, threw the car into gear, and headed across the road.

A bubble of shimmering air came at him like the thin veil of water in an automated car wash. He gripped the steering wheel with clammy hands.

*Whoosh.* The bubble swept over his car.

A motel appeared, identical to the one across the way—twins, just like in the crystal ball. *Seriously?*

Units three, four, six, seven, and nine in the new building flicked their lights on one after another like falling dominoes. Cars appeared out of nowhere—antiques like from Hal's era. They filled most of the parking spaces. A vacancy sign glowed above a lobby lit well enough to reveal someone standing behind the check-in counter.

Hal?

Stoddard?

*Abigail?*

The lobby brightened even more, providing a clear view of the girl inside. She wore a scarf and a faded country dress.

He rushed out of the car to greet Rebecca. Stopped just inside the building.

Blinked.

This blonde-haired, ponytailed kid in jeans was so not Rebecca.

"Hello, Brian."

They'd met twice before. Her name was…?

"I'm still Gabriella."

She had the creepiest eyes. Did he notice that the last time?

*Yeah.* He turned away, feigning nonchalance while planning to run like the wind once he escaped out the door. Forget about the stupid crystal ball. He could look for the cabin on his own.

"You won't find it this time."

"Yeah. Well, I better get going, anyway." He grabbed the door handle.

Gabriella closed in on him faster than should have been possible. "I'm here to help you."

He cringed. "Help me how?"

"By letting you see what this has been about." She grabbed his hands, sending warm tremors all the way to his elbows.

The world skipped a beat. The floor wobbled.

He yanked his hands free. "What the hell are you?" His words came out slurry.

"I could sprout wings to give you a hint." Gabriella's voice had a tinny echo.

He met her gaze and found a hint of sadness deep within those creepy eyes. Vulnerability, too.

"Give up, Brian," she said. "Go home. Rebecca only has one life left. After that, she'll fade into a future you can't possibly live long enough to see."

"I don't know what you're talking about." He turned to the door.

"Shall I show you?" Gabriella took him by the wrist, shooting tremors up his arm again, right through the sleeve of his jacket. "Come with me. You'll learn the bargain she made."

Like he had a choice. He let her lead him from the lobby into a hallway lined with doors on either side.

# CHAPTER FORTY

**WITH EACH STEP BRIAN** took, the dimly lit hallway stretched longer. Gabriella led him to one of the many doors along the way, opened it, and stepped into a leafy forest, in the dead of winter, crossing an impossible bridge from one set of time-space coordinates to another.

He hesitated. Behind him, Nebraska offered the security of a world he somewhat understood.

Ahead, the general murmur of a bustling settlement brought goose bumps to his arms.

*Colonial Salem, w*here answers waited? Yeah, like maybe telling him how to end whatever spell locked Rebecca inside the dream world when she wasn't hanging herself to get out.

He hurried after Gabriella.

"You won't like what I'm taking you to see," she said.

He gritted his teeth and kept going.

Warm, piney air carried the hint of summer. Night hadn't fallen yet, but the shadows were long. By the time they reached a clearing, half the sun had disappeared below the horizon, and a pale moon hovered over a scene so terrible Brian's knees buckled.

Three victims hung from a gallows with necks bent in a real bad way.

*Broken.*

He braced a hand against a tree, shut his eyes, almost puked. Abigail's prank wasn't some harmless spell. *People were dying.*

"Nineteen poor souls hanged in 1692," Gabriella said.

He turned away.

"You'll want to know what happened to Rebecca, Brian."

He dragged after her, along a path of trampled twigs and leaves, skirting the edge of the forest. Waning sunlight gave way to darkness. Burning tar soon thickened the air, followed by flickers of light in the near distance. A murmur of voices rose above the buzz of insects and caw of a crow.

Torches cast a glow over a circle of hand-holding, hooded women in a clearing. Rebecca and her mom sat on a bench in the center, dressed in white.

"Rebecca!" He started toward them.

Gabriella clutched his sleeve. "None of them can see or hear you. Not even her. You're here to watch and listen."

She pointed out an older woman perched on a wooden throne. "That's Angelique, the coven queen."

But the gathering wasn't all witches. Henry Stoddard sat on a throne on the opposite side of the circle. He was dressed in a ridiculous star-studded cape, like some colonial superhero.

The women on either side of him broke their circle of hands rather than hold his. Who could blame them? Rebecca might have referred to this guy as an ally, but he'd never come close to inspiring trust, in Brian's book. "What's he doing here?"

"Angelique invited him. She'll want to cut a deal to chase him out of the district. Witches and sorcerers don't get along." Gabriella settled onto a log and patted the space beside her.

Brian edged onto it.

The queen cleared her throat. "It pleases the court this night to deliberate high crimes against the Sisterhood." She pulled a parchment scroll from a pocket of her cloak, frowned at it for a long moment, then glared at Rebecca's mom. "Martha Church, what manner of parent allows her daughter to cast spells on innocents?"

Rebecca's mom looked down.

"The Puritans have gone on a hanging rampage over the effects of Rebecca's curse. Dost thou dispute the crime committed on thy doorstep by thine own flesh and blood?"

"Nay." The woman's voice barely rose above a whisper. She took Rebecca's hand.

Rebecca leaned into her and whispered.

Her mom flashed the hint of...a smile?

Brian caught a glint in Rebecca's eye, as if she and her mom were up to something.

*Hopefully.* Except the overall atmosphere was much heavier with menace than hope.

Angelique studied her scroll again. "We propose an exile to the far frontier. The powers of the Sisterhood shall bridge the netherland and whisk thee to a forbidding region of sand and hills." She glanced up at the witches. "Do ye say aye or nay?"

"Aye!" Voices rose all around the circle.

The queen gazed across at Stoddard. "Perhaps you wish a kinder fate for the woman foolish enough to welcome you into our district?"

The sorcerer stared at Rebecca...and winked? "'Tis no moment to me wouldst thou relocate a witch."

Again, some hidden meaning? Brian turned to Gabriella. "What am I missing?"

"Watch and listen," she said.

Two of the witches took Rebecca's mom by the hands and led her away.

Angelique leveled her sights on Stoddard. "These troubles started after *you* arrived in the district with imps in tow."

The sorcerer shot out of his throne. "Dost thou accuse me of mischief?"

"No. We simply offer a gift if thou wouldst choose to leave."

Stoddard swept his gaze around the circle. He arched his brows. "A *gift from witches?*"

"Aye. Young Sarah Chance shall serve as thy bride."

*Sarah Chance.* The image of a fading name on an old

gravestone popped into Brian's head. He shrugged it off as one of those weird memory flashes. Things recalled that never happened. Déjà something. Except, didn't he dream about—

A teenage girl stepped out of her place in the circle and headed toward Stoddard. She lowered her hood, revealing a shock of hair so achingly auburn an ice-cream flavor could have been named after her. Her eyes were blue enough to have fallen straight out of a midwinter sky.

The sorcerer touched her hair.

She shrank from him. "We haven't courted yet, sir."

"Then kneel beside me until we do."

Sarah slapped his face.

Shocked silence all around. The girl and sorcerer stared each other down. Then, "Be more respectful," she said. "Do you see legions of my sisters clamoring to deal with you?"

Stoddard doubled over with laughter. He started to speak. Stopped. Wiped tears from his eyes. "Aye, Angelique, a fair bargain this is."

But the queen had shifted her attention back to her scroll. She read in silence. Looked up. "Rebecca Church, thou art accused of unauthorized witchcraft. Spells, and curses in particular, shall never be cast without coven approval. You have ignited the fire of rage now scorching us all. What say thee to the charge?"

Rebecca met the queen's stare with shoulders squared and head held high. "I ne'er intended the consequences of my act."

Brian jumped off the log. "Abigail did it!"

Gabriella grabbed his wrist. "Can you not control your misguided urge to rescue this girl?"

*Misguided?* He pulled away from her. Took a step forward. "This gets better, Rebecca. If I can't help now, I *will* be there for you like I promised, when you come looking for me. You're everything to me."

A gust of wind caught him head on, pushing him back. But did he catch a hint of recognition in her face? A secret smile?

Gabriella got hold of his sleeve and tugged him onto the log. "*Watch* and *listen.*"

He clenched his fists. If the situation in the circle got any worse, he'd lower his head and charge, Gabriella or no Gabriella.

"Rebecca Church," the queen continued, "we sentence thee to serve five centuries in the World of Mortal Dreams."

"A word, Mum?" Rebecca said.

The queen glared at her. "Dost thou plead for leniency?"

"In a small way. Exile me until the sixteen-hundredth anniversary of the Pogrom of a Thousand Tears. 'Tis more than three centuries from now…certainly a harsh enough sentence for my crime."

*Three hundred years?* Brian had trouble breathing the heavy air. The math wasn't hard to do. Sixteen-ninety-two plus three hundred and thirty, give or take, and a gigantic puzzle piece fell into place. Rebecca had never been exiled against her will. She'd gone along with the sentence, using her time in the World of Mortal Dreams as a portal to *him.*

All of this time he'd been trying to rescue her and—

The queen's angry voice cut into his thoughts. "*We* shall decide the proper sentence for the crime. *Five* hundred years. "

Rebecca winced.

"Huh?" Brian turned to Gabriella. "Then how did she get off the bus so early?"

Gabriella mouthed the words. *Watch and listen.*

"Mother Angelique," Rebecca said, "you know the tenets of our code. An anchor is customary for those exiled to the netherland. I request the right to visit my mum in her cabin."

The queen scowled. "Very well. We need no reminder of our Code from the likes of a wayward witch who casts spells without permission. We shall grant a single visit during each solstice, and thou shalt ne'er stray more than twenty furlongs beyond the site."

And there it was. In more of a duh moment than wow, Brian now knew the meaning of the phrase he heard the day Sharon cornered him about her Witch of the Hills research. *Twenty furlongs but never more, the circle at the edge and the cabin at the core.* He'd already guessed some sort of spell bound Rebecca.

The fact she'd had a hand in its casting sure was news, though. Another kick-in-the-head announcement that everything had played out the way she wanted. Rebecca had never been looking for rescue by a hero.

Not that Brian would retire into a Clark Kent existence anytime soon. He and Rebecca had Abigail to deal with, didn't they? Or else the void would devour everyone's dreams. Didn't Rebecca warn as much the night of Club Intrigue? He'd seen Abigail interacting with a black fog earlier that night. It didn't take a Mensa to put two and two together and—

"I also request the cat's cradle," Rebecca said.

Gasps and murmurs rose from the group.

"What's that?" he said.

Gabriella shook her head. "I never should have tinkered with events in Salem. Now you're both bent on a questionable mission at best. But win or lose, she's lost to you."

He leapt from the log. Glared down at her. "What are you talking about?"

She took a deep breath. Sighed. "The cat's cradle allows a convicted witch to stray from exile if she's willing to hang herself each time. But only *nine* trips are allowed. After the last one, you'll never see her again."

White mist swept out of the trees, curling in smoky waves until it reached the witches and billowed into a cloud. They disappeared behind it.

A flash of light blinded him. He shut his eyes, reopened them, and gaped out his windshield. The penguin gazed down on him from the motel sign above.

*Vacancy*, with a burned-out letter C.

# CHAPTER FORTY-ONE

REBECCA SAT AT THE mushroom table in the corner of the Gallery of Secrets, researching the lore of the Sisterhood once again. She paused in the middle of a thick book to run her fingertips across a sketch of an angel with clipped wings.

The reading candle on her table flickered, and a shadow stained the page. She cringed. Although she'd asked the goblin caretakers to let her have privacy, they'd allowed someone to creep up on her from behind.

"Rebecca, do you remember the night you cast a sleeping spell on two girls and sent the moon dancing into a pentacle?"

*Gabriella.* Of course. The goblins wouldn't have the power to stop *her*. Rebecca refused to look up from the book, let alone leave her stool to kneel before a most unholy angel.

"Were you aware sightings were reported as far away as merchant ships at sea?" Gabriella said.

"I have a gift for illusion."

The creature peered over her shoulder. "What are you researching here?"

"Fallen angels."

Gabriella drew in her breath. "Figured me out, did you?"

"Henry Stoddard did."

Silence. Only the murmurs of other visitors at the far end of the gallery and the steady tick of a pendulum clock cut into the perfect quiet. Perhaps Gabriella had left.

Rebecca took a deep breath. The bothersome creature was dangerous and not to be trifled with. Best if she *had* gone away.

"I didn't." Gabriella stepped around the table, flashing the smug smile of a triumphant little girl. Only her timeless, brooding eyes gave her away as a menace, not an innocent child.

Rebecca didn't flinch. This creature's unsettling gaze held nothing to fear anymore. "According to this book, you fallen ones have been stripped of your powers. Do you even have substance?"

"My words are substance enough."

Yes, they were. Their magnitude took Rebecca's breath away. "You've taught Abigail how to harness her powers, haven't you? She'll grow the void until it swallows every dream. How will people survive without the World of Mortal Dreams to replenish their spirits?"

"Maybe mankind would be better behaved with only one dimension to worry about."

Rebecca sprang off her stool. "Then why did you come to my cabin that day in Salem? You told me where I'd find him, in *this* century. He and I would never have made a connection otherwise."

"A mistake," Gabriella whispered.

"No, it wasn't. I've had visions of how terrible the world would be without our dreams."

The creature folded her arms. "Visions? I've seen bombs. Big ones. I've been to Hiroshima. Don't try to tell me—"

"You're a menace, Gabriella." Rebecca headed to the doorway, steeling herself for the five-hundred-three step climb, the struggle across the forbidding badlands beyond, and then...

"You don't know how to save the world, Rebecca."

The room swam. Rebecca grabbed a railing to keep from falling. Gabriella was right. Rebecca had no idea how she and Brian could possibly stop the void from swallowing everything.

The fallen angel approached from behind. "He's looking for

you in Nebraska at the moment, not that the boy has any more clue than you do."

*Was Brian in danger?* She balled her fists. "Where in Nebraska?"

"Sandy Night Motel in Sidney."

# CHAPTER FORTY-TWO

THE VOID HOVERED TO the east, fiercely boiling and curling into itself. No sign of Abigail. Gabriella's phooka never seemed to travel into the past, but Rebecca kept a wary eye out just in case as she walked along the edge of a pond nestled within the rugged hills. A mile later, she reached her old home and found her mum on the doorstep with her knitting.

The sun brought out the red in her mother's hair. She'd never gone white, *not even at the end.*

Their eyes met, and her mother frowned. "I asked thee not to torture thyself by coming from the future to visit a ghost, Rebecca. Art thee not inside the cabin at this very moment to keep me company?"

Rebecca froze. What year had she entered, 1720, perhaps? What if her younger self *was* in the cabin using one of the quarterly allowances the coven queen had granted for visiting her mother? Rebecca dared not defy superstition by looking through the window to catch her own eye, so to speak. She averted her gaze to the doorstep. "I've muddled everything."

Her mother set her knitting aside. "Sit with me for a spell."

As they sat in silence, a pleasant chorus of birds, crickets, and frogs tried to thin the worries in the air. Rebecca attempted slow, steady breaths to calm herself. "I wasted a hanging to burn marks on the door of a girl who had eyes for Brian. I told him the marks were to ward off the phooka, but *that* was less than truthful." She sighed. "And how many journeys did I squander just for the joy of being with him? Only one visit remains, but Brian's no closer to realizing what I need. He thinks I want to be rescued!"

"And what dost thou need?"

"We're chasing a prophecy, Mum. I need to bring your dreams back and stop the void from devouring everyone else's. I need—"

"Love."

"Love?" Rebecca all but spat out the word. "Love has defeated me."

Her mother let out one of her long, deep motherly sighs. "No it hasn't. But perhaps your pride has."

Rebecca found Henry puttering in the garden outside his castle. She hid in the shadows and twisted her hands, over and over and over again.

She'd always relied on herself. She'd never asked anyone for assistance. *Especially him.*

The sorcerer plucked one weed after another out of the soil, tossing each into a growing pile. He picked a rose and placed it in a clay vase, setting it on a workbench.

Then he stopped...and chuckled. "Do you really think you can creep up on me, Rebecca? After all these years, I can sense your approach from a mile away." He turned to her. "The air sweetens, just a touch."

Was he greeting her with sarcasm? She'd never been good at reading his hidden meanings. Rebecca shifted from one foot to the other. Sarcasm would come soon enough when she told him why she'd come. Her instinct was to look down, but she squared her shoulders and met him eye to eye. "I've come to ask for help."

All went quiet. The birds stopped singing. The insects no longer buzzed.

Rebecca didn't waver. She held Henry's gaze even as he arched his brows and widened his lips to an annoying grin.

"What would your precious code say about this, Rebecca?"

Her mouth went dry. Did he have to bring *that* up? "Sometimes, Henry, events become larger than tradition can handle."

# CHAPTER FORTY-THREE

**THE AFTERIMAGE OF SALEM** witches faded. The piney scent of their forest hideaway staled into the not-so-new aroma of a Kia with plenty of miles. The crackle of torches became the gentle hum of an idling motor.

Brian opened his eyes. He'd parked here in the lot earlier, gone inside the motel lobby, and taken a three-century trip to Salem with Gabriella.

Now what?

*A rewind.*

He'd go inside again and—

He slumped in his seat. Why get hit on the head twice with the same bad news that for Rebecca this particular page of the calendar was a mere pit stop on a five-hundred-year journey? She had one more visit left before disappearing from his waking life forever.

*Unless covens allow parole for good behavior?*

Yeah. Uh-huh. The Salem witches didn't come across as the forgiving type. *Parole* wouldn't be a word in their language. Not in Ogham. Not in Shakespearian English.

Except…*that whole crew died hundreds of years ago, right?*

He sat straighter.

Rebecca's exile scheme had been brilliant. Confess to a crime

301

and get a ticket to the future. That's how they met in Nebraska. Now she just needed to shorten her sentence by stepping out of the World of Mortal Dreams and into the waking world for good. Who could stop her? Her original captors would have all died centuries ago. Maybe nobody served as backup.

Brian caught movement out the corner of his eye, inside the motel, over by the check-in counter. Rebecca this time? They needed to have a serious talk.

He hurried out of the car and into the lobby.

The lights were on, but the reception area was empty. Brian peered down the door-lined hallway where Gabriella had led him through the portal to Salem. "Hello?"

*Dinnnggggggggggggggggggggg...* The service bell at the registration counter went off on its own. The tinny sound stretched beyond a normal stopping point, tickling his ears, raising the hair on his arms.

*Nnnggggggggggggggg...*

It wouldn't stop.

*Nnnggggggggggggggggg...*

The bell's vibration crept down the back of his neck.

*NnnggggGGGGGGGGG...*

Brian covered his ears. He turned to the parking lot outside, where his car offered refuge from all things creepy.

*No.* He needed answers, and this place had provided a few already. Could Rebecca get out of her sentence early? If not, could he bust her out? He wouldn't find out by running away.

"Good." Somebody's gravelly voice rose from the check-in counter. "You never struck me as the quitting type."

Brian swung around.

Henry Stoddard grinned. Dressed in ordinary street clothes, this sorcerer, this author of cat riddles, this fellow time traveler—or incredibly old man—winked at him, as if meeting in the middle of time/space nowhere was the most natural thing in the world. He held up a folded piece of paper. "She left this for you."

Brian snatched the note and opened it.

*Brian,*

*You need to go home. I will NOT step one foot into my cabin with Gabriella lurking so close. Christmas Eve is only a few days away. I'll visit you at your parents'.*

*Love,*

*Rebecca*

She'd drawn hearts at the bottom and scented the stationary.

Brian couldn't find much cheer in that promise. Christmas Eve would be Rebecca's *last* visit.

Stoddard folded his arms. "I've got some advice for you."

"I'm all ears at this point."

"Not every damsel in distress needs rescuing, son."

"Yeah. I figured that one out already."

"Good. Then you know your real problem is down the hallway."

*Poof.* Stoddard was gone.

Or was he? Brian reached across the empty counter, grasped thin air. "What real problem?"

No answer.

He turned to the endless door-lined corridor. "Which one do I go through?"

Silence.

The glowing one. Had to be. Not glowing, exactly. Rays of light seeped in through the cracks between door and frame.

Brian went up to it. Turned the handle. Yanked it open.

*Whoosh.* A blast of wind shoved him backward and then reversed its flow, sucking him out of the hallway.

Brian flailed in the wind. He spun, tumbled, flipped, and rose, higher and higher. He flew across the Nebraskan prairie from night into day. Gasping for breath, blinking his watery eyes, he tried not to panic, tried to go with the flow, even as the landscape raced beneath him as if he were flying in a rocket ship.

The storm stopped so suddenly it knocked the air out of him. His heart pounded while he hovered high above the ground, a short distance from Rebecca's cabin.

To his right, sunlight blinded him. To his left, the darkest wave of nothingness he could ever imagine closed in on the cabin. Hills disappeared into its gloom. Birds. A deer. He shuddered.

A girl stood before the billowing darkness.

*Abigail.*

She pointed to the cabin, and the black fog sped in that direction.

"No!" Brian's words died in his throat.

The cabin went dark.

The scene dissolved.

Brian stood in the motel lobby. His ears buzzed.

Henry Stoddard grinned from behind the counter again.

Brian tried to speak. Nearly choked. Tried again. "What just happened?"

The sorcerer shook his head. "If you don't stop Abigail, every dream will be swallowed. We'll have nothing left. So go home like Rebecca told you and worry about how to win this war."

*Poof.*

"Wait! How do I beat Abigail?"

"Son..." The sorcerer's disembodied voice rose from behind the counter. "I wish I knew."

"You don't?"

No answer.

*Now what?* Brian tried to think of a plan. A set-one-foot-in-front-of-the-other kinda thing. But he didn't have enough ideas to even lift the first foot.

The guitar riff tone of his cell phone jolted him like a bolt of lightning. He stared at the caller ID—*Kara*—remembered he had a sister with that name, managed to find a voice. "Hey."

"Hey yourself, Brian. I need you in Kenosha. Mom and I agree it's time you knew something."

"There's a thought."

"Let's meet at Sacred Heart Cemetery tomorrow morning at eleven. This'll blow your mind."

Too late. His mind had already crashed like one of those knockoff smartphones they make in third world sweatshops.

# Chapter Forty-Four

**BRIAN TRUDGED ACROSS A** snow-covered lot to a warehouse he'd visited once before. The crumbly brick facade wasn't modernized by a canopied entranceway anymore, or brightened by blinking neon lights announcing Club Intrigue—a rendezvous point he'd been drawn to like a moth to flame, seemingly a dozen lifetimes ago.

This side of the building didn't even have a door now.

Did that make the entire scene of Rebecca's onstage poetry recital/hanging a dream?

He shrugged. Rebecca's ability to create reality out of nothing blurred all lines to the point where one state of existence became indistinguishable from another. Not that it mattered. Dreams and reality were different shades of the same color, just like his mom said back when he was a kid bouncing toy trucks off the lion claws of their dining room table.

Rebecca's appearance at Club Intrigue had been real. This completely different here and now was real. And the threat to the World of Mortal Dreams?

*Real.*

He headed around back—the first place he'd seen the black fog and the *last* where he'd encountered Abigail in the flesh. Not counting a horse in a cemetery dream he now remembered with great clarity. Or, much more recently, the illusion created by Henry Stoddard to deliver a message—*Abigail had to be stopped.*

*Stopped here?* Brian didn't know where else to look.

"Abigail?"

The wind whistled across a pile of snow-covered tires, beneath a deep, star-studded sky. Fog had blotted out those pinpricks of light the last time he'd been here. A black fog as absent now as the girl/horse/phooka he didn't have a clue how to find.

Or defeat.

His cell phone vibrated.

He yanked it out of his pocket. Read the text.

*Are you home yet, Brian?*

*Yeah, Kara,* he typed. *I'll see you in the morning.*

Brian jammed his hands into his pockets. Looking for Abigail here had been worth a shot.

Now what?

# Chapter Forty-Five

A GUST OF WIND lifted snow from the arch of the Kenosha graveyard's stone entrance and stung Brian's face with a thousand icy needles. He turned away from the next blast in time to see his sister drive up.

Kara got out of the car, spread her arms, spun in a circle, curtsied. "See anything different?"

"Yeah." She'd gone Christmas, shadowing her eyes green instead of black and donning a red ski cap. Normally this would be the time for a joke. Mockery even. But Brian couldn't get past the mission at hand. "Kara, how much do you know?"

She stared at him for a long moment before breaking into a grin. "I'm your big sister, and a witch to boot. Shouldn't that mean I know everything, from your perspective?"

He could only hope. "Including how to beat a phooka?"

"From what I've learned about Henry, I'm sure you've got it in you." She headed toward the cemetery gates.

Brian wasn't even sure where to start with the questions. "Henry, as in Stoddard?" He hurried after her.

They followed a shoveled path past mausoleums and well-kept graves until they reached a low-rent district dotted with plain markers bent by time into odd angles. A little fence separated them from an even older section where the gravestones had been weathered almost smooth.

Brian stopped. He'd been here before, in a dream he now remembered like it had really happened. A dream involving Rebecca, Stoddard...and a phooka. "Hold on, Kara. You're taking me to Abigail right now? I haven't figured out how to stop her yet."

Kara stepped over the fence. "I think you're supposed to find her on your own. We're here for something completely different."

He followed her in, shooting glances over his shoulder. He didn't see any sorcerers. Or shapeshifting horses. Nothing but ancient graves and snow.

The wind had swept everyone's footprints away. No wreaths decorated these graves, and the only flowers left for loved ones either were plastic or had withered to dead stems poking out of the drifts.

But Kara led him around a hill near the back and up to a grave decorated with actual live, blooming flowers.

*More of the phooka dream?* Brian stopped again. He breathed in a gulp of bracing air and let it out in a puff—white fog, not black. So far, the presumed location of Abigail's stomping ground was proving harmless. He came up alongside Kara and looked down at the grave. *Sarah Chance*—thanks to Gabriella, Brian knew who she was. He bent to read the inscription.

*Here lies my loving wife, resting now in Wis Con Sin. 1676 – 1756.*

The epitaph raised nothing but questions. How could this be the grave of Henry Stoddard's wife? Yes, Sarah Chance had been offered to the sorcerer as a bride in the scene he witnessed with Gabriella. But why would a Salem witch be buried in Wisconsin?

"Want to hear some history, Brian?"

Brian jumped at the sound of Kara's voice.

She picked one of the roses out of the snow and used its stem to trace a stick figure, then added two others wearing little triangle dresses. "Once upon a time, a witch named Rebecca told another witch named Sarah she'd been visited by a boy from the magical land of Wis Con Sin. I don't suppose you'd know who that boy was."

"Are you saying Sarah Chance followed me out here?"

"No, she married a sorcerer and stayed east. But on her dying day, she asked her husband to move her grave if he ever found the enchanting land she'd heard about."

"Looks like he did."

"Yeah, in 1830 when settlers started calling their new home Wisconsin. Before that, this region went by the Indian name, Meskousing."

"How do you know any of this?"

"From Henry. Let's go someplace warm, and I'll tell you the punch line."

They drove to a diner and found an empty booth by the window.

A perky waitress with a million-dollar smile hurried over and took their orders, coffee for her and hot chocolate for him.

Brian eyed Kara's laptop, unopened on the table between them. Obviously, she'd brought it in for a reason, but something out the window grabbed her attention. Probably the urge to torture him with a slow-motion act before revealing whatever secrets she decided to share. Kara had always been good at that.

Two could play that game. He waited her out by counting the ceiling tiles, sipping his hot chocolate when it came, watching a waitress behind the counter make a milkshake, and so on. But when Kara still kept her gaze averted after a ten-minute stalling act, he threw in the towel—game, set, and match in her favor. "Okay, I'll ask. What are you looking at?"

"Those sparkly things."

"Where?" He glanced out the window and caught a tiny blink of light, as if the sun had reflected against a piece of foil floating in the air. Another one flashed a few feet farther left. "What are they?"

"Portals to the World of Mortal Dreams. They follow witches and sorcerers around like pets."

"Who needs a portal? We go there in our dreams every night."

Kara gave her coffee a slow stir. She added a cube of sugar. Stirred some more. Glanced up at him. Shrugged. "Not body and soul, we don't. Think suspended animation. *Rip Van Winkle* without the beard...like in *Avatar* or *Prometheus,* which I think was the best Alien movie in the series."

"So we're talking Rebecca. And she can fit through a pinpoint of light because..."

Kara brought her hands together and then spread them wide apart. "Because it *stretches*. And because a coven of twenty gave her the power when they sentenced her. Short of a coven that size, she would have needed a sorcerer's help to do it. Or an angel's. Know any?"

"Uh-huh. I've been batted back and forth by the A team lately."

"So I hear." Kara started to open her laptop. Stopped. More torture games. She dribbled cream into her coffee, paused, added a touch more, and then started in again on the sugar cubes...dropping each one into her mug with maddening deliberation. She sipped, frowned, and reached for another.

Brian shot rays out of his eyeballs, but she wouldn't die. He drummed his fingers on the table.

"Let me enjoy the moment here, Brian."

"Knock yourself out." The time had come to try outwaiting her again. He grabbed a menu and studied the thing as if he couldn't care less about whatever story she planned to tell.

Kara snatched it away. "Never try that on your girlfriend."

"Why not?"

"She'll turn you into a toad for ignoring her."

"Kara, even Rebecca would have booted that laptop by now."

"Fine." She turned her computer on and angled it so they could both see the screen. "Back in February, I was channel surfing and got hooked on this cable show about genealogy. So I bought some software and researched our happy family. Did you know you're the only male in the line for over three hundred years?"

"No, I'm not. There's Dad and—"

"On Mom's side."

"What about Great-Uncle Charlie?"

"He was adopted."

"And you searched *three hundred years* back?"

"Legend has it someone of your kind is only born into a matriarchal line every few centuries."

Brian's stomach took a little roller-coaster ride. "Get out. And what do you mean *my kind?*"

The genealogy program opened. Kara fiddled with the menu and brought up a lineage chart so humongous it didn't fit the screen—row after row of little boxes, each with a name and date, all connected by a maze of lines.

"That whole thing's our family?" He couldn't follow it without getting dizzy. "There must be a hundred names."

"Way more. I uploaded tons of info from journals, diaries, and anything else I could get my hands on." She clicked one of the boxes, bringing up a black-and-white cameo of a woman. A short bio had been entered beneath.

"You must have spent ages on this, Kara."

She grinned. "Brad says it keeps me off the streets. I traced our family tree all the way back to the 1600s."

"Ireland?"

"Yeah, but Salem is the good part."

The roller coaster in his stomach crested and dived.

Kara pulled up another chart. "I had trouble finding the date of death for Sarah Chance's husband."

That took a moment to sink in. "We're related to *Sarah Chance?*"

"Not only her. Does the name Henry Stoddard ring a bell?"

Brian almost swallowed his tongue. Why not just hit him over the head with the laptop?

His sister couldn't have grinned any wider. "Your mouth is hanging open."

"No kidding."

"Henry Stoddard married Sarah Chance. They had a daughter who married and had her own children. Those kids married and had more, and so on all the way through the centuries. Everyone in the line was a girl except *you*."

"Hold on. Stop the world for a second."

Bad choice of words. The background clatter in the diner evaporated. Customers sitting on stools at the counter froze into a row of mannequins.

Kara snorted with laughter. "This is a witch's trick. Didn't Rebecca ever do it?"

"Yeah, once or twice, but this stopping the world thing isn't getting better with age."

"I didn't really halt it. I've put you into a dream."

"Swell. Can you spill me out of it?"

The clatter resumed.

*A witch's trick.*

"Okay, back to the news flash." Kara danced her fingers across the keyboard and brought up a copy of a ragged old diary page. "See Henry's name mentioned in the third paragraph? I found a few vague references in other journals, too, but he kept a low profile and dropped off the grid completely around the time Sarah died."

"Yeah, but he's still alive. I've met him."

"Me, too!" Kara's eyes gleamed with excitement. "Back in July, I came across records about Sarah's grave being moved here, so I drove up to take some pictures. The roses seemed *so* out of place in that old graveyard. Just as I bent to touch one, someone came up behind me. Henry sure made me jump."

"Join the club." Brian needed another freeze-the-world time-out to process the math. Henry Stoddard equaled great-great-great-great-grandfather? He'd probably missed a dozen greats, judging by the number of years since Salem. "Did he know you were one of his descendants?"

She nodded. "Yeah, but he couldn't place me. He said I reminded him of a woman named Elizabeth Danahey. When I told him she was our great aunt, his eyes lit up."

Kara pulled up a picture of herself posing with Stoddard. The sorcerer towered over her, smiling from ear to ear. "We had a nice chat right here in this diner, and when I mentioned your name, he nearly fell out of his chair. That's when he told me all about Rebecca and the prophecy. He never thought he'd be passing the enlightening rod to his own offspring. See how magical this all is? Everything happening was meant to be, Brian."

*Magical?* The sickening image of a hanging victim flashed through Brian's mind. "Did he tell you the bad part?"

"About Salem? Yeah, Henry feels *awful* about bringing a phooka to town. But he didn't know what she was!"

So Henry Stoddard *was* one of the good guys. Rebecca had said as much, too. Brian needed to reboot his mind, but the program just didn't want to compute.

"Don't look so creeped out, Brian. He's been helping you and Rebecca all along."

"Yeah? How?"

"Where do I start?" Kara took a sip of coffee. Stared out the window. Let out a sigh. "He gave me the crystal ball, for one thing, and he set up a billboard outside Sidney much earlier. Do you remember seeing Rebecca's image in Mom's mirror on Thanksgiving? Oh, and did you think your Kia really ran out of gas the day you met her?"

"I thought maybe Rebecca did that."

"Nope. She tends to rely on faith way too much. Henry's more practical. But Rebecca doesn't know anything about his involvement, so don't tell her."

Brian tried to think through the past few months and sort out who'd done what. "I've been falling backward into Salem lately. Because of Stoddard?"

"I'm sure that's all Rebecca. Henry is more of a behind-the-scenes kind of guy. He's been secretly helping her for ages…like the way he leaves books and magazines on her cabin doorstep. He's afraid the poor girl will lose her grip on reality if her only source of information comes from dreams."

"I can relate."

Kara snapped her laptop closed. "Well, that's the story. Now go beat the bad guys. It's magic time."

"Magic?" He still had no idea how to stop the void from swallowing every dream in the universe.

Kara laughed loud enough for heads to turn. "You're the only boy in a line of descendants started by a sorcerer. Wouldn't that make you one, too?"

"Not hardly."

"And don't hate me, Brian. I see it in your eyes."

"No, you don't. Or yeah, maybe a little, but why did you wait until now to—"

"Tell you all of this? Help you more along the way?" She slid out of the booth. "The prophecy is clear that Brian and Rebecca will act on their own to defeat the darkness. I hope Henry and I haven't helped *too much.*"

Brian's stomach flipped.

"Anyway, think about everything I told you from the minute we sat down here."

"Wait! Talk this through with me."

She headed for the door. "You'll figure it out."

Brian let her walk away. Why chase after her? He'd have more luck turning to the walls in the diner for answers than trying to pry information out of his sister once she'd zipped her lips.

The waitress came by with the check.

He set it aside and tried to analyze everything Kara just told him.

Portals, covens, Sarah Chance, Henry Stoddard. What else?
*Sparklers?*

He'd seen the little things before. The day he met Rebecca, his car had stalled. He'd thought the effort of pushing the Kia uphill had made him see stars. Much later, when Sharon cracked Rebecca's book open while sitting outside the condo with him, a spark shot out of it. Maybe something other than static electricity zapped her. And other times…

What if portals had been following him around for months, *just waiting for him to use them as passages into the dream world?*

And here was a thought—he shouldn't bother looking for the phooka in a waking location. If Abigail was working with the void to destroy the World of Mortal Dreams, she'd be right there on site, urging the black fog to eat more cabins.

"Yes!" Every head in the diner probably turned, but what did he care? Sorcerer or not—and he sure didn't feel like one—he'd finally put the last piece of a supernatural jigsaw puzzle into place.

Time to beat the bad guys.

Or die trying.

# CHAPTER FORTY-SIX

**TWO SPARKLES OF LIGHT** darted from the porch of April's condo, hid behind a snowdrift, then shot up to the highest branches of a nearby tree. Brian gasped. How many times had he seen these little things and mistaken them for something else? Stars, fireflies, tiny windblown shavings of metal, and who knew what? But never portals.

The flickers leapt to a snow-covered bush, where he lost them for a moment. Then they blinked again, racing away.

He hurried off the stairs, down the block, around a corner and...*grabbed one.*

The sidewalk spun. He lost his balance, fell back—

*Darkness.*

Then light.

And summer warmth.

The scent of fresh grass wafting in a puffy breeze.

Brian stood in the middle of a broad, peaceful meadow.

But he didn't come looking for peace. The void lurked in this realm. So did Abigail, for sure. Maybe not here, but...

How to get from point A to point B in the World of Mortal Dreams? Wish upon a star? Click those ruby slippers?

*Or just order off the menu?* "Abigail!"

A roar louder than a freight train made him jump. The black

316

void, miles wide, churned counterclockwise, devouring its prey like a Texas tornado. Bushes. Trees. *A cabin.*

Brian gritted his teeth and started forward. "Show yourself, Abigail!"

Rebecca's gentle touch came down on his shoulder. "You can't do this alone. We're supposed to be hand in hand."

Brian turned to the most awesome girl he'd ever known—beautiful, *magical.*

She wore the same long, faded dress as when he'd first met her. She brushed a lock of red hair out of her eyes. But she stared at him with steely resolve. "We have to follow the prophecy, Brian."

"Yeah. I know." He took her hand in his, and that simple contact eased the pounding in his ears.

The black void brightened. Shrank. Stalled. It hovered a few feet off the ground.

He chanced a step forward.

The void retreated.

"It's afraid of us," he said. "We can beat this thing."

"Not really." Abigail's voice sent a cold shiver down his spine. She appeared in front of them. First as a horse—a white filly, majestic and proud, until its eyes turned red—then a girl with arms crossed. The girl on the side of a highway in Wyoming whose angry words—*not with the likes of you*—rang in his ears once again.

Behind the phooka, the void widened and spun fast, ready to devour...

*Everything.*

A bolt of lightning shot out of it toward Rebecca. He stepped in front of her.

Wham! The bolt sent him flying into her. They both tumbled in the grass, side by side, like gymnasts in rewind mode. After a series of bone-jarring bounces, he ended on his back, gasping for breath. Rebecca's own harsh rasps energized him to scramble up, despite the pain in his neck and shoulders, even though he'd hit his head hard enough to see stars, and not the portal kind.

Nothing and nobody was going to hurt Rebecca. Not on his watch.

He lunged forward.

Wham! Another bolt shot him into the air. "Oomph." He landed a good twenty feet behind Rebecca. If there was ever a time to draw on whatever power a sorcerer's blood in his veins provided, the time had come. But how? Brian closed his eyes. He ignored the burning pain in his right shoulder, where he'd landed. Held his breath. Tried to focus.

"So you think you're a sorcerer?" Abigail looked down at him, leering with the meanest eyes he'd ever seen. "Even if you could summon some feeble illusion, how would you stop *this?*" She raised her arms.

The darkness behind her expanded a hundred times larger, stretching so high it blotted out the sun, turning the daytime into a dusky shadow.

Abigail grew to a terrible height—ten feet. Fifteen. Twenty. A scraggily-haired, mean-eyed monster.

Rebecca crawled toward him. Her forehead bled. Her dress was torn. Brian's heart caught in his throat.

Abigail cackled. "Go ahead, witch. Try to help this ridiculous boy somehow." She stepped aside.

Brian rose onto shaky legs.

A gust of wind knocked him back down.

He crawled.

"Brian." Rebecca's voice was weak but her eyes remained strong. She stretched an arm to him. "Remember the words of the prophecy. *Hand in hand.*" She opened hers, revealing the enlightening rod. "Henry thought you'd need this."

He reached up and closed his own hand into a fist around hers.

This simple ribbon, as she once called it, tingled his palm, and he remembered one of his dad's favorite sayings. *Pride cometh before the fall.*

Brian grinned up at the phooka. "Okay, Abigail, she wins."

Abigail stared at him with the look of confusion one might

show when digging into the source code of a computer program only to find all zeroes and no ones. As if he'd spoken Greek to her.

Or Ogham.

"*She* wins?" Her voice roared. The ground shook.

Rebecca gasped.

Brian gripped her hand tighter and tried to summon the calmest tone he'd ever used. He needed to project great confidence here. "*Gabriella* wins."

Abigail balled her hands into giant fists. "Gabriella doesn't win. *I do!*"

Lightning shot through the sky.

Brian rose to one knee. Looked her in the eye. "Yeah, well, here's the thing, Abigail. Destroying every dream in the world was *her* idea. Not yours. I suppose if you had put your own spin on it, then maybe—"

"Spin?" The roar of Abigail's voice spilled him onto his back.

Brian sat up and took a deep breath. He turned to Rebecca. Drew strength from her misty eyes. Then he locked in on Abigail again. "Yeah. For example, suppose the void swallowed only the good dreams. That could have been *your* spin. You'd leave nothing but nightmares."

Rebecca gasped. "No, Brian. What are you doing?"

"I'm *coaching* her." He stood, took her hand again, and pulled her up beside him while waiting for the phooka to process what he'd said.

"Only nightmares?" Abigail looked away for the longest time, thinking, pondering. "That would be *your* spin, wouldn't it? Maybe I'll do the opposite."

"The opposite? I'm not sure that would work. How about instead—"

"Silence!" The phooka's angry roar blew across Brian like a hurricane.

He held on to Rebecca's hand to keep her from being swept away.

"We'll do this *my* way." Abigail faced the void, raised her arms, and twirled them clockwise.

In an instant, the void turned from black to white. Its freight-train blare calmed to the rippling waters of a creek.

A swarm of butterflies flew out of it, scattering in all directions.

And Abigail…

*Disappeared.*

"Yes!" Brian punched the air where she'd been standing. "I tricked her!"

Rebecca looked around. Worry clouded her face. "This doesn't feel—"

A blare drowned her voice, like from a hundred air horns going off all at once.

Brian swung around and took in the sight of a *second* massive void. Blazing shards of lightning spat out the sides, igniting patches of grass, exploding bushes into flames, and incinerating even the earth itself—melting the ground into pits of black emptiness wherever they struck.

The monstrous form of Abigail reappeared, arms spread, menace twisting her features into an ugly snarl. "You took me for a fool!"

Brian's vision blurred. A ringing in his ears muted the phooka's angry voice.

The ribbon fell from his hand.

*No! He had to be strong here.*

He reached down to grab it and—

The ribbon began to grow.

To stretch.

To reshape itself into…

A wand?

Rebecca mouthed words he couldn't hear. She lifted the wand and repeated whatever it was that she said.

A violent, hot gust of wind shoved Brian backward. Away from the wand. Away from Rebecca…

Whose insistent lips moved again, and this time he got it. *Hand in hand.*

But *her* hand might as well have been a thousand miles away. As Brian struggled to approach her, the wind fought back, scorching his face and neck with blazing heat. He gasped but didn't quit, inching ever forward against the broiling maelstrom until he got close enough to grab Rebecca's hand where she gripped the wand.

Their fingers intertwined. Tingly warmth spread through his hand and up his arm.

A beam of light shot out of the wand toward a point on the ground midway between them and the void. An old woman materialized at that spot—tall, white-robed, wizened face. She stretched her arms toward the twirling hurricane of darkness and heat, her gray hair streaming back, exactly like an image he'd seen...where?

Blue rays of light shot out of the woman's fingers, and the void bent inward where struck by them. A *Star Wars* moment for sure.

"It's her!" Rebecca fell to her knees.

"Her?"

"Aislinn."

*Wow.* Brian recognized her from Rebecca's coin. That crazy enlightening rod was more than anyone thought. He and Rebecca were gripping an actual portal to the centuries-old mystic who foresaw this mess.

*Obi Wan Aislinn?*

The white-haired prophet continued sending rays of light into the void, but she shifted her focus to Rebecca. Something passed between them. An unspoken message Rebecca acknowledged with a misty-eyed nod of the head.

Next, the ancient witch looked into Brian's eyes.

Although he didn't hear a message in his head, his arms reacted as if *they* did, lifting and pointing at the void, his right arm bringing Rebecca's left up by the hand. In a moment, rays of power came out of him, too, tingling their way from his elbows to his fingertips until they exploded into green bursts of light.

Brian wavered for a moment, and the rays shooting out of his hands diminished.

The void bulged in his direction.

"No way!" He refocused and sent it bending backward.

*So this is what a sorcerer can do?* The electricity of this moment, this awakening of awesome power, sent him staggering backward a step. He'd inherited whatever this was from a long line of witches, from Henry Stoddard, and ultimately, from this old woman who'd found a way to travel over a dozen centuries forward in time.

And together, *he and Rebecca were living out a prophecy.*

The void diminished and Abigail shrank as well, from a towering monster to something less menacing, then smaller, and smaller still. "You can't!" She stomped a foot like the harmless, whiney little nothing she'd always been.

In an instant, the void, Aislinn, and Abigail disappeared as if they'd never existed.

The extraordinary calm of a sunshiny day swooped in to fill the gap. No churning tornado of evil, no lightning, no rays shooting out of his fingertips…just the chirping of birds and the ripple of a faint breeze across unsinged grass.

Dizziness forced Brian down to one knee, but nothing could diminish the thrill still racing his heart into overdrive. "I think we won this time!"

Rebecca just stared at the tranquil scene, no doubt completely mystified by his sudden show of force.

Brian had to explain, but he hardly understood a fraction of this. Where to start? Henry. Aislinn. *His ancestors.* "Rebecca, I…uh."

But she turned and limped away before he could get out another word.

Brian hurried after her.

Rebecca didn't slow, or even turn to look at him until he finally caught up and sat with her on a log by a stream.

"What's the matter?" he asked.

"Everything." Tears rolled down her cheeks.

He shifted closer. Moved his hand to her chin. "But we defeated the void, didn't we?"

She shrugged. "You heard Aislinn. Good always attracts evil."

"I didn't hear anything." Yet Brian had seen the look passing from Aislinn to Rebecca, and he certainly wasn't a stranger to mind melds these days. "What did she say?"

"Good always attracts evil. If Abigail and the void don't return, something worse will come along, sooner or later. And I'm to watch for it during the two long centuries stretching out before me."

Rebecca's sad, weary eyes burst Brian's bubble. He'd wanted to be her champion from the moment he first met her. Now he'd done this awesome thing…somehow…and yet…

Rebecca looked down at her shoes. "I've got two hundred years left to serve, Brian."

"But the coven who sentenced you…they're all dead by now, aren't they?"

"That doesn't release a pure witch from her vows of obedience." Rebecca's voice cracked. "I can only visit you one more time, Brian, and then I'll be gone."

"No," he said. "Let's talk this through. I've got this power now. I'm sure we can—"

Poof. Brian stood on the sidewalk outside his aunt's condo again. He'd lost the thread of the dream he'd entered.

*And he'd lost Rebecca.*

Forever?

# Chapter Forty-Seven

**REBECCA TRAVELED BACK IN** time to her earliest days in Nebraska. Thanks to Brian, her simple cabin and its occupant were no longer in danger, no longer threatened, a dream to linger forever. But her heart ached nonetheless. She'd soon lose him.

She settled onto the top step of the porch, beside her mother. Neither said a word.

Her mother set her knitting aside and gazed out at the hills. The black hooped dress and white bonnet she wore stirred centuries-old memories—of banishment and exile, angry witches, scheming phookas, a cabin in a strange new land, and a quest to find a fearless young man who, in the seventeenth-century era of this dream, hadn't been born yet. Brian hadn't yet found this cabin or listened to the "Vagrant" poem or kissed Rebecca for the very first time.

Rebecca broke into sobs.

Her mother settled a comforting hand over hers, still saying nothing.

Her mother always put up a brave front, but the woman's weary eyes revealed the pain of exile from their home in Salem. They'd both made great sacrifices. *Voluntary* sacrifices. Neither had been forced to follow the wishes of their coven.

*But pure witches always obeyed.*

"I only have one visit remaining, Mum."

"Make it a joyful one," her mother said. "Call on him Christmas Eve."

# CHAPTER FORTY-EIGHT

**BRIAN BRUSHED SNOW FROM** Sarah Chance's gravestone and sat on it to wait as long as the waiting might take. He'd learned so many secrets during these past few months—about ancestors and prophecies, phookas and sorcerers. But the question of how to keep Rebecca in his waking life came with no ready answers.

So...maybe a sorcerer would have an elusive one. Somebody who actually knew how to use his powers without the aid of an enlightening rod and an ancient, time-traveling witch.

He tightened his jacket and let the slow minutes pass, puffing clouds of warm breath into cold winter air.

A horse neighed somewhere behind him. Brian swung around and found himself face-to-face with Henry Stoddard.

The sorcerer chuckled. "Don't tell me a savior is afraid of farm animals. Abigail is long gone, son."

Henry Stoddard could have passed for an undertaker. The sorcerer wore a bowler on his dark head of hair and a black cape over his shoulders. He stood as tall as ever, and intimidation would have been child's play for him. All he had to do was frown.

But he extended a hand instead. "Call me Henry."

Brian met the sorcerer's probing gaze and tried to match his crushing handshake. "I'm Brian."

"Tracked me down, did you?"

"I figured I'd give this cemetery a whirl."

Stoddard nodded toward the grave. "You picked a special moment. My Sarah passed away on this date, back in 1756."

"Sorry."

"Don't be. Rumor has it that *almost* everyone from that era is dead by now. Rebecca's mother passed away the same day as Sarah, you know."

Brian caught his breath. He pictured the genealogy chart Kara had shown him. The lines connecting the boxes shimmered off the computer screen to stretch through time and space, Henry with him, and now, the sorcerer's late wife with Rebecca's mother. "That must have been a hard day for both of you."

"Tough on Rebecca. She was left all alone."

"Yeah, well, I don't want her to be alone anymore."

The sorcerer gazed up at the clear blue sky. A V formation of geese passed close enough to run its shadow across the grave. "That girl has always chosen a solitary path. She never wanted help from anyone until you came along."

"But you helped anyway, didn't you, Henry? What if I'd ignored your welcome-to-Sidney billboard and gassed up at the next exit?"

Still staring at the sky, the sorcerer lifted an arm. Clouds appeared out of nowhere and gathered into a swirl. Just as they began dipping toward the ground, he dropped his arm.

The storm evaporated in an instant, as if it had never been there.

Brian tried to hold steady against a wave of dizziness.

"You can't imagine the illusions I can conjure," the sorcerer said. "I would have reshaped Nebraska into a funnel and poured you out the spout in a northerly direction if I had to."

"Great. Can you point Rebecca in *my* direction now?"

"No." Henry scuffed an arrow across the snow with his shoe, leading away from the grave, toward the field where a harmless horse still grazed. "You're the one who needs pointing, boy. You've got my blood in you, don't you?"

"I guess."

"Then you'll live for centuries. Wait her out."

"Two hundred years?" Brian's head throbbed. "Come on. I need your help *now*. Throw me a bone."

"A bone?"

"Anything. How about another riddle?"

"Oh, I *do* love those." Henry looked past Brian for a long moment. He stroked his chin. "Okay, here's a good one. Twinkle, twinkle little star, how I wonder what you are."

"That's it?"

"Let's keep in touch now that you know where to find me."

A cloud of snow lifted from the ground, circling the sorcerer and masking him from view. The snow thinned and settled onto the grave.

Henry Stoddard had disappeared.

A shiny speck rose up, catching and reflecting sunlight in brief flashes. One burst. Then another. One more and...

*Bingo.*

Brian's heart pounded. He knew how to keep Rebecca in his life. The answer had been within his reach from the moment he first met her.

# Chapter Forty-Nine

**EARLY AFTERNOON ON CHRISTMAS** Eve, sparkly things suddenly glittered out the window like windblown confetti. Brian grabbed his jacket and hurried onto his parents' front porch. He shaded his eyes against the glare of the snow, looking right…then left.

Nothing.

But he'd seen dozens of them.

Hundreds.

*Portals.*

He headed down the stairs, glanced up and down the sidewalk, checked behind the house. A swinging motion from the neighboring yard caught his eye—*a rope and noose*, clinging to the limb of a sturdy oak tree. He swallowed.

"Brian."

He turned.

And there she stood.

Rebecca would have been the perfect image for one of those Currier and Ives paintings his mom liked hanging on the walls for the holidays. Light snow dusted her hair, her red cape, and the tumble of colorful Christmas presents balanced in her arms.

The sudden sight of her was so overwhelming he couldn't even choke out her name. He hugged her instead. Long and hard.

The perfect moment to freeze time. But the world kept spinning, and when they stepped apart, a tear trickled down her cheek.

He took her hand. Led her to the porch out front. Sat on the steps with her. "Weren't you holding presents just before we hugged?"

Rebecca managed a giggle despite the sadness in her eyes. "Maybe they're hiding under your tree."

"Next to the stuff we bought you?"

"You bought something for me? Do tell!"

"I've got something better to tell you. We'll be seeing a lot more of each other."

"No, we won't." Her lower lip trembled.

He smiled. Squeezed her hand. "Here's the thing. If I can't rescue you, there's another answer."

"Such as?" Her voice had fallen to a whisper.

Snow began falling in perfect little flakes, floating in the breeze, tumbling, rising again, *and turning silver.* He snatched at one and closed his hand around it. "I know what this is now."

Rebecca's eyes widened. "Tell me what you know."

"My sister told me these things follow witches and sorcerers like pets. I have a little of both in me, so they're mine, right?"

Rebecca gave him a hard look. He could almost picture the gears turning in her head...and jamming. "You do have a *witch's* blood in your veins. I'll grant you that."

Brian savored the moment. After all of the bombshells dropped on him, he finally had one of his own to deliver. "Henry Stoddard married Sarah Chance in 1693 after what I can only imagine was a deeply twisted courtship for the poor guy, judging from my personal experience with witches."

She poked his arm. "Why are we exploring colonial history, funny man?"

"Because they had a daughter named Agnes, who married somebody named Tom Johnson. They had two girls, one of whom later had a kid named Alice. And Alice had a girl named Beth. See where this is heading?"

Rebecca stared out at the street for a long moment. "You're

describing a matriarchal line. No surprise, since Sarah was a witch."

"Yeah, we're talking three centuries of falling dominoes. Girl, girl, girl, girl, girl, and more girls...until... Bingo! A guy named Brian comes along. Henry Stoddard is my ancestor, Rebecca. I'm part witch, part sorcerer."

She didn't speak. Just stared with an open mouth he absolutely had to kiss.

So he did. He closed his eyes, met her lips, and flew to the moon. The g-forces almost buckled his knees. An epic takeoff, two perfect orbits, and a fiery reentry.

She mumbled something over the roar in his ears as they glided back onto the tarmac.

"Hmm?"

Rebecca eased her mouth away but kept her hands nestled warmly against his cheeks. "Brian, please don't tell me I'm kissing a Stoddard."

"Get used to it."

They went at it again, and the entire world became Rebecca for a heaven-bound, time-warping cruise, until the sound of a car pulling into the driveway jarred him back to earth once more. Doors opened and closed. His family piled out of their SUV.

"Look who caught a lovebird," Kara called.

"Get a room," Brad shouted.

Brian's mom and dad would have done him a huge favor by shoving those two back into the car and heading out for some ice cream or something. He hadn't shared his plan with Rebecca yet.

But all four closed in on the porch.

"Hey, guys, meet Rebecca." Just saying her name made his throat lumpy.

Mom wrapped Rebecca in a hug. "You must be freezing! What sort of boy keeps his girlfriend sitting outside in the cold?"

"Brian finds ways to keep me warm."

"Within the guidelines of the code?"

"I've almost lost my way with him more than once," Rebecca said.

Kara elbowed Brad. "Lucky for you, I'm far more wanton."

Could this get any more embarrassing? Thankfully, his mom steered Rebecca up the stairs and away from the clowns.

"I can help with the meal, Cassandra," Rebecca said. "I'm only a fair cook, but I do have a wonderful old recipe for bread pudding."

"I'll bet it's old," Kara said.

As his mom fiddled with her key in the door, she shot a miffed glance back at Brian before turning to Rebecca with dewy eyes. "I don't like that scarf around your neck."

"It's nothing."

"How many times have you had to wear these little nothings of yours?"

"Nine." Rebecca's voice trembled.

"*Nine times*? My son's a dolt when it comes to sorting his future out in any kind of a reasonable timeframe."

The dolt grinned. Maybe he'd been slow, but he'd finally sorted his future.

Mom whisked Rebecca into the kitchen, where they busied themselves banging pots around and talking up a storm. Some major bonding was going on in there, so Brian ducked down the basement stairs to give them some space.

The Taj Mahal glimmered in its resting place on a shelf. His dad and Brad worked at the table just below, sorting pieces for a new model, and Kara sat on a stool beside them with her nose in a novel, waiting for the inevitable call to find a missing piece.

Brian hesitated to tell them anything. He'd thought of a great plan, the only road to happiness, but the sight of his family busted his heart.

He tried to rally. First of all, he'd given up the lion's share of his family life on the day he started college. This second move, although much worse, simply represented another step in growing up.

Didn't it? After all, if sacrifices of this magnitude weren't commonplace, why was he always hearing clichés such as manning up, toughing it out, taking one for the team?

Kara glanced up from her book. "What's the matter? You look ready to cry."

"No I don't." He grabbed the stool next to her. Tried to organize some of the little bricks. Felt everyone's eyes on him.

He needed to get on with it. Walk them through the scenario. And lighten the mood or he *would* bust into tears. "Hey, did I ever tell you guys how I fell asleep doing homework one night and typed a poem on my computer?"

Kara dog-eared a page and closed her book. "You mean you were sleep-walking?"

"Yeah, I guess. But suppose I started sending emails to everyone. You would have thought I was awake at my computer rather than wherever we go when we sleep."

Dad arched his brows. "Wherever we go?"

Kara winked. Maybe she got where this was heading. "Or you could leave a phone in a drawer and mind-meld somebody sleeping into sending texts for you…or Facebook posts, Twitter, whatever."

*She got it, all right.*

"Yeah. The possibilities are endless. Asleep or awake. I'd always be in touch. And you could write back."

Her eyes turned soulful. Deep. A little sad? "Would you always be asleep? For, like, a couple hundred years or something?"

Brian almost couldn't answer. He looked down at the floor. "Mostly, except for classes and maybe some holiday visits, I guess."

Brad shot off his stool and raced to the stairs in comic, hell-bent hurry. "Ma Danahey! I think Brian and Kara broke into the spiked punch!"

"Brad!" Mom's shout rang down the stairs. "Bring Kara up here and help Rebecca set the plates out."

Brad turned to Kara.

"Go ahead," she said. "I'll follow you in a second."

Brian waited for Brad to disappear up the stairs before turning to his dad. "How much do you know?"

Dad said nothing for so long he obviously knew everything. He took a deep breath, then rallied and slapped him on the back. "You've gotta chase your dreams, Brian."

Kara hugged him. "We're so proud of you."

Brian couldn't force any words past the lump in his throat.

After dinner was finished and the rest of the family made a discreet getaway to the kitchen or the basement or wherever, Brian sat with Rebecca on the living room couch. The most amazing girl he'd ever met hummed "Silver Bells" while straying her hands to the gifts he'd given her—a heart-shaped locket hanging from the gold chain around her neck and a turquoise bracelet decorating her wrist.

The blaze in the fireplace put on a light show, shifting up and down the color spectrum. Yellows, oranges, purples, and blues danced in sync with her tune.

"Rebecca?" he said.

"Hmm?"

"It's time for you to go."

"To...*go?*"

"Yeah, but not alone."

She turned to him and stared, lower lip quivering, eyes welling up.

"I'm coming with you, Rebecca, through one of the portals. We'll spend the next couple hundred years in exile *together*."

She had her arms around him in an instant. "Oh, Brian, Brian, Brian, I so wanted this! From the very beginning I hoped you'd join me. But I couldn't ask. I couldn't ask. I couldn't..."

"I love you," he said.

Brian glanced over her shoulder, saw one of the sparklers he needed, reached out to snatch it…

And all was right with the world.

A warm breeze ruffled Brian's hair. He gazed at his Kia, stuck on the side of the road where he once pushed it. He'd miss the old thing.

"Try lifting your hood again. That's a universal symbol for drivers in distress, isn't it?" The comment coming from behind had a hint of amusement in its delivery.

He turned to Rebecca. "The eclipse was a nice touch that day."

"I have a gift."

He took her hand and walked with her along the worn footpath. They passed the oak tree and eventually reached a fork he hadn't noticed before. The World of Mortal Dreams had a knack for evolution.

Rebecca pulled him left, away from the cabin, and led him forward until they came to a different tree. Maybe they'd find a 1920s writer dancing inside to the rhythm of a Scott Joplin rag.

Rebecca squeezed Brian's hand. "Agatha Christie has a window in her kitchen. I can show you how to cast your worries."

"I don't have any."

She supposed she no longer did, either…only anticipation, hope, and blinding love.

She steered him away from the tree. "Let's visit Agatha another time, Brian. I want you to meet my mother."

### *Did You Enjoy The Witch of the Hills?*

Please do this writer a solid, by hopping onto Amazon and leaving a reader review. The process is simple:

(1) Type The Witch of the Hills in the search box.

(2) Click the cover picture.

(3) Scroll to the bottom and click Write a review.

(4) Write a bit about your experience traveling through time with Brian and Rebecca. Who or what did you enjoy the most? You don't need to write much. Some reviews are only a few words in length. Others are longer. Just do what feels comfortable to you.

(5) Once you're finished, while you're still in Amazon, maybe you'd like to read Faulty Bones? You'll find an excerpt on the next page.

Thank you!
J.M. Fraser

*Excerpt from*

# FAULTY BONES

## by J. M. FRASER

ONE DAY, RUNNING ON empty and down to my last few dollars, I run into a friend of a friend who introduces me to another friend, who tells me about Hal, who knows some guy named Philippe. A French guy. Philippe has a scam going. Counterfeit chips.

Enter Philippe. We're at his joke of an apartment, and I'm sitting across from him at an ancient Formica table with wobbly legs, in a kitchen so old the appliances are colored yellow and green. Not white or stainless steel like the kind I'd buy if I could ever build up a bankroll large enough to cover anything more than a poker buy-in and the next meal. We're talking hard times all around, and that shouldn't make any sense to me, given the fact Philippe is supposed to be a successful counterfeiter and all.

But I'm a little too desperate for cash to worry about that. Besides this man's nationality has captured my entire focus, distracting me from all else, cuz for a poker player, there's nothing more important than the initial read. Ironic, huh?

Anyway, Philippe isn't French. He's an everyday, balding, older guy with tattoos all over the muscled arms bulging out of his dirty T-shirt. He looks like another Joe or Bob or Hank. A former seaman or retired cop who let himself go in his declining years. Until he opens his mouth to speak.

"What can I help choo weef and how much woudchoo pay me?"

Yep, he's Russian through and through, not only based on his accent, which I won't try to pathetically imitate anymore, but also the *give something to get something* attitude, especially the way he emphasizes the word *pay,* dragging it out slowly, the same way he'd undoubtedly prolong my torture if I fail to return every penny I'll ever owe him, notwithstanding the fact I'm a woman, and a pretty one at that. Uh-huh, that's a brag, but I work long and hard at taking good care of myself. We're talking six miles of roadwork a day, minimum. I eat the right foods, barely any at all, and thanks to the unfailing wisdom of my late mom, I brush my hair to a shine at least once a day. She always said what a man finds the most appealing in a woman at first glance sits north of her forehead. My mom insisted on that, so don't believe anyone who claims they're a tits man or a legs man. That all comes after the initial impression.

I know all about reads, believe me.

I gaze into Philippe's eyes, cool as can be, and I silently count to twelve before answering, just to convey how unintimidating I find his subtle menace and the overall dire situation I may be getting sucked into. Who in their right mind goes to a man who isn't only Russian but undoubtedly mobbed up, to get involved as a mule for his dastardly counterfeiting enterprise? Yes, my right knee is beginning to tremble in its hiding place under the table and out of view, but I command it to hold steady. *Not one inch of my body* can even hint at the absolute terror causing my heart to pump a thousand miles per hour.

Otherwise, I'm sunk with a guy like this. He'll have me for breakfast if that half-empty bottle of vodka at his elbow hasn't satisfied his appetite already.

"I don't like the feel of you," I say in a steady voice, "so let's just say I came for a visit, and I choked down a nice glass of vodka with you, but now I'll be on my way."

That's what's known as a bluff, folks.

I start to rise from my chair, but quick as an eyeblink, he has me by the wrist with a powerful hand. Anyone...*anyone* would scream at this point, but I've commanded all body parts, including my throat, to behave, so I merely whimper, and then I bust out crying.

*Faulty Bones* is available now on Amazon and other online retailers in both ebook and paperback formats.

# About the Author

**J.M. FRASER** is a businessman and writer. He's living the dream with his better half, Mary, in the suburban prairies west of Milwaukee. When not doing whatever it is that they do, they spend as much time as they can with their two daughters, Carolyn and Natalie, and a cute little grandson named Colin.

www.ingramcontent.com/pod-product-compliance
Lightning Source LLC
Chambersburg PA
CBHW020330180626
46812CB00001B/125